Dear Reader:

I'm delighted to present to you the first books in the HarperMonogram imprint. This is a new imprint dedicated to publishing quality women's fiction and we believe it has all the makings of a surefire hit. From contemporary fiction to historical tales, to page-turning suspense thrillers, our goal at HarperMonogram is to publish romantic stories that will have you coming back for more.

Each month HarperMonogram will feature some of your favorite bestselling authors and introduce you to the most talented new writers around. We hope you enjoy this Monogram and all the HarperMonograms to come.

We'd love to know what you think. If you have any comments or suggestions please write to me at the address below:

> HarperMonogram
> 10 East 53rd Street
> New York, NY 10022

Karen Solem
Editor-in-chief

FORBIDDEN DESIRE

"What are you asking me?" Wynne asked.

"I'm asking you to trust me," Drew said.

She leaned against him. Her cheek rested against his steady heartbeat and his hands stroked her arms and back. He'd asked her to accept him as a man. Lord help her, but she did.

"I want you," she whispered into his shirtfront.

His arms closed around her. She felt his lips move against her hair. He whispered back, "Oh, love."

"Does that mean yes?"

"It means I can't say no to you any longer. You've won, sweetheart. I'll come to your bed, but not when you snap your fingers. On my terms, when we want each other, anytime we want each other."

Harper Monogram

All My Dreams

Victoria Chancellor

HarperPaperbacks
A Division of HarperCollinsPublishers

HarperPaperbacks *A Division of* HarperCollins*Publishers*
10 East 53rd Street, New York, N.Y. 10022

Cover illustration by Jean Restivo Monte

First printing: November 1992

Printed in the United States of America

HarperPaperbacks, HarperMonogram, and colophon are trademarks of HarperCollins*Publishers*

❖ 10 9 8 7 6 5 4 3 2

To my family,
especially Chuck,
who never doubted me

To my friends,
especially Becky,
who encouraged me

And to those who believed in this book:
Susan Wiggs and Carolyn Marino

Thank you for making my
dreams come true

Prologue

The Tower of London, February 1759

The hour was late, the night wind cold. It seeped through the hallways of the Tower, beneath the heavy closed door, and mingled with the heat of the stone hearth. The fire burned low; there would be no more wood until morning.

On the table two fat tallow candles burned, making the faces of the men seated there appear yellow-gold in the stillness of the cell. No matter that nobility were allowed small comforts, it was still a prison.

Andrew Leyton raised his eyes from the document spread before him. "And Barrows has found no trace of the man in Calais?"

"None," his father answered.

"Damn the man!"

"My investigator or the elusive highwayman?"

Drew ran a hand around his neck, beneath his long, dark hair, trying to massage the tension from his shoulders. "I'm sure Barrows is doing the best he can—the best that can be done. But this wait!" He raised his head, looking his father in the eyes. "I dread that I've ruined our family name."

His father shook his head. "It will take more than a false charge of robbery to ruin the Leyton name, or the title, for that matter."

"Still, not every earl's son is charged with so serious a crime. How is Mother taking it?"

"Well, as always. She has more faith in justice than most. The sentiment is turning, son. I've heard rumors that even without finding the actual highwayman, the charges will soon be dropped."

"I hope to God they will. I can hardly stand it at times, when I think about everything that's happened in the last few months. James's death, these charges . . ."

Drew's father, Robert Leyton II, Earl of Morley, leaned forward and patted his son's arm. "I know we haven't talked about it much, but we miss him too. He was a fine lad, Drew. You did the right thing in bringing the boy to your estate."

"Even if I did have the housekeeper raise him?"

"A bachelor household is no place for a young boy."

"If I hadn't interfered . . . if he'd stayed with his mother . . . perhaps he'd be alive today." Drew hung his head.

"You don't know that. His lungs were weak. You can't blame yourself for the fact his mother was greedy."

"I could have just given her the gold."

"Money was never enough. She was after blood—your blood." He paused for a moment. "She wanted to hurt you, son. You were more than fair to her, a parlor maid. I think sometimes she wasn't quite sane," the earl whispered.

Drew turned to look at his father. He had thought as much sometimes. But if he'd never acknowledged the flirtatious glances of the dark-haired maid at his friend's estate, James would never have existed; and if it was only for a brief time, Drew had loved his son. Even now, he couldn't call him "bastard."

"I must be going." The earl rose, straightening his cloak around his shoulders. "Newcastle's strength in Parliament is weakening. Pitt has the foreign situation under control, and soon we'll see the tides turn. Don't despair; you'll be a free man again before long."

"I hope so, Father. Send my best to Mother and the rest of the family." Drew walked with his father to the door. "Perhaps we'll all be together at Moreton Hall before Lent." Drew knocked on the door, signaling the guard.

"Get some rest, son. I'll talk to you in a few days, sooner if I hear any news from Barrows."

Drew leaned against the door after it closed, listening to the heavy bolt slide home, hearing the lock click as it was secured. He'd heard it a hundred times in the past two months, and yet he still wasn't accustomed to the sound.

He blew out all the candles but one, then walked to the bed, more of a cot really, hoping he could rest for the remainder of the night. It wasn't always easy for him to sleep, especially after a visit from his father. Sometimes he dreamed of James's happy shouts as he ran through the meadows, other times imagining his son's tired, labored breathing in the cold of winter, seeing him lying alone in the wet earth in a newly dug grave.

When he had first learned of James's death, he sought forgetfulness in alehouses and inns, drinking himself into a stupor many evenings, staying wherever he happened to stop for the night.

That was what caused the charge of robbery. He happened to stop at a particular inn where a highwayman was visiting his love, a maid who tended to bar customers and straightened the upstairs rooms for overnight guests. Local authorities were apparently after the highwayman. In a stroke of criminal genius, he planted some stolen articles on Drew, had the girl notify the sheriff, then slipped away. Drew learned later that the man went to Dover and caught a ship for Calais the next evening. The maid had gone with him.

So he had been hauled away to Newgate to stand charges of robbery. At first, the authorities wouldn't believe that the bleary-eyed, rumpled and disheartened man was a peer of the realm. After almost a week, they finally notified his father, who spent several more days getting him transferred to the Tower. The whole thing had been a nightmare.

He managed to fall asleep before dawn. The sound of footsteps in the corridor woke him. The door hinges creaked. He sat up, startled by the intrusion. A guard stepped into the room; his features indistinct in the dim light from the single, sputtering candle.

"Time to leave, Milord."

The gaoler's voice was not familiar to Drew. "Where to?"

Another entered the room and whispered, "Wot's keepin' ye?" the second man whispered.

"I repeat, where are we going?"

"Out of the Tower. They want to see ye. Come along now."

"Who wants to see me?"

"Bloody hell, I don't know! I do what I'm told. Ye do want to leave, don't ye?"

Want to leave? He'd give almost anything to breathe clean country air again.

"I'm not going back to Newgate."

"Yer not going back to Newgate, Milord."

Drew crossed to the chair, retrieved his greatcoat and approached the door. The first man stepped back, nearly colliding with the second. "Let's go."

"Yer hands," the first man said. "I have to cuff them."

"We don't want trouble," the second man added. Shackled, he walked out of Beauchamp Tower, flanked on either side by the two uniformed escorts. The wind coming off the Thames was bitterly cold. Ice and snow covered the protected recesses along Queen Elizabeth's Walk. By the time they got to Bell Tower, his lungs burned with the frigid air.

"Down the stairs," his escort ordered.

They stepped down into the darkness of an interior corridor as quiet as a tomb. When they came out, they were in the chamber behind Traitor's Gate. Drew stopped and raised an eyebrow.

"Aye, we're going by boat," the first man said.

Cautiously, Drew stepped into the small craft. It bobbed and dipped as the other men entered, taking up oars at each end while he sat in the center. Soon they passed through the open gate and under the wharf tunnel into the river. He hadn't seen another soul. Odd, but he always thought there would be more guards about. When he had arrived at the Tower, there had been rows of them around the inner ward.

These two must not be Yeomen of the Guard. Their uniforms were ill-fitting beneath their cloaks. Where could they be from? He racked his brain for an answer, but could think of nothing to explain this unexpected journey into the Thames.

The sun was just beginning to rise and they headed straight into it. Alarm registered for the first time. They should be traveling west, not east, to reach the courts or public buildings.

"Where are we going?"

"Yer full of questions, Milord. Why don't you just relax and enjoy the fresh air?"

The second man chuckled.

Ahead, he could make out the shapes of ships along the many docks. He swallowed the panic that threatened. He was so close to being cleared! Surely a few more days and he would be out of the Tower.

"Who hired you?"

"Now why would ye be thinkin' we're hired?"

"We're headed for a ship, aren't we? It was Newcastle's supporters, wasn't it? What did they pay you to get me out of the Tower? Whatever it was, I'll double it. Just row this boat over there"—his head dipped toward the north shore—"and you'll have your money soon enough."

"Ah, we can't do that, Milord. Besides, they paid us to kill ye, not send ye on a pleasant little trip," the man said, laughing.

Drew tried to stand. The dark depths of the river looked more inviting than an unknown ship, a foreign shore. He might be able to swim far enough to make the bank. He might—

He heard chains rattling, then a blow to the back of his head caused his knees to buckle. The last thing he saw was the sun rising over the masts of the ships docked along the north shore. Then the world dipped and rocked like a small craft in a gale, and the sky was blacker than midnight.

1

Williamsburg, Virginia, April 1759

The carriage pulled out of the Raleigh Tavern onto the Duke of Gloucester Street, past stately homes bordered by brick walls or picket fences, past black-barked trees with new green leaves. Wynne Carr slowly opened her small purse and withdrew a stack of silver coins, their slightly dull color nearly the same shade as her grey kid gloves. The coins shifted in her hand, the stamped surfaces rubbing together with a cold, metallic sound that grated on her nerves.

She placed the coins back in her purse, dropped that in her drawstring bag, and placed it on her lap beside a hand-painted fan. Her traveling gown was grey also, an inconspicuous color that wouldn't draw attention to her or her purpose in coming to Williamsburg. Only when her unsteady hands were folded sedately over the bag did she glance up. Focusing on the silver in her purse did nothing to settle her nerves; in fact, it made matters worse.

It didn't take long for the carriage to travel the mile or so to the dock at Queens Creek. An auctioneer, who bought servants by the lot off the ships from England, then resold their bonds to the planters along the James and York Rivers, waited at the Public Warehouse.

As soon as they came to a stop, Wynne's butler climbed down from his place alongside the driver and opened the carriage door.

Wynne gave him a slight smile, more for her own assurance than his. Still, she needed his cooperation; she wanted his approval. Smythe was more than just her butler, he was also a friend. He was the only other person on Waverley who knew why she was here. And he was absolutely loyal. Wynne put her hand in his and stepped down.

They walked in silence near the warehouse platform, close enough to see the men and women without becoming offended by the odor of unwashed bodies or infected by the ill humors clinging to the wretches. This auctioneer obviously had not taken much time to groom the bonded people, or spent any coin to bathe or clothe them. Snapping open her fan to further hide her face, Wynne gently stirred the air. Perhaps this auction was not going to be any more successful than the others she had attended in the last few months.

She dismissed the first bondsman as unsuitable, then walked farther down the line, Wynne's tall, well-endowed figure draped in a sedate gown that made her look stately rather than seductive. The matching veiled hat effectively hid both her youthful features and thick, blond hair.

She slowed, watching a man who seemed to be scanning the passersby and finding them lacking. Even though his posture was relaxed, Wynne sensed an underlying tension in his tall body. When she stopped in front of him, standing maybe fifteen feet away, he stared right at her. She felt her breath catch. Her eyes roamed, taking in the width of his chest, straight legs, and proud stance. He was impossibly dirty, his face half-covered with a heavy, red-brown beard, but there was something in the way he stood that said, "The world be damned." Wynne understood the sentiment; she felt that way much of the time.

"That one, Smythe." Wynne pointed discreetly with her fan. "Go see about buying him."

"Madam, really. Surely I should ask some questions first."

"You're right. See if the auctioneer knows his background. Especially where he's from, his age and education. See if he has a family—children" Wynne paused, looking again into the bondsman's eyes. "I do believe he's the one," she whispered to no one in particular.

Smythe frowned and went off to find the auctioneer.

The way the bondsman stared at her was disconcerting. Although she knew the man couldn't make out any details of her features, she felt as though she were being appraised in return by that somber, unblinking gaze. She didn't like the feeling, had not liked it, since the day six years ago when the way people looked at her had changed from admiration to scorn.

She would never forget how it felt to be looked down upon, to be judged by someone else and found wanting. She wouldn't do that to the bondsman, but she would expect cooperation and discretion. She could offer him a pleasant life, a few years of service instead of the normal seven years of bondage, and a settlement to see him far away from Waverley.

Wynne looked for Smythe and saw him questioning the auctioneer, who had walked over to stand in front of the bondsman. She couldn't hear their voices but saw heads nodding. She knew her butler would never say anything to indicate how the bondsman would be used, what her intentions were. Still, just knowing it herself made her uncomfortable.

What if she made a mistake, misjudged the man? What if he turned out to be diseased, depraved, or worse? She shuddered in the warmth of the spring day.

Wynne resisted the urge to tap her foot or shift her weight. She did let out an audible sigh, causing the veil to flutter like the curtain of an open window.

Finally, when she thought about breaking all rules of propriety and approaching the men herself, Smythe finished his interrogation. He walked, slowly and with dignity, to where she stood beside the carriage.

"Well?"

"He is from Sussex, more or less, convicted of robbery according to the auctioneer, although the man adamantly denies it," Smythe reported with emphasis on his skepticism. "He speaks four languages—fluently—and claims to write those, plus one more."

"How impressive for a bondsman," she whispered, taking another look at the man. She tapped her fan on her opposite forearm, distracted and fascinated at the same time. "What is his name?"

"Andrew Philip Leyton."

"And his age?"

"Thirty. Or so he says."

"You doubt it?" Wynne looked again. It was hard to tell beneath his dirty hair, which appeared brown, and his bushy beard, which appeared . . . disgusting.

"My search for an honest man would not begin with convicted felons," Smythe said.

"But he spoke the truth about his education? He can speak four languages?"

"Yes, madam, but—"

"I'm not looking for a terribly honest man, Smythe. I'm looking for . . . other traits. Did the auctioneer guarantee he was free from disease?"

"Yes, he assured me the man suffered from nothing more than the normal rigors of transport."

"And family?"

"I believe so."

"Then buy him, Smythe. Purchase his bond, and let's get on with it."

"Madam, are you sure? It is not too late to reconsider your idea."

"Smythe, just purchase his bond. Then take him to the physician for a certification that he is free of disease. Also, get him measured for some new clothes before those fall off his body." The man was absolutely ragged, one sleeve torn half off, a trouser leg ripped. "Perhaps Mrs. Campbell has some men's clothing that was left behind at her tavern. He needs something to wear until I can have some made for him."

"Yes, madam. Anything else?"

"I'm going to Waverley as soon as I finish my errands. I'll leave the wagon to get the supplies we need. You and the bondsman can follow tomorrow."

"I will see you then, Mistress Carr, with your bondsman," Smythe replied politely, if somewhat coldly. He walked back to the auctioneer.

My bondsman? Yes, I suppose he is, Wynne thought. And may God have mercy on my soul.

Waverley Plantation, Virginia

"Samuel? Can you hear me? I have something important to tell you." Wynne perched on the mattress, one knee drawn up, her firm hands grasping the cool, soft ones of her husband. She watched his eyes for movement, and finding them focus on her for a moment, continued. "Do you remember the plan I told you about? Where I would look for a suitable man . . . a bondsman? Well, I found him yesterday in Williamsburg, and Smythe is bringing him back today."

Samuel Carr's eyelids blinked.

"He is well educated, Samuel. Speaks four languages." She frowned. "I forgot to ask Smythe which ones. And he's very tall, with good posture. I can't tell too much about his features since he was so dirty, with a beard, and I didn't get very close, of course."

Samuel blinked twice.

"Don't worry about that, though. Smythe is taking him to the physician for certification. As soon as he gets here, after he's cleaned up and well fed, I'm sure he shall do nicely."

Wynne cocked her head, looking for some sign, any sign, of emotion or understanding from her husband. He had been lying like this, more or less, for over five years. Only God knew how many more years Samuel would be made to suffer because of one small sin committed so many years ago in India. He probably didn't even remember which camp follower he took to bed to get this horrible disease, but it had ruined his life, and through no fault of his, it was ruining hers.

She smoothed a strand of grey-white hair over his mostly bald head. "Please be happy for me, Samuel."

Wynne stopped a moment, tears beginning to fill the corners of her eyes as she stared at her hand, clasping Samuel's.

She whispered, "I'm so sorry things turned out this way for us." She paused and wiped away the tears before they slid down her cheeks. "I'm truly proud to be your wife."

Wynne left shortly after that, after sitting quietly with her husband for several more minutes, and promising to visit again soon. Samuel's long-time valet waited in the main room of the hunting lodge where Samuel had spent the last five and a half years.

"Sethti, he looks very good. You have been taking excellent care of him, as always."

The Hindu smiled. "Thank you, memsahib. I give him the medicine daily, and he eats the food well."

"Good. I'm sure he knows you are with him." *I only wish I knew what he thought of this plan,* Wynne said to herself as she pulled on her riding gloves. *I wish he could counsel me now like he did in the past, when he taught me how to run the plantations, how to ignore that which I couldn't change, and make the most out of what I had. I need you now more than ever, Samuel,* she thought as she pushed the small pearl buttons through the leather holes. She pulled her jacket sleeve over the gloves and looked up.

"I must be going now. Smythe will be back later today, and Annie is there if you should need anything."

"Yes, memsahib. I am glad you visited today."

"Thank you, Sethti."

Wynne used the mounting block beside the old hunting lodge to position herself on the sidesaddle of her bay gelding. She had a lot to do before Smythe arrived with the bondsman. As her horse broke into an easy rolling canter, she thought of the tasks awaiting her. The cheese must be tested, the meat in the smokehouse inventoried, a count of the shingles at the sawmill . . .

Riding in the wagon beside Smythe, Drew enjoyed the sunlight, fresh air, and stillness of the forest. It was a land where small flowers peeked shyly from beneath thick beds of pine needles, new blades of grass grew beside the rutted road, and hundreds of birds chirped and sang. Insects buzzed lazily over stagnant, shallow pools of rainwater left in the hoofprints of horses who had traveled the road before the last spring shower. And when the wind shifted, he smelled freshly turned, damp earth so strong it brought to mind hundreds of acres on his own land, prepared for planting.

They had left Williamsburg early that morning, traveling all day through mostly forested wilderness. Occasionally he would glimpse cultivated fields and houses through the trees, but for the most part, he'd been thinking.

There was no need to ignore his situation, nor was there a need to announce who he really was. Apparently these people knew nothing of the affair in Sussex, a world away from this colony. He would keep quiet about his family, his father's title, and his wealth. There was no need to bring further shame on his family, or possibly expose himself to another political threat if Newcastle found out he was alive.

Over a mile later, the road that carried them west from Williamsburg turned and continued northward. They left it, traveling south through tall, straight pines and newly blooming and budded trees. Ahead he could see the trees thinned, then a clearing appeared.

The road curved to the left and Drew got his first look at the house. It was an impressive rose brick with rustic stone lining the front door. Six chimneys accented the grace and symmetry of the house. The front entrance faced west; a wing looked as if it had been added along the northern wall of the original rectangle. Drew took in the architecture and landscaping as the horses plodded slowly around the curving drive. The lawns and shrubs surrounding the house showed a history of careful maintenance. It looked very much like any other country estate in England. Only this is Virginia, he reminded himself.

Smythe was just as meticulous as the house and gardens. A man perhaps eight to ten years older than himself, Smythe sat straight as a board on the wagon seat. He looked like the kind of man who kept his thinning, light brown hair combed at all times and his starched shirt free of wrinkles. His expression was usually carefully blank, but like any other well trained butler, he could frown and look down his nose with the best of them.

The wagon stopped at the back of the house. Smythe gestured for Drew to get down. "Take these bundles to the kitchen"—he motioned to the separate building down the brick walk—"and then tell the cook to heat water for your bath. There is no doubt that you need one. You will find lye soap in that small bundle and a change of clothes in the larger one." He frowned again at Drew. "I do presume you are accustomed to cleanliness?"

"You presume correctly, Smythe. A bath would be most welcome." Drew scratched at whatever was biting him beneath the waistband of his breeches.

"Good. I will inform the mistress that we have arrived, although I suspect she is well aware of that fact already."

Drew gazed at the house, noticing a faint movement of a lace panel upstairs. She probably smelled me coming, he thought, but didn't share his observation with Smythe.

"To the bath, Smythe, and with great delight."

Wynne watched the arrival of her bondsman from her bedroom window. He was lean beneath his ragged clothing, his movements slow and measured, as if he was unsure of his strength. But his eyes—she thought she would always remember them. She had recognized the intelligence shining there even before Smythe had quizzed him.

She watched him disappear into the kitchen. No doubt Smythe had sent him to bathe before coming near the house. Wynne smiled as she thought of the proper butler in the company of the wretched bondservant. Smythe would likely start another moral lecture. He'd been with Wynne on Waverley since she came here and before that he had started his career with her father. She respected his loyalty and his opinion, but about this one subject she heeded her own counsel.

A discreet knock interrupted Wynne's thoughts.

"Smythe has arrived, ma'am, and awaits your presence in the study," announced the maid.

"Tell Smythe that I'll be down presently," Wynne replied in a distracted, quiet voice while she continued to stare out the window. The yard was empty now.

Wynne smoothed her day dress of mauve silk as she sat down on the dressing table bench and tucked a few stray strands back into her neatly arranged hair while gazing into the mirror. Her reflection was one of a confident, graceful woman in the prime of life. She had wealth, style, beauty, and a heart that was so empty she wondered if anything would fill it. Oh, she loved Samuel, whom she used to call "Uncle Samuel," Waverley, and Virginia. But it wasn't the same as loving your own flesh and blood. Or being loved in return.

Smythe was waiting, as she expected, standing by the green-veined marble fireplace like a soldier at attention. "Everything has been unloaded, madam. Those things that were fit for the house have been brought inside. Everything else is still being scoured."

"I should think, Smythe, that he would be doing his own scouring."

"Indeed. I believe that is accurate."

Wynne smiled slightly at Smythe's reply. "Tell me what else you've learned about our new 'acquisition'— Andrew Leyton, wasn't that his name? I want to know about his attitude."

Smythe took a seat after assisting his mistress. He drew a long breath before beginning. "Andrew Philip Leyton, in full. And upon which subject would you like to know his attitude, madam?"

"In general," Wynne replied, slightly flushed. "What is his opinion of his situation? Do you think he'll be reasonable?"

Smythe seemed uncomfortable, looking at anything in the room except her. He cleared his throat. "It is difficult to tell. He did not attempt to run, or make my job harder, but he has the ability to view situations in the absurd. Indeed, he has a slight smile that can be most annoying."

"Smythe! He was able to annoy you? How delicious!"

"Really, madam, I do not consider that occasion to laugh. He can be most exasperating. I do not believe he will take orders well."

"Then I'll try not to give him too many," Wynne replied, becoming serious again. "There's only one thing I require from him, so perhaps we'll not be communicating too much."

Smythe looked taken aback. "With all respect, madam, I would think you should be communicating to an extreme."

"I don't know why you would say that. It's not as if he will be a field servant or a coachman. I will not have to instruct him, surely."

"Madam, really! I do not believe you are aware of what we are discussing."

Well, maybe I'm not, Wynne thought. Only Smythe realized how little she knew about the "duties" of the new bondsman.

"Thank you for the report and information. I don't need to tell you how much I appreciate your help, Smythe." Wynne rose as gracefully as possible and preceded her butler to the study door.

"Madam, please reconsider your decision. I truly do not think it is in your best interest."

Wynne turned and bestowed a sad smile on the man who had been through so much with her. "My friend, I don't know if it's in my best interest either. However, I must do what I can to preserve Waverly. My father and Samuel worked too hard to build it for me to lose it through a whim of the Fates."

"Yes, madam. I understand your position. I will get Mr. Leyton settled then. Would you like him to be moved into the bondservant barracks?"

"I think the former overseer's room would be sufficient."

"I will see to it immediately."

"I'll meet Mr. Leyton at nine o'clock in the study. Please make sure he has a good meal. And Smythe? Thank you again for your concern."

"You are most welcome."

As soon as Smythe left, Wynne walked quickly down the hall from the study to the family parlor, then up the stairs. She didn't really want to go through with this plan. She wanted to run and hide, forget the bondsman, and pretend the last years were nothing but a bad dream.

"Andrew . . . Philip . . . Leyton," Wynne murmured as she trudged up the stairs. A fine, fancy name for a bondsman. It probably wasn't his real name anyway.

"Mistress Carr."

Wynne stopped and descended far enough to answer. "Up here, Faye."

"Ma'am, Cook needs to know about dinner this evening. How many will be dining?"

"Just one," Wynne finally answered. "And, Faye? Have the overseer's room cleaned immediately."

"Yes, ma'am."

Wynne heard the light tapping of Faye's steps as the maid went down the stairs and through the parlor. Let the staff think what they wanted; the bondsman would live here in the house. It would make things more convenient.

Drew settled back against the tub, savoring the second round of scalding, cleansing water. He had thrown out the first in disgust. Now he was beginning to feel like himself again, except that the soap was not scented, and there would be no servant to offer a warmed, soft towel. No evening clothes, or even a lounging robe. No dinner on fine china, with brandy served afterwards in crystal. Despite all that, he closed his eyes and enjoyed his bath.

More than just his physical comforts had changed, Drew realized. When he had wakened aboard the ship, still shackled, lying in darkness, he thought for a brief moment he might go mad. Then he listened for clues, movements, and heard the sounds of other chained men shifting. He felt the roll of the ship, not the sideways rocking of a docked vessel, but the gentle plough of one at sail. Had they left the Thames yet? He had no way of knowing, so he asked his fellow passengers.

He was aboard a transport ship, on his way to Virginia. He almost laughed out loud. He was finally visiting the colony that produced all that tobacco he invested in each fall. It was ironic.

Well, it could have been worse. The bumbling guards that Newcastle's men hired could have killed him. Perhaps he could make the most of being transported. His father would find him, or he would find his father. All he had to do was stay alive.

His new "home" was at least prosperous. The people he had met so far, although not exactly friendly, were not abusive. It would only be a few months, six or seven at the most, and then he would be going back to England. Home, to Sussex and his estate, Rother Hall; to his family estate, Moreton; and to London, with all its amusements and distractions.

There was that small complication of the robbery charges, but Drew was sure that would be taken care of by his father's investigators and solicitors. It was strange, but being a bondsman had somehow improved his attitude. He was alive, he had survived arrest, confinement, and now transportation to Virginia, and he had hope.

He missed James. There was a large, empty place in his heart that ached at the loss. But grief couldn't bring his son back, and Drew knew he had been given a second chance at life. Perhaps it was time to look for a suitable young lady during the next London season.

"Are you not finished? You have been here close to an hour." Smythe entered the bathing room quite unexpectedly, and with his usual disapproval.

"I thought you wanted me clean? It took a while. I do hope your mistress understands," Drew replied in a caustic tone as he flexed his broad shoulders against the tub.

"What I hope, Mr. Leyton, is that you understand your

position here. Whatever you were accustomed to in London" —he paused at Drew's raised eyebrows—"you are not going to have here. And I do believe, Mr. Leyton, that you were accustomed to much, much more. Am I correct?"

"You are, Smythe. Quite correct."

"I will be blunt. You stated in Williamsburg that you were not guilty of robbery, although you were convicted of that crime. What were the specific charges?"

He wouldn't argue with Smythe about the assumption that he had been convicted. Let these people think what they would. "According to our fine courts, I'm a notorious highwayman. Does that surprise you?"

Smythe seemed to ignore the reply, his eyes focusing instead on the filthy pile of rags Drew had been wearing. "And are you a notorious highwayman, Mr. Leyton?"

"Hell, no. But I would be surprised if you believed me. After all, most of England preferred to think the worst. As a matter of fact, I'm surprised you didn't read about it in the London papers."

"We rarely get the London papers. Mistress Carr prefers the local press. The weekly *Virginia Gazette* is more relevant, you understand."

Drew nodded , then rubbed the droplets of water that ran down his forehead. "No matter, then. Smythe, I was snared like a rabbit in a trap, if you care to know. That really doesn't change my circumstances, does it?"

"No, it doesn't, and I'm glad you realize that. I hope you can become adjusted here at Waverley." Smythe's tone had changed somewhat, Drew realized. He was not hostile or unfriendly, just guarded. "It is a pleasant plantation: prosperous and peaceful for the most part. I would like to see it stay that way."

Drew gazed at the butler thoughtfully. "I'll do my best, Smythe. That's all I can promise."

"Well, then. That is enough for now." Smythe turned to leave, then stopped as if he had just remembered an additional point. "You will meet Mistress Carr soon. She is a lady. I want you to remember that."

"Of course," Drew answered, puzzled. "Is there something about your mistress I should know?"

"Yes," Smythe replied, his tone colder. "She is your mistress now also. Please do not forget it." He turned, walked toward the door, then added, "As soon as you finish here, get Cook to fix your dinner. I will return later." With that final command, he left.

Drew finished his bath, then managed to talk Cook out of a large meal of roasted chicken, early vegetables, and the best rolls he had ever tasted. He pushed back from the crude table and bestowed a genuine smile to the matronly woman.

"That's the best meal I ever had, and that's the truth," Drew grinned at the flushed cook.

"Go on with ye, now. You're nigh to starved, that's why."

"No, I'm serious. I never tasted better, even from the best French chefs at court."

"Mr. Leyton, really. You're a tease, I'm thinking."

"Please, call me Drew. All my friends do."

"Then Drew it is. And ye can call me Annie, although most everyone calls me 'Cook,'" she said, placing a large slice of buttermilk pie before Drew.

"This place looks very established. How long have you been here, Annie?" Drew inquired casually as he tasted the pie.

"I was with Mistress Carr before she came here, with her father," Annie replied, returning to kneading dough for tomorrow's breakfast. "He was a fine gent, Colonel Palmer."

Drew stopped chewing and swallowed. "Palmer? But your mistress's name is Carr. She's married, then?"

"Oh yes, married she is, but . . . ."

Drew hadn't heard Smythe enter, but suddenly he stood in the doorway. "Leyton, there you are. I'm sure Cook has been entertaining you, but Mistress Carr wishes to see you." Smythe gave Annie a hard look, upon which she raised eyebrows but didn't comment. "If you are finished, that is."

"Of course, Smythe." Drew took his last bite of pie, pushed his chair back, then turned to Annie and took her plump, flour-covered hand in his much larger one. "Thank you for the fine dining experience." He kissed her hand and made a courtly bow. "Until later."

Smythe snorted, then grabbed Drew's elbow. "Mistress Carr is waiting, Mr. Leyton. Enough of your fine manners."

Drew followed Smythe's measured tread on the brick walkway to the main house. "Mistress Carr is something of a mysterious lady, Smythe. At least, she seems to be so far."

"Mistress Carr is not 'mysterious,' Mr. Leyton, just discreet. She is a true lady, as I mentioned earlier, and does not feel compelled to scamper about her business in the manner to which you are obviously accustomed. She works very hard on this plantation and oversees each detail personally."

"Then there is no Mr. Carr to see to these details? Is she a widow?"

"She is a married lady," Smythe stated firmly.

Great, Drew thought to himself. She sounds like a veritable saint. He envisioned the rigid, tall, austere woman who had stood by while Smythe asked questions the headmaster at Eton would have been proud of. She had worn a severe grey dress, a veiled hat that hid her features, and, when the wind shifted just right, the intoxicating smell of jasmine. She was probably middle-aged and ready to rap his knuckles with a stick if he were naughty. He chuckled.

"Something you would like to share, Mr. Leyton?"

Drew looked down at the other man, smiling. "No, Smythe, I don't believe I do."

2

Inside the study, *Wynne paced* nervously in the space between her massive desk and the fireplace. She glanced at the multipaned windows overlooking a fountain and the darkened garden. The windows reflected the scene within the room: two comfortable chairs, a bookcase for the ledgers, and her tall, pale figure. She moved to straighten one chair, which was angled slightly wrong. What was keeping Smythe? She glanced again at the wall clock. One minute past nine. Perhaps she should be seated at the desk. That would be more authoritative.

As Wynne moved from behind the chair to take her place at the desk, Smythe opened the study door and announced, "Mr. Leyton, madam." After urging Drew forward, he discreetly closed the door.

Wynne didn't move for a moment, thinking perhaps Smythe had brought the wrong man to the study. But she looked into his eyes and knew; this was the bondsman from Williamsburg. Good God, but he was so much more than she had anticipated. He was more than she had wanted.

More than handsome, the only word that described his features was beautiful.

Wynne recovered her composure, straightening her spine, schooling her face. It took only a few seconds for the mask to slip into place, hiding her shock at the bondsman's changed appearance.

"Mistress Carr?" he asked softly. No fire crackled, and even the crickets seemed silent.

Before she spoke, Wynne drew a deep breath. It was a trick she had learned from Samuel, when she was too shy to speak, too angry and embarrassed by the "great scandal" to talk to their neighbors. "Mr. Leyton, I presume?"

"At your service, madam," he replied in a velvet baritone that seemed to vibrate through Wynne's body.

She blushed at his words. All thoughts of how this should be going had vanished. She could only remember why he was here, not how she was going to explain her situation. Was she staring? It didn't seem to matter, because she couldn't stop looking. *His eyes are blue,* she thought. *As clear as a summer sky, as deep as the ocean.*

After several moments, he asked, "Mistress Carr, are you well?"

"Yes, Mr. Leyton, very well. Thank you." She dropped her eyes from his, then moved behind the desk as originally planned, taking her seat. She motioned for him to take one of the chairs, conscious that his eyes followed her every move.

I cannot think! What was I going to say? Wynne pasted a slight smile on her face, which she was sure Mr. Leyton could tell was false.

"Did you wish to discuss something with me, mistress?"

"I . . . just wanted to inquire if you had been made comfortable, Mr. Leyton. I understand that you've just arrived . . . that your circumstances are somewhat reduced."

"I'm beginning to feel more comfortable, Mistress Carr. Everyone has been most kind."

Wynne allowed herself to look below the wide shoulders and saw immediately that the simple homespun clothes that Smythe had procured for Mr. Leyton in Williamsburg were inadequate. The shirt strained across his chest, exposing a smooth expanse of muscles and flesh between the laces. There were lines radiating across the fabric, pulling it taut. Even his arms strained the simple garment. She swallowed, then blushed furiously when her eyes returned to his face and she realized he was aware that she had been evaluating him in a most unladylike manner.

Wynne felt the sudden urge to end this interview. She rose quickly. He followed her example almost immediately.

"Well, Mr. Leyton, if you have no questions, I believe I shall talk to you another time. I'm sure you are most fatigued from your long journey."

"But my duties, Mistress Carr. Did you wish to discuss them now?"

No! Wynne felt like screaming the word. Instead, she shook her head. "Not tonight, Mr. Leyton." Not tonight, nor tomorrow, nor the day after that, if I could avoid it, she thought. "Perhaps tomorrow, after you're rested."

"Good night, Mistress Carr." He bowed to her. "I'm at your disposal."

"Yes, Mr. Leyton, I know. Good night."

Wynne felt the heat of a blush warming her cheeks as she watched Andrew Leyton walk through the doorway.

As soon as he was gone, Wynne slumped into the chair and suppressed the irrational urge to burst into tears. This is insane, she thought. He is my property! He cannot make me feel this way, like . . . what? He'd done nothing improper. Except, of course, for that one infuriating, slow perusal when he first walked through the door of the study.

The poor man couldn't be blamed for the way that inadequate shirt fit his muscular body. Nor could he be blamed for the way the breeches clung to his thighs, outlining his long muscles when he stood or moved. But, Lord, why did he have to look like that? Like some statue of an ancient warrior come to life. Wynne lowered her head to her folded arms and gazed into the black void of night. What have I done? she thought. And what will I do now?

Drew made his way up the back staircase to the north wing of the second floor, running his hand along the cool, highly polished mahogany banister. His steps were slow, as if reluctant to leave the presence of the lady below. And a lady she truly was, just as Smythe had promised. He still couldn't reconcile the beautiful woman he'd just met with the stern, efficient mistress Smythe described.

He turned the brass knob to his room, leaving the dimly lit hallway for his comfortable, if somewhat small, bedroom. Smythe had told him earlier that this was the former overseer's room.

For a while he had thought Mistress Carr might want him as a tutor for her children, especially when Smythe had asked all those questions about Latin, French, and classic literature. Yet there had been no mention of teaching, and anyway, the woman in the study below couldn't be old enough to have a child of schooling age. Perhaps he had been brought to Waverley to serve as overseer. Yet that didn't make sense either, for Mistress Carr knew nothing of his ability, or lack of it, in running a plantation. And then there were those awkward questions about his family, about children.

Perhaps she didn't know as much about managing a plantation as Smythe wanted him to believe. Drew's own impression of the lady was not one of authority, but rather of naïveté. Drew crossed to the bedside lamp and turned up the wick. Apparently a maid had been here earlier to straighten and prepare the room, because the soft, worn quilt was neatly folded next to the footboard. A porcelain washbowl and towel had been left on the stand in the corner. It was infinitely more appealing than the hold of a ship.

So this was the former overseer's room. It didn't look recently occupied. There wasn't one personal item in the small chest, on the washstand shelf, or on the bedside table. There were no books, candle stubs, or quills. Had Mistress Carr served in the capacity of overseer in the absence of a man? That might explain Smythe's reference to her hard work and diligence. And, come to think of it, where *was* the lady's husband?

Suddenly too tired to contemplate the enigma of his mistress, Drew sank to the feather mattress and began to remove his clothing. The plain leather shoes and bleached cotton stockings were dropped beside the bed. After a moment he stood to unlace and remove the ill-fitting shirt. He struggled out of the garment, almost ripping the seams as he tugged it over his head. The effort left him breathing hard and he shook his head in dismay.

On his country estate, he would have risen early, met with his estate manager, gone over ledgers and plans, then toured the grounds, checked on the cattle, and perhaps ridden to Moreton for dinner. During his bachelor life in London, he could have fenced away the afternoon after riding to the hounds at dawn, then danced, dined, and drank his way through various clubs before joining his current mistress in a rousing romp. No longer, it seemed. He'd lost strength with each meager meal aboard the transport ship. His bruises had been slower to heal than his attitude.

Regaining his breath, Drew stretched and walked to the stand to wash his face and hands before retiring. Clean water was such a luxury—one he had not viewed as such until his incarceration. He ran the tepid water through his hands, still slightly calloused from his various sports. What kind of labor would these hands see at Waverley?

Drew stood beside the bed, ran his hands over the cool, soft, sheets and smiled. Again, a small pleasure that he had previously taken for granted. They were not the embroidered Irish linen to which he was accustomed, but they were clean and covered a very soft mattress. He couldn't think of anything more appealing at the moment.

Slipping out of the tight homespun breeches and between the cool sheets, he released a sigh. He turned down the lamp and fell back against the pillows. Soon he was soundly asleep, dreaming of a beautiful woman with guarded green eyes and an aura of mystery.

Wynne woke to the pale sunlight of dawn entering her bedroom through the wide windows on either side of one of the fireplaces. She struggled beneath the twisted covers, her legs tangled in a long, white nightgown. She'd had dreams last night, of her nanny, Samuel and her father, all condemning her. They pointed their fingers, taunting her, accusing her. More than once she awakened, hating what she had to do to secure Waverley. If the magistrate, Sir Francis Wolton, ever found out Samuel was permanently disabled and she had been running the plantation for almost six years, she could lose control of everything in the courts. And her other fear, of being alone in her older years, also haunted her.

Dressing quickly without her maid, she made her way downstairs, through the back hallway, and into the early morning splendor. Dew still clung to the closely cut grass. Flowers in the small garden surrounding the fountain were just beginning to open as the sunlight touched their petals. It was the kind of morning that made nightmares vanish.

Taking a seat on one of the stone benches facing the slowly gurgling fountain, Wynne thought about Andrew Leyton. She definitely had to obtain the upper hand at their next meeting. Not that he could be faulted in manner or speech. It was she who had failed. She'd been reduced to mindlessness by the mere presence of a bondsman from the block in Williamsburg.

Who are you, Andrew Leyton, to make me feel this way? Am I so lonely that any man would look good? Wynne sighed, glancing at the second-story window which looked down on the garden.

He was up there, perhaps even watching her. He could be standing there in his rough garments or even without his shirt. Was his flesh as smooth all over as the glimpse she had seen through the lacings? Did he still smell of soap and man?

"Stop it!" Wynne cried aloud, then covered her mouth with a fist as she realized what she was doing. Even in the quiet of the garden she couldn't escape his presence. Something had to be done, and quickly.

Marching with determination into the house, Wynne entered the dining room, startling the servant who was laying out breakfast on the cherry sideboard. "Have someone waken Mr. Leyton and instruct him to join me for breakfast. I'll expect him in twenty minutes." Wynne marched out of the room as fast as she had entered, leaving the flushed kitchen maid without a backward glance.

*   *   *

Drew followed the smell of ham and freshly baked rolls to the dining room. He found the aroma of a substantial breakfast so familiar, the sight of covered, silver serving dishes so refreshing, an ache for the pleasant family breakfasts the Leytons had shared at Moreton overcame him. He stopped just inside the door, reminding himself that only the setting was similar.

Wynne returned to the dining room exactly twenty minutes after she had told the maid to waken Andrew Leyton. She'd changed into a pink-and-grey-striped morning gown that seemed very appropriate for a breakfast chat with a bondsman.

He was standing by a window, looking at the garden and the fountain. "Good morning, Mistress Carr. It's a lovely day."

"Good morning, Mr. Leyton." Wynne tried not to look at him at all. Her first brief glance confirmed the suspicion that she still suffered from the same affliction that had beset her last evening. He moved to the sideboard. "Can I fill your plate, Mistress Carr?"

"No thank you, Mr. Leyton. Please help yourself. We're quite informal here at Waverley in the mornings," Wynne replied, her voice betraying none of her unidentifiable emotions. As soon as he finished, she took a plate and served herself.

After she was seated at the head of the table by the bondsman, who obviously knew his manners, he returned to his place at the side of the long table. They ate in silence, the only sound in the room the clink of silver against china. He coughed softly and Wynne quickly raised her head.

"Are you well, Mr. Leyton? The crossing can be very damaging to one's health."

He placed his fork beside the plate and turned his full attention on her. "It's just the lingering effects of the damp sea air, I believe. I'm not ill."

"Good. That's very good," Wynne returned. She remembered the helplessness she felt when her father's health rapidly deteriorated, the frustration of losing Nanny Richards, and this terrible disease of Samuel's. She could not abide any more sickness.

Returning their attention to their plates, they finished the hearty breakfast. Finally, she very neatly placed her napkin beside the plate and waited for the maid to clear the table. She poured another cup of coffee, sweetened it, and allowed her gaze to rest on Andrew Leyton.

"I understand from Smythe that you were convicted of robbery, Mr. Leyton. Is that correct?"

"That's what I was accused of, yes. It's not what I'm guilty of, however," he replied with assurance.

"And of what are you guilty, if I may inquire?"

He chuckled, then threw back his head and had a hearty laugh. Wynne scowled at him and he sobered. "Forgive me, mistress. It just struck me as humorous. Of what am I guilty? I would have to say that I had the extremely poor judgement of being in the right place at the wrong time." He looked steadily at her. "I am no highwayman."

"What are you, then? I know what you are not, but nothing about who you really are. You were not a poor man, Mr. Leyton. That is apparent."

"No, I wasn't poor. You could say I was a man of business, an investor, or any number of colorful titles. In fact, I've had my hand in many ventures."

Wynne regarded him for a few moments. He was definitely hiding something. He wasn't a common criminal, of that she was fairly certain, and yet he'd been convicted. Could the courts be wrong?

"Last night you asked about your duties. You're probably wondering why I purchased your contract."

"The thought crossed my mind. Seven years is a long time."

Wynne took a deep breath. The conversation was going well. The verbal defenses and inquiries were allowing her to concentrate on reason, not physical appeal.

The maid returned. "Would you care for anything else, ma'am?"

"No, that will be all. Please close the door when you leave."

"Yes, ma'am."

Wynne fidgeted with the lace-edged table linen. Quickly, before she lost her courage, she began. "Mr. Leyton, I have some questions to ask you. They're important questions, or I wouldn't inquire. Would you please indulge me?"

"I will do my best as your humble servant, mistress."

"Sarcasm is not becoming. I don't appreciate it." She felt an unaccustomed burst of anger at his remark.

"I'm sorry," he said with a slight smile. "Please begin. I'll try to answer your questions." Wynne drew a deep breath. "You said before that you aren't ill. In general, are you in good health?"

"Yes, usually I'm in excellent health, as I'm sure the physician certified. The conditions aboard the transport ship were most unpleasant and the food was very poor. I'm not fully recovered from that experience."

"Of course not. Well, I'm sure our cook will solve a portion of that problem."

"Yes, Annie is an excellent cook. You are to be commended on choosing such a talented woman," he said smoothly.

Too smoothly, Wynne thought, for a bondsman. "I don't want to discuss Annie, Mr. Leyton. I would like to discuss you."

"What else can I tell you, Mistress Carr?"

"I understand that you're not married."

"No. I'm not currently, nor have I ever been married."

"Do you have any children, Mr. Leyton?" Wynne raised her eyebrow.

"As I just mentioned . . ."

"I would like to know if you have any children inside or outside of marriage. Smythe indicated you may have some family besides parents, brothers, or sisters."

Wynne watched an array of emotions cross his face, the most significant, one of hurt, of sadness. He turned away finally. "I had a son," he whispered. "James."

A son? An illegitimate child? "Is the boy in England, Mr. Leyton?"

He turned to look at her again, his blue eyes hard and bright. "He's buried in England, Mistress Carr. Any more questions?"

"I'm sorry. Truly I am."

"So am I."

An uncomfortable quiet descended on the dining room as he avoided looking at her, obviously lost in his own thoughts. Wynne felt his sadness, sensed his loss, and knew he'd loved his son. Would that influence how he felt about her proposal?

"I have a few more details to explain to you."

"I hope your details are less personal, Mistress Carr. I find your questions to be in poor taste."

"I will be the judge of what's in poor taste in my household, Mr. Leyton. I'm sorry about your son, about bringing up such an unpleasant memory. But as I said, these questions are important. I hope you can understand."

"No, I don't understand," he said, "but I'm sure you will tell me sooner or later."

"Yes, I'll try to explain the entire situation in as few

words as possible. If you have any questions, please wait until I finish, then we'll discuss them calmly. Is that acceptable?"

"It seems I have no choice."

Wynne glared at his reply, but decided not to start an argument. She added more coffee to her cup, then stirred, watching him as he shifted in his chair again. The spoon clinked against the china cup.

"I've been married for six years, Mr. Leyton. My husband, Samuel, is a hopeless invalid."

"I'm sorry."

"Please do not interrupt."

Wynne continued after taking a sip of coffee. "I've decided I would like a family. Two children should be sufficient."

He simply sat there and stared at her.

"I cannot have children with my husband. He'll never get better." The irrational emotions were returning. She remembered how she'd reacted last night in the study. How she couldn't sit in the garden without thinking of his very manly physical attributes. She swallowed.

He stared. Wynne fidgeted. She took another deep breath. She glanced at him, then her courage failed. She couldn't say the final few words to make him understand. Why couldn't he see?

"Mistress Carr?"

When she looked up the next time, she knew her eyes reflected the near-panic she felt.

"Mistress Carr, do you wish me to help you adopt children? Are you trying to find children to adopt?"

I must tell him, she thought, taking another deep breath. "No, Mr. Leyton." Wynne shook her head. She looked at the pattern of lace. She looked at him. He was so handsome and seemed so confused. "No, I do not wish to adopt."

"Then I don't understand. How could I possibly help you?"

Wynne rose from her chair, her back straight, the tension of the quiet room grating on her nerves. She rushed ahead with her explanation before she lost her courage.

"What I wish you to do, Mr. Leyton, is . . ." She stopped for a moment, rephrasing her response. "I want you to get me with child—twice. I hope it won't take too long, perhaps three years. Then I'll sign your papers and you'll be a free man. It's really quite simple."

There was dead silence at the breakfast table as he stared at her and she defiantly stared back. His eyes narrowed as if considering her announcement and finding it repulsive.

"Are you serious?" he asked in a quiet, almost menacing tone.

"Quite serious, Mr. Leyton." She hoped her confusion didn't show.

He shook his head. "In all my years, I haven't been surprised by very much. But you, madam, have well and truly caught me unawares." He rose from his chair and threw his napkin on the table. She could read his anger through his tightly controlled movements and clenched jaw. "We have nothing to discuss."

"I have not dismissed you, Mr. Leyton," Wynne informed him.

"You lack any understanding of what you were discussing. For my own good, and yours also, I'm leaving this room. If you wish to beg my forgiveness for your indecent proposal, I'll be in my room." He turned and stormed across the dining room.

Wynne stood and stared at his retreating figure for a few moments before she found her own voice. It had taken that long to compose her thoughts. No one had ever spoken to her like that! "Come back here!" she yelled as she watched him march through the doorway and into the hall. She leaned against the table to steady herself, knocking over her empty coffee cup. He was halfway across the main hall when she picked up the delicate piece of china and threw it at him. It hit the base of the staircase in front of him, breaking into a hundred fragments and scattering across the pink-veined marble. He paused for a moment, then walked on.

Aghast at her own behavior, as well as her bondsman's, Wynne stared at the doorway for a few more moments while she trembled in impotent fury. She was mistress here. She wouldn't accept his dismissal of her plan.

Wynne stormed to the front entrance and called, "Smythe!"

Her butler appeared almost instantly by taking one step forward from the doorway leading to the drawing room. "Yes, madam?"

"That man . . ."

Smythe cocked his head and waited patiently.

"He . . ."

"Yes?"

Wynne turned in a swirl of pink and grey and brushed past Smythe into the study. He followed more slowly as she paced in front of the fireplace. Every few strides, Wynne started to speak, then lowered her eyes to stare at the carpet and pace some more.

Finally, she gained control and took her seat in one of the chairs facing her desk. She motioned for Smythe to do the same.

"He refused me! He practically laughed in my face,

insulted me, and left the room without my permission. I
tell you, Smythe, he is intolerable!" Wynne ended on a
high note, emphasizing her outrage.

Smythe's expression betrayed no emotion. He calmly
asked, "What would you have me do, madam?"

"Order him. Tell him he must obey me. I purchased
him, didn't I? He must do my bidding."

"With all due respect, Mistress Carr, I do not think any
magistrate would agree that your bidding in this case was
either proper or a task that could be performed at your
will."

Wynne considered his reply thoughtfully before con-
ceding, "Maybe not proper, but certainly something he
should be capable of." She jumped from her chair in agita-
tion. "Would someone please explain to me why you men
find this so unusual? Can you deny that a young man's
very objective in life seems to be compromising women?
Even an older man! They're all alike in that regard. You
know what happened six years ago with Henry Wolton. I
was the one blamed for that—that scandal! No one said
Henry was wrong when it was he who tried to . . . to . . ."

"That was different, madam."

"Pray tell me what is different. I simply don't understand. They want to compromise me and I don't wish to be
compromised. Now, I wish to be compromised, and he
says he doesn't wish to do so. There is no logic here!"

"Please, madam, be seated and calm yourself. I will
attempt to explain to the best of my abilities. This is, however, hardly a proper conversation to have even with a male
family member."

"Foolishness! There's very little proper left in my life.
You know that."

"Aye, I know. That is why I will try to explain a man's
mind."

Smythe remained silent while Wynne again took her seat, smoothed her skirts, and sat straight in the chair. She raised questioning eyes to Smythe.

"You are correct that men are attracted to women and some attempt to compromise them. This is especially true when the lady is young and attractive."

"But what about Mr. Leyton?"

"Men prefer to be the aggressors. A man insists on deciding upon the lady, the circumstances, and the time. That is one reason I urged you to abandon this plan. This game was not initiated by Mr. Leyton; therefore, he is not willing to accept your rules.

"The man always wishes to be in control. If the lady is willing to play the game, the man may allow her to set the stage, but he continues to be the playwright. She becomes an actor in his production."

"That is ridiculous! Why would a man go to such lengths to compromise a woman?" Wynne was incredulous.

"Seduction is not a simple act. It is merely one act of the play," Smythe replied.

"You speak in riddles, of plays and such. Men are men. They waste time and effort in the staging of such games."

"That may be, but it is how the game is played."

Wynne was thoughtful for a moment. She had never considered that these silly games played by most men, married and single, old and young, were a necessary prerequisite to the actual physical relationship. In trying to simplify the outcome, she had apparently overlooked a major ingredient. Comprehension dawned, flowing over her face and neck as a gentle blush, lighting her eyes with an inner spark.

"How can I make Mr. Leyton want to play this game, Smythe? You are a man. Tell me what I must do."

Smythe looked positively horrified.

"Come, tell me. I know you've at least ideas on how I may achieve this goal." Wynne smiled innocently at the butler. "We must write the play. What is the first act?"

"Madam, I have no idea!"

"Of course you do. You just don't realize it yet. Let's think of a solution together. You've been my adviser since Samuel became ill," she added quietly. "You know he would help me were he able."

"It is not my place to advise you on this matter. We are speaking of your good name."

"We are speaking of my children. And you know I have no one else to ask, Smythe. Please, not as a servant, but as a friend, help me. If I have to participate in a man's ridiculous game to gain what I need, then I will."

Smythe sighed. Wynne smiled.

"If you are sure . . . ?"

"I'm sure."

"Then, madam, here is what you must do. . . ."

3

After talking with Smythe for much of the morning, Wynne felt better. She recovered from her anger and confusion quickly, concentrating on the ideas they had formulated in the study. It wasn't as carefully drawn as a battle plan, but to Wynne, it was just as important.

The late afternoon found her relaxing in a tepid bath, the scent of jasmine floating around her freshly washed hair and glowing skin as she reviewed her day. After leaving Smythe, she had met with the visiting shoemaker. He was in the process of making serviceable footwear for all the slaves and servants, a task that would take him almost three months. Then she discussed the impending weaning of calves with the stockman, the cabin repairs with the carpenter, and the new iron hinges with the blacksmith. All in all, it had been a very productive day.

She had received a letter from a Mr. Barton MacClintock, a factor from the Scottish firm of William Cuninghame and Company out of Glasgow. She had never sold Waverley's tobacco through that particular firm, using instead the contacts Samuel had established before his illness. MacClintock had visited Waverley last month, reviewing the rich fields and newly transplanted tobacco crop. He was also interested in the other crops produced on the plantation and told Wynne he would be especially interested in purchasing corn or wheat if she had a surplus.

Now he wanted to visit her again on a "matter of mutual interest." Wynne wasn't sure what that could be. It was too early in the season for firm commitments and she was confused by the wording of the letter. He almost implied she *must* meet with him, but that was unlikely. He probably had just received a shipment from England and wanted to find buyers. She dismissed the man from her mind as she splashed in the cool water.

She'd thought a lot about what Smythe had said earlier, about making a man feel as though he were making an amorous conquest. That was a difficult act to perfect, since she wasn't at all interested in having any attention from the bondsman, amorous or otherwise, except what was absolutely required to have a child. But still, when she thought of Andrew Leyton, it was difficult to suppress the feeling of anticipation and exhilaration that caused her skin to overheat and her breath to catch. Of course, it must be because she was so anxious to have a child. There was something exciting about him that she couldn't deny, that she responded to on a level she had never experienced before.

From Smythe she learned that Mr. Leyton had appeared downstairs for luncheon, which he took in the kitchen in the company of Annie, the cook. Afterwards, he had retired to the drawing room with a Greek tragedy. He undoubtedly wishes to irritate me by behaving like a guest rather than a servant, Wynne thought, but he won't succeed.

He had also used the bathing room again, and had enlisted the aid of one of the maids to alter his very limited wardrobe. Wynne made a mental note to obtain more suitable clothing for the man.

Stepping out of the brass tub and drying quickly, she donned a sheer chemise and rang for her maid. She would dress with particular care. Smythe had mentioned that Mr. Leyton had believed her to be a widow at first. Perhaps she did wear grey and lavender often, but those colors had always suited her mood. She did *not* feel like grey this evening.

Several minutes later, Wynne's maid fastened the last button. "This is a beautiful gown, Mistress Carr. It reminds me of Waverley in the spring."

"Indeed, it's very springlike, isn't it, Millie?" Wynne smoothed the grass-green silk and adjusted the fitted, stiff bodice, embroidered with pink and white flowers from the square neck to the pointed waistline. She smiled at her reflection in the cheval mirror. "This should do very nicely."

Millie collected the discarded towels and day dress. She remarked casually, "Cook seems to think very highly of the new bondsman."

"Oh, yes," Wynne said, swirling in front of the mirror. The green silk was parted in the front to reveal a pale pink quilted petticoat.

"I heard he reads books. He probably writes and figures too."

"Yes, I think he does. Oh, Millie, get the small locket from my jewelry box."

Shaking her head, Millie walked across the room and found the necklace. When she returned to fasten it around Wynne's neck, she had to wait while Wynne splashed perfume on her wrists.

"Would you like me to prepare any bedchambers for guests, ma'am?"

Wynne looked at Millie, puzzled by her question. "Why would you think we are having guests?"

"Well, I just thought since you were getting all dressed up . . ."

Wynne suddenly realized how unusual her behavior must seem to the servants. She sometimes dressed for dinner, but very rarely, and never in such an elaborate gown. And wearing jewelry was an equally odd thing for her to do. Surely they wouldn't think she was dressing for the bondsman!

"Millie, I . . ." Wynne turned around and retrieved a lace shawl, draping it over her arm. "I just felt this beautiful spring weather was worth celebrating. There won't be any company coming tonight."

"It's a shame to waste that beautiful gown, eating dinner all by yourself."

Wynne gave Millie a hard look. "If you're finished, you may take the wet towels to the laundry."

"Yes, ma'am," Millie replied, her plain, thin face blushing.

Someday, Wynne thought, I must do something about that girl's inquisitive attitude. But tonight she was feeling too happy. The weather was beautiful, the tobacco crop was growing well, she had a plan, and the bondsman was, after all, only a man.

There were no doubt several basic necessities she could provide for the bondsman. One was excellent food. She had ordered a delicious dinner of chowder, veal, creamed peas, tender greens, candied roses, cheese and fruit, and, of course, wines to accompany the various courses. In addition, Annie had promised a dessert to please the most sophisticated palate, which Mr. Leyton no doubt possessed.

Depending on how well she could follow Smythe's suggestions, perhaps she would see to Andrew Leyton's other needs later.

Upstairs in his bedroom, Drew was pondering anything but the various dinner courses. In the hours since breakfast, he had alternately raged, contemplated, condemned, and been intrigued by the absurd suggestion of his owner. He refused to believe that she was serious, yet she had seemed so direct. No woman came right up to a man and told him that he would service her the way a stallion does a mare.

Surely she was slightly crazed. After all, Smythe had told him she lived a virtually secluded existence on this plantation. Perhaps the lack of civilization had adversely affected her mind. Still, she had seemed so sane for a few moments. Perhaps that was a symptom of her illness.

Drew turned to the small mirror over the oak chest. Who was he fooling? Not only had she looked sane, she had looked more beautiful than any woman he could remember. She had been a shining beacon in his sea of discontent, and now his traitorous mind refused to think of any defect to her loveliness.

Perhaps she was not the fascinating creature he had created by his imaginings. Perhaps she was a vain shrew who believed that the world would do her bidding. She may have tried this approach on many unknowing and innocent men. Maybe she was this dictatorial in all her dealings with other people.

Or perhaps she was telling the truth.

Drew pulled on the rough-spun, altered clothing. It was the only change he had, and although it now fit his greater height and more muscular body better, he was still uncomfortable in garb more suited for a laborer. Overall, he was irritated and confused; it was not a good combination.

Earlier he had asked Annie to trim his hair, and now that was at least more presentable. He'd taken another long, soaking bath with the strong soap Waverley seemed to prefer. He'd not seen his mistress since leaving the dining room that morning, and he'd looked in the house, the kitchen, the garden and across the lawns. She had virtually disappeared, yet everywhere he went, there was evidence of her presence. Smythe said she was with the carpenter, the carpenter said she was at the house, and Annie swore she was "out and about." The woman was either a whirlwind of activity or she was effectively avoiding him.

Then, late in the afternoon, the shy maid who had altered his clothing appeared at his door. He was invited—not ordered—to dinner at seven. His mistress had sent her apologies for not yet providing more formal dinner attire, but assured him that he was welcome despite his clothing. That was very cordial, considering these clothes were provided by her, Drew scoffed.

Still, he had dressed with care. He was both interested and repelled, and at the moment he couldn't decide which was the stronger emotion. One thing was certain: He must learn the truth about her.

A knock sounded on his door. He opened it.

"Mr. Leyton, if you're ready, the mistress will see you in the family parlor below, just down the stairs," the maid said.

He nodded in agreement. "I'll be right down."

The family parlor was located in the same wing as his bedroom, only downstairs. He had not previously spent any time there. Mistress Carr was no doubt formulating new plans for his next seven years.

* * *

Confident. Masculine. A diamond in the rough. These descriptions flashed through Wynne's mind as her bondsman slowly made his way down the stairs. His muscled thighs strained against the fabric. He moved with loose-limbed grace and precision. He dominated the scene, and what was so disconcerting to her, he seemed to know it. A hollow feeling began in Wynne's stomach, spreading downward and making her shift on the padded seat.

Apparently the day of rest and good food had done wonders for his health. He appeared stronger, more sure of himself. He looked more formidable. She could read nothing in his cool blue eyes as she observed him from her seat on the damask settee. She took several calming breaths, ordering her heart to stop pounding.

"Mistress Carr." He bowed formally at the bottom of the stairs.

"Mr. Leyton," Wynne graciously replied. "Please have a seat. Would you care for sherry?"

"Thank you," he replied politely. It was as if they had just been introduced in London, as if this morning had never occurred. It was as if he were truly an honored guest in her home.

She rose from the settee and walked to the sideboard. Her movements were careful, measured, and controlled. It was hard for Drew to believe that this was the shrew who had propositioned him and then angrily thrown a china cup at him from her breakfast table.

She returned with a glass of sherry. "Is there something amiss, Mr. Leyton? You seemed deep in thought."

His eyes passed over each detail of her dress, skimming with interest over the creamy expanse of bosom and shoulders, up her long neck and to her blushing cheeks. His eyes returned to her bright green ones, and he smiled with lazy self-indulgence. "No, nothing at all seems amiss, Mistress Carr."

She blushed even more. "You forget yourself, Mr. Leyton."

"Do I?" Drew took the sherry, then captured her hand before she could draw it away. He lowered his head to kiss that soft, white flesh as she began to resist in earnest. He ignored her attempts as he placed a brief kiss above her knuckles. She gasped just as he released her.

Now I've shocked her, Drew thought as she stepped quickly backwards, almost colliding with the settee.

"I thought you invited my attentions. Pardon me if I misunderstood this morning."

Drew raised an eyebrow and sipped his sherry. No telling what she was thinking about him now. She probably considered him a decadent womanizer. Even so, she apparently thought she could play with him as a cat does a mouse. Well, they would both see who was the predator.

She placed a hand on her chest as if to still her racing heart and made an obvious effort at composing her features. "Did you have a pleasant day?"

"Quiet, but pleasant. It seems my duties as bondservant have been temporarily suspended."

"I thought a day or more of rest would be in your best interest."

"Indeed, I was not up to strenuous activity."

"Mr. Leyton, we will discuss your duties at another time. I would like to have a pleasant evening and a good meal. I hope your desires run in a similar path."

Drew didn't miss the slip, nor did he miss the brief flare of panic in her eyes when she recognized the double entendre. "It's always best when two people's desires are equally matched, but I don't think that is the case this time," he said, gazing intently at her rigid features. "What do you think, mistress?"

"I think . . ."

"Yes?"

"I think we should adjourn to the dining room for our evening meal," she said harshly, placing her sherry glass on the low table.

Drew followed her example, feeling that he had won the first skirmish.

The meal was both a successful culinary feat and a personal disaster. The conversation was limited to passing the condiments and complimenting the cook, while the unspoken issues screamed for release. Wynne knew they both remembered the morning meal, and by silent decree did not discuss the "misunderstanding."

As a consequence, Wynne was almost grateful when her head groom arrived in the dining room, breathless and with hat in hand. Smythe was apologetic as he interrupted their meal, but they had just finished dessert. "I'm sorry, Mistress Carr, but Riley said it was important."

Wynne folded her napkin with customary care, placing it beside the gold-rimmed plate. "What's the problem, Riley?"

"It be the old mare, mistress. She been tryin' to foal for nigh onto six hours, and that foal don't want to be born," Riley replied, twisting his shapeless hat and shifting from one sawdust-covered foot to the other.

Immediately Wynne jumped from her chair. "Have more coffee prepared and brought to the stable. I'll be with you in just a moment, Riley."

Drew rose also and told the flustered Riley, "I'll go with you."

Wynne stopped and turned. "I don't have time to argue with you, Mr. Leyton. We are in the middle of a crisis."

"Pardon me, Mistress Carr," Drew replied. "May I have your permission to join you in the stable?"

"Can you help?" Wynne asked seriously.

"I have some experience with horses. I can try."

"Then you may go with Riley. Let us not waste more time." Wynne glided out the dining room doors, then lifted her skirts to bound up the stairs with unladylike haste.

In the stable, in a large stall designed for foaling, a sweat-slick bay mare labored to produce the latest addition to Waverley's limited racing stock. She rolled her eyes and strained her neck, but the foal would not make its entrance. Her strength was obviously failing.

Riley entered the stall and the mare gazed at him with large brown eyes dulled with pain. Drew followed, taking in the situation in a glance. "How long has she been like this?"

"For more than an hour. I knew it'd be hard for the old girl, but not like this. She's always been easy to foal." Riley shook his balding head. Drew knelt in the sawdust near the mare's head. He placed his hand over her extended nostrils, both to let her get his scent and to judge the shallowness of her breathing. It was not a promising discovery.

Drew rose and moved to her flanks, running his hand along the distended sides and moving to the mare's rump. He pushed her wrapped tail aside and was just about to examine her when Wynne burst into the stall, grabbing the corner post to stop her headlong flight. The tired mare shuddered and snorted at her intrusion.

"Must you startle her so?" he asked harshly. "She's in distress."

The frosty glare returned to her bright green eyes. "I am well aware that *my* mare is in distress, Mr. Leyton, without your expert opinion."

"Then I suggest, Mistress Carr, that you do not distress her further by running around like an empty-headed child," Drew retorted.

Wynne had changed into a plain, serviceable gown and was standing with hands on hips just inside the doorway. Her cheeks were flushed as she glared at him.

Wynne turned to Riley, apparently deciding to dismiss a "mere bondsman" as an inconsequential irritant. "What do you think, Riley? Will she be able to foal?"

"I just don't know, ma'am. I need to turn the foal, but my old hands be all crooked, and, well . . ."

"I'll turn the foal, Riley," Drew volunteered.

Wynne's flashing eyes settled on him as she whirled to face him. "You? Why should I trust this mare to you?"

"Because she'll be dead if you don't," Drew said frostily.

Wynne seemed to consider him as he knelt in the thick, fragrant bedding. Did she see that he was confident of his abilities? He couldn't tell; mostly, she looked disgusted with the whole affair.

"Go ahead—if you know what you're doing. This foal is very special." Wynne walked softly to the mare's head, kneeling also and stroking the damp, dusty blaze. "Her sire was Monkey. Do you know who he was?"

Drew looked up from his contemplation of the mare's feeble efforts. "Maybe." He well knew the reputation of the Virginia racehorse, who was also famous in England.

"She's in foal to Jolly Roger."

"The Duke of Kingston's champion?"

"He's a Virginia horse now, Mr. Leyton."

Drew returned to his examination. "Hold her head. I'm

going to see how the foal is positioned." With that, Drew rolled up his sleeves and went to work.

"Do you think he will live?"

The bondsman looked at the wet bundle of horseflesh that was attempting to rise on unsteady legs. "I think they'll both live if she has no internal bleeding."

Feeling his eyes on her, Wynne glanced only briefly at him before returning her attention to the mare and foal. She wondered how she looked to him now as she sat in the sawdust, no doubt dust-streaked where sweat had pooled at her brow, her lip, her neck. She made an effort to wipe away the grime, knowing his eyes were on her. It was a mystery how he could make her feel so confused with only his presence. It was much safer to concentrate on the foal

The mare was still lying down, but as Wynne watched, she straightened her front legs and hefted herself upright. She shook the dust from her coat and hung her head as she breathed deeply. "What's the mare's name?" he asked.

Wynne shook her head and laughed a little. "It sounded very sensible to a four-year-old. Her name is Colonel Nanny."

"I beg your pardon?"

"I named her myself after my father and I had arrived in Virginia. She was just a little thing, a few days older than that fellow," she explained, pointing to the foal. "My father said I could name her, so I picked the names of the two people I cared most about: my father, the Colonel, and my nanny, Mrs. Richards."

He continued to look at the foal, who was now being licked by his mother. "It's good she's showing interest in the foal. Maybe she's stronger than I thought."

"Of course she's interested in the foal. He's her own flesh and blood!" Wynne replied indignantly.

"That doesn't mean so much. I've seen many mothers, human and otherwise, who had very little interest in what they gave birth to." He turned to look intently at Wynne. "Haven't you?"

"No, I haven't. It is instinctive for a mother to care for her offspring. To be otherwise is unnatural."

"If you truly believe that, you've led a very sheltered life." He continued to look intently at her, but she turned away, irritated.

"You are a true cynic, Mr. Leyton, to have so little faith in women."

"Maybe, though I prefer to think of myself as a realist. Tell me the truth, Mistress Carr. Haven't you known other women, neighbors perhaps, who didn't even name their children, hold them, or spend time with them, until the child was over one year of age?"

"No. I am glad to say that I do not know anyone like that, Mr. Leyton. Perhaps your acquaintances are more varied." She still thought it inconceivable that a mother, someone who had been blessed as a parent, would not love her child.

He stared at her until she looked away. The stable was quiet in the early morning hours, silent and strangely intimate.

"How long did you say you have lived here, in Virginia?"

Suspicious, Wynne countered, "Why do you ask?"

"Oh, just curious. It would tell me how old this mare is, for example," he replied innocently.

Or how old I am, Wynne thought. She glared at him, as if daring him to ask the question himself. He only raised that one eyebrow, and continued to look innocently at her.

She decided to take the dare. "Twenty-one years, Mr. Leyton. The mare is twenty-one."

"Ah, I see. Well, that is quite old, especially to have a foal."

"She's not too old to foal! Why, she's a very healthy horse. You should see her run around the pasture."

Wynne stopped her headlong rush of words to look at him as he sat quite still and continued to smile.

"You just don't know her that well. You would change your mind."

"Are we still talking about the mare, Mistress Carr?"

Oh, how easily he had turned the tables. He seemed to find her weaknesses and turn them to his advantage. Wynne flushed with anger and embarrassment.

"Well?"

"We are discussing the mare, Mr. Leyton. Only the mare. And I believe the conversation is exhausted."

Before she could rise to leave, he captured her arm and pulled her against him. She felt the beat of her pulse accelerate as he held her to his side. She experienced the heat of a flush, smelled the sweat of the horse and the scent of the stable. He smelled of soap, man, and earthly pleasure, and suddenly she was very, very afraid of the sensations stirring in her body.

Wynne continued to look into his intense blue eyes, filled with a message she couldn't decipher. He bent his head, blocking the light from the single lantern, and then she knew the message. He was going to kiss her, really kiss her, and she didn't have the will to say no.

His lips were warm and surprisingly soft, gentle, and persuasive as they touched her mouth. He moved smoothly, slipping his arm to her back and pressing her closer. His lips continued to move, coaxing a response from her, but Wynne was so shocked by the experience that she couldn't react. She felt faint, as if she had been spinning in circles, and that frightened her so much she groaned and pushed away.

His eyes flew open, all the softness gone. Wynne read anger and perhaps scorn in his set features. "So, you really are made of ice. I wondered about that, since you show fire on occasion. You must be one of those women who are either cold or angry—never anything in between," he taunted cruelly.

Wynne tried to slap him, but they were still too close, and her attempt was easily stopped. "How dare you! How dare you try to take advantage of me in the stable, like a rutting animal!"

"Rutting animal? Really, Mistress Carr, you are too clever." He rose with fluid grace to his feet, leaving her sitting in the sawdust. "Let me clarify the situation for you, since you are having so much trouble putting this into perspective." He continued to glare at her and she glared back, too angry to speak.

"This morning you informed me that I had been purchased to . . . what was that phrase? . . . Ah yes, 'get you with child.' I was to impregnate you twice, I believe?" He bent at the waist, until his nose was about a foot from hers. "Just how would you compare your earlier instruction with a rutting animal, Mistress Carr?"

"It's different," she sputtered. "We are two adults, you fool. Can't you see the difference?"

"Was I just to throw you down on the dining table and get the job done? Or perhaps you thought I would politely ask if I could lift your skirts after dessert? Just what did you have in mind? I would really like to know."

Wynne, so embarrassed and angry that she could barely speak, glared at him. He continued to glare back, unblinking, until she knew she must answer.

"It should be done in a civilized manner, Mr. Leyton. Something I'm sure you know little about. I would evaluate the optimal time, you would be informed, and that would be that."

He broke eye contact, shaking his head. "You are truly mad if you think that would work. Either that, or you know nothing of men."

"Smythe said you'd not agree to that."

"By God, you discussed this with Smythe!"

"Of course. He helped me purchase you, didn't he?"

His eyes were so cold, Wynne shivered as he questioned her further. "What else did Smythe say?"

"Well," Wynne hesitated, "he said that men didn't like to be approached by women. He said men like to take the initiative. It all seems silly to me, but he assured me that you would feel that way. It seems he was right."

"Right! By God, woman, you do not know the meaning of the word." He ran a hand through his hair, which had worked loose from the leather thong, strands hanging almost to his shoulders. "You didn't want to be kissed?"

"Of course not," she said indignantly. More gently she asked, "Is it a requirement?"

"A requirement!" he burst out. He turned and paced the stall, hanging his arms over the half-door. "You really do want to have children, don't you? This isn't some ridiculous scheme to acquire a lover for a few pounds?"

"Mr. Leyton, I assure you I'm quite serious. Did you question my motives? I was telling you the truth. It is my intention to have two children, and I would like to have your cooperation." Flashes of her earlier conversation with Smythe penetrated her thoughts, and she tried to control her temper and appeal to Leyton's sense of duty.

"You said yourself you are healthy. And you're an intelligent man. You're not unattractive. Those are qualities I want in my children. That's why I purchased you, Mr. Leyton. You *are* suitable."

"Where is your husband?"

Wynne blinked, startled by the question. She had known he would ask sooner or later, but she'd hoped to postpone that particular question until she could devise a good answer. It would be a lie, of course, but what else could she do? She couldn't admit that her invalid spouse was less than a mile away, secreted in a hunting lodge in the dense forest.

"I don't believe that's your concern. The only thing you need to know is that he cannot harm you." Wynne paused, taking a deep breath. "He has been ill for a long time."

He continued to stare out the stall door until the wobbly foal ambled forward. The bondsman guided the foal to his mother and helped to steady his steps.

When the foal found what he was seeking, Leyton turned to her again. "I can understand your motivation, even though I don't agree with your methods." He paused, looking up at the planked ceiling, then back to the newborn foal.

"I don't think I could service you like Jolly Roger did this mare, then never see the product of that union." He paused again. "I also don't know what kind of relationship you've had with your husband, or anyone else for that matter. However, I couldn't make love to a woman I didn't desire. Passion involves more than the act of coupling, and if my kiss was so distasteful to you, then I'm sure we've nothing else to discuss."

He turned to leave, then stopped. "Perhaps you can return me to Williamsburg, Mistress Carr. You can always tell the auctioneer that I was unsuitable."

With that he left, closing the stall door behind him.

For a long time after he left, Wynne continued to sit in

the stall and watch the mare and foal. The sun rose and diffused the light from the lantern, but still she didn't rise. The mare watched her with tired eyes, nuzzling the spindly legged foal.

Riley returned from his brief rest, rubbing his sleepy eyes, obviously surprised to see her still sitting there. "Is the old girl doing all right, Mistress Carr?"

Wynne looked up in confusion, then rose to her feet. Her legs were cramped from sitting.

"Colonel Nanny is doing fine. I really don't think her age is that much of an issue," she replied with a huff.

4

"Mr. MacClintock, how nice to see you again."
Wynne led the wiry-framed tobacco factor to the chairs
before the fireplace in her study. "To what do I owe this
visit?"

Barton MacClintock settled into the comfortable
upholstered chair. Wynne watched his eyes scan the
room, taking in the modest oak wainscoting; the thick
carpet of subdued colors; the furniture produced by local
artisans. Apparently he did not find the decor to his
taste.

MacClintock smiled, but there was nothing friendly in
his eyes. "I came to talk with you about a future business
relationship, Mistress Carr. I think we could help each
other a great deal."

"It's too early to contract for my tobacco. The other
crops are not ready for harvest yet either. I believe it premature to discuss our possible business."

"Oh, I don't think the business I have to discuss could
be considered premature," MacClintock replied with just a

hint of innuendo. "We can talk about much more than the crops."

Wynne rose with grace, anger replacing her usual composure. "You may leave now, Mr. MacClintock. Smythe will show you out."

"Don't think I want to do that, ma'am. And after I tell you what I know, I don't think you will want me to go either."

Wynne paced to the open window, near the corner of the house that framed the fountain. She listened to the calming water, clenching her fists in the folds of her skirts.

"What do you wish to discuss, Mr. MacClintock?" Wynne asked quietly. She believed that she already knew the answer. She had dreaded this day for six years.

"Only one very isolated house, with a very helpless man living there. I was just asking myself, 'MacClintock, why would that man be living way out there in the woods, when he could be living at that nice big house?' And then it came to me. If he was up here, why, everyone would know the truth. You wouldn't want that, would you, ma'am?"

Wynne looked away from the garden and returned her attention to the miserable little weasel sitting in her study as if he owned the world. In a way, he did. He was currently in firm control of her life, her livelihood, and her future.

"No, I wouldn't want that. The question is, what do you want?"

"Oh, just your cooperation with a little side business I have."

Wynne continued to stand by the window, staring at the man. She would not beg for his answers; she would not solicit his unscrupulous demands.

Apparently undaunted, MacClintock continued, "Now, I have a sort of contract to deliver certain goods to my clients on the western frontier. They're anxious to get their hands on what I have, but we have a problem." MacClintock paused as if he expected encouragement from Wynne before he continued. Receiving none, he marched ahead.

"The problem is, I can't quite deliver these items to the Queen Mary's Dock or up College Creek. I've been looking for a good spot to dock below the fall line on the rivers, but until I visited you last month, I was beginning to think I would never find it. Then, lo and behold, I found this nice, deep creek flowing right into the Chickahominy. Quiet and isolated.

"Now, ma'am, what do you think I found near one of those creeks?" the Scot chuckled.

Wynne continued to stare. When he remained silent, she gave in and answered, "We both know what you found, MacClintock."

"Yes, well, I suppose we do. The only question is, can we help each other? Now, you have a lot to lose. If any of your fine neighbors accidentally found out that your husband wasn't away on business like you always claim, then the courts might just appoint a guardian for you."

"That will never happen, I assure you," Wynne returned with a confidence she didn't really feel. It had always been her fear that Sir Francis Wolton might discover Samuel's illness.

MacClintock's eyes narrowed and he replied maliciously, "You had just better think that it might, Mistress Carr, because I assure you that it could. Just a word here and there, and the magistrate will appear before you can pack that poor old man off to another hiding place. Why, the move alone might kill him. Then you'd be a murderer as well as a liar."

Wynne glared at his assurance. Yes, she could see that happening, and it scared her more than she would ever admit.

"I might even get appointed the guardian of the estate, come to think about it." MacClintock smiled cruelly. "We could have a good time out here, far away from everyone else. We could become good friends."

"I have no intention of becoming your friend, Mr. Mac-Clintock, so get down to the business you want to discuss." Wynne moved away from the window, walking to the desk. She sat with erect dignity, folding her hands on the desktop and staring at the Scot. MacClintock apparently didn't know that Sir Francis would never appoint another man as guardian of the estate. If he had the chance, he would save the honor for himself, or maybe his son. Wynne barely controlled her shudder at the thought.

"Let me outline what I think you want. You wish to land some supplies, probably weapons for the Indians, on my land as your dock. You'll then carry these items overland, or someone will meet you here to take possession of them. In return, you'll remain quiet about my husband and our situation here at Waverley." Wynne paused. "Is that correct?"

MacClintock slapped his knee, smiling widely. For the first time, a spark of true delight reached his eyes. "Very, very good. You keep quiet and I keep quiet. We are going to get along fine."

"No, MacClintock. We are not going to get along at all. You conduct your business and I will continue to run Waverley."

The Scot shook his head. "If that's what you want, then I guess we'll do it your way. As long as we both get what we want, I can't complain." MacClintock rose, reaching for his hat.

"I'll be going, then. You probably won't see me for a while, but when I return, I'll use the creek beside the hunting lodge. My men will continue upstream, and they won't disturb you."

Wynne nodded absently, anxious for this awful man to leave.

"Good day to you, Mistress Carr. You have made a wise choice." The door closed behind the little man.

Rising, Wynne returned to the window. There was a rustling of the bushes at the corner of the house, but no sign of any person in the garden. Probably the wind, she thought.

"A wise choice," Wynne remembered him saying. No, she had not made a good choice. She really had no choice, and that was the saddest thing of all.

Drew entered the front hall, intent on finding Smythe and having his letter posted. Before he had walked ten steps, the butler intercepted him.

"May I help you, Mr. Leyton? You appear to be lost."

Drew chuckled. "Always the proper fellow, aren't you, Smythe?" He paused and looked around the spacious hall with the rose marble floor and the palest pink walls. It was a room designed to please a woman. The furnishings were sparse, but graceful in design and strategically placed to encourage intimate conversation.

"No, I'm not lost. I figured that if I ventured into restricted territory that you would find me immediately. In fact, I was looking for you."

Smythe straightened even more and asked chillingly, "What did you require?"

"I need this letter posted as soon as possible." He hand-ed the thick envelope to Smythe, who gave it a very thor-ough perusal.

"And how will you pay for the posting, Mr. Leyton?"

Drew's eyes narrowed. For the first time he considered how the packet must appear to the haughty butler. It was addressed to his father's solicitor in the most exclusive business section of London, but it contained several letters to his family and business manager. He hoped an explana-tion would not be demanded; he had no suitable reason for the correspondence that he wanted to share with Smythe.

Besides, his ability to pay for anything he desired had never been questioned. It irritated him that he had no idea how a bondservant paid for something.

"Well, Mr. Leyton?"

Drew placed his hands on his hips and replied, "Your mistress will pay. Tell her if she wants my cooperation, that letter *will* be posted. And, Smythe, I know you understand my meaning." Drew's hands clenched into fists, and he turned and left the room with deliberate strides.

Drew continued to the back of the hall, meaning to escape from the man who reminded him of his bondage. He would visit Annie in the kitchen. She appeared to be the only normal person he had met since coming to the colonies.

Before he made it out the back entrance that led to the covered walkway to the kitchens, he was intercepted by the object of his frustration. Her cheeks pink from the slight exertion, Wynne hurried toward him from the other hall-way, holding her skirts up slightly. He could see her soft kid shoes and just a hint of pale stockings. Her voice was soft and breathless.

"I heard you in the hall, Mr. Leyton. I thought perhaps

you would walk with me to the stable to visit the new foal."

"Why?" he asked abruptly.

"Why? Why, to name the foal. Since you delivered him, you should have the honor of naming him."

What was she up to now? She acted as though the scene in the barn the previous evening had never happened. While he had pondered his dilemma, standing by his open window, staring at the night sky, she'd probably been dreaming up new ways to confuse him. His anger faded as he considered his options. Two people could play this game.

"I would be honored to name the foal, Mistress Carr." He offered his arm in his best courtly manner, knowing he was challenging her to accept.

She placed her well-manicured, soft hand on his rough sleeve and gave him a faint smile. "Well, let's go to the stable then. I'm anxious to see how the mare is faring this morning."

"Yes, let's check on the old girl," he replied, smiling innocently. Let's see how long your cool composure lasts today, he added silently.

He saw her frown as they started down the brick walkway to the stable. She obviously didn't play these games often, else she would be more adept at controlling her feelings. Her emotions showed clearly in her expressive green eyes. He had seen everything reflected there except passion and love.

What would she look like, lying in a rumpled bed, her lips swollen from his kisses, her eyes glazed with satisfaction? He felt the blood rush to his groin at the very thought. Damn, but he couldn't be serious about bedding the woman! She was crazy, or close to it. She was trying to use him, a Leyton, and nobody did that! The last thing he wanted was another bastard child, especially one in Virginia, a land that he planned to leave at the first available moment.

Still, he wanted Wynne Carr as he'd wanted no other woman. There was a mystery lurking behind her eyes, hiding in the house somewhere. That must be the reason he found her so fascinating.

Both mare and foal were doing fine, as they saw when they arrived at the large box stall. Riley had just fed a bran mash to the mother, so she was munching contentedly while the still wobbly foal nursed. Mistress Carr glowed with a rare, sweet smile at the pair, and Drew found it impossible to look away. Damn, but she was beautiful. He wished he could call her by her first name, at least to himself.

"Isn't he wonderful? It always amazes me that they are up and around so soon." She turned and he knew she saw the naked desire in his eyes before he schooled his features.

He felt disgusted for revealing so much. He didn't want to talk about the foal. He wanted answers, not more complications. He continued to look ahead, at the foal, and tried not to think of the woman standing so close at his side.

"Do you have a preference in names, Mistress Carr?"

"No, not really. It might be good to use his sire's name, to identify him."

"Yes," Drew replied cooly. "It is common to give the offspring the father's name."

"That's not what I meant, Mr. Leyton. I meant, his sire is a famous racer. If he is promising, we would do well to play on the name."

"Of course. He's your horse, after all." Drew paused, thinking. "How about Roger's Folly?"

Her forehead wrinkled, her brows drawn together, she

repeated, "Roger's Folly. Roger's Folly." The foal quit nursing and turned his head to look at her.

Drew laughed at her expression of delight. "I think he likes it. What do you say?"

"I think it's a fine name, Mr. Leyton."

"Thank you." Drew pushed away from the stall door to face his owner. "What about me, Mistress Carr? Will you call me by my given name?"

She turned around so her back was against the stall door, clasping her hands behind her, leaning her shoulder blades against the wood. Her breasts pushed against the fine, pale yellow silk of her gown.

"What would you have me say to you . . . Andrew?"

He gasped as she whispered his name. It was like a caress, like her soft, white hands lightly tracing his spine. His name had never sounded so sweet.

He had no answer to her question. What could he say with words? Drew stepped forward, slowly raising his hands to clasp her upper arms gently. His body moved forward until he touched her lightly and her skirts brushed against his arousal, but he doubted she felt how much he wanted her. Not yet. Her head rose to stare unflinchingly into his eyes.

"Say nothing. Show me." Drew ran his hands up her arms, across her shoulders to the bared flesh of her neckline. His fingers splayed outward to caress her neck and jawline, then continued to her hair and small pink ears. Everything about her was soft and beautiful.

Wynne closed her eyes as he caressed her. She'd never dreamed that touching could feel this way. She wanted to sink down, clasped to him, and lie on the dirt of the stable with no thought to the time or place. She wanted him to continue to work his magic, for indeed it must be an illusion of the senses.

He leaned into her, crushing her against the wood with his weight as he lowered his head. "Say it again," he whispered. "Say my name again. Call me Drew."

Wynne closed her eyes at the flood of sensation his body inspired. His breath was another caress, seeking an answer. "Drew," she said. "Drew, Drew . . ."

His demanding kiss stopped further speech. His mouth slanted across hers, parting slightly to allow his tongue to probe her closed lips. Without thought, she opened her mouth to his quest and was rewarded with a rush of feeling as he entered her soft lips, tracing her teeth, pressing, throbbing.

Wynne responded, driven by an elemental need that she didn't understand but refused to question. As he continued to kiss her, his hand drifted down her neck to her breast as he shifted his weight slightly. She thought for a moment that he meant to pull away, but then he stroked her nipple through the fabric with expert care until she thought she must go mad.

She moaned, then broke away from the kiss as she gasped for air. Her eyes tightly shut, she unconsciously moved closer to Drew, wanting more contact with his lean, hard body. Her legs were so weak she would have surely fallen if not supported by his weight against the door.

"You're not made of ice, sweetheart," he whispered into her sensitive neck. "You're a flesh and blood woman." He placed little nibbling kisses along the smooth, flushed flesh of her shoulder.

Mindlessly, Wynne shook her head. Why did he want to talk now? This was too wonderful to spoil with words. She gasped in pleasurable shock as he lightly bit where her neck joined the shoulder.

"This is what you really want, isn't it? You want a man."

"No," she breathed. "I want a child. Children."

He stopped his caresses, yet his demanding body kept her pinned to the stall door, his hands holding her arms securely. Wynne raised her eyelids slowly, staring at his face, knowing only that these questions must be answered somehow.

"Tell me that you want me as a woman does a man," he demanded.

Wynne shook her head again, attempting to clear the muddled thoughts that raced through her mind. It was difficult to stop the sensations that flowed like strong wine in her veins. She wanted him to continue.

"I want children," Wynne breathed. "Please don't stop."

"This is not how you planned it, is it? You didn't know how it would feel to have a real man make love to you." He moved his hands up her arms, over her shoulders and down, until he held her breasts. He squeezed lightly and Wynne knew he was watching her. He lightly rolled her nipples. Her eyes closed and her mouth opened with a sigh.

"You want me now, and it wouldn't matter what time of the month it was. It wouldn't matter if you were already seven months along with child." He ground his pelvis into hers as though torturing her into a confession. It was sweet, sweet torture.

"You lust after me, Mistress Carr. Like a rutting animal."

Wynne's eyes flew open and she began to struggle. His words finally penetrated the passion-induced fog of her brain, and his insults dashed cold water on her raging desire. How dare he! He did this to me, she thought, and then he condemns me for my response. The lecher!

"You bastard," she spat. "How dare you do this to me?"

"You wanted it as much as I did," he replied, grasping her flailing fists as he continued to pin her to the stall door.

She struggled and kicked, but could inflict no serious injuries.

"I did not! You made me feel those things. I didn't want to! I didn't," Wynne sobbed.

He let her go. She sank some few inches before her legs held her upright.

"You meant to use me and then discard me, and no one does that to a Leyton. Not for any reason. Do you understand?"

"I'm not using you! I'm offering you freedom!"

"Tell yourself that if you want, but we both know better. Remember this when you lie in your lonely bed tonight and every night. Come to me when you admit you want me as a man, not a stud. When you're woman enough to admit that, let me know." Drew turned and strode away.

That night, after Drew had eaten a hearty supper with Annie in the kitchen, and Wynne had hardly touched the tray that had been sent to her room, the big house was silent except for the ticking of the grandfather clock in the hall. Drew stood at the staircase and gazed upward into the darkness. A wall sconce was left burning in the hall, in case of the appearance of a guest, he supposed, but the upper floors were dark. He hadn't ventured upstairs in this wing. Although his wing was connected at a right angle to the main part of the house, the upstairs ballroom separated his bedroom from the other living quarters.

He wasn't quite sure what he expected to find. Ever since he'd overheard the end of the conversation between Mistress Carr and the blackmailing little Scot, he'd been intrigued with finding her elusive husband. Was he upstairs in one of the bedrooms, confined to bed or guarded like a criminal? Only a search could tell for sure. Since she never ventured away from the plantation, it seemed best to go ahead with the search while she slept.

Smythe was snoring loudly in his bedroom, downstairs in the other wing. The house was quiet and dark, and there was no time like the present. Drew took a deep breath and started up the stairs. There was no illumination except the faint moonlight that entered the hall from the open doorways. Almost all the doors were open, allowing the cool breezes to drift through the open windows.

Drew turned to his left, to a pair of doors that were closed. Slowly, he turned the latch and saw the ballroom. It was a large room with highly polished wood floors and many windows. The moonlight played on the two chandeliers. The room smelled clean, but closed and unused. He shut the door.

Turning back to his right, he continued down the hall to the next closed doorway. It was a single door, and upon opening it, he discovered the nursery. It also smelled clean and vacant, but unlike the ballroom, it was filled with a soft, thick rug and many furnishings. Drew couldn't make out all the toys in the dark, but there was a large rocking horse in front of the window. There was a rocking chair with comfortable cushions next to the crib. How long had this room been ready for a child, a child she wanted to create with him? If he complied, this would be the room of his son or daughter.

James's room had been much like this one, except there had been a small bed instead of a crib. He had come to live with Drew when he was three, stolen away from his mother after she continued to make unreasonable demands. James had been a happy boy, with wide blue eyes and dark, curling hair. Despite the fact that his mother had been a maid and that his birth was illegitimate, James was loved by the staff at Rother Hall and by his grandparents just as though he had been a legitimate son, an heir.

Drew moved further into the room, drawn by the vacant crib that symbolized all of Wynne's hopes and dreams. Drew ran a hand over the painted railing of the baby bed, then lightly fingered the fine wool of a knitted blanket folded at the end of the mattress.

He heard a faint whimper. Startled, Drew looked around the room, then back at the crib. Had he imagined the sound? Then it came again, and for the first time he noticed a very faint line of light under a door connecting the nursery with another room.

Drawn by the light, he tiptoed to the door and stopped to listen again. He heard the whimper, faint and muffled, from the next room. He turned the knob slowly while he held his breath.

The room was bathed in the faint golden glow of a candle on the nightstand. Because of the bedhangings, he couldn't see the occupant, but he believed it was Mistress Carr.

Moving across the floor on silent feet, he walked around the corner of the bed and gazed at the form there. The light cast a glow on her pale features and blond hair and reflected off the tears on her cheeks.

She shifted, opening her eyes slowly, looking lost. Drew expected surprise or outrage; she showed neither. Instead, she seemed only sad.

He moved silently to the bed, sitting beside her as she moved over. He reached down to capture a tear that hung like a dew drop on her high cheekbones. She turned her head toward his hand.

"Why are you crying?" he whispered.

"I had a bad dream. It's nothing to be concerned

about," she whispered in reply.

Drew felt the intimacy of being alone with her, in her bedroom, in the dark of night. He could take her now and she wouldn't say no. He could join her in that soft bed and ease the constant ache of wanting, making love to her, if he was careful, without risking a child.

But he didn't know if he could do that. Did he even possess that much self control? And at this moment, he would be taking advantage of her vulnerability, making him the dishonest and disreputable fellow she'd accused him of being more than once.

Instead, he curved his hand around her face and stroked her temple. "Would you like to tell me about it?"

She shifted. "I don't think so."

"Tell me," he demanded lightly.

She stared at the flickering candle so long that he began to think she wouldn't answer. Then she began in a soft voice, "I was born in India. My father served there—Colonel Winston Palmer. I'm named after him, you see."

She paused for a moment and Drew continued to stroke her face, her hair.

"My mother's name was Elizabeth. I'm named after her too. Elizabeth Wynne. She died when I was two. I think it was some sort of fever." Her brows drew together. "My father loved her very much. He said I look like her, only taller. I think that's why he always called me 'Wynne.'"

Her voice dropped to a whisper. "It must be wonderful to love someone that much."

Drew smiled, although he knew she could not see. Her story was rambling, childlike in what it revealed, yet he wouldn't have asked her to tell it any other way.

"After my mother died, my father, my nanny, and I moved here to Virginia. He bought the plantation next to

Waverley so he could be close to Samuel, since they were old friends from India. I really don't remember living anywhere else.

"It was great fun growing up. There were parties and trips. There was a young man, Henry Wolton."

Drew felt a shudder run through her as she closed her eyes for a moment.

"My father arranged a betrothal with his father, Sir Francis Wolton. Everything was going to be wonderful, I thought. Henry was much like any other man, I suppose. Wealthy, spoiled, and always looking for some sport."

"Did you love him?"

"Oh, perhaps I was in love with the idea of being in love. It was expected that I marry, so why not Henry? He was quite a catch due to his father's position as magistrate. But no, I didn't love him. I know that now."

"What happened?"

"It was the night of the betrothal ball. The house was full of guests. The servants were running around, getting everyone ready for the feasting and dancing later. I needed to get away from it all, but there were people everywhere, laughing and congratulating me. So I went for a walk, out past the gardens, just wanting some peace and quiet.

"I heard a noise then, a crash like something hitting wood. Then a woman screamed. It was almost dark, but I thought it came from the gardener's hut. I suppose I wasn't thinking clearly. All I wanted to do was help. I was far away from the house, and the scream sounded so terrible."

"I understand," he said quietly. But he didn't, not really. The thought of putting herself in danger like that made anger and fear race through him.

"I ran to the door and threw it open." She stopped,

closing her eyes as if reliving the scene. "Henry was inside, on the floor. He was laughing, holding a girl's arms down, kneeling—"

"You don't have to tell me if it upsets you."

Wynne didn't even appear to hear him, although she opened her eyes and gazed straight ahead. "He didn't see me at first. She was crying, begging him not to hurt her. He seemed to enjoy it, having her beg for mercy. He slapped her and she stopped crying. Then I yelled for him to stop.

"I'll never forget the way he looked when he faced me. He seemed like an animal. I could see his eyes gleaming in the dark, hear his heavy breathing. It was disgusting and horrible. I couldn't believe this was the same man who was frivolous and carefree, the man I was supposed to spend the rest of my life with."

"Sometimes you never know someone's true nature."

"But this was *Henry*! We'd grown up together, even though he was older than I. He was angry then. He tried to hit me, but I backed away. The girl got up and ran, so Henry got even more angry. He asked me if I wanted to take her place, if I was jealous." She paused again as her voice broke, but went right on. "Jealous! I told him I was repulsed by what he was doing, that I thought he was terrible. He laughed at me and tried to grab my arm. I was against the wall, and he came toward me. I touched the wood, then I felt the handle of a tool. When he came at me again, I swung it.

"He yelled. I didn't know then what I had done, but Henry kept yelling. I don't know how many minutes passed, but I was so upset. I wanted to run, but I was afraid I had really hurt Henry. I tried to see, tried to get him to quit yelling, but his hands were holding his face. When he turned toward the door, all I could see was the blood."

"He deserved whatever you did, sweetheart."

She didn't seem to hear. "Then my father and Sir Francis were at the door, along with many of our neighbors and my friends. They must have been standing three deep trying to see in the hut. Someone had brought a lantern and they handed it inside."

She shuddered again, turning her face toward Drew's hand. Her voice was soft when she continued. "I'd cut Henry's face open from above his eye all the way to the other side of his jaw. There was blood everywhere, on his clothes, even on my hands. I just stood there while they tried to stop the bleeding, but Henry wouldn't be quiet. He started telling them that I'd asked him to meet me at the hut, that it was all my idea."

Drew wanted to ask where Henry was now so he could kill him, but he didn't. Wynne needed comfort, not more violence. And he felt this was probably the first time she'd ever spoken about the incident that had no doubt changed her life.

"I told them no, but they believed Henry! I said he was trying to rape a girl, that she'd run away. But later, when they questioned all the servants and slaves, no one knew anything about it."

"They were frightened."

"Yes, they were. Sir Francis was very powerful, and no one wanted to speak out. I couldn't prove what I'd said. Henry was so convincing, so sincere, that everyone except my father and Samuel believed him. The next morning our guests left. I've never spoken to most of them since that night."

"They were wrong. It wasn't your fault."

"I know that, but it didn't help much at the time. A few months later my father suffered an illness of his heart. He made Samuel promise to take care of me and the plantation. You see, he'd borrowed heavily from Sir Francis to put on the betrothal ball, to buy my gowns and everything. The money wouldn't be coming in until after the tobacco harvest. He was afraid of what Sir Francis would do."

"And did Sir Francis try to hurt you?"

"Oh, yes, he tried. But Samuel was always there, especially when my father died. We agreed, Samuel and I, that the only way to protect my estate was for me to marry him. That way, Sir Francis couldn't ruin me financially as Henry ruined my reputation."

"So you married a man old enough to be your father."

"It was the only way. Samuel was more like an uncle, a truly kind and wonderful man. He helped me through so much."

"I'm sure he did." Drew tried to keep his voice calm, but the thought of Wynne giving herself to a man that old caused a burst of jealousy and anger. Still, he understood. She'd done what she had to do to survive. "And the dream? Was there more to it?"

She nodded. "Sometimes I dream of what Henry did, of him raping the girl, of the blood. But then my father, Samuel, and my nanny come in. Instead of believing me, they start scolding me. They tell me it's wrong to want to save Waverley, to have a child. Everything gets so confused in my mind."

"I don't think you're wrong to want to save Waverley. I think you're doing what seems best to you. But, Wynne, you're still young. You can't be sure how long Samuel will live, can you? Any man would be proud to call you his own."

"Anyone except you," she said sobbing, and turned away.

"Ah, Wynne. That's the problem. You're not mine. You belong to a man I've never met."

"I can't help it. You don't understand."

"I understand more than you think. I know that if people find out Samuel Carr is incapacitated, you could lose control of everything. You see, I know what you're going through."

Wynne's sobs dissolved into hiccoughs. "You do?"

"Yes, sweetheart, I do." Drew smiled at the childlike picture she presented.

"You called me that before."

"Sweetheart?"

"Yes. Why? I thought you didn't even like me."

"I thought so myself. I was wrong," Drew replied, his gaze soft on her reddened eyes, her pale face and soft pink lips.

He lowered his head until his lips just faintly brushed hers. She was soft and yielding beneath his mouth, and it took all his willpower to break away before intensifying the kiss. Now was not the time to take advantage of the passionate woman he knew Wynne to be. Now she needed a friend.

Drew raised his head and saw confusion and vulnerability clearly revealed in her expressive green eyes. He released her now relaxed hand and pulled the covers back up over her chest. "Can you sleep now?"

"I believe so. Thank you."

Drew smiled. "You're welcome. Good night, Elizabeth Wynne."

"Goodnight, Andrew Philip Leyton."

Drew tiptoed toward the door, but stopped and looked back at the bed. He was barely able to see Wynne, curled beneath the covers, but the candlelight played across her tousled hair and painted her pale skin golden. Like a child, she was probably afraid of the dark. As he watched, her eyes closed, her face relaxed, and a faint smile played about her lips. He watched until he was sure she was asleep, then reluctantly left. He could have stayed and watched her all night. He could have curled beside her in the bed, fitting his body against hers, waking beside her in the morning.

He spent the night in his narrow bed, trying not to think about her pleas to have a child.

5

Drew was sitting at the dining table the next morning when Wynne came in for breakfast. He raised his head and put down his fork when he heard the rustle of her skirts and petticoats coming down the hall, the slight click of her heels on the hardwood floor.

Wynne paused briefly when she entered the dining room. Their eyes met for only a moment and he saw her confusion. Then her gaze shifted to the sideboard, where the covered dishes had been placed. She took a deep breath, which swelled her breasts above the stiff bodice of her gown. Drew swallowed, his throat suddenly dry.

"Did you sleep well, Mr. Leyton?"

He took a sip of his coffee before replying. "Tolerably well, Mistress Carr. And you?"

"Tolerably well," she replied, with the trace of a smile.

"Do you mind that I helped myself to breakfast? I found that I had a tremendous appetite this morning."

"No, not at all."

Drew rose to pull out Wynne's chair as she finished filling her plate. Her eyes met his briefly, but again, she turned away. He filled his cup with fresh coffee, then returned to his seat.

They ate in silence for a few more minutes. Outside there were muted sounds of laundry being done, voices raised in conversation, an occasional horse's neigh and a persistent fly near Drew's plate. The silverware clinked and Drew slurped when he tried to sip his hot coffee.

"Excuse me," he apologized.

"That's quite all right," Wynne replied automatically.

Drew put down his cup and looked at Wynne until she was forced to meet his gaze. "I would like to help you around the plantation. I've some skill with ledgers, and with horses, as you know. I would be willing to learn."

"Of course you need something to occupy your time," Wynne replied after a long pause.

"I want to do more than occupy my time, Mistress Carr. I would like to help you with the running of this plantation." Drew watched her take another sip of coffee, then look out the window. It was difficult to remember his "place," especially after last night. He was ready to take charge, to tell her he insisted on contributing. Not because of his bond, but because he wanted to. He also had a strong urge to tell her about his background, that his father was an earl, that he had extensive holdings in his own name. But he doubted she would believe him now; she would doubt his motives..

"Very well. I need to do an accounting of the stock, then survey some timberland that I'm thinking of clearing." She hesitated only briefly. "Would you like to come with me and help with the books?"

"When do we leave?" Drew tried to maintain his calm demeanor, but in truth the thought of spending the entire day with Wynne was very exciting. He had never considered counting cattle to be a stimulating activity before.

"Right after breakfast. I'll need to change. We'll be gone until early afternoon."

"I'll have Annie pack a picnic basket," Drew remarked. "That is, if it's agreeable to you, Mistress Carr."

"A picnic? Yes, a picnic basket would be nice."

"Good. I'll meet you in the stable in, say, half an hour?"

"Fine. I'll be ready, Mr. Leyton."

Drew rose to leave the table, pulling Wynne's chair back as she began to stand. He couldn't resist letting his hands stray from the chair back to her small waist. At her startled gasp, his hold tightened and he leaned forward to whisper in her ear, "You can call me 'Drew' again if you want. I promise I won't take advantage of your familiarity."

She tried to pull away, giving him an indignant look, but he held her firm. "I like it when you show a little temper. It puts color in your cheeks." Drew let go of her waist, then stepped back before she could respond physically.

She spun around, but he was already halfway to the door.

"Half an hour, Miss Wynne," he taunted as he strolled into the hall.

The horses were in fine spirits as they left the stables. Wynne sat erect on the sidesaddle, expertly handling the high-stepping bay mare. Drew followed on a roan gelding that was equally lively, though not as showy. The sun was bright; the temperature was mild and the breeze light as they headed northwest to the fields.

Near the house almost all the trees had been cleared. There were a few large, ancient oaks, but for the most part the land stretched clear and almost flat, covered with lush spring grass to the point where pines grew thick, straight, and tall. There was a well-worn path and Drew could see the bare footprints of the field hands who had passed this way several hours before.

Separating the house from the fields was a parklike stand of pines with an opening for the path. From a distance, the ground looked freshly turned and hoed. As Wynne and Drew traveled closer to the field, the newly transplanted tobacco plants made slight green slashes in the dark, rich soil.

Drew stayed slightly behind and beside Wynne, enjoying the play of sunlight on her blond hair. Her small hat was tilted forward to provide protection to her face, leaving the back of her head and neck open to observation. He remembered kissing that neck only yesterday and shifted uncomfortably in the saddle.

She reined in her horse to pull beside him. "We are almost there, Mr. Leyton."

"Drew."

"I cannot call you 'Drew' when someone may overhear. Surely you understand that!"

"No one is listening now." He raised his eyebrow and swiveled around in the saddle. "No, we're quite alone."

"Very well, but I'll call you 'Drew' only when I'm certain we are alone."

"Only if I can call you Wynne at the same times," he replied nonchalantly.

Wynne flounced forward, causing her mare to sidestep and pull the reins down. Regaining control of her horse, Wynne said, "You won't accept a small concession, will you? You want everything to be on your terms." She paused and took a deep breath. "I am trying my best to be cordial to you, Mr. . . . Drew."

"And I appreciate it, Wynne. Really I do. I just think that it would be inequitable for me to call you 'Mistress Carr' when you are whispering 'Drew' into my ear." He made a valiant effort to keep the grin off his face, but he had to settle for a small smile.

"Sometimes you are insufferable!" Wynne cried, putting her heel to the mare. They galloped forward through the trees.

Drew urged his horse forward to pull even with the lady. Perhaps, he thought, this time I was a little pushy. Still, he loved to banter with her.

"Hold up," he urged. When Wynne's mare slowed, he continued, "Look here, I'm sorry. I forgot myself."

"You certainly did. You forget yourself with great regularity. Sometimes you are terribly arrogant, yet at other times . . ."

Drew laughed, causing Wynne to turn to look at him. "I don't have the proper experience to be a respectful bondservant."

"Just exactly what *do* you have the experience for?" She made a face at the leer he gave her. "Never mind. I don't think I want to know." Drew watched the fleeting expressions crossing Wynne's face. He could only imagine what she was thinking, but he was sure that it involved his unknown past and her unresolved present.

"Wynne, please don't get in a huff. I'm not a bad sort of fellow. Why, in London I was considered to be quite popular." He paused at her glare. "By both men and women."

"You're my bondsman. I'm not required to find you amusing."

"I doubt if any of what you require from me is legal, much less moral," Drew answered. He wasn't ready to get into another debate over her needs and desires. A definite change of topic was necessary. "Let's not fight. It's a beautiful day and you can spend the entire time impressing me with your knowledge of tobacco growing."

"And timber production. Then there's wheat farming, grazing and cattle management. Should I go on?"

Drew laughed. "Please, please, that's enough. My poor bondsman's mind won't be able to absorb all that. You must go slow. Have mercy, mistress," he pleaded with great theatrics.

Wynne laughed. "Very well. We'll cry truce for the remainder of the day."

"And I'll be on my best behavior. I promise." Drew crossed his heart and smiled, thankful they hadn't resorted to another heated discussion of his status.

They rode in silence for a few more moments, skirting the field and following a path of sorts that circled the dark, turned soil. The smell of the earth was strong. The sounds of hundreds of birds filled the skies.

Wynne stopped her horse and pointed at the far boundary of the field. The tree line was barely visible. "This is the closest field. Beyond the trees is another, then they spread out in both directions. We have to make allowances for the streams that intersect, and the lay of the land."

"How about the trees? Clearing the land must be a tremendous job," Drew observed.

"It is. That's why so many field hands are needed to run a plantation this size. We clear land in the fall and winter, and some in the spring after the tobacco is seeded in the beds."

"Seeded in beds?"

"Yes. You can't just plant the seeds in the fields. First, you start the seedlings in beds, then transplant them to rows. After that, it's constant care until late summer. Then there's drying, cutting, and curing." Wynne took a deep breath. "It takes a lot of work to produce tobacco, but it's the best crop we have."

"And each year it's the same?"

"Not really. You can only plant tobacco in the same field one year out of three. In the other years, we plant wheat or corn, then leave the field fallow for a year." There was pride in Wynne's voice as she spoke of her land, the pride of accomplishment. "You have to be careful, though. If you leave a field fallow too long, it's gone before you know it. Swallowed up by the forest." She laughed, and Drew watched the sparkle of her eyes and the slight dimple in one cheek.

"You are an incredible woman," he said quietly.

Wynne shook her head. "No, I'm not. I just love this land."

"Well, it's beautiful land." And you are beautiful, too, he thought. Beautiful, and smart, and I think I'm starting to care too much for you. He waited for the thought to leave him cold and shaking, panic-stricken and ready to run. That didn't happen. Instead, it crept into his mind and his heart like a well-versed song, one that had been sung many times before. It was definitely too soon to speak of his feelings. And besides, this was the worst time to complicate his life with a woman.

He turned his roan back to the path. "What's next on our journey, Mistress Carr?"

When she didn't answer immediately, Drew twisted in the saddle and caught her look of confusion. Then her expression cleared as though she no longer pondered any problems. "I'll race you to the corner of the field," she challenged.

Before he could comprehend her meaning, she was racing along the path, sending great clumps of black dirt flying. Drew took off almost immediately. He'd gone no more than ten strides when the roan started crow-hopping down the path. Drew looked behind him as he tried to stay in the saddle. One of the straps holding the picnic basket must have come loose. The wicker container bounced against the flanks of his horse, digging into his sensitive sides.

Drew clung with his muscled thighs, but the months of inactivity in the gaol and aboard ship had taken their toll. He came flying off the horse and fell with a muffled thud into the soft dirt.

Wynne noticed in a few moments that she wasn't being followed, so she turned in the saddle and slowed her mare. She was treated to the sight of Drew, struggling to rise, cursing the horse and the basket roundly. Turning her mount around, she cantered back to the site of the mishap.

"Are you all right?" She reined to a stop and jumped down. She moved to brush off the side of his back where he had landed. He flinched as if struck.

"I'm just trying to help."

"Your property is not permanently damaged."

"Well, it certainly damaged your disposition!"

"I'm not in the habit of falling off a horse!"

"Maybe you need more experience riding."

"Like hell! Who do you think won the steeple-chase at . . ."

"Steeplechase? You raced in England?"

"No, don't pay any attention to me. My pride is more damaged than anything. I haven't ridden in a while."

"Let me off brush this dirt." Wynne moved around to his back and started moving her hand over the rough texture of his shirt. His back was as hard as a rock. She slowly traced the area where the soil clung, then moved her palm over the muscles below his shoulder blades. He felt so warm, so alive. Before she realized what she was doing, she was rubbing the dirt into the fabric rather than removing it.

Drew slowly turned as Wynne continued to caress his back. She didn't even look up, but kept her hand in place until it was lightly resting on his chest. Her eyes rose to his intense blue gaze.

"I think I'm fine now," he said quietly. "My clothes will have to be washed, you know. The stains won't brush off."

"No, no, of course not," Wynne replied as if in a daze. She blinked her eyes, trying to clear her head. Why did he always have this effect on her?

"Let's get back to work, Wynne. We do have a lot of ground to cover, don't we?"

"Yes, we do. We should get back to the . . . back to . . ."

"Right." Drew chuckled. "I'll help you mount."

They continued to the rolling pastures where cattle grazed: cows with new calves and yearlings that would go to market or table. The terrain here was more uneven, with limestone outcroppings on some gently sloping hillsides. Most of the trees had been cleared, but some massive pines and maples remained to provide summer shade for the animals.

The sun was high overhead when Wynne suggested they stop for lunch. The place was much like any other; there was a shade tree, and the newly lush grass covered the rich soil of an area that had not been cultivated for tobacco or any other crop. The picnic basket was removed from the roan, the contents only slightly damaged due to the short but wild ride. Both Wynne and Drew were silent as they spread the blanket and removed the parcels and jars of food.

"Annie packed enough for an army," Drew commented when everything had been assembled. "I fear the dessert is ruined, though." He continued to unwrap the fried apple pies that had broken apart, leaving their sticky filling on the greasy paper.

"Umm, delicious." Drew licked the spicy apples from his fingers. "Maybe they aren't ruined after all." He scooped more of the spilled filling on his index finger, then extended it to Wynne. "Want to try?"

Wynne sat back from spacing the utensils and napkins on the blanket. The image of licking apple filling from his fingers, using her tongue to get every drop of the sticky substance, was a shock to her composure. She relied on the predictable, "Really, Mr Leyton!"

"Drew."

"Really, *Drew*. I believe your manners are lacking again," she criticized mildly. He looked so young, so boyish sitting there, smiling innocently at her. The backdrop of a lush green pasture in springtime seemed the perfect setting for this man. He was as elemental as nature, as changeable as the weather.

"Manners are fine things. You just have to learn when not to use them. Trust me; I have a great deal of experience in this area," Drew teased.

She reached for the roasted chicken and uncovered the browned pieces. "We have a very hearty meal to consume. Annie will be disappointed if we don't finish most of this."

They ate in silence, the morning ride increasing their hunger by a good margin. Annie's lunch disappeared with amazing haste.

Drew stretched his long legs out and leaned back on his elbows. "I feel like a Christmas goose—stuffed." He patted his lean ribs. "I'll say one thing; the food here is almost worth the trip."

Wynne laughed. "You do have a way with words, Mr. Leyton."

"Drew."

Wynne was silent for a moment, studying her bondsman. After his visit last night, she had slept well, with no more bad dreams to interrupt her rest.

"Very well, Drew, would you tell me how you came to be in my bedchamber last night?" Had he gone there to finish what he started in the stable? If so, he had certainly changed his mind. He was the one who had pulled away last night, not her.

"I couldn't sleep, so I thought to borrow another book from your library. I heard a noise upstairs and, since everyone else was asleep, I went up to investigate. That's when I heard the sounds from your room." He turned to his side, bracing his head on his hand. He smiled that boyish, disarming grin. "I hope you didn't mind."

Wynne tried for a very proper response, but all she could remember was the feeling of relief and security his presence had elicited. Instead, she began to fidget with her napkin.

"It was improper for you to be in my bedchamber," Wynne replied in a small voice, pleating the napkin.

"Improper? Why, we can't have that!" Drew returned with good-natured sarcasm.

"And, I was going to add, under the circumstances, I was very grateful. You were most . . . kind."

"Why, I do believe that's the first nice thing you've ever said to me," Drew remarked. "Except that observation that I was 'suitable.'" He reached over to take Wynne's hand. She glanced up nervously.

"I was glad to be there," Drew said, stroking her hand. "You were very upset, you know. Would you like to . . ."

"No," Wynne said abruptly, removing her hand from his gentle grasp. "I really don't care to discuss it further."

They began packing away the remaining food and empty jars.

"Would you tell me about the man who visited here yesterday?"

"Why do you want to know?"

"If I'm to help you with Waverly, I need to know the men of business with whom I might deal." Drew paused. "I assume he was here on business."

It took a moment for her to reply. "Oh, he's a tobacco factor who wants my crops. I told him it was too early to contract, but he's trying to convince me to sell to his firm." She turned and walked a few steps. "You may see him from time to time, but don't bother with his business. I'll deal with him."

"I rather got the impression from Smythe that the Scot— was his name MacClintock?—wasn't thought of too highly." Drew left the statement open for comment.

"Well, the Scots aren't real popular here in Virginia, if you really must know. The feeling is mutual, that is, between the English and the Scots. They only care about their work and their strict religion. Why, the English call them 'Cohees.'"

"'Cohees?' That's an unusual word."

"Yes, I think it came from their saying 'quote he' all the time. At least, that's what I heard." She looked uneasy. "Let's talk about something more pleasant than those dour Scots."

Drew's tension disappeared and he laughed. "Why, Miss Wynne, I do believe you're learning to flirt."

Wynne twirled the riding crop in her hand and looked at him from lowered lashes. "You may just be right, Mr. Leyton."

"Drew."

He walked toward her with purposeful strides. Put up your defenses now, Miss Wynne. Let's see how immune you are to me. He stopped just inches away, his body moist with the day's warmth.

"Drew . . ." she whispered.

He stared at her a long time. Was she really the coolly composed woman of means, or was she the young girl looking for her first love? Perhaps she didn't know herself, but he was determined to find out. At least her responses were becoming more consistent. She wasn't at all immune to him, any more than he was to her.

"We'd best be getting back," he said in a low, calm voice. "The clouds are building in the south and we may be in for a drenching."

Drew knew she was watching his lips move. It took all of his control to keep from kissing her breathless.

"What?"

"I said, beautiful dreamer, that we should get back before it rains," he teased.

She blushed scarlet. She turned and walked to the horses, with Drew following closely. He lifted her into the sidesaddle, his hands lingering, then mounted his own horse as she adjusted her leg and skirts. They rode toward the house in silence.

6

"*And I tell you, the mistress has taken* herself a man. Bought and paid for, I say!" Millie emphasized the point by slamming her palm on the kitchen table.

"Just because he's young and . . ." Faye trailed off, her pale complexion heightened with color.

"Aye, he's a fine-looking man, that's for sure," Annie commented. "But he's a gent, and he's not the kind to be sneaking up the back stairs in the dead of night."

"Hah!" Millie scoffed. "You just don't see what I do. She wanders about that big room, just a-dreaming and thinking." The maid pushed back her chair and stood upright, imitating Wynne to the best of her ability. "She just moons around, fingering them nice dresses she never wears and looking at herself in the mirror." Millie posed in front of an imaginary mirror and ran her hands over her own nearly flat bosom. She sighed loudly and dramatically.

Faye, the shy maid who had altered Drew's clothes last week, giggled into her hand.

Annie sliced the air with her hand and ordered,

"Enough with ye! It's jealous ye are, saying those things about the mistress. She's a fine lady and he's a gent, even if he is a bondsman. I'll not have ye badmouthing either in my kitchen!"

Seemingly unconcerned, Millie strolled across the room, batting her stubby brown lashes. "Oh, Mr. Leyton, will you help me with the books after dinner?" she repeated in a more high-pitched, sticky-sweet imitation of Wynne's voice. "Oh, Mr. Leyton, will you go with me to the stables?" She paused and turned, theatrically tossing her head. "Oh, Mr. Leyton, will you come to my bed and—"

"Enough!" the cook roared. She hefted her weight from the chair and hurried across the room, grabbing the broom. She chased after Millie, brandishing the weapon, while Millie squealed and circled the table.

At that moment the door opened and Smythe entered. Calm and self-assured, he raised his eyebrows and questioned, "Ladies?"

Annie immediately lowered her broom while continuing to glare at Millie, who had resumed her seat at the table. Faye stared wide-eyed at the butler, who had not moved from the doorway. Annie lowered her eyes and started to sweep.

"I hope you have not been engaged in improper conduct," he addressed the room at large. "Respectful and discreet behavior is required."

"Aye," they replied, almost in unison.

"We were just playin' around, Smythe. No harm done," Millie offered.

"Well, I certainly hope so. I would not like to dismiss anyone from Waverly, but if I must, then it will be done." He paused. "Is that clear?"

"Aye," they replied again, this time more quickly.

Smythe backed up, closing the door.

Annie, who had stopped the unnecessary sweeping, leaned the broom against the wall and glared at Millie. "I hope ye're satisfied, ye little tart."

"Well, I for one will not take back a thing I said. The woman bought him to warm her bed, that's for sure, and ye can't tell me otherwise," Millie responded with a huff. She flounced out the door.

The kitchen was silent for a moment, as though a storm had just passed. Faye stood and gathered the dishes. "I'll help you with these, Cook."

"Thanks, me girl. It's good to know that at least ye are not believing the lies of that green-eyed Jezebel."

Annie washed the dishes and Faye dried. They were almost finished when Faye said, "Millie must believe what she says, Annie."

"Hah! Yer too sweet for yer own good."

"And I think her eyes are gray, not green."

Annie laughed as she picked up a rag and wiped off the table. "Thinkin' don't make it so, lass. If ye thought ye could have whatever ye wanted, what would it be?"

Faye sat down at the table and propped her chin on her folded hands. "I'd have my parents back," she said sadly. "I'd make sure they stayed in England, that they never got on that ship where they died and left me alone."

Annie sat across from her. "Aye, that was a bad time for ye. It's a sorry practice, making the child pay for the parents' passage if they die. Just be glad Mistress Carr bought yer bond and not someone else."

"Oh, I do, Annie. I thank God every day for my life here. I only wish . . ."

"What, girl?"

Faye blushed and dropped her hands to her lap. "I sometimes wish Mistress Carr were more friendly. Or maybe she's just not happy. For her, it's always work, work, work."

"Maybe that'll change now that Mr. Leyton is here," Annie said with a smile.

"Do you think he's to be an overseer? I don't ever remember Mistress Carr having one before."

"He and Mistress Carr rode out yesterday to look over the property. Today they're in the study, goin' over the ledgers and such. It wouldn't surprise me a bit if he took over some of the work around here."

"That's grand, Annie." Faye paused a moment, staring at the pattern on her skirt. "He's a fine looking man, that's for sure."

"Aye, he is. Fair of face and form, that's Mr. Leyton."

"Mr. Smythe is awfully nice, too."

Annie looked sharply at the maid. In a moment, she replied, "Mr. Smythe is a fine man, Faye. A good and fair one too."

Faye blushed again as she rose from the chair. "I'd best be getting on with my chores."

Wynne paced the long, elegant bedroom; she paused in front of the cheval mirror to stare at her reflection; she stopped to review the dresses in her wardrobe, frowning at the mostly somber colors. Outside, the day was sunny and sweet, smelling of earth, grass, and wildflowers, but Wynne could appreciate none of its beauty.

It had been over a week since their picnic, and Drew had continued to be polite, if teasing. He worked diligently on the ledgers, attempting to understand the harvests and yields, the expenses and profits, the seasons and planting cycles. He was more than Wynne had bargained for—much more than she had wanted. Or so she kept telling herself.

He was amazingly quick with numbers. What took her several hours, he seemed to comprehend in less than half that time. He was interested in and commented upon every aspect of the crop production, timber cutting, and plans for expansion. To Wynne, who had lived so long with only her own counsel, his involvement was almost disturbing.

While she worked beside him at the large desk, exceedingly aware of his masculine presence, he seemed to be able to dismiss her as a woman. Every now and then, he smiled or made a lighthearted comment, but there were no stolen kisses, no caresses.

Four days before, Wynne had sent Smythe and Faye to Williamsburg to get the clothes she had ordered for Drew. She'd commissioned the tailor to make breeches and silk stockings, linen shirts and stocks, waistcoats, vests, and frock coats. She ordered more changes and variety than was probably necessary, but she wanted no repeat of that heart-pounding reaction to his tight, ill-fitting clothes or bared skin. Drew had gained a few pounds and was again straining the seams of his garments.

Faye was also told to choose some lightweight, colorful fabrics for Wynne's new gowns. She had ordered a few new sacques and morning gowns when she was in Williamsburg that fateful day when she bought Drew's bond, but now she felt the urge for some more new gowns. She had asked Faye to chose some matching chip hats and bonnets from the milliner and some lightweight kid slippers from the shoemaker.

Her excuse had been the warmer weather and an upcoming visit from the newest neighbors, Lady Grayson and her son. Wynne hoped these recent Colonial arrivals wouldn't know about the scandal that kept so many others away. But in truth, she knew the desire for new clothes was because of the bondsman. She would *make* him notice her. She would be more womanly, more desirable . . . and soon she would be with child.

Late that afternoon, the carriage returned to Waverly. A travel-weary Smythe and an excited Faye entered the kitchen with laden arms and empty stomachs. The smell of Annie's chicken in a flaky pastry filled the warm air.

Faye placed her bundles on the table and smiled at the cook. Annie was sitting at the workbench, a crockery bowl and wooden spoon occupying her attention. "It was a grand trip, Annie. We stayed at an inn in Williamsburg, and I had my own room!" Faye glanced at the closed door, lowered her head, and whispered loudly to Annie, "Smythe was a real regular fellow, Annie. He gave me some coins for ribbons and the like."

Annie smiled at the girl's excitement. "Ye have a kind heart and a pleasant face. Ye deserve a beau of yer own, and soon." She winked at the blushing girl. "Did you behave yourself?"

"O' course I did, Annie! You know I'm a good girl."

Annie chuckled. "Of course ye are." She continued to stir the sponge cake batter. "Maybe the mistress will let you go back this summer."

"Do you think so?" Faye asked with excitement.

"Aye, I think so," Annie replied, placing the batter in the cake tins. "What do you have there?"

"Oh, these." Faye stacked the scattered bundles. "The mistress ordered all sorts of things for Mr. Leyton. Why, he's got enough clothes now to last him forever."

"He just needs enough for seven years, missy. That is, if he stays that long," Annie remarked.

"What do you mean, Annie? O' course he'll be here seven years. He's bonded. He won't run, do you think?"

"Just what are ye thinking about our fine new bondsman?" Annie inquired.

Faye blushed to the roots of her mousy brown hair and looked down at the toes of her sturdy boots.

"Come on, girl. Are ye thinking about that man for your own?"

"Oh, Annie," Faye responded despondently, "a man like that wouldn't look twice at me." She looked at the neatly stacked packages of fine clothes. "If Mistress Carr weren't married, he's the sort I'd think would come to call."

Annie moved over and placed a motherly arm around Faye's thin shoulders. "Well, maybe he's not the man for ye, but there'll be someone. You're a right bonny girl, Faye, and there'll be a special beau in your life."

Faye turned hopeful eyes at Annie. "Do you really think so? Mr. Leyton, he's such a fine gent." She paused and smiled timidly. "He's a real proper sort, and speaks so fine. Do you think he's gentry?"

"Wouldn't surprise me a bit, me girl. Now"—Annie gently pulled the maid from the chair—"why don't ye take those bundles up to Mr. Leyton. He's probably in the study or in his room. Ye can leave them on his bed. I know he'll be happy as a cat with cream to get some clothes that fit."

Faye grinned and picked up the packages. Annie held the door open for the girl. "Come back for your dinner," she called, closing the door and chuckling.

Smythe returned within moments. "What was that about, Cook? The girl was almost . . . skipping."

"I sent her to Mr. Leyton's room with his new clothes. She seems real taken with the man." Annie turned a hard gaze on the butler. "I'm thinking that isn't a good idea."

Smythe returned her even gaze. "No, no it isn't. That won't do at all." He turned and left the kitchen, carrying the rest of their purchases to the house.

7

Wynne had asked Drew to join her for dinner that evening. The days were growing longer; the lamps had not yet been lit when she made her way to his chamber, intent on seeing if the clothing fit. She knew it was improper to visit his private quarters, but she hoped to have a word with him away from the inquisitive ears of the servants.

She wanted to know what she had said or done to make him change the way he treated her. He'd been polite yet distant. She wanted to recapture those feelings of comfort and intimacy they had once shared, but she had no idea how to approach the subject. She could only think that if he were well fed and clothed, he would be more agreeable. Perhaps he would calmly come to her, fulfill her wishes. She wanted none of those intense, confusing emotions, she insisted to herself.

Her steps were slow as she climbed the stairs from the family parlor to the second floor. There was a window near the stairwell; it cast an orange-pink glow on the coral flowered light muslin gown that had been brought from

Williamsburg. It was a simple dress, but the neckline was low enough to reveal the upper slopes of her breasts and the valley between. The skirt was full and rounded with petticoats, but no hoops or panniers. Wynne was well pleased with her purchases.

Drew's door was ajar and she heard sounds of the man moving around inside. She was just beginning to knock when she heard a giggle escape. A flush of anger hardened her heart; it was unexpected and intense. She pushed the door open.

Drew was standing in the muted light of sunset while an amused Faye tried to play valet. They obviously didn't notice her standing there, because Drew continued to struggle into the coat sleeves while Faye held the garment by the collar as she stood behind him.

"Am I interrupting something?"

Wynne's chilling voice had its intended effect. They appeared almost guilty as the amusement fled from their faces.

Drew recovered quickly and responded. "Faye was just trying to help me so I wouldn't wrinkle this fine new coat. She was kind enough to press it for me."

"Really? Yes, I can see that was most kind of her."

Drew's eyes narrowed as he finished struggling into the coat. Faye stepped away, as though she felt the tension sparking between Wynne and the bondsman.

"Faye, why don't you leave now," Drew said.

The maid hurried out the door. When she was gone, Drew walked over and closed the door, brushing past Wynne.

"How dare you! Open that door immediately!"

"And have the whole house hear you make a fool of yourself? No, I think not."

"You are calling me a fool? After dallying with a maid

beneath my very nose?" Wynne was so angry she felt ill with it; her ears burned with heat and her fists clenched within the folds of her skirts.

"That poor girl," Drew said indicating the closed door, "has no idea what you are raving about."

"Oh, doesn't she? I saw the way she was looking at you."

"She's little more than a child," Drew attempted to explain, holding onto his temper with fragile threads. Wynne's reaction was startling; he had no idea she could be jealous.

"A child? And I suppose I'm an old woman?"

"You, Mistress Carr," Drew began as he moved closer to her, "are a very jealous young woman."

"I'm not—I never have been—jealous."

"You're jealous of that poor, lonely maid. A girl who's just beginning to understand that there's an attraction between men and women. An innocent." He continued more gently, "You have nothing to be jealous of."

A sound between a gasp and a sob escaped Wynne. Drew tilted her face up to look at him. He knew she didn't want to meet his eyes and did so only when it became obvious that he wouldn't release her immediately.

"You're upset. You shouldn't be. I promise you that I'll not dally with a maid beneath your roof, nor will I willingly do anything to hurt someone else."

"But she looked at you with such . . . hunger."

"As you do?" he questioned lightly.

"Me? Of course not." She drew herself up. "I do not 'hunger' for you."

"Do you not? I see hunger in your eyes when you think I'm not watching." He gauged Wynne's reaction, noticing her anger had been replaced by a blush. "Sometimes I feel that I may be consumed as dessert."

"You are crazy! I do not look at you that way," Wynne insisted.

"Oh, yes you do. You have a lot of passion locked inside."

"I simply want you to fulfill my original request. It does not involve any passion on my part. If you feel the need for passion, I assume that . . ."

"You feel passion," he repeated.

"I do not!"

Drew turned and walked away, moving to the window and looking at the sunset. It was beautiful; the deep orange of the horizon faded to yellow, pink, and then blue as his eyes scanned upwards to the evening sky and the sun dipped lower. Soon it would be night.

"Tonight." Drew was surprised that he had spoken aloud, but his course was clear. She must be made to understand. "Tonight I will come to you."

"You will?" Wynne asked numbly. "Tonight?"

Drew turned to look at the surprised woman. Her skin glowed with the colors of sunset. Her green eyes were wide and innocent, searching his face for the truth. She was beautiful, but he must not let that influence him.

"Yes," he replied quietly. "After the house is asleep, I'll come to you." He paused for a moment, his tense body outlined by the sunset. "You will be ready."

Wynne nodded slowly. "Yes, I'll be ready. Tonight."

"Do you still wish to have dinner, Mistress Carr?"

"Dinner? Yes, we should go to dinner." She turned to open the door. "If we didn't, the servants would talk. I can't have that."

Drew laughed. "No, you can't have that."

She stood at the door, watching him like a combatant who wondered at her enemy's strategy. Did she think this was a stroke of good luck? Did she imagine that he had somehow capitulated to her overwhelming reason? He almost smiled at the thought. She had been so sure of what she wanted when she approached him. Children—with no emotional complications. No feelings, no caring, no passion. Well, she wasn't going to get what she asked for. He was going to give her what she needed.

"Until dinner then, Mistress Carr."

Despite being married for over six years, Wynne had no experience with the kind of passion Drew expected. Samuel had always been like an uncle to her; and besides, he would never have approached her, suffering as he was from that horrible disease.

What would it be like with Andrew Leyton? She wondered. He could be forceful, but he didn't seem cruel or violent. He could also be incredibly gentle.

Since the tense dinner, where Drew had remained remotely polite, Wynne's nerves had been stretched taut. She'd mechanically ordered a bath, donned a nightgown and wrapper, and prepared for bed. She wasn't sure what else was involved in getting ready, so she paced the floors and waited for Drew.

On the table by the windows lay a book she had retrieved from the library earlier. Her eyes gazed at the gold letters, her fingers traced the embossed leather. She stiffened as she realized the book was an anthology of Greek plays from Aeschylus. Greek plays; he read Greek plays. She threw the book across the room, where it landed against the double doors.

Drew paused outside Wynne's bedchamber. He'd quietly made his way from his bed, down the hall to the back entrance of the upstairs ballroom. He had walked on silent, bare feet across the gleaming wood floor, through the dou-

ble doors, and down the hall to the master's chamber. Just
as he paused before opening the door, he heard the dull
thud of an object striking the wood. Damn, but the woman
threatened to waken the entire household by throwing
things in the middle of the night!

He turned the latch and stepped into the room. He
retrieved the discarded book, padded across the thick Per-
sian carpet to the large bed, and sat down near the candle.
Wynne watched him from across the room, much the way
a lamb watches a wolf, as he calmly looked at the title.

"Greek plays?" He turned the pages idly.

Wynne stayed rooted to her spot, standing between the
bed and the chairs.

"Come here," Drew demanded quietly. He settled back
against the headboard, pushing the pillows more comfortably into position and stretching his long legs out. When
Wynne made no move to comply, he repeated, "Come
here. I promise I don't bite."

She walked slowly forward, moving around the end of
the bed toward his side. She stopped about three feet away,
standing ramrod straight and looking so tense he wondered
if her knees were trembling beneath the gown.

"I . . ."

"Come here," Drew repeated patiently. He reached out
his hand.

She complied, allowing him to pull her down gently
until she was sitting on the bed. Near, yet so far. He felt
her shudder.

"I won't hurt you, Wynne. Do you believe that?"

"I don't know." She paused and studied her perfectly
shaped nails. "Sometimes you get very angry."

"Why should I be angry tonight?"

"Because," she said with apprehension, "because I'm
making you do something you do not wish to do."

Drew chuckled and she looked quickly at him. "You aren't forcing me tonight. Well, that's not really true. Let me put it this way." He paused and searched for words. "Circumstances have put me in a situation I have little control over. You are trying to serve your best interests. However, if I didn't wish to be here, tonight, in your bedchamber, I wouldn't have come." He paused again. "Do you believe that?"

She studied his face as if she could discern the truth in his eyes, his brow, or the set of his lips. Finally she said, "I believe you."

"Good. Now, we must feel more at ease with each other."

"What do you mean?"

Good Lord, what kind of man had she known? Had her husband truly come in, thrown up her gown and rutted like an animal? Drew found it inconceivable that any man could treat an exquisite woman like Wynne in that manner. Even so, she seemed to know nothing of the manner of courting and seduction.

"First, I want you to come and sit beside me. We'll just sit here for a while, talk, and get relaxed." At her startled expression, he explained, "It's better when both people are relaxed."

Drew grasped her under the arms and pulled her back against the wall of his chest. She let out a small squeal. "Relax. Lean back against me and get comfortable. We'll probably be here for a while."

Drew picked up the book again and resumed his review of the pages. His arms circled Wynne. When he found the passage he sought, he held the book in his right hand and lowered his left so it rested at her waist. She had no idea what to do with her hands, so she folded them in her lap. She concentrated on relaxing; she listened to his deep breathing, felt his chest rise and fall, and listened to the cadence of his voice as he read.

When he finished the passage, he dropped the book to the mattress and turned her in his arms. His lips took hers in a compelling kiss, drawing away her breath, her resistance, her very soul. His hands wandered at will, touching her through the thin material of her gown, molding her body more firmly to his.

She felt Drew's heart race as she rested against the soft linen of his shirt. He held her for a few moments, then pushed her gently from his chest.

"Do you have any doubts?"

Yes, she felt like screaming. You kiss me and I feel like melting. I'm terrified of these emotions running through my body. Instead, she shook her head, afraid to trust her voice.

"Then take off your gown for me."

No, surely he didn't expect her to disrobe. It was embarrassing enough to be alone with him like this, but to let him see her . . . no, she couldn't.

"Wynne?"

"I can't. Please, just turn down the light and get on with it."

He frowned then, looking into her eyes as though he could read her thoughts. "I'll not compromise on the gown, but you can turn down the lamp."

She did, walking on shaky legs to the table, dreading what came next. This was much more difficult than she had imagined.

"Come here," he said softly from the shadow of the bed-hangings.

She stood beside the bed and waited as he lifted the hem of the gown, slowly pulling it up and off, leaving her visible to whatever light filtered through the windows. She closed her eyes.

"You're very beautiful," he said with a certain reverence. Then his hands, hot and searching, molded over her ribs, her breasts, her hips, as though he could see through his fingertips what was denied his eyes. He pulled her close, her chest even with his head as he knelt on the mattress.

His lips kissed her, his hands held her, and when he took her nipple into his mouth, her knees gave way to a rush of pleasure. When next she became aware, she was lying on the mattress, Drew stretched out beside her.

"You do enjoy this," he said with something akin to wonder. "There's more, love, much more."

And he showed her, using his body, his lips, his words. She vaguely thought that he should remove his breeches, but then he distracted her with delicious caresses that brought forth a moan from deep inside. She'd lost the will to resist this pleasure, and she had no strength to try to find it again.

Her mind was spinning, so lost that she barely felt his hot breath on her neck. But she could feel the urgency of his desire, responding to it herself until she couldn't think any longer at all. When the most intense sensation she had ever experienced burst upon her, she lost herself completely to it, sinking into the comforting black void of unconsciousness.

Drew rested his head on the pillow next to Wynne, his hand still touching her intimately, feeling the small aftershocks of pleasure that rippled through her body. He took a deep breath, inhaling the scent of Wynne as he'd never experienced before. The jasmine fragrance, surely, but also desire he'd intentionally brought forth.

Lord, why was he torturing himself like this? To teach a lesson to a woman who denied their attraction to each other, who thought making love should be a cold act between two strangers? His body begged for release, but he wasn't about to give in. Not yet. First, she had to admit she wanted him on his terms.

He roused himself in a few moments, half expecting Wynne to berate him for not completing the act. He shifted on the bed, but still she didn't stir.

He got up and lit a candle, just as he knew she liked to have beside her during the night. In its flickering light he could see that a small smile touched the corners of her mouth. Her breathing was even and deep. Incredibly, she was asleep.

He wasn't sure what he felt about that: relief that she hadn't pressured him to finish the deed tonight; pride that he'd caused such a profound response that she had actually fainted, although he had heard that the reaction was possible. And regret that he couldn't see her green eyes glazed with passion, softened with love.

He pulled the sheet over her body with remorse, because he could look at her all night without growing tired of the sight. It would be best if he left, going back to his own room and allowing her some needed rest. He smoothed the tangled strands of hair over the pillow and trailed the back of his fingers along her cheek. Staying away was becoming harder and harder.

8

Wynne stretched, arching her back, reaching for the headboard with her arms. She'd had the most wicked dream last night concerning the bondsman. He'd come into her bedroom, just as he did that first time, only this time he didn't stop with a few chaste kisses. He had stroked her body, kissed her passionately, touched her in places where she'd never imagined. She had a vague recollection of feeling on fire, of thinking she would explode into a thousand stars. Then the dream stopped. The dream had left her deliciously relaxed, infinitely rested and . . . very naked.

She sat upright, losing the sheet and gazing with horror on her naked breasts. She gasped at the implication—she remembered everything. Leaping from bed, she searched for her nightgown, which she found bunched between the mattress and the bedhangings at the foot of the bed.

Wynne quickly donned the gown, glancing nervously at the lightening sky. Dear God, but it hadn't been a dream! Soon Millie would be here with warm water for her morning toilet. She must not be seen like this. The entire household would know.

She rushed to the mirror and looked critically at the image reflected there. Her cheeks were flushed; her hair was loose and tangled; her eyes were wide and bright. She grabbed her hairbrush and tried to restore order there. Millie knew that she always braided her hair before retiring.

He had come to her just as he had said. And she—she had come to him. Wynne moaned as she remembered his urgings and her frantic response. She slumped in the chair, the brush dropping loudly to the floor as she buried her face in her hands, trying to block the words and images.

He had whispered "Come to me" and she had, willingly and wantonly. She'd moaned and cried aloud, like the most loose woman of the streets. He'd touched her where she'd never thought anyone would dare, where she now realized she would never have dreamed of being caressed.

And she had loved it.

Millie knocked lightly and opened the door, carrying a large pitcher of heated water and fresh towels. Wynne looked up briefly but did not acknowledge the girl. She remained sitting in a chair, half draped over its arm, hiding her head between her folded arms.

Millie rushed forward after setting the pitcher on the washstand. "Mistress Carr," she said gently, "What's the matter? Are you ill?"

Wynne knew her eyes were red and her face was no doubt as white as a sheet. "Yes . . . yes, I believe I must be ill."

"Why don't you come back to bed, ma'am? I'll have Cook fix something for you. How about some tea and toast?"

"Yes," Wynne replied faintly, rising from the chair. "Tea and toast."

Millie placed an arm around Wynne's back, helping her to bed. "I'll go tell Cook, ma'am. Should I send for a doctor?"

"No, Millie. Just bring the tea and toast. I'll be fine soon." No, I won't, she thought. I'll never be fine again. I'll never forget what he did to me. I'll never be able to face him.

She rolled over and tried to go back to sleep. Anything to stop the memories.

Drew wakened late. He had slept little during the night. After leaving Wynne, he'd returned to his room, only to toss and turn.

Last night, Wynne had burned with desire. She'd been soft and womanly. What would she be this morning?

Drew made his way to the kitchen, intent on a cup of coffee and a relaxing chat with Annie before beginning his morning review of the timber cutting. He was just about to turn the corner and open the door when he heard the cook's voice raised in anger. He stopped. Annie was never angry.

"Ye stupid chit!" she bellowed. "How can ye say such a thing about the lady?"

"I tell you, she's sick this morning. It's a sure sign o' breedin', my mother always says," Millie insisted, proud of her knowledge. "The poor lady is weepin' and moanin' upstairs, and here you are, yellin' at me!"

"The lady's not with child," Annie asserted. "Her husband's not been here and she's not visitin' the man. How could she be with child?"

"Are you forgettin' the bondsman? He's done his job

real good, I'd say. Not three weeks yet and she's already losin' her breakfast."

"Don't ye say a word of this to anyone else," Annie threatened. "If she's not with child, ye'll look the fool. Keep quiet about this business with Mr. Leyton. He's nothing to do with this."

"Sure," the maid returned saucily, "that's what we're supposed to believe. When she looks like a melon, you'll know I was right." Millie grabbed the tray and walked out the door.

Drew made no move to hide himself. He was shocked by the conversation he had overheard. First, Wynne was ill. Secondly, the servants, or some of them, knew why he was here. Smythe would never tell, so the maid, Millie, must have guessed. Thank God for loyal Annie, who didn't give in to the wild speculation of a frivolous maid. Even if she was right.

Millie rounded the corner and almost ran into him.

"Mr. Leyton!" she gasped. "You near scared me to death."

"From what I just overheard, you should be more than scared," he said.

Millie had the good sense to blush and keep quiet.

"You're wrong about me, Millie. If she's with child, it's not mine. I don't care about defending myself to you, but I'll not have the lady's name dragged through the mud because of your imagination."

"I never said anything bad about the mistress."

"Perhaps your mistress should know about your loose tongue. I could take that tray upstairs and let her know," Drew threatened. "How long do you think you would stay at Waverley?"

Millie paled, her whole demeanor changing. "No, don't tell her that," she pleaded. "She'd send me away for good."

Drew fixed her with a hard stare. "If I hear one thing about this, I'll know who started the rumor. And believe me, it's just a rumor." He pointed a finger at the girl. "You'll be gone so fast your shadow won't be able to find you."

"I promise. Nary a word."

"Good. Make sure you remember that." Drew moved around the girl and entered the kitchen. Millie's rapid footsteps could be heard on the brick walkway as she raced inside.

Drew paused a moment to collect his thoughts. Wynne was sick—because of him. He'd not anticipated so strong a reaction to the activities of last night. He'd only thought to teach her a lesson about the fire she was playing with, showing her she could be burned. He had never meant . . .

"Drew!" Annie greeted him. "What's the matter, boy? Ye look real poorly. Maybe there's an ill humor in the air. The mistress be feeling poorly herself."

"No, Annie, I'm not ill. I just didn't sleep well." He moved to the table. "Do you have some coffee left?"

"Sure I do." She poured some of the strong brew into a mug. "What's bothering ye, Drew? I can tell it's something powerful to make ye act this way."

"I heard Millie. I know what she thinks."

"The girl has a powerful imagination."

"Yes, she does," Drew replied. "I threatened her, Annie. I told her to keep quiet or I'd tell the mistress what she was saying."

"Good for you!"

"I hope so. I would hate for Wy— Mistress Carr to hear those rumors."

"Well, rumors have a way of bein' based in truth many times," Annie observed quietly. "Other times, not. Mistress Carr's affairs are her own, I say." Drew watched Annie take a sip of her coffee. "Don't ye worry, Drew. Ye probably put the fear of God into the girl. She'll be quiet."

"I hope so, Annie. God, I hope so." Drew finished his coffee and rose from the table. "I'd best be getting to work." He left the kitchen, still deep in thought as he made his way to the stable.

When James was born to a maid who worked on the estate of his friend's family, he accepted responsibility for him and her. He bought them a house near his family's estate, Moreton Hall, and gave Sally a generous allowance. It was never enough; she meant to bleed him dry. She had never managed money, so she spent it frivolously and freely. Merchants took advantage of her; dressmakers made a fortune from her seasonal fittings. And she wasn't even a good mother, in his opinion. Eventually, he had removed James from her care, still supporting her, but not excessively.

James was six when Sally came to his house to steal the boy away. Drew was gone on business on the continent and didn't get her barely legible ransom note for over a week. In that time, James's lungs became congested, his fever soared, and Sally, ignorant of medicinal cures and scared to take the boy out lest they were detected, tried her best to nurse him herself. It wasn't enough. He had died within two weeks of being whisked away from his home.

Drew had grieved; his whole family had loved the boy and they all were deeply saddened by his death. But as much as he'd loved the boy, he'd never considered him his heir. His mother's position kept him from taking a place in society, even though Drew had intended for him to be educated well and placed in business upon reaching his maturity.

But Wynne was not some ignorant maid; she was a woman full grown, educated and intelligent, running her own plantation. She would make an excellent mother, since she had so much love to give. She was his equal, someone he could and would marry if she only were free.

If only she were free. The thought kept coming back, stronger each time, fueling his frustration. Where was Samuel Carr? Did he even exist? What if Wynne had kept him alive in her own mind, both to fool society and to give legitimacy to any children she might have? If Samuel were dead, that meant Wynne was free. And if she were free *and* with child, she could marry him.

At that very moment, a barge was being poled up the shallow stream that passed through Waverley land. It was riding low in the water, heavy with tarp-covered boxes. The two men poling were silent; the water barely rippled as they passed through the muddy green current. In the front of the barge, Barton MacClintock knelt on the rough wooden deck.

He scanned the woods: the landmarks were concealed by the heavier foliage. Through the grove of trees to his right was the frame and brick lodge he sought. He rose and walked carefully to the rear, where the men waited for instructions.

"Up ahead," he said, "there's a bend in the creek. Past that house"—he pointed to the dark colored building— "you need to look for a pool of water off the creek. That's where we'll leave the barge."

The silent men nodded. Their heavy bodies strained to walk the polls from mid-barge to the rear. Their faces were covered with thick, unkempt beards, and their clothes were the skins and leather of backwoodsmen.

MacClintock looked at the hunting lodge, which they were passing slowly. It had been luck that had brought him here the first time. After he'd returned to Williamsburg from finding Samuel Carr, he had made inquiries. Yes, people there knew the man. He owned Waverley, a prosperous plantation up the Chickahominy. He traveled extensively, sometimes to India and the Orient, and was gone for years at a time. No one could remember seeing him recently, but his business interests were conducted from London. He had attorneys who managed his various interests. The woman? Yes, Samuel Carr had a young, beautiful wife.

A beautiful wife with much to lose if anyone discovered she ran the plantation.

9

After having been assured that Mr. Leyton had ridden to the new timber-cutting camp, Wynne made her way to the study to meet with Smythe. She'd come to a decision after falling into a fitful sleep, spending half a day feeling sorry for herself, then trying to pull herself together. She'd scrubbed her body to remove any trace of the night's activities and splashed cold water on her swollen eyes until they were back to normal.

When she glided into the study, she was once again a woman in control. She walked immediately to the desk and seated herself before looking at Smythe, who occupied one of the chairs in front of the fireplace. He had risen when she entered, and she motioned to him to be seated.

"I've come to a decision regarding the bondsman, Smythe. It seems you were right. My action was precipitous. I've made a mistake"—she paused and drew a deep breath—"and now I must take steps to correct it."

It took a moment for Smythe to reply. To Wynne, it seemed he was unusually solemn. "What did you have in mind?" he finally asked.

"I want you to take him"—Wynne found that she could not even say his name—"back to Williamsburg. I want him off this plantation."

"Has Mr. Leyton done something improper?"

Improper? Wynne felt like laughing. Oh yes, it was very improper. And degrading. He had set out to prove he was right, and he had succeeded. Now he would see that she could also be a formidable opponent. He wouldn't feel so smug when he was slaving under the hot sun, weeding tobacco seedlings and searching for cutworms. He wouldn't be so sure of himself when he felt the overseer's whip on his naked back.

Wynne pressed the back of her hand to her mouth, stifling a gasp that the image provoked. She didn't want him whipped. She didn't want that smooth, solid flesh marred by the lash.

"Madam, if I may be so bold," Smythe questioned gently, "would you like to discuss what the bondsman has done to make you want him gone from Waverley?"

"He . . . he is insolent. And disrespectful," Wynne explained. "He's entirely unsuited to this way of life."

"And what way of life is that, madam?"

Wynne blushed. She knew to what Smythe referred. He had told her this was a bad idea, and she had blithely ignored his counsel.

"All right, Smythe. You want me to admit that I was wrong," she began. "Fine. You were right. I was wrong. It was a bad idea. I must have been mad even to consider such a thing. Now I realize that I cannot go through with it, and I want him gone."

"It is hardly Mr. Leyton's fault that you changed your

mind," Smythe calmly observed.

"I don't care! He won't be any worse off than if someone else had originally purchased his indenture. It will be as if he had never been here," Wynne declared.

"Will it? I wonder."

"Smythe, I want him off this property in the morning. He can take his new clothes. I'll give him tonight to say goodbye to his friends here." She paused as the vision of the adoring Faye leaped into her mind. "But at sunrise, I want you to take him back to Williamsburg."

"If that is your wish, you know that I will comply. However," Smythe pointed out, "I would ask that you also consider this. You may be placing Mr. Leyton in a very unpleasant situation by this rather rash action."

"Don't argue with me, Smythe. My action is not rash." No, not nearly as rash as the bondsman's last night.

"Very well, madam. If that is your final decision, I will inform Mr. Leyton when he returns," Smythe replied with an air of resignation. "Will you excuse me?"

"Yes, of course," Wynne returned distractedly. "Tell him when he gets back. Just get him off my property, Smythe. I don't think I could stand to see him again."

Drew shook the water from his hair and began to towel dry his body. The quick bath had removed the sweat and dust of the day. If only he could remove the feeling of foreboding from his mind as easily.

Riding back from the timber-cutting camp, he had made a decision. He would ask politely to talk to Wynne. He would try to explain his motives for the midnight visit. He would try to take the feelings away that were making her ill and replace them with more tender memories. He would reason, beg, or promise, but somehow he would make her understand his feelings regarding siring another child. He didn't believe she was ready to hear about his feelings for her.

Surely she had some tenderness toward him. She was so responsive, so passionate. She obviously wasn't that way for every man or she would have been more experienced than she was. When she wasn't yelling at him or trying to keep him in his place, Drew could tell that she genuinely enjoyed his company and conversation.

Dressing carefully in his new clothes, which in his eyes were much more suited to his needs, he bundled his dirty garments and made his way to the laundry room. He left the soiled clothes and decided to stop by the kitchen. The hour was getting late, but he had been detained by the timber boss longer than he'd anticipated. A delicious aroma was drifting through the building. Annie was no doubt fixing something special for dinner. He was hungry enough to eat two helpings and hoped that the cook would give him a taste prior to the evening meal.

"Ah, Annie, that smells delicious," he observed, taking a deep breath of the warm, fragrant kitchen air. "What are you fixing?"

"Braised veal, ye vulture. And ye'll not be getting any early, either. Lady Grayson and her son be comin' for dinner tonight." Annie waved her wooden spoon like a broadsword.

"Vulture, is it? Is that any way to greet a hungry, hard-working man, home from the fields? I rode hard just to come and see you," Drew teased, but his mind wasn't on the banter. Who were the Graysons? Wynne hadn't mentioned them, so she obviously had no intention of introducing him to her friends.

"To see me or my food? If ye ever grow into yer appetite,

we'll have to build ye a house with great, wide doors and sew yer clothes from canvas tents."

"Ah, you wound me, woman! And all along I was just forcing myself to be polite and taste all your dishes."

"Hah," Annie returned, a broad smile on her ruddy face. She resumed stirring the sauce for the veal.

"Who are the Graysons, Annie? Are they neighbors?" Drew asked nonchalantly.

"Aye, neighbors some twenty miles hence." She pointed her spoon toward the west. "Lady Grayson be a widow. She and her son been here in Virginia . . . not quite a year now."

"From England?" Lord, he hoped not. All he needed was to be "discovered" by family friends before his name was cleared and his father contacted, or before he resolved his relationship with Wynne. The very thought caused a brief moment of panic.

Annie stopped stirring and looked up toward the ceiling, apparently thinking hard. "Wales, I think."

Drew almost let out a sigh of relief. Perhaps they wouldn't recognize him, even if they did see him. He didn't recall a widow named Lady Grayson. He vaguely remembered his mother mentioning an old friend named Grayson, but surely that lady could not be in this remote section of the Virginia colony.

"I'll see you later, Annie," Drew announced, taking a freshly baked roll from the bread box. "I have some things to discuss with Mistress Carr."

"Well, good luck to ye," Annie replied. "She's hardly left her room all day, but Millie said she was dressed now and working. Maybe ye can cheer the lady up."

"I'll try, Annie. Lord knows, I'll try my best." Drew made his way out the kitchen door and toward the house.

He entered the study after a brief, quick knock on the door. Wynne wasn't at the desk, but the butler sat in a chair near the fireplace.

"Smythe. I was looking for Mistress Carr."

"She's not available right now. Sit down, Mr. Leyton." He gestured to the matching chair.

Drew walked slowly into the room. Smythe rarely spoke to him, and this evening the butler's demeanor didn't look encouraging.

Drew seated himself and returned Smythe's even perusal. It was unsettling; the man obviously had something to say.

"Mistress Carr has made the decision that your purchase was not . . . wise. She has decided that it would be in her best interest if you left Waverley. Tomorrow you and I shall be returning to Williamsburg, where I will seek someone else to purchase your papers."

Drew's lips tightened and rage filled him. "No!"

"I beg your pardon? I assure you," Smythe instructed, "that you have no say in the matter. She has made the decision after consulting with me."

"Damn it, man! I don't care what she thinks right now. The woman is upset, maybe rightly so, and she's lashing out at me." Drew rose and paced the room. "She's punishing me, Smythe."

"If she wanted to punish you, Mr. Leyton, she would have you whipped," Smythe observed. "She wants you to leave Waverley."

"I'm not leaving under these conditions," Drew emphatically stated, leaning an arm against the mantel. "I want to talk to her."

"She won't see you. She made that very clear."

"She will see me! I'll not be shipped off like an errant bull," Drew roared.

"Mr. Leyton, you forget yourself. I repeat, you are in no position to dictate the terms of your departure."

"We'll just see about that, Smythe." Drew whirled and strode quickly out of the room. Smythe jumped up and followed him.

The butler caught up with him in the great hall. "You will not see her!"

"I'm going upstairs. You can't stop me." Drew paused at the bottom of the stairs. "Don't make me hurt you, Smythe."

Smythe grabbed Drew's arm, as though that would stop him. Drew shook him off and continued upstairs.

"Stop, Mr. Leyton. She does not wish to talk to you."

"Leave it be, Smythe," he replied, climbing slowly. "You don't know what this is about."

"I know what *you're* about. You may have given in to her demands, but that does not give you any special privileges."

Drew stopped and turned around. "Give in?" he replied incredulously. "Is that what you think this is about?" He laughed, a vicious, cruel sound. "I wish it were that easy. No, Smythe. Mistress Carr has not stolen my virtue."

"Then what?" Smythe abandoned his usual cool manner and rushed up several steps, raising his voice. "What has happened?"

"Smythe, I'm not going to tell you. I'm not going to confirm the petty rumors of the maids or the speculations of the staff. I won't tell you what goes on behind closed doors." He continued up the stairs.

Smythe ran ahead, reaching Drew at the top of the landing. "Let me talk to her first. I know that I cannot stop you, but there is something wrong."

"Only I can fix it, Smythe. I caused it and I can fix it."

"You admit it? You caused her this pain?"

"I never meant to cause her pain," Drew stated quietly. "Quite the contrary, as a matter of fact." He shook his head, his manner subdued. "It doesn't matter. I just want to make her understand. If she decides after I talk to her that she wants me to leave, I'll do so."

Drew continued walking toward the double doors of the master suite. Oh, he would talk to her and more, if necessary. And if that failed, he always had his trump card—the truth of his identity.

Wynne gazed out the window, watching the sunlight play across the water of the fountain. The day had been very warm, without a cloud in the sky. The dancing water of the fountain looked very inviting.

Wynne heard the door open quietly, then close. She didn't turn from window, but continued to watch the garden. Thinking it was Millie, she asked, "Would you prepare my bath?"

"I'll be glad to," a deep voice replied.

Clutching her wrapper, she whirled around at Drew's voice. Her mouth opened but no sound came forth.

"Please, Wynne, don't be alarmed. I only want to talk with you."

Wynne darted from the window to the fireplace, her earlier shock replaced by panic. Her only thought was to protect herself. She wouldn't let him touch her again!

She grabbed the first handle she touched: the poker. "Don't come any closer," she threatened. She held the poker in front of her.

"Wynne, please stop this. I didn't come here to fight with you."

"Get out!"

"Not until we talk."

"I want you off Waverley," she stated frantically. "Where is Smythe?" She cast a pained glance at the doors. "What have you done to Smythe?"

"Nothing. I explained to Smythe that I wanted to talk to you," Drew said levelly. He advanced a few more steps. Wynne backed toward the doors, her only thought to escape from his presence.

"Put the poker down and let's talk," Drew said calmly.

"No! Never. Get out!"

"As I said, not until we talk."

Drew advanced, his eyes intent on her face. Wynne barely controlled her trembling under his steady gaze.

"Wynne, I want to explain about last night."

"No! Don't try to tell me any of your lies. Just get out!"

She turned and ran for the door. Drew rushed her, grabbing her from behind. He pinned her arms to her sides and the poker fell to the floor, the sound muffled by the carpet.

"Let me go, you animal!" she yelled. "Let me go," she sobbed, twisting frantically in his arms. Drew stood there and held her firmly, not tight enough to bruise, but she was well aware of his lean strength. She kicked and twisted, cursed and cried, but he wouldn't let her go.

Soon she was exhausted. She sank into his arms, her curses turning to sobs. Oh, why wouldn't he just leave her alone? This had all been a terrible mistake. She should have been guided by her instincts, not the cool logic that said this was the only way. Now she'd put into motion events which threatened her calm existence, her peaceful life.

Drew picked her up easily, carrying her to the nearest chair, easing down, still cradling her.

He stroked back her damp hair. "Now we're going to talk."

"I don't want to talk," Wynne repeated lifelessly. "I just want you to leave."

Drew held her, wiping the tears from her cheeks and rocking slowly. They sat that way for a long time, until Wynne relaxed and unconsciously snuggled against him.

"I'm sorry you were sick today. I wanted to talk to you earlier, but I thought it would be best to let you . . . well, get over the shock." He spoke quietly.

"It was you who made me sick," Wynne returned, showing none of her usual spark. "Every time I think about what you did, I just want to die."

"What did I do that was so terrible?" he returned. "I made you feel like a woman. I tried to make you understand a part of what happens between men and women." He paused at her shudder. "Was that so bad?"

"Yes," she replied vehemently. "It was horrible. How could you do such things to me?"

"Wynne, I didn't do anything bad to you."

"Yes, you did. That kind of behavior is not normal."

"How would you know? I think I'm in a better position to know what is 'normal' and what's not. After all, the only man you've known is old. Just because he didn't make love to you like that doesn't mean it's abnormal."

"Oh, and I suppose you've made love to hundreds of women!" Wynne struggled to rise from his lap. "And they all enjoyed the things you did to them."

Drew appeared to be contemplating her words. He looked down at his fingers, mentally tabulating. "Maybe not hundreds."

Wynne drew back her fist to hit him, but he captured it easily. "I was only teasing."

She glared at him, her old spirit back in full force. He grinned at her expression.

"I like it better when we fight like this. You're no fun when you're serious."

"But this is serious. You have to go."

"Dear Wynne, I do not wish to go."

"You have to."

"Even if I promise to do whatever you want?"

"Like what?"

"Anything," he replied with a twinkle in his eye.

"You are a horrible man," she whispered.

Drew hugged her tightly. "I know I am." He rocked her back and forth, continuing to hold her securely. "I didn't mean to make you angry or to hurt you in any way. I just didn't realize how you would feel this morning."

"I felt . . . *feel* awful."

"Maybe I should have stayed with you all night. That way we could have talked this morning."

Wynne gasped at the picture that remark inspired. To wake up with him in the same bed! It was bad enough that he had done those . . . things to her.

"Wynne, Wynne, what am I going to do with you?"

"Mr. Leyton, you are hardly in a position . . ."

His kiss effectively silenced her very proper remark. All thoughts of scolding the man fled as his mouth moved across hers, as his tongue outlined her lips and sought entrance. She opened like a flower in spring, welcoming his invasion with returning passion.

Drew broke away first. "Do you really want me to go?" he asked softly.

Wynne didn't know what to reply. Yes! part of her cried. Get out of my well-ordered life and leave me alone. No! another part yelled. Make me feel and love and laugh. Work your magic on my senses.

"I don't know."

"Then let me stay." He hesitated, stroking her hand. "You said that you trusted me once. Trust me again."

"I don't know."

"I want to explain something to you, Wynne." He shifted her weight in his arms, his body more tense. She saw pain in his blue eyes. "I told you before I had a son— James. His mother was a maid on . . . an estate in Sussex."

"Did you work on the estate also?"

Drew smiled slightly, then his eyes closed. "No . . . no, I didn't. However, I did visit there once, and I met Sally, James's mother. When I found out she carried my child, I got her a small house. I supported them, Wynne. I went to see James often."

"Why didn't you just marry her?" she asked, her tone more harsh than she intended. The thought of Drew making love to another woman, even years ago and thousands of miles away, caused jealousy to rip through her, leaving pain and anger in her heart.

"I couldn't. It wouldn't have been wise. But that's not the point. What I want you to understand is how I felt about James. He was my *son*. I loved him. Eventually he came to live with me. When he died, I nearly went mad."

Wynne reached up and touched his face, her anger gone, replaced by empathy for a man who had lost someone he loved. She knew the feeling well . . . too well. She had lost everyone she loved in the last six years, because even though Samuel still lived, his mind, his counsel, were lost to her forever.

"I don't want to go through that again. I don't think I could stand to lose another child," he whispered.

"But Drew, don't you see that he *wouldn't* be lost.

Any child I conceive would be brought up with all the benefits Waverley can provide. My children will inherit all this someday." Her arm stretched wide. Then she placed her hand tentatively on his shoulder. "You must admit that I could provide a better life than that of a . . . a . . ."

"The word you're searching for is 'servant,' I believe."

"I don't mean to be cruel, but you must face the fact that my children will have advantages."

"How about the advantage of a loving father?" he asked angrily. "Who will be the child's father, Wynne? Some phantom figure of Samuel Carr? Does he exist, or is he someone you've created to give you the freedom you want? It's not every woman who can have *all this*"—he slashed the air in an imitation of her earlier gesture—"without the responsibilities that usually accompany marriage."

Instead of his anger fueling her own, she felt sympathetic to his plight. If she had his child, the baby would have more benefits than Drew. It must difficult for him to accept.

"Samuel exists. He's not here right now, but he is real."

"And what would he say if he walked through your door right now? How would he feel about your sitting on my lap, about your asking me to make love to you?"

Wynne ran her palm over his tense muscles. "He would understand. I'm sure Samuel wants an heir as much as I want a child. As I said, he's ill, unable to . . ."

"Make love to his passionate wife?"

Wynne blushed and removed her hand from his shoulder. "Please try to understand. If I do have a child, I'll care for him and love him with all my heart. Surely you won't regret helping me in this if you know how good his life will be."

"Oh, Wynne, what can I say? I know you mean well. You just can't possibly understand my situation."

"Then tell me. I feel there are secrets about your past that you refuse to share."

"Sweetheart, I wish . . . No, let me rephrase that. I would tell you if I could, if I thought it was for the best. But this decision must be separate from my status or background. Can you understand that?"

"I'm not sure. I think you're asking me to trust you again."

"Yes, I suppose I am."

Wynne leaned against him, relaxed into his hardness. Her cheek rested against his steady heartbeat and his hands stroked her arm and back. He had asked her to want him as a man, accept him as a man. Lord help her, but she did.

"I want you," she whispered into his shirtfront.

His arms closed around her. She felt his lips move against her hair. He whispered back, "Oh, love."

"Does that mean yes?"

"It means I can't say no to you any longer. You've won, sweetheart. I'll come to your bed, but not when you snap your fingers. On my terms, when we want each other . . . any time we want each other."

Her eyes misted as she looked at him, at the creases in his forehead, the laugh lines by his eyes. She noticed the darkness the sun had caused in his complexion, the golden highlights in his freshly washed hair. How had he come to mean so much to her in this short time? How could he sit here and hold her like a child and tell her they would make love?

She wanted the pleasant warmth of his kiss, the tenderness she felt when he held her. She didn't want those overpowering, intense feelings he had made her feel.

"I don't want to feel like I did last night," she stated firmly.

"How did you feel last night?" Drew murmured innocently. "I need to know so I won't make you feel that way again."

"I felt . . ." she began, then stopped. "Are you teasing me again? Because if you are, I don't think it is either funny or in good taste."

"I'm serious." He smoothed a strand of hair back from her temples. "Talk to me," he urged, touching his lips to her forehead. "Tell me why last night scared you so."

"You made me feel things . . . things I never knew existed," Wynne confessed. "It was too strong, too intense." She reached up to touch his slightly rough cheek. "All I ever wanted was to conceive children. I didn't want a lover. I didn't expect a friend."

He crushed her to his body as Wynne sobbed into his chest. She felt as though a weight had been lifted from her, as though she'd been relieved from a heavy burden carried too long.

After a long while of sitting in the chair, coming to an unspoken understanding, Wynne sat up shakily. She pressed a hand to his damp chest.

"I've gotten your new shirt all wet," she said. He smiled in reply and Wynne continued, "Do you like your new clothes?"

"Very much. Thank you."

"You're welcome."

"Annie said you were having company for dinner tonight."

Wynne had almost forgotten about the Graysons. Now that she and Drew had reached an understanding, how could she just ignore his presence, send him to his room like an errant child?

"I could introduce you as my new overseer."

Drew leaned back, his expression unreadable. "Yes, I suppose you could."

"Would you like to have dinner with us?"

He smiled, the genuine warmth of his feeling evident. Again, Wynne was surprised at how boyishly attractive the expression made him appear. "I'd like that very much."

"I didn't mean to exclude you. To be honest, I'd forgotten their visit."

"I suppose under the circumstances that's to be expected." He again stroked her hair, then lightly caressed her cheek. The feeling was so exquisite that she almost moaned aloud. "I've put you under much strain lately. It wasn't my intention."

"It wasn't my intention to cause problems with my request either. It seemed so sensible, so logical. Only after you came here, when I saw . . ."

"Saw what?"

Wynne felt her face heating again. She had never blushed so much in her life as she had in the last two weeks. Drew's arms tightened around her. "Tell me, woman. If you don't, I'll be forced to take desperate measures."

"Such as?" Wynne flippantly replied, thinking that he might threaten to kiss her into submission.

One of his hands moved to her waist, his fingers splayed, creeping upward. Her breath caught in her throat. The now familiar tension began to build as her blood began to race.

Suddenly, his fingers dug into her ribs, moving quickly, tickling her senseless. She hardly suppressed a scream, but couldn't control the laughter that bubbled out. "Stop!" she pleaded.

He laughed at her response. "Not till you tell me what you saw."

"Very well!" She let out a whoosh of breath as he stopped tickling her. "Please, no more."

"Tell me," he urged.

Wynne took a deep breath, unable to meet his eyes. "When I saw you for the first time, clean and shaved, standing in the doorway of my study, I thought . . ."

"You thought what?"

"That I might have been mistaken about my decision. You see, in Williamsburg you were just another dirty, nameless bondservant. I couldn't even tell if you were . . . what your features were."

"You mean you didn't know if I was ugly as the very devil?"

Wynne giggled. "That's about the truth of it." She traced the stitching of his shirtfront, loving the feel of his chest beneath the fabric. "You definitely aren't ugly," she whispered.

"Ah, I feel another compliment coming on."

"Oh, very well. You must know you're as handsome as any man has a right to be."

Drew laughed. "You little vixen. So you were so overcome with my striking good looks in the study that first night that it struck you speechless?"

Wynne let out an indignant sound and smacked him firmly on the chest. He responded by resuming his tickling. She laughed aloud, the feeling was so wonderful after her life of restraint and moderation.

"Drew, stop!" she managed to get out between giggles. "I must get ready—"

"You look ready to me," he remarked cryptically, and nuzzled her neck.

Wynne threw her arms around his neck and laughed

again. She was just about to kiss him soundly when the door burst open.

They both looked up . Wynne felt as if all the air had left her body. Smythe stood in the doorway, a look of shock on his face.

"Madam! I heard your scream and thought to investigate. I never imagined . . . I beg your pardon." He backed up one step and slammed the door. Drew and Wynne immediately burst into laughter.

"Poor Smythe," she finally said. "He's never seen anything like this before. I've probably shocked him out of ten years of his life."

"I should hope so! The man is entirely too stuffy, even for a butler. He's more proper than—"

"Who?"

"Never mind."

There was certainly much more to Andrew Leyton than met the eye. She was in much too good a mood to pursue it tonight, however.

"I really should get up and get dressed." She glanced out the window and saw that the sun had nearly set. "Lady Grayson and her son will be here any moment."

"Yes, and I must restore feeling to my legs if I'm to join you for dinner tonight."

"Why, you! Are you saying that I weigh too much?"

"No, not too much." She felt his eyes burning her as he inspected every inch. "Just right, I would say. However, I'm unaccustomed to having a woman sit in my lap for extended periods of time. My feeble condition, you know."

"Feeble condition, indeed! There's nothing wrong with your condition, Mr. Leyton."

"Ah, another compliment." He kissed her swiftly on the lips. "But, alas, I must prepare myself also. Pray get up, wench, else I'll be forced to dump your impressive curves on the floor!"

Wynne giggled at his frivolity. She swung her legs over the arm of the chair, onto the floor, and reluctantly left the comfort and security of his arms. She found she was shaky from sitting with him so long, so much so that she longed to hold him to her for a few moments more. She resisted the urge.

"Do you need help to rise, Mr. Leyton?"

Drew threw back his head and laughed deeply. "No, that doesn't seem to be a problem when I'm around you."

She had no idea what he meant, but he seemed to find it very amusing. She smiled. "Then come," she extended a hand. "You must be ready in a few minutes."

He laughed again, so she patiently explained. "For the Graysons' visit. For dinner."

"Ah, yes. Dinner." He rose from the chair with grace, despite claiming to have suffered from her weight. "I had better go talk to Smythe. He'll be worried."

"Smythe! I had forgotten about him."

"Don't worry. I'll explain that we've reached an understanding."

"He probably thought you were murdering me," Wynne laughed.

"Never that, sweetheart," Drew murmured, pulling her to him. "I could never hurt you."

"I believe you," she whispered.

Drew gently pushed her away. "I had better get ready for your guests and talk to Smythe or they'll find two famished, exhausted people in the morning." He smiled at her confusion. "I was teasing again."

"Oh," she replied, never knowing when he was serious. Drew moved across the room, opened the door, and strode into the hall. Wynne heard him call for the butler as she smoothed her wrinkled gown. She quickly went to the vanity to brush her hair, thinking what a lucky woman she was to have chosen a man like Drew.

10

Drew stopped just inside the doorway of the formal parlor. His earlier feelings of unease returned. Sitting daintily in a chair near the fire was a lady whose face was vaguely familiar. Had he seen her before? Did she seem familiar only because he had predisposed himself to possible recognition as the earl of Morley's son? It was impossible to tell.

Standing behind her, leaning against the mantel, stood a man perhaps five or six years younger than himself. He had the same dark blond hair as his mother, the same proud bearing. It was that, more than just knowing Lady Grayson was visiting, that identified them as peers. Suddenly Drew wondered how well *he* had fooled anyone, especially if he dressed and acted as he'd been raised to do.

The lady turned, catching him with an inquiring look that begged for an introduction. She had friendly eyes and intelligent features. Drew liked her almost immediately. The feeling of vague unease grew, however, when he realized that the lady reminded him more and more of someone he'd met before, perhaps when he was still a lad. She was of an age to be friends with his mother. Was she? If so, she would surely recognize his name. And if she did, how would Wynne react when she learned that her bondsman was a peer of the realm? That he'd lied by deception after asking her repeatedly to trust him.

"Mr. Leyton," Wynne called to him from the sofa, "please come in and meet my guests."

He stepped forward, alternating his gaze between mother and son, knowing that the young man, at least, was fairly bursting with questions about the name Leyton.

"Lady Carolyn Grayson, please allow me to introduce my overseer, Mr. Leyton."

Drew gave a small bow to the lady, hoping he conveyed a message with his eyes that cautioned the woman to say nothing if she knew. "Milady, it is an honor."

"And this is her son, Michael." Drew turned to the young man and gave another bow. "Mr. Grayson, an honor also."

"Leyton?" Lady Grayson questioned. "Is that with an L-E-Y or L-E-I-G-H?"

"L-E-Y, milady. Andrew Leyton."

"I knew some Leytons in London," she said with a raised eyebrow. "Quite the family, I must say."

"I am from Sussex, Lady Grayson."

Her eyes narrowed slightly, as though she were sizing him up. "Indeed. Well, I am sure the name is common, even though the family is not."

"It's an old name, to be sure. As you said, fairly common," Drew replied nonchalantly, hoping to end her interest.

Michael Grayson gave his mother a confused look. Drew noticed that Lady Grayson moved her head slightly, asking silently for her son to remain quiet. Drew gave a sigh of relief. For whatever the reason, he was safe for now.

"Would you care for a sherry, Mr. Leyton?" Wynne asked, reaching for the decanter on the low table in front of her. She wore a pale blue dress with cream lace, her hair upswept, her posture perfect. Drew found it difficult to imagine that this was the laughing woman he had held and tickled no more than half an hour ago. She was once again the coolly proper mistress of Waverley.

"Sherry would be fine, Mistress Carr."

"Have you been in the Virginia colony a long while, *Mr.* Leyton?" Lady Grayson asked before taking a sip of her wine.

"Only long enough to learn the bare essentials of the plantation, milady. I find it very refreshing here."

"Indeed, I imagine it is quite different from Sussex. That is where you said you are from?"

"Born and raised there," Drew answered truthfully.

"Your sherry, Mr. Leyton."

"Thank you, Mistress Carr." Drew took a small sip and smiled slowly at Wynne. Lord, but he loved to look at her. How could anyone with so much passion locked inside appear so calm and proper? She had to be strong beyond any woman he had ever known to have such control. It wasn't as though she were acting, trying to manipulate others to her will. It was more like a shield she erected, a way she put distance between herself and the world.

"Lady Grayson has been here only a short time herself. And, of course, Michael," Wynne added with a smile. A smile, Drew thought, that was slightly warmer than Wynne's usual demeanor. Did she have a *tendre* for the Grayson boy?

"How do you find the colonies?" Drew asked Lady Grayson.

"We have enjoyed it so far," she replied, reaching for her son's hand and giving it a little squeeze. "Michael meant it to be an investment, but it has turned into a fine home."

"Indeed, it is," Michael added, speaking for the first time. "Much different, I imagine, from Mr. Leyton's life in England."

"I'm an adaptable sort, Grayson. I find that I enjoy my time here more each day." He gave Wynne a meaningful look. "Waverley is just beginning to fully bloom."

"Well," Wynne said quickly, rising from the sofa. "Dinner should be ready now. Mr. Grayson, would you be so kind?"

"I would be delighted, Mistress Carr." He offered his arm, Drew noticed, in a very friendly manner, one which Wynne was more than willing to accept. Drew felt an unfamiliar spurt of jealousy. He wanted to take Wynne's hand in his and pull her away from the young man, but of course he couldn't. Calling him her overseer was stretching the truth. Identifying him as a bondsman would certainly give him even less reason to lay claim to her hand. Or anything else.

He walked to Lady Grayson, bending and offering his arm for her to rise. "Milady?"

Wynne and Michael were already passing through the door as Lady Grayson lingered in her chair. "My pleasure, Mr. Leyton. Or should I say, milord?" Her eyes were intense, probing, as she whispered, "Does your father know you are here, masquerading as an overseer?"

"My father?" Drew felt his heart stop for a moment, then race.

"Yes, your father—the earl," she said quietly and with assurance, rising from the chair with the aid of his arm.

"Milady, I ask you not to repeat that information to Mistress Carr." They began walking slowly across the room.

Lady Grayson raised a pale, arched eyebrow. "She knows nothing of your background?"

"She knows me as a bondsman."

Lady Grayson stopped suddenly. Her eyes were wide as she stared up at Drew.

He urged her to continue through the hall. "Have you heard nothing of the charges that have been brought up against me?"

"Nothing," she confided. "But we are very isolated here."

"I would like to speak with you later."

"I normally take a stroll before retiring."

"Mr. Leyton? Our dinner will grow cold before you arrive," Wynne chided.

Lady Grayson answered, "I'm sorry, my dear. I find that I move more slowly of late."

"My apology, Lady Grayson. I assumed that Mr. Leyton was exhibiting his usual high regard for the 'weaker' gender. He seems to feel that we women are not capable of managing without a man's guidance."

"Ah, but then we do have men to lean upon," Lady Grayson added with a smile. "I have Michael," she explained, "and you, my dear, have Mr. Leyton now."

Dinner was long and filled with tension for Drew. Lady Grayson complied with his wishes, making no mention of his background. He wished to be anywhere except sitting with these people, making polite conversation while he watched Wynne sip daintily of her wine, spear small pieces of veal and chew them slowly with her even, white teeth. It was almost more than he could bear. He wanted to whisk her away from here, from Waverley and Virginia, to take her someplace where his background and her marital status had no importance. Somewhere only lovers visited.

But he made the correct responses to their questions,

made witty comments on occasion, and in general comported himself as befit his station—peer, not overseer. No one seemed to notice, or if they did, they didn't comment on his manners. He noticed Michael Grayson watching him carefully, but the young man obviously took his cue from his mother and remained silent about Drew's background.

After dinner they resumed their places in the parlor, except that both Drew and Michael took seats facing Wynne. She had urged Lady Grayson to play the latest sheet music on Wynne's Woolfinden spinet. It sat in the corner, illuminated by a silver candelabra. Lady Grayson played beautifully, but Drew's attention was again drawn to Wynne's smiling countenance. The candlelight made her hair glow like highly polished gold, made her skin appear even more flawless.

He wondered what she would do if she found out he was the owner of an estate and title, although minor, in England. Would she hate him for the deception, or would she understand that he had done what he thought was best at the moment? Would she understand that his primary concern at first had been his family's good name and the political treachery of the Duke of Newcastle? If he told her he had come to care for her, would she understand that he wanted her to care for him as a man, not as a peer or as someone to sire her children?

There were too many questions to answer and none that he could ask outright. He would again wait, gauge her mood and his standing, before revealing anything else about his past. But what of Lady Grayson, who played so calmly upon on the spinet? Would she keep his secret safe for long?

The music ended and Wynne clapped appreciatively. Drew joined in, praising Lady Grayson's abilities.

"I haven't played in quite some while. Michael has

ordered a harpsichord, but Heaven only knows when it will arrive."

Smythe entered then, carrying a tray bearing a carafe and cups, a decanter and glasses for wine.

"Would you care for some port, Mr. Grayson, Mr. Leyton?" Wynne asked as soon as the butler had placed the tray on the table in front of her.

"Thank you," they both said at once. Drew gave the younger man a scowl.

Wynne looked from one to the other. Something was amiss. She had been in Michael Grayson's presence before and never found him so reserved, so solemn. And Drew acted like Michael was some sort of adversary.

"I'll just take some coffee, my dear," Lady Grayson said, filling the silence. "With cream and sugar, please."

Wynne watched Drew carefully. Although she was not accustomed to doing much formal entertaining, she recognized Drew's impeccable manners. He fit in more here, in this setting, than he did in the stable or the study. In fact, the only place she could think of that he seemed even more at ease was in her bedroom. She felt her cheeks grow hot as she remembered how very well he comported himself there.

"Have you enough timber for all the tobacco hogsheads you'll need?" she asked the Graysons, deciding that she had had enough of thinking about Drew's characteristics.

"I believe so," Michael answered, "although if the weather holds we may have a record harvest. If that is the case, I expect we will have to buy some."

"Mr. Leyton is overseeing the cutting of the trees close to the river. We should have spare timber if you need additional hogsheads built. I've been meaning to cut that particular stand for several years, but with Samuel being gone,

I haven't had the extra time to oversee the operation myself."

"Have you heard from Samuel recently, my dear?"

"A letter occasionally. He may arrive home soon, though. It's difficult to tell."

"It seems a shame to leave such a lovely wife alone for so long," Michael remarked, his eyes resting on Drew.

"Thank you, Mr. Grayson," Wynne said. "But it takes so long to reach India that he must make the most of each trip. I understand. Now, with Mr. Leyton here, perhaps I can accomplish more around Waverley. And of course Samuel will be pleased to find such a bountiful crop when he returns."

"Of course," Drew tightly commented, taking a large sip of port.

Lady Grayson placed her cup on the table. "I find that I must retire now, my dear. It has been a long day."

"I'll show you to your room," Wynne said, rising from the sofa. "If you gentlemen will excuse us?"

The men said their good evenings to the ladies. As soon as the women's footsteps could no longer be heard on the staircase, Michael turned to Drew.

"What are you doing here, *Mr.* Leyton, playing the part of the humble overseer?"

"What do you know of it? Perhaps that's my station in life."

"You were graduating from Cambridge with top honors the last I saw you. If I remember correctly, your father, the Earl of Morley, was there, along with the rest of your esteemed family. Don't try to confound me with your play-acting."

"Ah, so you were at Cambridge while I was still there. And your mother? She claims to know my identity, yet says nothing either."

"I'm sure my mother has her own reasons, which I have yet to understand. But understand them I will before this visit is over."

"I'd hoped to talk with your mother before retiring. She says she walks before taking her rest."

"My mother is a sensitive woman. If she wishes to remain silent, I will honor her decision. However, if I find that you are deceiving Mistress Carr for some dishonorable reason, you will have me to answer to."

"Your feelings for Mistress Carr . . . do they extend beyond neighborly concern?" Drew asked, placing his wine glass on the low table and strolling toward the fireplace.

"That's hardly the concern of her overseer," Michael replied with a sneer.

Drew changed his tactics, realizing that he had no good answer for that statement. "And how is it that you recognize my name and family, yet I have no knowledge of yours? There seems to be a mystery there also."

"Grayson is my family name, as Leyton is yours. What title my father had is no concern of yours."

"Then you refuse to say?"

"It is of no concern," Michael ground out.

Smythe entered then, quietly and efficiently. "Mr. Grayson, may I show you to your room? Your mother requested a word before retiring."

Michael placed his glass on the table, straightened to his full height, and adjusted the lace at one sleeve. "Until tomorrow, Mr. Leyton." He turned and followed the butler up the stairs.

Drew waited in the moonlit garden. Where was Lady Grayson? The invitation to join her had been unmistakable. A low-burning lamp remained on in one of the guest bedrooms, but Drew didn't know which one Lady Grayson was in and which one Michael occupied.

The distinct sound of footsteps crunching shells carried to his ears. Drew dropped his arms, straightening his sleeves and waistcoat, ready to step out and greet Lady Grayson.

The footsteps grew closer, then paused. Was she looking for him? He stepped from the shadow into the moonlight, his own steps muffled by the lush grass.

"Lady Grayson?"

There was no answer from the figure standing a few yards away, because it was not, as he realized immediately, Lady Grayson. That tall figure and blond hair could only belong to Wynne.

"My pardon. I was out for a bit of fresh air and thought you were Lady Grayson."

"Really? It sounded more to me as if you were expecting Lady Grayson!"

She was angry again, Drew realized. Angry and jealous. "Why would you think that?" He stepped closer.

She held her ground, standing even straighter, taller, if possible. "You are beginning to make a habit of being caught with women in what some would say are compromising situations."

Drew chuckled. "Is that what you think?"

"As I said, it may only seem that way."

He saw no sign of Lady Grayson, so he took Wynne in his arms and retreated into the shadows of the arbor. "I've been wanting to do this all night," he murmured before crushing her to him, slanting his mouth across hers and kissing her thoroughly. "You nearly drove me crazy, sitting there so sedately, looking so beautiful."

Wynne didn't reply, but instead clung to him, pressing her head against his chest.

"Wynne, Wynne," he whispered into her jasmine-scented hair, "what are we going to do?"

"Do?"

"About this attraction we feel. About this madness."

"You know what I want you to do," she stated simply.

Drew was silent for a moment, his arms tightening around her. Then he whispered, "I know."

The sound of footsteps interrupted whatever he might have said. He wasn't sure what he would have promised her at the moment. "Wynne, you must go. Someone is coming."

Not questioning his suggestion that she should be the one to leave, Wynne gave him one quick, confused look before turning and softly running through the back of the rose arbor, across the damp grass that muffled her light footsteps.

A few seconds later, Lady Grayson stepped into view. She was wrapped in a light cloak to chase away the chill of the night. "Mr. Leyton?"

"Yes, I'm here, milady." Drew stepped onto the walkway.

"I hope I didn't keep you waiting too long."

"Of course not."

"Michael felt obligated to tell me his thoughts. I asked him to come to see me so I could explain why I didn't reveal your identity to Wynne. Apparently you and he spoke after I went upstairs?"

"Yes, we did. He wanted to let me know he was aware of who I was—who my father is."

Lady Grayson laughed. "You seem to be a bit confused. You are still part of the Leyton family? You haven't been disowned or anything foolish?"

Drew shook his head, speaking softly. "No, nothing like that." He looked around and spotted a bench just a few yards down the path. "Would you care to sit for a while?"

"Of course."

When Lady Grayson was comfortably seated on the mortar bench, Drew told his story. He gave her a shortened version, of course, omitting much about why he was in the inn that night. Lady Grayson, although she no longer lived in England, apparently kept up with the politics of the court. She knew of the power struggle between the Duke of Newcastle and William Pitt. When Drew told her of the night he was taken from the Tower, she gasped aloud.

"But then why are you still here? Why haven't you told Wynne who you are? She seems to be a reasonable woman. She or I could give you passage back to England."

Drew was silent for a moment. How could he explain what he couldn't quite understand himself? He couldn't tell Lady Grayson what Wynne wanted of him, and he certainly couldn't admit that he was seriously considering complying with her wishes.

"It's difficult to explain. You see, I want my name cleared. I thought to give my father time to have the incident investigated further. I wrote to him. The letter has been posted. I thought it best to keep my identity a secret from Mistress Carr until I can be more sure of my status."

"Your status? Somehow, I think you are telling me more by what you omit than what you say. Are you thinking of your situation or hers?"

"What . . . ?"

"Your eyes betray you. You care for her."

"She is a married woman. I do not intend to shame her or myself."

Lady Grayson smiled and placed her small hand on his arm. "Honor is bred into you, as it was with your father and his father. Did you know that your mother and I were friends, that we had our coming-out balls in the same season?" Lady Grayson laughed softly. "She knew she wanted to marry your father almost immediately. It frustrated her to no end that he was so intent on doing everything properly, taking all the steps necessary to ensure a suitable match."

"That does sound like my father. He can be most relentless when approaching a challenge."

"I think you are much like him," she said, patting his arm.

"Then you know that I will do nothing to hurt Wynne."

"I know that you will do nothing *intentionally* to hurt her. But you must realize she is a very lonely young woman, for all her talk of her plantation and her absent husband."

"You truly have never met him?"

Lady Grayson shook her head, then stared off into the night. "I know what you are thinking. I have pondered the same thing myself. I asked myself why she would create stories about the man, why she would pretend to see him, correspond with him. But then I realized how very vulnerable she is. Do you know anything of the scandal *she* suffered five or six years ago?"

"She's spoken of it."

"She probably doesn't realize that I know about it, but others have spoken of it to me. However, after meeting her when we first arrived, then her invitation to Waverley, I can't imagine she was at fault. I've never been one for gossip. But I will say this. Sir Francis is still magistrate, even if he does leave her alone for now."

Drew felt a surge of anger. "No one will harm her while I'm here," he swore.

Lady Grayson waited a moment to reply, as if she knew his inner battle for control. Then she whispered, "But what about when you leave?" She rose from the bench. "I must go in now, for the night grows more chill." She reached down and took his hand in hers. Her fingers were thin and cold. "Think about what you really want, Andrew Leyton. And think about what she needs."

11

It *had been a day and a half* since the Graysons had departed. Amid promises to call again soon and invitations to come and visit, they climbed into the carriage after spending one night and drove away, leaving Wynne alone with her thoughts.

Drew had mentioned over dinner that evening that he planned to take another walk in the garden before retiring. Wynne knew it was an invitation, although she'd not said she would meet him there. Not exactly. She believed she'd said something like "Oh, really?" He was asking her whether she planned to renew her vow to have the kind of relationship he wanted. Her fear had kept her from answering before. The problem was, she still felt fear—of the unknown and her response to it.

Wynne slipped her feet into green kid slippers that matched her gown and let herself out of the room, glancing both ways for servants. No one was upstairs at this hour.

Drew was waiting in the shadows of a dogwood tree. His shape was clearly revealed by the moonlight, yet his features were in shadow and Wynne couldn't tell his mood. Please don't try to make me lose control like I did before, she prayed. She closed her eyes for a moment to calm her rapidly beating heart.

The smell of the garden was almost overwhelming; forsythia and honeysuckle, hundreds of roses and freshly turned soil competed to bring early summer to Virginia. Wynne breathed deeply and hugged her arms to chase away the slight chill of late evening.

"Let me offer you my coat." He moved out of the shadow. His face remained unreadable as he advanced and shrugged out of the tan poplin coat, spreading it over Wynne's shoulders. His hands lingered and he held her loosely as his eyes searched her face.

"Let's walk," he said gently, and she turned away to the crushed-shell walk, a carefully weeded path through the boxwoods. The shrubs formed low borders for the roses and flowering bushes, with occasional ornamental trees that had been pruned for an appealing symmetrical design. Drew kept his hand at her elbow. The heat from that touch reminded Wynne of their intimacies. They were quiet as they strolled through the formal gardens, taking in the peaceful night and enjoying their companionship. As they walked farther from the house, the small topiary garden Wynne had started five years ago became visible.

Drew stopped and Wynne tried to look at the garden through his eyes, at the shapes clearly revealed by the bright, white moonlight. There was a rabbit, three toadstools of varying heights, and a turtle. The walkway formed a circle around the shapes. On the other side of the circle was a stone bench between two tall evergreens resembling giant curved horns.

"Would you care to sit for a while?" Wynne asked. At

Drew's nod, she lowered herself to the bench and watched Drew. He continued to review the topiaries, smiling at the art forms.

"I like your garden. It reminds me of . . ."

"What?"

"Nothing," he replied distractedly. "It just looks similar to a place I saw once in England."

"Oh," Wynne responded, clearly disappointed. She had been sure that he was going to tell her something about his previous life.

Drew sat beside her, close enough that she could feel his body heat. She shivered and he pulled her closer. She immediately stiffened in his grasp.

"Relax. I promise not to ravish you in the garden," Drew teased.

Wynne tried a weak smile. "I know. I suppose I'm nervous."

Drew placed both arms around her, holding her. He rested his chin on her head.

"Did you know that I remembered smelling the jasmine scent you wore when you bought me more than anything else about Williamsburg?" As Wynne shook her head, he continued, "I love your smell. I believe I would recognize it anywhere, for the rest of my life."

"That's a long time," Wynne whispered.

"I know, sweetheart. Forever is a very long time."

"So is seven years—for some people."

"Seven years doesn't seem nearly long enough," Drew murmured. His lips moved to her ear, placing tiny kisses around the shell and moving lower.

"Don't!" Wynne cried and jumped up from the bench. "You don't have to do that!" Her skin tingled; her nerves were stretched taut. Why did he always want to make her feel this way—so unlike herself? Suddenly her decision to come to him on his terms seemed a terrible mistake.

"I know that. I did it because I wanted to," he calmly explained. "Please come and sit down beside me."

"We . . . we should really go in," Wynne said, backing away from him, hugging her arms over the large coat.

"So you weren't serious about how you want me," Drew accused.

Wynne turned and began walking rapidly down the path. Her heart raced, keeping time with her footsteps. The yellow light from the windows of the house beckoned and she began to walk more quickly. Drew caught up to her in only a few strides.

"Stop it!" he demanded, grasping her arm. "You're trying to fool yourself again and it won't work."

"You're wrong! Let me go."

"You think that if you can keep me at a distance you won't feel anything when I come into your body. You think you can keep this impersonal, like a casual acquaintance that you accept into your bed for a few minutes whenever you think the time is right." Drew paused and took a deep breath, his eyes burning into hers. "Well, it doesn't work that way."

"It would work very well if you would let it!" she returned sharply. "You could be very happy here for a time. Why can't you accept what I have to give without always asking for more? We are not courting! We are not husband and wife! We have nothing in common except your indenture papers!"

She saw his temper flare at her words, his anger reflected in his eyes.

"Fine. Get upstairs and into your fine bed. Turn down all the lamps and blow out the candles. Lie there and get comfortable, because it will be a cold day in hell before I join you."

Drew brushed past her and stalked toward the house. He was almost out of sight before Wynne began walking, then running toward his retreating figure.

He rounded the corner of the house and stormed through the back entrance, not trying to be quiet. The heavy wooden door slammed against the brick. He took the stairs two at a time.

Wynne entered the house just behind him, then followed him quickly up the stairs. Just as he was entering his room, she grabbed his upper arm and turned him around. He raised his other hand, ready to strike out.

"Don't!" she commanded. Her hand relaxed on his arm and the grasp became a caress. "Don't . . ." she whispered. "Drew, I'm sorry. I'm just so frightened."

He turned and pulled her close, clutching her painfully to his chest. "You can't say no again tonight," he growled. "Leave now or accept my terms. There'll be no turning back."

Wynne twined one hand around his head, pulling the velvet ribbon and loosening his hair. She urged his head lower, capturing his lips with her own. "Kiss me," she murmured, and he did. They sank against the doorframe to his room, lost to the moment and the passion.

Drew's hands roamed almost desperately over her body. Wynne's knees refused to support her and she sagged in his arms. Her head thrown back, her eyes tightly shut and her fingers still twined in his heavy, silken hair, she felt Drew press fevered kisses to her throat, nuzzling aside the wrapper and continuing downward.

"Wynne . . . Wynne," he whispered into her neck. "We must not stay here." He nibbled at the swell of her breasts above the gown.

"Come to my room," she whispered in reply.

He reached for her shaky legs, swinging her up into his arms and striding down the hall. They moved through the ballroom with purpose; Wynne's head turned toward his neck as she returned his earlier kisses with her own. Each time her tongue stroked his heated skin Drew gave a little shudder. Soon he stopped, staggering against the mirrored wall.

"If you don't stop that we'll never get to your room," he murmured teasingly.

She stroked his cheek, then combed her fingers through his hair. Good Lord, but she cared too much about him. How would she feel after tonight, after they had shared more than she had ever experienced with another man? She must get herself back in control.

As soon as they entered the bedchamber, Drew firmly closed and locked the doors. Wynne made her way to the bed and removed her wrapper, folding it at the foot of the bed as she did each evening, thinking about how very normal the action seemed.

"Is something wrong?"

Her head jerked up. "Wrong? No, what do you mean?"

"You seem different somehow. Are you having second thoughts?"

"No, no second thoughts. I agreed to your terms."

Drew moved into the room and turned down the lamps until only the moonlight illuminated the room. "You did, didn't you? I only wonder if you are aware to what you agreed."

He came to stand before her. His movements were slow and deliberate as he unbuttoned the shirt, pulled it off, and tossed it carelessly by her wrapper. Drew sat on the bed and took off his shoes and stockings. Standing, he reached for the front flap of his breeches, his gaze never leaving her face as he undid each button.

Wynne was both curious and appalled. He intended to remove all his clothes! She closed her eyes briefly as the memory of his bare chest against her breasts came flooding back. Opening her eyes, she realized that he had paused and was watching her carefully.

She let her eyes roam over his chest, his arms, his stomach. There was nothing to mar the solid planes and curves of his physique. His body was a magnet that kept her coming back again and again until she was afraid she would never be able to separate from him.

Wynne watched as he finished the last button on his breeches.

The sense of panic returned. She was alone in her bedroom on the verge of making love to a man she had known less than a month! But many brides barely knew their husbands, and this was not so very different, she told herself.

"I've been told I'm not all that unpleasant to the eye," he teased her lightly. "Surely you aren't still frightened?"

Wynne shook her head in response, not trusting her voice.

Drew went to the bed and sat back, pushing himself away from the edge and fluffing the pillows behind him. He looked perfectly at ease and natural reclining in her chaste bed.

When she still stood in the middle of the floor as though frozen, he reached out a hand. "Join me," he requested.

The time has come, she thought. He will take me now and I will let him. She shuddered again and moved to the bed, sitting on the edge and looking at his sculpted face. "What do you want me to do?"

"Would you take off the gown?" he asked quietly.

"If it's important to you." At his affirmative nod she reached for the straps and slipped them from her shoulders.

He leaned forward and helped her undress, then opened his arms. She came willingly. He leaned back into the pillows and pulled her across his body, stroking her back and smoothing her hair over her shoulders. "I want this night to last forever," he confessed.

"Nothing lasts forever," Wynne reflected, her words muffled into his chest.

He began kissing her then, deep, drugging kisses that trailed downward from her lips to her neck. She braced a hand against his shoulder, her world spinning as he unleased the same sensations she'd felt the other time.

"No, wait," she pleaded breathlessly.

He raised himself up from where his tongue swirled along her collarbone. "No more waiting, Wynne. You said this is what you wanted."

"I do, really. But—"

"No." He said it simply, with finality. Wynne closed her eyes and sank back into the mattress, her heart beating faster. Soon she clutched his shoulders instead of bracing against them. She ran her fingers through the crispness of his hair as he kissed the tip of one breast, then the other. And when his hands strayed lower, she moaned aloud so that he began kissing her lips again, taking the sound into his own mouth.

"It's been so long, love," he murmured. "I wanted to wait, but I can't."

He touched her where she was nothing but sensation. She knew she should resist these feelings, but they were too strong, too wildly compelling. Her skin felt on fire, as hot as his seemed beneath her fingers. She let herself explore his back, his arms, anywhere she could reach.

She felt a moment of panic as he raised above her, spreading her legs with his own. She should have told him, she vaguely realized. Did it matter? But then his manhood was pressing against her, his hands and lips commanding her to respond.

He pressed into her slowly when she would have surged against him. He stopped, his arms trembling with effort as he braced above her. He kissed her tenderly, his eyes speaking a thousand words.

When he thrust forward, it happened so quickly she barely had time to gasp and recoil against the pain. She felt tears run down her cheeks as her eyes stayed tightly shut. But then she heard his soft words and felt his hands smoothing over her face as her body began to accept his swift invasion.

"Love, why didn't you tell me?"

"I wasn't sure it was important." She sniffed, trying to reassure him at the same time she was so uncertain about her own feelings. "I wasn't sure you could tell."

"Then Samuel never . . ."

"He was ill."

Drew kissed her again, more passionately and possessively than ever before. His hips thrust forward, more gently this time, and it seemed her body adjusted to his size and weight. She moved against him, tentatively at first, then with more enthusiasm. Those wonderful feelings returned, only intensified where their bodies were joined.

She felt a further swelling, then his cry of completion hung in the air even as she strained toward the goal he had taught her so well before. But then she realized his movements had stopped, his breath heavy against her neck as he collapsed into the pillow.

"I'm sorry, love."

"Sorry?"

"That I was so selfish that I couldn't wait for you to join me."

Embarrassed, she turned away from his steady, burning, gaze. "That's all right, really. It wasn't necessary."

"Wynne, love, look at me." He coaxed her to meet his eyes with a gentle hand. "It *was* important. This first time . . . I can't find the words to tell you how much it meant to me. To know that no other man has ever touched you like this. To know you've given to me what you can never give again to another. Wynne, I love you."

Her breathing stopped, her body stiffened. "Don't say that."

"What? That I love you? It's true, it has been true, from the first time you faced me in the study, so flustered yet trying to be the stern matron you like to portray. You infuriate me, you entice me, but I can hardly keep from loving you."

She pressed against his shoulders as if that would budge him. "That wasn't part of the plan."

"Damn the plan! I'm talking about our future. Don't you understand? I love you. I want to be with you always."

"No." She shook her head in denial, unable to meet his eyes.

"Your husband never consummated the marriage. You could have it annulled. We could be together."

She shook her head, knowing that she had to stop him from believing they had a future. "No, we couldn't. This is *my* plantation. When Samuel and I married, we combined the land my father had with Waverley. I've worked for it for six years. I'm not about to give it up."

He tensed, then pulled away abruptly. "Not even for what we could have together?"

"Drew, I've never given you any hope that we could be together. You're my bondsman—"

"And that's all you want, isn't it? A man you could control, someone who wouldn't give you any trouble."

"I didn't mean to hurt you," she said softly. Lord, but this was difficult. She hadn't realized he might feel this way, that he would become so possessive.

He rolled across the mattress and grabbed his breeches from the floor. "No, I don't suppose you did. At least, not in so many words."

"What does that mean?"

"You think about it, Mistress Carr," he said with banked anger as he pulled on his shirt and stuffed it into his breeches.

"Drew, don't—"

"Don't expect a repeat of this night. I doubt I could generate much enthusiasm for a woman who thinks I'm only after her plantation."

"I didn't say that."

"You didn't have to. Goodnight, Mistress Carr."

He didn't slam the door, but shut it with such firm finality that Wynne knew he meant what he said. She'd known all along he was a proud man, a man accustomed to more than what she wanted to give. And now she'd hurt him, thrown his declaration of love back in his face with careless disregard. Oh, he probably did think he loved her. But it wouldn't last. Not like Waverley.

On trembling legs she walked to the basin and washed away the traces of lovemaking. Then she removed the gown she'd donned for the purpose of seducing her bondsman, folded it gently, and placed it in the bottom drawer, where she wouldn't have to see it again.

When she crawled back into bed moments later, dressed in plain white cotton, she pushed away the pillow that smelled of Drew and cried herself to sleep.

12

Wynne sat at the desk early one morning and studied the numbers that had been prepared for the anticipated yield from the tobacco harvest. Calculating the hogsheads from that yield and the rate per hogshead, she came to the conclusion that the quitrent to the crown would be paid again this year in tobacco rather than silver.

She closed the ledger and leaned her head on her hands. Paying in pounds sterling for the bondsman and in silver coin for his clothing and hers had drained her ready supply of currency. There was never enough currency in Virginia for the imports the colonists wanted to purchase, but with the recent expansion of Waverley's production acreage, she should easily be able to meet the tax.

She rose wearily from the desk and walked to the window that looked over the garden. The grey light of dawn had not found its way into the small courtyard, and it still appeared as dark as night. The full moon

had waned to a quarter, and she was no closer to rec-
onciling her feelings toward the bondsman.

When he'd left her room on that fateful night, she
had again been tempted to take him back to Williamsburg, to get him off her property. A thousand thoughts
had raced through her head, yet none brought her the
neat, orderly solution she desired. Why did this have to
be so painful? Why couldn't he just accept what she had
to give and allow her some peace? There didn't seem to
be any justice in the world, at least where her life was
concerned.

After Wynne stopped feeling sorry for herself, she realized she would never be the same after the two nights in
his arms. She had wanted to establish a friendship of sorts,
but he wanted more. He wanted her love, which she dared
not give, and her plantation, which she would never risk
losing.

So she had gone on, limiting her contact with the man
and never consulting with him alone. Always Smythe or
Riley or Millie or someone was with her. He wouldn't
dare to voice any personal matters in their presence.
When she would briefly glance his way, his eyes would be
troubled and questioning, but she did not give in to the
emotions that caused her stomach to plummet and her
skin to flush.

Wynne moved away from the window and decided to
visit the kitchen. Cook would no doubt be making breakfast and she always prepared coffee early. Millie didn't usually come with a tray until well after sunrise, and Wynne
was hungry now. She walked slowly down the hall and out
the door.

The mornings were still slightly cool, and with the
dampness in the air, Wynne hugged her arms and
wished she had thought to bring a shawl. She watched

the red brick walkway, since the foggy air made it difficult to see five feet in front. She was brought up short by a figure that suddenly loomed in her path.

Strong hands grasped her shoulders and she panicked, twisting in his grip and trying to turn away.

"Why run, mistress? Surely you don't find my touch so distasteful."

"Let me go," she ordered coldly. "Remove your hands!"

"Not until you talk to me," Drew returned in an equally cold voice. His chilling tone frightened her more than the strength he held in check.

"I have nothing to say to you. Now, if you don't mind, I was on my way to the kitchen."

"But I do mind, Mistress Carr. You see, your humble servant is confused over his duties."

"I told you before that I didn't appreciate your sarcasm, Mr. Leyton. Let me go," she demanded.

"Not until I prove something to myself," he stated with finality as his mouth descended on hers like a hawk on a sparrow. He pulled her shocked body close and wrapped his arms around her. His lips ground into hers with bruising force as his tongue invaded and withdrew in what Wynne now understood was an imitation of a more intimate joining.

She tried to resist his kiss, but felt betrayed by her body. Her mouth opened and welcomed him, her hands rested on his chest, grabbing his shirt as a moan escaped her lips. He broke away, breathing hard, as Wynne shuddered in response. He held her at arm's length and looked deeply into her startled eyes.

"What did you prove?"

Drew continued to stare into her eyes, as though he searched for the answer.

"Well, what did you prove?" She balled her hand and

beat ineffectually against his chest. "What are you trying to do to me?"

He grabbed her fist and held her easily. "Don't!" Then, more gently, he added, "I never tried to hurt you, Wynne."

"Well, you did! With your demands and attitude that you were always right. You think you can move into my house and take over everything I've worked for, everything I've built, just because my marriage . . . But then, I must have seemed like a very vulnerable target to you."

"No, you didn't. You aren't a target at all."

"Don't try to tell me again how much you care."

"Very well then, I won't," he answered coldly. He paused for a moment, then turned away and walked into the swirling mist.

The mist cleared and rolled away to the river; the strong sunshine burned away the last of the fog from the lowlands and caused the rich scents of spring to rise from the meadows. Drew was standing by the study window, looking absently at the blooming garden, when the dusty, travel-worn wagon pulled up to the kitchen.

On the wagon seat was a haggard woman holding a bundle that could only be a swaddling babe, and a young boy driving a pair of large, rawboned mules. The boy wiped his forearm across his eyes and wearily put on the brake as he pulled the team to a halt. The woman barely glanced at her surroundings.

Drew hurried down the hall and out of the back doorway to see what these people needed. They were standing beside the wagon when he reached them.

"Hello there," he greeted them. The boy drew himself up in height, pushing out his thin chest and hitching up his rough britches. "Name's Williams—Peter Williams."

Drew stopped a few feet away and studied the boy. He was obviously the man of the family and took his responsibility seriously.

"Glad to meet you, Peter Williams. I'm Andrew Leyton. Welcome to Waverley."

"We're on our way to Williamsburg, Mr. Leyton. Do you have some work I could do in exchange for lodging and food for my mother and sister?" His request was asked with such inherent pride that Drew momentarily forgot his position on the plantation.

"I'm sure we can work something out, Peter," he began. Out of the corner of his eye he saw a flash of lavender against the green shrubbery.

Peter stared in open-mouthed wonder at Wynne as she approached. He quickly smoothed his long, unruly hair back from his forehead and closed his gaping mouth. Drew couldn't suppress a smile.

Wynne stopped before the boy and gave Drew a hard look. The uncomfortable silence was broken when Peter respectfully introduced himself.

"I'm Peter Williams, Mrs. Leyton. This is my mother, Sarah, and my baby sister, Bess."

Wynne's normally pale complexion was bright pink as she turned accusing eyes to Drew. "What did you tell Master Williams, Mr. Leyton, to have him assume your status here at Waverley?"

"Why, nothing," Drew replied innocently. "The boy's obviously bright. He came to his own conclusions."

Wynne continued to drill holes through Drew with her icy green eyes. Again, Peter broke the silence.

"Mrs. Leyton? Excuse me, ma'am, but my mother is powerfully tired from the trip. Could you spare a cool drink for her?"

Wynne turned to the boy as if seeing him for the first time. Her detached politeness returned. A smile formed that did not reach her eyes.

"Of course." She and Drew both glanced to the kitchen doorstep. Annie watched and listened from beside the kitchen. Wynne motioned to her. "Please prepare some lunch for our guests, Annie."

Wynne stepped forward, still smiling at the boy. "However, Peter, you have been misled on one point. My name is not Mrs. Leyton. I am Mistress Carr. This is *my* plantation, Waverley, and I'm glad to meet you."

"Carr? Then who is . . . yes, ma'am. Thank you," Peter stammered and blushed.

Drew watched the exchange and tried not to smile. His gaze moved back to the poor woman leaning against the wagon, clutching her bundle protectively. She had probably not even been listening to the conversation. She looked almost dead on her feet.

Apparently Wynne was concerned about her as well, because she walked forward and opened her arms. "Can I help you?"

Sarah Williams turned her tired hazel eyes on Wynne. Sarah was thin to the point of emaciation. Her grey-streaked hair was pulled beneath a cap, and her clothes could have originally been any color from brown to grey. They were now faded and dusty, travel-stained and worn from previous washings. A wet stain showed where the baby had been held on her lap.

Sarah closed her eyes and sagged against the wagon just as Wynne reached for the baby. Drew rushed forward to catch her before she fell. He looked into Wynne's eyes and saw, for the first time in days, an emotion other than fear or anger.

There were strange sounds coming from the guest bedroom. Drew and Smythe exchanged dubious glances as they moved to the doorway. Drew pushed the door open and looked at the scene within, Smythe right against his shoulder.

Wynne was leaning across the high bed, fussing over the infant. She made cooing sounds and hummed snatches of songs, obviously not yet aware of the two men in the doorway.

"Poor wee babe," she crooned. "Your nappy is all messy!"

Drew turned quickly to Smythe, raising his eyebrows. He mouthed the words "Your nappy is messy?" as Smythe shook his head.

Drew cleared his throat.

Before Wynne could school her expression, she turned to the sound. The expression on her face was one of joy. Her eyes were alight, her features animated, her smile genuine. "The baby was wet," she proclaimed.

There was silence for a moment, then Smythe replied with his usual demeanor, "Indeed, madam?" Drew continued to look at the domestic scene. Wynne turned her attention to the infant, tenderly cleaning her and applying cornstarch to her slightly irritated bottom. She expertly folded a clean "nappy" and covered the infant.

She continued her nonsensical cooing and crooning. Drew watched her as the bright light of morning streamed through the gauzy curtains. Could she already be carrying his child? The thought caused a curious ache in his chest.

Smythe silently turned and walked away.

Drew moved into the room and stood behind Wynne as she placed a clean gown over the infant's small body. "She's awfully small, isn't she?"

Wynne turned to look at him over her shoulder. "She is small. I believe her mother can't feed her properly. I'm hoping she will stay with us for a while so I can get one of the women to nurse little Bess."

"I guess they're all small at first," he replied. He tried not to think of Wynne birthing a child—his child—but the image was strong. Would she tenderly hold his child, care for it, nurse it at her breast?

Wynne picked up the now clean and dry baby and held her. Bess's thin blond curls glistened as Wynne snuggled the baby close. He could almost imagine this was their child. Would the baby be a boy or a girl, have blond hair or brown? Green eyes or blue?

"You look very . . . maternal," Drew observed.

"I do? Well, I guess it must be the baby," Wynne replied, smiling at him.

"Must be." Drew reached out and stroked the fine baby hair. His eyes met hers and the yearning for what could have been was so strong that the need overrode all caution.

"Wynne . . . ," Drew murmured. "Love, I'm sorry for the way I acted this morning. I had no right—"

Wynne captured the hand that was absently stroking Bess's curls. "I'm sorry too, sorry I snapped at you, sorry things can't be the way you want them to be. But maybe we could have something together." She looked into his eyes. Drew saw an abundance of hope reflected there.

"Something? Yes, we could at least have something. It might not be everything; it might not be forever; but it would at least be something," Drew replied softly.

"Oh, Drew. I never meant to hurt you either," Wynne cried.

"Shh, love. Things will work out." I'll make them work out, he vowed to himself. Drew moved his hand to Wynne's cheek and felt the heat radiating from within. Her eyes were misty as he traced a finger over her fragile lower lid, to the corner of her eye and into her hair.

"Will you come to me tonight?" she asked softly.

Drew hesitated only for a moment. "I'll come."

Sarah Williams slept most of the day. Toward evening she awoke and cried out for Bess. Faye immediately jumped up from her bedside watch and tried to soothe the woman.

"Please, Missus Williams. Your baby is just fine. The mistress has taken real good care of her while you were resting."

"My son?"

"He's been resting too, although I think he went to the stables not too long ago to check on your mules," Faye assured Sarah.

The older woman slumped back against the pillows, exhaustion still written on her face. "I'm thankful for all your help."

"We were glad to help, Missus Williams. Would you like to speak with Mistress Carr now?"

"That would be real nice."

"My name's Faye. Call me if you need anything else. I'll go get the mistress now." Faye hurried out the door and down the hall.

A few minutes later Wynne appeared in the chamber where Sarah was resting. She pulled up a chair next to the bed and smiled at the older woman. "Bess is fine, Missus

Williams. I've been seeing to her comfort. She has been bathed and fed."

"How did you feed her, mistress? Cow's milk never did agree with the child."

"One of my women has a child about Bess's age. She has plenty of milk for both children," Wynne explained.

"Is this woman white? I don't want any black woman's milk in my child," Sarah declared.

Wynne, momentarily speechless at Sarah's outburst, sought to assure the other woman. "Bess is taking the milk just fine, Sarah. You mustn't upset yourself."

"Is the woman white?"

"Well, no, she's not. But she is a good, upstanding person. She's very healthy and will take care of Bess's needs until you're feeling better," Wynne calmly assured her.

Sarah shook her head. "No, I can't have a black woman feeding my child. You just have her brought here for her feedings," she firmly insisted.

"But, Sarah," Wynne tried to reason, "you're in no condition to nurse a child. You need to rest and recover your strength. Bess needs—"

"Bess needs her *mother,* Mistress Carr. And how do you think I'll feed the child when we leave here? I can't let my milk, weak though it is, dry up."

"I'll help you, Sarah."

"Can you give me more milk, or make it come back after it dries up? No, I don't think so. I do thank you for your kindness, but I'm a God-fearing woman who takes care of her family. I'll not have Bess suckled by a heathen black woman."

Wynne clamped her mouth shut. It would obviously do no good to explain that the woman was a Christian who had one of the most kind dispositions Wynne had ever seen.

"I'll have Bess sent to you when she awakens from her nap. Will that be suitable?"

"Thank you kindly, ma'am. Our ways might be different, but they've served us well these past ten years in the heathen wilderness. Lord knows, we all could have been murdered by the savages."

"Where did you come from, Sarah? Where were you living before you decided to travel to Williamsburg?" Wynne asked.

"We had a homestead near Staunton, just off the Wilderness Road. My late husband, Thomas, and I settled there with young Peter after we traveled from Scotland with James Patton in Forty-nine." Sarah paused as if collecting her thoughts.

"You don't sound Scottish, Sarah."

"Thomas's mother's family was Scottish. That's how our passage was arranged. Anyway"—Sarah paused to push herself up in the bed, leaning back against the pillows—"anyway, the savages started murdering along the frontier a few years after we settled there. James Patton himself was killed in Fifty-five at Draper's Meadows. My own Thomas wanted to join up with the Virginia militia then, but I talked him out of it. The children were younger—we had another boy and girl between Peter and Bess—and we needed him at the homestead."

"It must have been very difficult for you," Wynne observed as Sarah paused in her speech.

"Difficult? It was a nightmare. I never knew when those savages would sneak up and kill us in our sleep. Thomas finally went with Andrew Lewis's company in Fifty-six against the Shawnee. The good Lord looked out for him though, and he returned safe to us."

Sarah paused again, glancing at the ceiling and clasping her thin, worn hands. "He went back with another company before the first frost last year. Never came back." Sarah shook her head. "I miss that man. He was good, for all his warring ways."

"I'm sorry, Sarah. It must have been very hard on you and Peter. He's a good boy."

"Ah, he is that. That's why I'm taking him back to my relatives in Williamsburg. I don't want him going to war against the savages and the thieving French as soon as he can hold a musket."

"No, I don't blame you there," Wynne replied.

"Do you have any children, Mistress Carr?"

"No, I don't." She immediately thought of Drew and the coming night.

"Well, I've lost two little ones to fevers. I've lost my man to the savages. I just want to live in peace and raise the two the Lord chose to let me keep."

"The Indians are certainly difficult to control. Surely the French are far north of the frontier?"

"Well, I don't know where they are, but I'll tell you this. Someone or something keeps things stirred up out there. The savages have weapons—axes and knives and muskets—and they must be getting them from the French. Who else would give things to the savages that could kill loyal, faithful Englishmen?"

Who indeed? Barton McClintock. And that made her, Wynne, just as guilty.

Wynne stood up suddenly. "I must be tiring you, Sarah. You must rest and regain your strength. I'll be back later to check on you." She almost rushed out the door.

* * *

Later that evening, after the household had been fed independently, after Sarah Williams had pitifully nursed the small Bess, Wynne paced the floor of her bedroom and waited for Drew to appear. She wasn't sure of her emotional state. Was she upset due to anticipation of his visit, or had Sarah's story made her think of things she didn't want to face?

The room was dark and silent. Only the bedside candle burned to illuminate the room. A damp breeze, warm in the near-summer temperatures, drifted through the open windows. Wynne continued to pace the beautiful, thick carpet in the sitting area of her room.

"You'll wear out the rug that way," a soft voice admonished.

Wynne turned, billowing the white cotton gown out like a bell. An uncertain smile lit her face, then faded. "I wasn't sure you'd come."

Drew moved into the room after locking the doors. "It took a while to get young Master Williams settled. It seems he took a nap this afternoon and was reluctant to leave my company this night." Drew chuckled. "That boy wants to hear every story and learn every detail that a person will share."

"It's nice of you to take some time for the boy." Wynne moved closer to Drew. "His father died last fall and I believe he's lonesome for male company."

Drew moved to stand before her, reaching out to stroke her bare arms. "I enjoyed talking to him. Do you think a bondsman is suitable company for the lad?" .

Wynne lowered her head and tried to turn away. Drew slightly increased his hold. "I'm . . . sorry about what I said earlier. I was . . . distraught."

Drew leaned closer and whispered into her ear. "Did it upset you to think of us as a married couple? I think of it often, far more often than I should."

"Don't. Please don't think of it. I already told you it cannot be," Wynne murmured. She leaned into his solid chest and closed her eyes. "Just hold me . . . please."

Drew's arms closed around her and he pulled her against him. Gently, he guided her to the bed.

13

"Remember, call me when she goes to sleep," Wynne whispered to Faye outside the guest bedroom where Sarah Williams would soon be napping after lunch.

"Of course, ma'am. As soon as she's good and asleep."

"Good. I'll be in my study." Wynne turned and glided down the spacious hall to the front stairs.

Upstairs, Faye opened the door quietly and stepped into the guest room. Sarah was finishing her luncheon of broiled chicken and spring vegetables, fluffy rolls and jam cake. Smiling at the older woman, Faye seated herself by the bed and waited for Sarah to finish.

"The food here is the best I've tasted," Sarah commented, wiping her mouth.

"Everyone says so, ma'am. Our cook is a real jewel, she is."

Sarah pushed back the lap tray and the maid rose to gather the dishes. "Are you ready for a nap, Mrs. Williams?"

"In a moment, girl. Could you bring my Bess to me? I've a mind to see the babe."

"I'll fetch her, ma'am." Faye walked quickly out the

door to the guest room next door. Although there was a fully furnished nursery, Wynne had not allowed the baby to be moved in there.

Faye picked up the sleeping baby and took her to her mother's room. Sarah's face glowed as she looked on her daughter, making her look younger than her greying hair and weathered skin usually indicated. Faye placed the child in her mother's arms and left with the dirty dishes.

Fifteen minutes later Faye returned and removed the sleeping child from her slumbering mother's arms. Sarah slept soundly, snoring lightly. Faye carefully carried the baby downstairs to the study.

Wynne bent over the ledgers, scanning the entries Drew had made. His bold but neat penmanship matched his personality but seemed out of place with the image of a bondsman. He knew too many things, did too many things well, to be a merchant, as he had once intimated. His manners were impeccable, his speech cultured. Even his movements exuded a natural command in almost any situation. She wondered again if he was some lord's bastard. Somehow, she needed to find out more about his background. Dropping her quill, Wynne dreamily recalled the last two nights when Drew had come to her bed. Her cheeks burned, but the heat was no more intense than the fever he had caused in her blood. He could ignite the flame of desire with a glance, fan it to an inferno with his tender caresses, and send it spiraling out of control when he brought her to a shattering climax.

He made her respond, made her hold nothing back. He broke down every barrier she tried to erect between them. When she would withdraw, he would advance with patience and skill.

A slight knock at the partially opened door brought Wynne out of her contemplation of the enigmatic bondsman. Faye entered with Bess, whispering again to keep from awakening the child. "Her mum's asleep, ma'am. I thought I would bring her to you since I didn't want to wake the poor little thing."

"That's fine, Faye," Wynne murmured, taking the sleeping baby in her arms. She smiled into the sweet face. How long would it be before she could hold her own child?

"I'll take her to Mary now. You can visit with Cook for lunch until I get back." Wynne rose and walked slowly out the door, her actions totally centered on the baby.

Outside the temperature was warming in early June. The fruit trees had almost finished blooming, but there were many other bushes, plants, and flowers that kept the landscape a riot of color. So absorbed was Wynne in gazing at the baby that she barely observed her surroundings.

Drew felt more frustrated than he believed possible. After making love to Wynne, lying next to her in sleep and watching the rise and fall of her breast, holding her in her dreams and waking her to his kisses, he was no closer to finding an answer than he was a month ago. That he loved her was a given fact; that he wanted to spend the rest of his life with a woman who thought him far below her in status was a dilemma he could not solve. He was beginning to doubt that Samuel Carr even existed, yet Wynne wouldn't talk about getting an annulment.

What must he do to win her love? He'd declared himself, but as a pauperish bondsman. Should he admit he was a baron, his father an earl, to prove himself worthy? Should he tell her of his riches, in land and investments? Even if she did believe that he had wealth and position, would that cause her to love him in return? And, finally, did he want her love, knowing that she only gave it to a man she could consider a suitable husband?

Drew almost laughed. If only the ladies of King

George's court could see him now, mooning over a colonial woman who considered him just above her cattle in value. Andrew Philip Leyton of Morley Hall, one of the most eligible bachelors of the realm, had been reduced to the most desperate kind of bondage—a bondage of love.

Pushing away from the arbor, Drew followed Wynne as she skirted the garden and continued to the servants' quarters. Even here the evidence of her orderly, neat lifestyle was apparent. For the free families there were small cottages with gardens; for the indentured servants there were barracks and cottages; for the slaves there were rows of small houses where older women watched the many young children playing in the sun.

Wynne entered a small house in the row of slave buildings. The exteriors were whitewashed and in front of this house flowers bordered by painted stones gave an inviting appearance. Drew followed slowly, careful to keep out of sight. He stopped around the corner from the open door and listened, curiosity overcoming caution.

"I brought little Bess, Mary. She's been sound asleep for some time now."

"You sure do like that baby, Missus Carr."

"She's such a good baby, Mary. She hardly ever cries or complains, even though her mother can't give her enough milk."

"I'm glad to help out."

The women were silent for a few minutes while Drew waited impatiently for more conversation. He scanned the yard; no one was about in midday to see him standing outside Mary's house.

"I'm going to meet Samuel in Norfolk soon. His ship will be docking there, but then he must leave again for the Caribbean almost immediately."

"Well, it's a real shame that he won't be coming to the plantation. It sure is pretty this time of year, with all the tobacco planted and the trees so nice and green."

"Yes, I'm sure Samuel will miss seeing Waverley."

So, she was spreading the news that her husband would be home. That she would be with him. What had he expected? Drew asked himself. If she was with child, she would need to ensure that everyone, from the neighbors to the servants, believed it to be Samuel's. Damn it, but the child would *not* be Samuel's! It was his.

"You're goin' to miss this little one when she leaves with her mama."

"Oh, I know I will. I haven't been around children that much, but I've so enjoyed having Bess in the house. How I hope that I can have one of my own soon."

Drew heard the wistful quality in Wynne's voice and winced. He'd known all along what she wanted, but it sounded strange to hear her speak to someone else about it.

"Well, perhaps the Lord will bless you soon."

"Yes, perhaps He will," Wynne replied so quietly that Drew had to strain to hear the words.

"She's full now, Missus Carr." Drew heard the chair squeak and knew Wynne would be coming out soon. He walked quickly away from the small house, cutting across the wide yard to the edge of the garden, where he leaned against an ancient oak.

Leaving the cottage, Wynne stopped immediately when she saw Drew propped up against a tree as though he had nothing better to do. She suppressed the breathless smile that was forming.

"Mr. Leyton," she said, striving for nonchalance.

"Mistress Carr," Drew replied. "Out for a stroll?" He joined her as she walked toward the house.

"You know perfectly well that I'm bringing this poor baby to Mary for her feedings."

"Yes, and if her mother finds out, there'll be hell to pay."

"Mr. Leyton!"

"Sorry. Didn't mean to offend your sensibilities," Drew apologized insincerely, a twinkle in his blue eyes.

"I don't intend for the woman to find out. She can't possibly feed the baby herself, in her condition."

Drew looked her over appraisingly. "You look to be in pretty good shape."

Wynne's eyes flew to his face. He knew perfectly well what kind of shape she was in.

"Do you plan to feed your own baby?"

Wynne sputtered, "That's none of your concern!"

Drew leaned close and pulled her behind the rose arbor. "Oh, but I think it is. The vision of you nursing our child, your beautiful breasts swollen with milk, makes me anxious to be a father."

Wynne's heartbeat raced; her face flushed and she felt damp in the midday heat. Surely even the baby could feel the thudding of her heart against the thin muslin of her dress. Her lips parted to voice a protest.

Drew took advantage of her silent outrage. His kiss was light and seductive, yet full of yearning. His hands caressed her arms, then moved to cup a breast and tease the nipple. "You will be even more beautiful then." He leaned down to place his warm mouth over the peak of her breast.

Wynne's knees buckled and she would have dropped to the ground if Drew hadn't caught her. He took the child from her limp arms and smiled into her eyes, his own dark with passion.

"Come with me, love," he murmured into her neck as they slid lower, kneeling on the lush grass.

"Where?"

"To . . . damn it! This baby is wet!"

Wynne's eyes cleared and she laughed, sitting back on the grass and clasping her middle. At Drew's dark expression she only laughed harder.

"It's not funny, woman," he growled.

Wynne rolled to her side, tears pooling in her eyes. Drew apparently finally saw the humor of the situation and joined her on the grass. He smiled as her laughter subsided. "I suppose it's difficult to be romantic with a wet baby between us."

Wynne wiped away the tears of laughter. "Yes, I would say it's almost impossible. I wonder how couples ever manage to have more than one child?"

"Babies sleep a lot," Drew replied, reaching for her hand. He gazed deeply into her eyes. "Let's get inside. We both smell like wet baby and, in this heat, I think a change of clothes is definitely in order."

Wynne grasped his hand and used the leverage to pull herself up. She reached out her arms for Bess. "Are you sure you want to carry this bundle?" he asked, looking askance at the smiling child.

"Absolutely. I love having her here. I hope Sarah and Peter stay for a while."

"You know that they'll leave soon, sweetheart. They can't stay forever."

"I know," Wynne replied softly. "I just want them to stay a little while." And she did, she told herself. Even more than having another woman's company, having Bess here had firmed her decision to have a baby of her own. Or two, she thought, looking at Drew. Two babies with dark, waving hair and sapphire blue eyes. At the rate they were currently going, it shouldn't be long before she could hold her own child.

"Let's get inside. I think I'm developing a rash," Drew teased, and Wynne laughed as they continued to the house.

Wynne swatted at her nose, reluctant to open her eyes to the new day. The irritation persisted, rousing her from a deep sleep and causing her to toss upon the pillow. She moaned deeply and waved away the bothersome tickling.

Strong male laughter finally awakened her. Slowly, reluctantly opening her eyes, she saw Drew lying on his stomach, angled across the bed, elbows propped on the mattress. Carefully he waved a long white feather beneath her nose, circling around to touch and touch again.

"You're a lazy wench to lie abed all this glorious day," he taunted.

Wynne closed her eyes and tried to push him away. "Leave me alone. I've had a miserable night."

"And was that my fault? You yawned me away after dessert." Drew attempted a hurt expression. "I spent an entirely lonely evening with only my own company. As I have the last several nights."

"Go away, you buffoon. I have no need of your humor this morning." Wynne opened one eye and gazed at the window. "How early is it, anyway?"

"It's time for a morning ride, that's what time it is," Drew returned, apparently unaffected by her ill spirit.

She inhaled deeply and stretched. The morning *was* glorious—sunny and sweet-smelling, with the promise of wonderful things. And she smelled him too, clean with soap and the scent of sunshine on his laundered shirt.

Drew settled more closely to Wynne on the bed, placing his arms around her and resting his chin atop her head. "There are two horses waiting for us at the stable. There's a picnic basket with ham and sausages, boiled eggs and fresh scones. I personally packed blackberry jam and fresh butter. What more could you want?"

Wynne smiled at his good mood. What she really wanted was about four more hours of sleep, but how could she resist his plan?

"And where is my maid this fine morning? She's usually here by now."

"All taken care of." Wynne tilted her face up to see him and Drew further explained, "I simply told Millie that you'd come down to the study early, but decided to go back to bed since you didn't sleep well. You are not to be disturbed until noon."

"Noon! I've never slept until noon in my entire life."

"Well, that's too bad. This morning you won't get to sleep, either. I'm taking you on a ride and a picnic." Drew's expression changed and he looked lovingly at her. "You've been working too hard, taking care of the Williamses, the house, and the crops."

"There's so much to be done," Wynne murmured, snuggling against his warm body. He held her closely for long moments, until her eyes grew heavy again and she was just about to succumb to sleep. She'd never wakened with him beside her in bed, in the sunlight. When he stayed with her at night, he was always up before the dawn to slip back to his own room. Then she would roll over and hug his pillow close, inhaling his scent, sometimes falling asleep with dreams of their loving the night before. Or sometimes he would waken her in the dark to kisses and caresses, joining their bodies even before she was fully awake, bringing them to sweet passion and staying with her, inside her, until she drifted off to sleep again. But never had he been in her bed in the morning as the sun shone brightly through the windows.

"Wake up," he whispered in her ear. Drew placed light nipping kisses on her neck, nuzzling aside her white cotton gown to reach the sensitive area of her shoulder. "Wake up," he whispered again as she stirred restlessly on the mattress.

Wynne moaned again, although not in sleep or annoyance this time. She shifted and came into contact with his arousal, pressing insistently against her hip. She had missed feeling his passion these last five days as she suffered her monthly woman's curse.

Drew stirred, growling, "Get out of this bed now, wench, or I'll not be responsible for my actions. Noon could come and go without our notice."

Wynne rolled away abruptly and smiled lazily. "Where are we going for our picnic?"

Drew waited several moments before replying, his gaze obviously focused on her thigh, revealed by the twisted nightgown. "You have beautiful legs."

Wynne moved to cover herself but he caught her hands. "Don't be shy with me." He paused as though carefully choosing his next words. "You are not with child?"

Wynne's smile faded and she shook her head. She'd searched her soul and found that the knowledge was not devastating. For all her wishing and planning, she had discovered something that she wanted almost as much as a child: Andrew Leyton.

"No matter. We'll not speak of it again if it bothers you," he commented.

"Yes . . . that would be best."

"Then let's go on a picnic and forget work and worries for a day."

"You certainly have a way about you, Mr. Leyton. I swear that you could talk the birds from the trees," Wynne returned saucily.

Today, she thought, I'll get him to tell me about his life in England. I'll find out who he really is.

Two hours later, replete with good food and companionship, Drew and Wynne lay beneath towering pines, massive oaks, and delicate dogwoods, watching the bright green leaves of summer flutter in the breeze, making shadows move lazily across the thick quilt. They lay apart, their fingers entwined.

Wynne glanced at Drew; his face was relaxed with a slight smile, his dark brown hair waved loosely, and his lean body appeared content. Now is the time, she thought. He'll surely tell me about his background if I ask him. "Drew?"

He turned his head to smile at her, love shining in his eyes. "What, sweetheart?"

"Tell me about yourself . . . please?"

Drew turned away, seemingly intent on the canopy of leaves.

"Please?"

His silence stretched on, driving Wynne to distraction. "Drew?"

"What do you want to know?"

Wynne rolled over to look at him better. There were frown lines between his brow and he was no longer smiling.

"I just want to know who you really are. I want to know what you did before you . . . came here. I want to know about your family and . . ."

He was silent so long Wynne thought he wouldn't answer. Finally, he took her hand in his and replied, "I was born in Sussex, near Horsham. I spent a lot of time in London."

"Did you attend school in London?"

"No . . . not in London."

"All right. Tell me about why you were convicted of being a highwayman. You said you were innocent."

Drew gave her a hard look. "I was traveling around the countryside, near Tunbridge Wells. I stopped for the night at an inn. I was alone."

"All alone?"

"Well, not exactly. That's how I got into trouble." Drew paused and turned to his side, bracing his head on his hand. "There was a comely barmaid at the inn, a very friendly girl."

Jealousy flared in Wynne and she knew she disguised it very little.

"She was also the lover of the highwayman that worked the area." He went on. "He robbed a coach that very night and hid the gold and jewelry at the inn. Fool that I was, and a drunken one at that, I went to her room and passed out in her bed."

"Passed out in her bed? I've never known you to drink to excess!"

Drew laughed at her expression. "Yes, I passed out. When I came to, there was a musket pointed at my head."

"But the girl . . . didn't she tell them who you were?"

"Why should she? Her lover was free and I was arrested. She told the magistrate that I robbed for the fun and excitement. She realized that I didn't need the money."

"Didn't need the money? But how—"

"So I was convicted based on her testimony, before I could prove my innocence."

"And then you were transported?"

"Actually, I was being held while I appealed. I had been moved to the Tower—"

"The Tower? But only high ranking prisoners are held there."

"A prisoner is a prisoner, no matter where he's held.

Anyway, before the appeal could be processed I was taken out through Traitor's Gate in the dark of night and put aboard a ship bound for Virginia."

"But why would anyone . . . ?"

"Wynne, my love, you have more questions than the magistrate at my hearing." Drew paused and reached out his hand. "I can't tell you more about why."

"Can't or won't?"

"All right, then, I won't," he replied. "Can't you be content with that?"

"But who are you, really? You have money . . . you didn't need to rob people. You have enemies who had you sent to Virginia. Who are you?"

"Andrew Philip Leyton. Your bondsman."

The silence stretched on, creating tension in the summer air. "You're not going to tell me, are you?" Wynne asked.

"No, I'm not. What does it matter? I am what I am now. What I did, who I was in England, matters little. You purchased my contract. You have my love. What more do you need to know?"

Wynne had no answer. Truly, what difference did it make? Whether he was a commoner or a bastard son of the nobility, he was still the man she had chosen to father her children. He was the man who made her laugh and soothed her when she was upset. And she realized, with certainty and a sense of forever, that she loved him.

She rolled away, turning her back on him so he wouldn't see the moisture that had welled in her eyes.

"Wynne? Don't be angry, love." He pressed his body against her rigid back. His hand caressed her from shoulder to wrist, then moved to her waist. He swept over her rounded hip and upper thigh before pausing, bringing his hand back to her shoulder.

"I'm not angry," she whispered. "It hurts that you won't

confide in me, although I suppose you have your reasons."

"Yes, I do," Drew whispered, nuzzling her neck.

Wynne smiled and took his hand, wrapping it more securely around her body and settling back against him, no longer wishing to discuss his past or their situation.

She slept, relaxed in his embrace as the noonday heat increased.

Wynne stirred first. Oh, what she would give for a cool bath right now, she thought. Then she remembered they were close to the shallow stream that separated this far meadow from timberland that would be thinned sometime in the future.

Rising slowly and carefully so Drew wouldn't waken, Wynne walked a short distance to the slowly moving stream. The water was no more than two feet deep and moved lazily across stones that were well worn from an eternity of submersion. The sunlight danced across the brown, gold, and tan of the streambed.

Wynne unbuttoned her bodice and skirt, draping them across a bush to dry in the slight breeze. Her petticoats felt hot and heavy in the summer heat. She removed them and flung them over another bush. Standing in her thin shift, she entered the cool water.

It was heavenly. The current was as light as Drew's caress and as relaxing as his softly spoken words when their passion had been spent. After splashing in the refreshing water, she settled on a large, flat rock that was warm from the sun. Stretching back, Wynne dangled her legs and arms in the water and watched the branches overhead sway across the blue sky.

She was nearly asleep when she became aware of a presence. Startled, she opened her eyes and attempted to rise, but was pushed back to the rock by two firm hands. Drew stood over her, blocking the sun.

"My love," he murmured, "you would tempt a far more saintly man than I." And he proved his words by standing up only long enough to finish unbuttoning his white cotton shirt, flinging it to the bank, and then starting on his breeches.

It seemed an eternity since they'd made love, but in reality it had been only five days. One week without his loving had left her hungry in a way she had never dreamed possible.

Drew lowered his body slowly, bracing first his knees and then his hands on the smooth rock. He continued to watch her face as her body arched upward, longing to touch him. When he was suspended above her, their flesh barely touching, he moved lower still to tenderly kiss her parted lips.

Gentleness gave way to passion as Wynne urged him closer with twining arms and clutching hands. Her breath came in short, panting sighs as she moved against him.

"Easy, love," Drew entreated. He kissed her face, her lips, her neck. "Go slowly," he urged as his lips moved to her shoulder.

Drew removed the shift and slid his hand down her body, resting lightly where she ached. "Are you really ready for me?" he asked huskily, his breath searing her oversensitized skin.

"Yes . . . yes. Oh, please. Oh, Drew!" she cried as he entered her in a smooth lunge.

She surged against him, oblivious to the hard bed they shared. His hands moved to her back, raising her shoulders and rocking her tightly against his straining body.

Her breath came in fast gasps, her mind whirling. She choked out, "I love . . . you!"

Their bodies still joined, Drew turned so he was on the bottom. Wynne slowly rose, bracing her hands on the rock and gazing questioningly into his eyes. He smiled in reply and arched within her.

Wynne returned his smile, delighted by the change of tempo and position that allowed her more freedom. She moved her hands to his firm chest and positioned her knees more comfortably before beginning the movements that would bring him satisfaction.

Drew closed his eyes as he heard her words again inside his head. She loved him! He'd waited to hear her admission of love, half afraid she never would. He moaned as she moved on him, the intensity building until he thought he might die from so much pleasure. He was aware of everything, it seemed. The fresh air, dampened by the stream; the fragrance of summer grass and flowers; the call of the birds and the sound of the water. All this he knew, but love he felt for this woman overruled all others.

He opened his eyes to her beauty, watching the look of concentration on her face. A low groan built within him, forcing its way out through his clenched teeth as he erupted within her tight body.

"Good Lord, woman. Someday you will be the death of me," Drew murmured in a shaky voice.

He shifted his weight, belatedly realizing his backside, shoulders and knees were chafed raw by the rough rock. But even that didn't dim the ecstasy he felt. She loved him. The words kept coming back, kept giving him hope.

"Do you remember what you said, love?"

"What I . . . what do you mean?"

"You said you loved me."

Wynne turned her head away, but he held her fast. She tried to pull away, but he wasn't about to let her retreat. Not now. "Will you deny it now?"

"Don't . . . please."

"I must, sweetheart. I must know. Do you love me?"

"Please, Drew. Don't try to force me—"

"Force you? My God, I love you. I only want you to admit that you love me too, that what we have is special. How can we go on with all this unspoken between us?"

He felt Wynne's hand clench, then he heard her small sob and his hands stroked her back, combing through her wet, tangled hair.

"Don't cry, love."

She took a deep breath, then released it in a long sigh that rippled over his damp skin. "You're right," she whispered, so low he barely heard her.

"Tell me," he urged softly.

"I love you."

He gently turned her face toward him, seeing her eyes bright with unshed tears, shining with a glow that could only be love. He leaned upward, urging her lips toward his, and kissed her gently. "I love you, too. For now and always."

14

Wynne hummed to the wiggling Bess as they moved along the shell walkway from the stable to the house. The sun was descending in the west, warming her and brightening her spirits. She'd told Drew she loved him, fully expecting that disclosure to leave her depressed and vulnerable. Yet she didn't feel that way at all. Her heart soared, her spirit flew free for the first time in many years.

Wynne laughed aloud as she thought about visiting young Peter at the stable. Drew was attempting to halterbreak Roger's Folly, and the young man was taking much delight in watching the headstrong foal battle the equally stubborn bondsman.

How much she enjoyed having a child around! Bess was such a good baby and was gaining weight each day. It was obvious that Mary's milk agreed with the infant. Wynne hugged the gurgling baby as she neared the back entrance to the house.

Standing in the doorway was Sarah Williams, a frown on her face.

"Good day, Sarah. The weather is certainly lovely," Wynne greeted her.

"Lovely is as lovely does, Missus Carr," the woman returned coldly. "Where have you been with my baby?"

Taken aback, Wynne could only stammer, "Why . . . why, we've been down to the stable. Peter is working with—"

"You've been visiting that heathen woman, letting her nurse my Bess!" Sarah accused. "Against my wishes you've put my child to a savage's breast!"

"Mary is no savage, nor is she a heathen," Wynne returned defensively. "Bess needs the nourishment, Sarah. Surely you can see that. She's improved so much."

"All I know is that I told you not to take my child to that woman and you ignored my wishes." Sarah's voice rose in anger. "She's my child, not yours. Do you hear me? She's mine!"

Sarah made a grab at the baby and Wynne backed up in reflex. "Please, Sarah, calm down."

"Give me the child," the older woman demanded.

"I will. Just please don't be so upset."

"I've a right to be upset! Don't tell me to be calm when you've done me wrong!"

Wynne moved around the fountain, holding Bess firmly, patting her back and trying not to convey her own fear. "You may think I did wrong, Sarah, but I did what was best for the child."

"It wasn't your decision!" Sarah screamed.

Drew rounded the house at a run, followed closely by Peter. Wynne watched him from the corner of her eye as she kept her distance from Sarah. Help me, she silently pleaded to Drew. One quick glance confirmed that he knew what was going on. They were bound by feelings deeper than words could express.

"Mother!" Peter called. "Mother, please stop."

Peter ran to the woman, grasping her arm and attempting to stop her advance. "Leave be, Peter," she commanded. "This is not your business."

"Mother, please," the boy pleaded. "Mistress Carr only did what was best for Bess."

Sarah whirled on her son, anger flashing in her hazel eyes. "So you knew, too. You knew, and you didn't tell."

Peter let go and stepped back, his fear apparent. "No, Mother, it wasn't like that. Bess needed . . ."

"Go to your room, young man," Sarah ordered. "Go there and stay until I come for you."

Peter glanced at Drew, then Wynne, still holding the crying Bess, then back to his mother. Obviously undecided, he stood his ground.

"Go!"

"Peter, why don't you go inside," Drew stated calmly. "Your mother and sister will be fine."

Peter reluctantly left as Sarah glared at her two opponents. Wynne thought she saw not only fear, but genuine hate, in Sarah's eyes.

Wynne took a calming breath. "Sarah, let's go inside and talk about this."

Sarah stood her ground until Drew approached. She eyed him warily.

"Sarah? Please come inside. Wynne means no harm to your little girl."

Slowly, her eyes still showing uncertainty, Sarah turned and entered the house. Wynne followed when Drew approached. He took her elbow and gazed with compassion into her eyes.

"What will she do?" she whispered.

"I'm not sure, love. Let's go talk to her. Perhaps everything will be fine."

Yes, perhaps, Wynne thought. Maybe she could talk Sarah Williams out of doing anything rash, taking Bess away from the nourishment she needed. Perhaps, but she had serious doubts. She felt the weight of her actions descend like leaden rain on her heart, wondering how she had so fully lost control of her life.

Late that night Drew held Wynne in his arms as the breeze rippled over the curtains, bringing the scents of summer into the bedroom. The pale moonlight played across Wynne's sleeping form, making the white gown look ghostly in the darkness.

The confrontation with Sarah Williams had left her drained and downhearted. She hadn't even eaten dinner, retiring early instead. When he'd slipped into her room, she was lying awake in bed, looking lost and empty. He had settled beside her, still dressed in a loose shirt and breeches. They hadn't made love; she needed comfort, not passion.

If he could have changed anything about the situation, he would have done so gladly. But he was incapable of stopping her heartache over losing the Williams baby. Every time he looked into her haunted eyes, he prayed to God that he could make her smile again, but it was a futile prayer. Wynne had become too close to the child, too involved with the family to be objective. And now she suffered for her soft heart that yearned for a child to love.

Drew bent his head and kissed her hair, smoothing the strands away from her neck. He loved her so much—too much. He had never thought of love as being painful or ill-fated. When he'd imagined being in love, before coming to Virginia and meeting Wynne, he had conjured up images of the quiet respect and smiling companionship his parents shared, or the calm yet happy relationship between his sister and her husband. Never would he have believed that when he fell in love, it would be a desperate kind of madness that made him want to confront Samuel Carr, then carry Wynne away, far away, from society and conventional behavior.

She needed him. Like air and water and food, she needed his love. The only problem was, she was too stubborn to admit it, too involved in her plans to see that they could be happy together. Of course, he silently admitted, she did think of him as a bondsman. That would color her perception of the situation. But it shouldn't be a barrier to their love, to their future. God, but what a fine mess things had become.

He closed his eyes, reminding himself to awaken in a few hours to slip back to his room. Wynne would never forgive him if her maid found them together in her bed. And he would never forgive himself if he caused Wynne one moment of pain.

The next morning the Williamses left. A very subdued Peter drove the wagon to the front door, where a silent Sarah carried her daughter outside in the bright summer sun.

Wynne had insisted the wagon be packed with fresh food, clean linens, and comfortable pillows. Sarah reluctantly agreed, partly because, Wynne guessed, Sarah considered herself the wronged party and felt that this was little compensation for the hurt Wynne had inflicted upon her and Bess.

She had steadfastly refused the coins Wynne tried to give her. As they hitched the team, Drew gave them to Peter to have in case of an emergency. The boy had no qualms about accepting the currency.

As the morning sun climbed overhead, Wynne stood beside Drew and waved at the departing wagon, knowing that she would probably never see the sweet baby again. Tears threatened and she sniffed quietly. Drew moved closer and placed a comforting arm around her shoulders before she allowed tears to fall over her cheeks.

"Please don't cry, love," he said. "There was nothing else you could do."

"I did everything wrong," Wynne sniffed. "I should have listened to you. I should have been more careful."

"You did what you thought was best for the child." Drew hugged her tighter as they watched the wagon disappear down the dusty road. "I think you did the right thing. Bess could have died without Mary's help."

Wynne turned reddened eyes to the man who had helped her through so much. "Do you really think so?"

"Yes, I do."

"I'm so sorry to see them leave. I feel like I owe them so much."

"Owe them? How so?"

"They've been through so much, have suffered so much. The Indians killed Bess's father and drove them from their home."

"You didn't cause that. How can you blame yourself?"

"Because I . . ."

"What is it, love?"

"Nothing . . . nothing. I'm just upset." Wynne turned away abruptly so Drew wouldn't see the lie on her face. She had come dangerously close to telling him everything, and that would not do. As possessive as he felt about her, as commanding as he could be, he would never allow her to remain involved with Barton MacClintock. And, she suspected, he wouldn't compromise one small measure, even if it meant having Samuel's condition exposed. "Let's go inside," she suggested calmly. "I think I would like some sherry."

Wynne was very subdued all through dinner that evening. Drew's concern and attempts to cheer her were appreciated—he was dear to try so hard—but her feelings were numb. It was as if she had turned inward, away from love and joy and passion. She knew what she had to do. She must sever her relationship with Barton MacClintock. But she also needed to protect Samuel and Waverley. She must move him to another location, where he would be safe from prying eyes and MacClintock's accusations.

She'd felt this way once before, when their "friends" and neighbors had turned their backs on her and her father. When she'd been condemned and scorned by almost everyone for trying to save the virtue of one slave girl. The numbness was threatening, frightful in its ability to over-power her other senses, but she didn't have the strength to fight it right now. It was much easier to withdraw.

Wynne bade good night to Drew in the hallway after dinner, saying that she was retiring early. As soon as he was out of sight, she walked back to the butler's pantry looking for Smythe. He was just locking the silver safe when she entered the small room.

"Madam?"

"Please come to the study. I have something to discuss with you."

Wynne walked to the chairs in front of the desk and waved distractedly for Smythe to join her. "I must go to Williamsburg on business. I've already told several of the staff that I'm meeting Samuel soon."

"Of course, madam. What would you like me to do?"

"Have the carriage ready to leave at dawn. Tell everyone that I've gone to visit my husband in Norfolk, where his ship has docked. Tell them he must continue to the Caribbean, so I'll only be gone for a few days."

"What should I tell Mr. Leyton?" Smythe inquired calmly.

"Mr. Leyton? Just tell him I had to leave unexpectedly on business," Wynne returned, looking intently at her hands, folded in her lap. If she really was so numb, she thought objectively, why did her hands want to shake and her body to tremble when she thought of Drew's reaction?

"He will talk to the servants, madam. They will tell him you are visiting Mr. Carr," Smythe pointed out.

"Yes, yes, I know. Tell him that although the others think I am visiting my husband, only he knows the truth about my leaving on business. Warn him not to discuss this with them."

"Very well." Smythe paused, then continued. "If I may inquire, madam, where will you actually be? Just in case I must reach you."

"I'll stay at the Raleigh Tavern again if I can get a room, Mrs. Campbell's if I can't."

"Will you take Millie?"

"No." Wynne paused and stared blankly at the intricately embroidered firescreen. When had she stitched it? She couldn't remember. "Tell Millie I must travel fast to meet Samuel. Or tell her that I just want to be alone with him." She sighed, tired from all the lies. "Or just think of something to explain why I'm going alone."

"Madam, are you sure you are well enough to travel?"

Smythe's question brought her out of the lethargy that had taken over her senses. "Well? I'm perfectly fine. Just a bit tired."

"Perhaps it would be best to postpone this trip."

Wynne shook her head. "No, I must visit the office of William Cuninghame and Company. Do you remember Barton MacClintock?" At Smythe's nod, she continued, "I have some matters to discuss with him."

Wynne rose from the chair and paced the room, her grey skirts swirling against the tables and bookshelves that lined the walls of the study. "So you can see that we're not really telling Mr. Leyton an untruth. I do have some business to conduct."

"I might expect, given the circumstances, that Mr. Leyton would accompany you on business," Smythe replied casually.

"Not this business. This has nothing to do with him."

"He will be insistent, madam. I do believe he has more than a small amount of fondness for you."

A bubble of panic surged through her. Drew must *not* question her on this. "Promise me, Smythe, that you will tell him nothing. He must not know about Barton Mac-Clintock, or my husband, or anything else, for that matter."

"Of course I will not tell him. Please do not be concerned. I will handle the situation here."

Of course he would, Wynne realized. Smythe could manage almost anything. The only thing that disturbed her was that Andrew Leyton also seemed perfectly capable of not only handling any situation, but also making it to his advantage.

"I know you will, Smythe. I think I'm still upset over the departure of the Williamses." Wynne moved to the desk and lovingly traced her fingers over the inkwell stand and quills. How many hours had she and Drew spent at this desk, using this same inkwell, recording the figures of production and expenses with these feathered pens?

"I don't want to lie to him, Smythe, but I can't admit the truth. It's important that the staff think I visited my husband." Wynne blushed slightly. No one must question the paternity of her child. No one.

"And I must also visit Mr. MacClintock. There's no need to involve anyone else. So please do not tell Mr. Leyton any more than you must," Wynne entreated.

"Who will accompany you, madam?"

"See if Mary's husband is able to leave. With the tobacco doing so well, he should be available for a few days. If he can't go, then get Riley. Talk to him tonight, please." Wynne watched her own reflection in the darkened panes of the glass, thinking again about how very complicated her life had become. She sighed wearily. "Is there anything else we need to discuss?"

"No, madam, I believe that covers everything."

Although Wynne had been lethargic and apart from the world as she went through the motions of dinner and conversation, the thought of going to bed alone made her restless. She rose from bed and moved to the windows, looking out on an evening as calm as she was pensive.

She missed Drew's presence here, tonight, and every time they were apart. It was a terrible feeling, yet one over which she had little control. They hadn't made love since the day at the stream; just that one memory made her want him as she never would have dreamed possible. Her arms ached to hold him. Her lips yearned for his kisses. Her body burned for his possession. She longed to tell him again of her love.

With an audible sigh, she gave up the fight with her conscience and her body. On silent footsteps she moved to the doors, down the hall, and and through the ballroom to Drew's room.

His door was closed but not locked. Wynne turned the

knob slowly and pushed it open. She searched the bed for
his shape, but found only rumpled sheets and the quilt
folded neatly at the footboard. She barely breathed his
name in the silent room.

He stood by the window, his naked form tense in the
meager light of the bedside candle. Wynne watched the
glow reflect over the bones and muscles of his body, now
so well recovered from his transportation. She looked at
him appraisingly, eagerly, and without reservation. She had
never come to his room before.

He turned toward her slowly, like a pivoting statue
come to life. No words were necessary when Drew opened
his arms. Wynne ran to him, wrapping her arms around his
waist and up his back, clinging to him as an anchor. He
held her firmly.

"I love you," she whispered. His lips descended and she
closed her eyes. And then he was lifting her, walking to the
bed with sure, swift steps. He was a tender but silent lover,
building their passion slowly to a blinding intensity. When
it was finished, Wynne clung to him as though she would
never let him go, as though she would never leave him.
They slept entwined as the night birds sang and the crickets chirped in the garden below.

Sometime in the dark hours before dawn, Wynne wakened and left his bed, careful not to disturb Drew's sleep.
The candle had long since burned out. She smoothed the
tousled hair off his brow and straightened the tangled
sheets over his nakedness before silently slipping out the
door.

She dressed efficiently, packing a large valise with simple yet elegant traveling outfits. Tiptoeing downstairs and
running to the stable, she stopped to glance at the dark
upper window, regretting the deception she was forced to
follow. Would he understand? Probably not.

Smythe and John, Mary's husband, were waiting for her inside the stable. They left before the first rays of dawn lighted the sky.

Upstairs, Drew watched the carriage roll away with eyes that reflected all the hurt and sorrow he felt in his soul. He clenched his fist, tempted to put it through the glass panes of the window or the smooth plaster of his wall. But it would do no good—she was already gone. To meet her husband, as she'd told Mary? He didn't think so. But if not to Norfolk and Samuel Carr, where? And when would she return?

15

Wynne stopped for lunch at Chriswell's Ordinary, reserving a room for her return trip so she wasn't forced to sleep on a pallet in a room with other women. She still avoided strangers and those who might know of her scandal six years ago. Alone on Waverley, she could almost believe she'd never been socially ostracized. But out in public, seeing the speculation on the faces of others, she suddenly felt nineteen and scared again.

From Chriswell's to Williamsburg took four long, hot hours. John guided the carriage past the College of William and Mary, down the Duke of Gloucester Street, toward the Raleigh Tavern. Since Williamsburg was much closer to the water and surrounded by marshes on two sides, it was humid and the air was still. Wynne longed to bathe the dust and sweat from her body before eating a light supper and sinking into a soft bed.

She thought briefly of trying to locate the Williams family, but as they hadn't encountered the wagon on the road and she didn't know Sarah's relatives, it would be almost impossible to find them. And Sarah Williams would not welcome her visit, Wynne was sure.

The tailor was in residence, taking measurements in his room as Wynne hurried up the stairs. She wanted to avoid the stares of the men laughing and talking in the upper hallway. Wynne again had the upper chamber overlooking the street, a room that isolated her from the other travelers. She could close her door and know that although they might speculate on why a lady would venture out alone, they would not approach her.

She bathed as best she could from the basin. The cool water felt refreshing as it trickled over her skin. The drops rolled beneath her arms, down her breasts, and over her ribs. It reminded her of Drew, how he had held her in the chair and tickled her when she was so upset over their first intimate encounter.

Perhaps she should have sent him away before their intimacy progressed, before she fell in love with him and before he declared his love for her. It was now so complicated, not just dealing with their feelings but how it affected her future after Drew left. And he would leave eventually, when he realized that she would never marry him, even if she could. A man wouldn't want a woman who insisted on controlling her own property and destiny. He would resent her money and position in society, a heritage he didn't fully share. No matter how well educated and noble he was, the stigma of bonded service would follow him forever. She couldn't subject him or her children to that burden.

No, Drew must leave as soon as he could, as soon as she had the child she wanted, so that he could start his life over. He could find a good woman to bear him sons, to work the land. Wynne decided that she would give him as much silver and currency as she could, which would allow him to buy some land or gain a position at another plantation, perhaps further north. He would be gone, seeking his happiness elsewhere, and she would have memories to last a lifetime and children to bring comfort to her older years.

Wynne pulled a clean nightgown over her head, then jumped as a mockingbird called out next to her window. The sun had set, allowing the breeze to flow over the land like a herald signalling the night. She settled into the narrow bed, hugging her pillow and dreaming of Drew, trying not to cry herself to sleep.

It was still early when Wynne had breakfast in her room. She had sent a message to John to have the carriage brought around. Barton MacClintock must be confronted and there was no time better than the present.

Coming down the steps, she saw the proprietor, Anthony Hay, in the shadows of the stairwell.

"Mr. Hay, good morning."

"Mistress Carr," he nodded. "I trust you had a pleasant sleep."

"Yes, the room was fine, as always. I need to visit William Cuninghame and Company. Do you know where the offices are located?"

Hay nodded. "Down the Capitol Landing Road, very near the Public Warehouse. It is a small building with a single center chimney and a porch in front."

"Thank you, Mr. Hay. I'll return later and spend one more night with you."

Wynne went out the back door and took a deep breath, smelling the heady fragrance of yeast breads baking in the large brick kitchen and hickory fires being lit in the smokehouse. A few sheep bleated in a pasture nearby and a horse seemed to answer from several lots away.

John brought the carriage up from the rear just then,

hopping down to help her into the vehicle. She smiled at the black man who did so many jobs around the plantation. Before Drew came, John had been too busy with various tasks. Wynne realized that now, but before Drew's arrival she hadn't known that things could run so much more smoothly. Damn the man for making her rely on him so much, for making her love so many things about him.

The distance was short, less than a mile, Wynne guessed. John pointed out the office just as Wynne was reading the sign hanging out front. He slowed the horses, pulling alongside the building.

Now that she was here, her courage seemed to desert her. All she wanted to do was drive away without confronting the little weasel Barton MacClintock, go back to Waverley, and launch herself into Drew's protecting arms. But that was the cowardly thing to do and she would never be able to live with herself. She had to walk into this office and tell Barton MacClintock to stay off her property and stop his shipments to the Indians.

She stepped down from the carriage. Her feet seemed leaden as she took one step, then two, then more. Her footsteps sounded as hollow as she climbed the stairs toward the door. Dear God, she prayed, give me the courage to do this.

The door opened easily and prompted a bell to ring, making her jump at the unexpected noise. The pale, freckled clerk, a young man already stooped from his labors, greeted Wynne. "Can I help you, ma'am?"

"I'm here to see Mr. MacClintock. Is he available?"

"I'm sorry, ma'am. He's not in the office at this time. May I ask who is calling?"

"Mrs. Carr," Wynne replied distractedly. "Is he in town?"

"He is expected in a few days, Mrs. Carr. Would you

care to leave a card? I'm sure he'll contact you immediately upon his return."

"No . . . When did you say he would return?"

"I'm not sure, ma'am. Perhaps in three days."

Three days. She couldn't wait that long. "May I use some paper? I'd like to leave a message."

After writing a directive to meet her near the hunting lodge one week from today, Wynne folded the message carefully and placed it in the envelope the clerk provided.

"Would you seal this, please?" she asked the young man.

He complied and soon the message was resting in a pigeonhole that served to hold MacClintock's correspondence. So much for confrontation, Wynne thought.

When she stepped outside, the smell of strong spirits assailed her nose. Ahead a workman had dropped a barrel of rum. The heady aroma dispersed rapidly as the air warmed and the liquid seeped into the red brick walkway and ran in rivulets through the dusty road.

There were more people out now, from all parts of England and Scotland, from Africa and other colonies. With this much activity, it was little wonder that her husband could get conveniently "lost" in the confusion. Until Barton MacClintock, no one had even questioned her stories of Samuel Carr's whereabouts or business dealings.

"John," Wynne said, "we need to go by the *Virginia Gazette* office. I have a letter for Mr. Parks to post."

"Yes ma'am," John replied, tapping the horses lightly on their rumps.

The letter was evidence that Samuel Carr was alive and well, conducting business as he docked in Virginia before continuing on to the Caribbean. Just one additional lie in a life that was becoming more and more distorted by untruth.

She would spend one more night in Williamsburg and leave the next day for Chriswell's, where she would spend a night before returning to Waverley. If people were to believe she was visiting her long-absent husband, she couldn't return too quickly. Wynne sighed. Nothing had really been resolved, and she still had to face Drew when she went home.

"Where in the hell is she, Smythe?" Drew demanded.

"I assume you are referring to Mrs. Carr?"

"You're damn right I am. She's been gone two days! Anything might have happened."

"Would you care to continue this conversation in a more private setting?" Smythe coolly asked.

Drew gave the man a fierce look, turned on his heel, and stormed into the study.

Smythe followed and closed the door. "Mrs. Carr is fine. Of that I am sure."

"How can you be sure? She's not here. Lord knows where she is or what kind of trouble she might be in."

"Mr. Leyton," Smythe said coldly, "as difficult to believe as you may find this, Mrs. Carr has lived most of her life without you. I have done my best to look after her since her father's death and her marriage. She is a very sensible woman." He paused a moment, but Drew wasn't overly impressed with Smythe's statements. There was a mystery here, somehow related to the Williamses. Their departure had devastated Wynne, and she'd felt guilt over their circumstances.

"You really should attempt to develop some faith in others, Mr. Leyton."

"I have faith in some, Smythe. Most of them don't live in Virginia, however."

"Mr. Leyton, this may be none of my business." Drew raised his eyebrow and Smythe continued, "But I am going to give you some advice. Mrs. Carr is a very independent woman. We both know why you are here. Although I disagreed with her decision, I have reconciled myself to the situation. But this is only a temporary circumstance.

"When you are gone from Waverley—and I believe that will be sooner rather than later—she will remain. I will remain. If she has a child, it will remain here. In short, Mr. Leyton, you are a temporary resident at Waverley and a short-term fascination for Mrs. Carr."

"How dare you presume to know what transpires between us?" Drew growled. "How dare you . . ." He found he could not continue.

"How dare I? Tell me this. Has she ever indicated to you that this relationship will continue? Has she sworn eternal devotion? Well?"

"I know what she feels for me, and it's not a temporary fascination." Drew paused for a moment. "Nor is my feeling for her."

"Still, if you could leave here today, walk out the front door a free man, would you not do so?"

"If I were a free man, I would take her with me."

"She would not go," Smythe stated firmly.

Drew had no answer. Smythe had just given voice to Drew's own dark doubts. "I love her, man. Can you understand that?" Drew whispered. "I love her."

Smythe moved closer and hesitantly placed a hand on Drew's shoulder. "I understand. Many of us love her, but in a different way, I'm sure. Still, she will not leave Waverley. Not for you. Not for anyone."

"We'll see, Smythe. I'll not let her go easily," he said. "I fight for what is mine."

"Is she yours? I do not believe so."

"Nevertheless, if she's not back by noon tomorrow, I'm leaving to find her. Whatever she's doing can hurt her, of that I'm certain."

"A bondservant cannot travel freely. Surely you know that," Smythe tried to reason.

"Noon tomorrow—bondservant or no!" Drew turned and left the study.

Noon of the following day found Drew saddling a sleek chestnut gelding with a wide chest and long legs. Riley wouldn't help him, but neither did he attempt to stop Drew's determined quest.

Smythe hurried into the stable. Drew gave the butler a quick look before continuing to tighten the girth on the gelding.

"I'll not stay here, Smythe. I'm going to look for her."

"I realize that. I won't try to stop you. However, I have something you will need."

Drew tucked the end of the leather strap under the girth. He lowered the stirrup and leaned against the horse. "And what would that be?"

"Papers. You will need them if you are stopped on the road to Williamsburg," Smythe revealed.

"Williamsburg? Then she really did go there," Drew mused.

"Yes, but that is all I can tell you. Mrs. Carr does not confide everything, even to me."

Drew chuckled. "Not even to you? Then I suppose I'm in very illustrious company."

"Humph . . . well, she is an independent lady, as I have already stated."

Drew led the horse outside after accepting the papers from Smythe and tucking them inside his waistcoat. After testing the saddle one more time, he mounted and looked down at the butler.

"She's a bit too independent, even for my tastes," Drew confided. "The lady has a lot to learn."

Smythe nodded. "You might check with Chriswell's Ordinary, about three hours' ride from here. She may stop there for a meal or the night."

Drew nodded his thanks, then rode away, looking back only once to salute Smythe. The chestnut had a good even canter that would eat up the miles. Despite his mission and trepidations, it felt good to have a fine horse between his knees and feel the sun and wind on his face. It had been far, far too long since he'd journeyed without restrictions. The freedom he felt was an intoxicant in his blood.

After leaving Waverley, Drew slowed the gelding to a trot, automatically responding to the horse's gait as he let his mind wander. It was a long ride to Williamsburg, but he would arrive before dark now that the days were longer. He had taken a handful of shillings from the strongbox in the study. Little though it was, it would purchase a room and a few hot meals.

And Annie had insisted upon packing food for his trip. His saddlebags were stuffed with small meat pies, cheese, and the first green apples from the orchard. The horse would probably get those, he thought, and he patted the chestnut's neck. There was a bottle of wine and a larger one of ale.

The heat increased as the afternoon wore on. Drew slowed the sweating horse to a walk, and after a mile or so he came to a grove of trees along a flowing stream.

Damn, it's hot, he thought. He was as sweaty and dusty as the horse and probably smelled no better than a field hand. The flies became more persistent in the sticky heat, and Drew's temper grew noticeably short.

Slapping at a particularly vicious insect, Drew removed the ale and uncorked it, taking a long swallow. It was warm but pleasant—strong and malty. He took another long drink.

"Damn," he swore as the fly continued his assault. He looked at the chestnut, who seemed to regard him with little interest.

"Let's get back on the road, my fine fellow." Deciding against replacing the coat, he secured it over the saddlebags and gathered the horse's reins. Only then did he realize he'd forgotten to return the ale. He shrugged and mounted the gelding, holding the reins in one hand and the bottle in the other, bracing it against his thigh.

Drew left the shade of the streambed, where willow and pines afforded protection from the sun, and resumed his ride southeast to the capitol. How in the hell would he find one woman out of the hundreds who would be there? The sun beat down on his back and shoulders and he cursed again. He put his heels to the chestnut and soon they were kicking up dust. At least the flies had been left behind.

He soon came to Chriswell's, but saw no sign of Wynne's carriage or of John in the stableyard. He had the bottle of ale refilled, watered his horse, fed him one of the apples, and set out again. Perhaps Wynne was still on the road, trying to get back to Waverley before darkness. If she was going to travel at night, he intended to protect her. Hell, that was what men were supposed to do—keep their women safe and happy.

The journey continued. Drew alternately trotted and walked the gelding, but didn't stop to eat. He let the strong ale sustain him.

Toward late afternoon the ale bottle was empty. Drew's linen shirt was damp and clung to his chest and sides. He passed another inn but saw no sign of her there. The joyous feelings of freedom had been replaced by the bitter truth of his search. He might not find Wynne at all.

Would she think he'd run? Drew laughed, startling the horse. "It's all right, son," he explained to the gelding. "I'm just thinking about my mistress." He chuckled again at the jest. "Hell, she's your mistress too."

Drew patted the gelding's neck. "Mistress of Waverley," he shouted, and hurled the empty ale bottle through the air. It hit the trunk of a large pine, shattering instantly with a loud crash that made Drew admire his aim.

The tired horse bolted sideways, away from the sound of breaking glass. Drew tightened his knees and hung on, tempted to throw his arms around the chestnut's neck as his alcohol-befuddled brain tried to react.

"Whoa," he commanded, trying to steer the horse in a circle. "Quiet down, damn it!" The horse shied again, but Drew kept up the pressure of his knees and pulled back on the reins. The gelding backed up, off the road and down into a slight ditch.

Drew attempted to guide the horse out of the ditch, touching his heels to the chestnut and throwing his weight forward. The horse shot up onto the roadway as Drew clung gracelessly to the reins.

They almost collided with a carriage.

The chestnut skidded to a halt as Drew tried to right himself. He looked up into bright green eyes, alight with amusement.

"Having trouble with your mount, Mr. Leyton?"

"Wynne!" he exclaimed, at once delighted to see her. His smile faded at her disapproving look. He glanced at John, who was scowling fiercely.

"Aren't you a little far from Waverley?" Wynne asked coolly. She obviously wasn't happy to see him. Did she think he was running away?

His anger resurfaced at her cold remark. By God, she was the one who should be answering his questions. She'd left without a word—without a clue—in the dark hours of morning. She had left *him*, and she dared to question his mission!

"Damn it, woman!" he shouted. "Where have you been?" He watched her through bleary eyes: her flushed skin, flashing eyes, and clenched fists.

"That tone will *not* be tolerated, Mr. Leyton. I will talk to you later, at Waverley."

Drew angrily turned the agitated horse in a circle, bringing it up beside Wynne in the open carriage. "We'll talk about it *now*."

"We will not!" she ground out.

In a move so quick she had no time to respond, Drew reached out and grabbed her, dragging Wynne across his thighs and holding her on his lap.

"Yaa!" he yelled to the horse, kicking him with his booted heels. They lunged forward at a gallop.

"Let me go, you barbarian!" Wynne flung her arms around his neck, holding on as though her life depended on it.

Drew looked back at John, who attempted to turn the carriage and pursue them.

Drew pulled the heaving chestnut to a halt and took a deep breath.

"You're drunk," Wynne accused.

"Am not."

"You're drunk and you're on the road to Williamsburg. Why?" she questioned softly.

"You left. You were gone so long. Smythe wouldn't tell me why." He shrugged. "I was worried."

Wynne looked at him for a long time. He wanted to say so much to her, about his frustration, about how angry he was, but he was suddenly tired. His tongue felt thick and his head ached horribly.

John bore down on them then, jumping from the carriage and grabbing the chestnut's bridle.

"That won't be necessary, John. Will it, Mr. Leyton?"

"No . . . no, that isn't necessary. I'll not harm her."

John dropped his hands. "What you want to do now, Missus?"

Wynne sighed. Drew felt her relax just slightly, leaning against his chest. How he wanted to comfort her, but not with John present. Wynne was always so careful. She guarded her reputation at all costs.

"We're all tired, John. Why don't we just continue to Chriswell's Ordinary, as we planned? I'm sure we'll all feel better in the morning."

He relaxed his grip on Wynne and she slid from the horse.

"Mr. Leyton, I believe your horse is winded. Would you care to ride in the carriage?"

"Yes, ma'am," Drew replied wearily. God, why had he drunk all that ale? He didn't even care for the stuff. The last time he'd drunk too much had landed him in gaol.

John helped Wynne into the tufted leather seat, now hot from the late afternoon sunshine. Drew followed at a respectful distance and tied his horse to the back of the carriage, slightly loosening the gelding's girth.

"Sorry, old fellow," he mumbled into the chestnut's ear.

He moved to the open entrance to the buggy and looked at Wynne sitting there like a queen. The ice queen. The passionate goddess of his nights. Good Lord, he was going mad. He rubbed his brow, troubled by a persistent throbbing.

"It's the sun and the strong drink," Wynne explained. "It can cause a terrible headache."

"As if you would know," Drew returned testily.

"So I've been told, Mr. Leyton. There are many things you may understand without experiencing them yourself."

"And many more you must feel to truly understand," Drew returned, watching her blush. She still looked naïve and innocent at times.

"So true, Mr. Leyton, so true," she returned softly. "And now," she said in a louder, more commanding tone, "please be seated so we can continue."

He sat down across from Wynne, trying to concentrate on her face, but it waved and blurred. His head pounded dreadfully. He closed his eyes and leaned against the cushioned leather. He was vaguely aware of Wynne, a look of concern on her beautiful face, before he gave up the struggle and relaxed in sleep.

16

Drew awoke to a dark, unfamiliar room and a pounding headache. He was sure that several small men with axes were chipping away from the inside of his skull. That, coupled with the fact that he felt disoriented and famished, didn't make for the best of moods.

He rose slowly from the single bed and tried to look out the small window across the room. Nothing. Absolutely nothing looked familiar.

Checking his clothing, he found that he was still dressed in the dusty, sweat-stained clothes he had worn . . . that was it! He'd been searching for Wynne, drank that abominably strong ale, lost control of his horse, and almost carried Wynne away in a fit of temper.

Drew cradled his head in his hands and moaned. Lord, he wished he could remember exactly what he had said and done. No doubt he'd made a total fool of himself and the woman was angry enough to send him back to Williamsburg for sure this time.

There was no water in the room and he had a terrible thirst. And he smelled—oh, how he smelled. The bitter, malty taste of the ale seemed to be coming from his skin, his clothes, everything. Drew opened the door and stepped into the dimly lit hallway.

The sounds of a common room came up the stairs, coupled with the heavy smoke of pipes and cigars, the appetizing aroma of roasting meat, and the smell of years of spilled tankards. He made his way carefully down the single flight of steps, walking lightly to avoid jarring his aching head.

Conversation didn't stop when he entered the room; indeed, most of the diners and drinkers weren't even aware that he was there. There was an empty table away from the wide hearth, and Drew took a chair there. Soon a barmaid arrived to take his order.

"What ye be havin', sir?"

"What can you suggest for a bad case of too much sun and strong ale?" Drew asked, barely looking at the girl.

"I'll fix you somethin', sir, if you trust me to. It's none too tasty, but ye'll feel better soon."

"Fine," Drew replied distractedly. "Bring whatever you have." He looked around the room, not really expecting to see any familiar faces. Where was Wynne now? Had she gone off and left him again?

Drew motioned for the man behind the bar to come over.

"Can I help you, sir?" The man paused and looked intently at Drew. "Why, you're the man that came through here earlier looking for Mistress Carr."

"That's right. I found her, too, farther south on the road, but I seem to have misplaced her again."

"Oh, she's here all right. Took a couple of rooms upstairs, and her man's in the stable. Had her dinner sent up a while back." and turned back to the counter.

The barmaid returned with a mixture and handed it to Drew. "This will help ye, sir."

Drew raised the tankard and took only a brief glance at the liquid before draining it. It was strong and bitter, but anything that might help was welcome. He only hoped he could keep it down long enough for it to work.

Checking his pocket to ensure that the shillings were still there, Drew ordered supper. He stepped outside for a fresh breath of air and some cool water. The night was warm and pleasant, with only a slight breeze from the east. Drew walked toward the stable, intent on finding John.

He stopped at the well and drew a fresh bucket of water, taking a long drink from the ladle. John stepped out of the barn then, his shadow falling across the stableyard as he stood in the open doorway.

"John," Drew greeted, "how are the horses?"

"Jus' fine, Mr. Drew. How are you?"

"I've been better, John." Drew rubbed his neck. "I've been better." He paused and walked closer to the barn. "I wanted to explain about this afternoon."

"Oh, no need, Mr. Drew. The missus already explained about the ale and all. It happens like that sometime."

"Thanks, John. I don't want there to be hard feelings," Drew said. "I behaved very badly toward Mrs. Carr. I don't want you to believe it was out of disrespect or . . . familiarity."

"Don't worry, Mr. Drew. The strong drink can make a man act crazy. It don't mean nothing."

"I'll see you in the morning." Drew turned and walked back to the common room. More travelers had just arrived, and he wanted to reclaim his table and have his dinner before they came in.

The barmaid was in the process of setting his plate down when he walked in. He suddenly realized that he felt better.

"Your cure seems to have worked."

"Near to always does," she replied.

Drew counted out several coins from his pocket and pressed them into her hand. "For the dinner and the cure. The rest is for you."

The barmaid looked into her palm.

"Thank ye, sir. Thank ye kindly."

Drew watched the new arrivals settle near the hearth. They were a talkative lot, apparently with news from Williamsburg and beyond.

"We're on our way to claim some property near King William City. Glad to be away from the continent, I can tell you that," one of the men was explaining to a Virginia planter.

"More fighting?"

"Aye, the French are all stirred up from their victory over Ferdinand of Brunswick in April."

"It's true," the other man chimed in. "If they're not spending it on court furnishings, they're off to war." He shook his head. "Give me a good solid Englishman any day."

"Hell," the planter proclaimed loudly, "give me a Virginian!" The room erupted into cheers. Even the two English travelers responded.

"Aye, to Virginians—men and women all," another raised his tankard in toast.

"Aye," was the reply at large.

The planter took a drink, then proposed a toast. "To Virginia—our land free, our men honest, and our women fruitful!"

The room cheered again and even Drew chuckled. God

save him from fruitful women. He lowered his head and finished his beef.

Later, after Drew had bathed as well as he could from the horse trough and changed into clothes he'd packed into his saddlebags, he returned upstairs to his room. At least, his intention was to return to his room. He saw the light from Wynne's room seeping under the closed door. He heard her soft humming, off-key, and he didn't even try to resist.

Trying the door and finding it locked, he knocked softly.

"Who is it?" Wynne asked quietly.

"Your humble and repentant bondservant."

Wynne leaned her forehead against the heavy door and smiled. He had often teased her, sometimes, in her opinion, unmercifully. How much teasing should she give him before admitting that she forgave him?

"What is it, Mr. Leyton?"

"Can we talk?" came the muffled reply.

Wynne unlocked the door and opened it a crack. She tried to look slightly frightened. "Are you certain that you won't carry me off again?"

"You have my promise. May I come in?"

Wynne opened the door wider and looked into the hallway. It was empty except for Drew. "Come in."

Drew slipped inside and shut the door. Wynne stood beside it and turned the lock. He raised his eyebrows.

"You can't be too careful. Lots of scoundrels abound in these inns," she explained, suppressing a smile at his appearance.

Drew walked over to the bed and sat down, clasping his hands between his wide-spaced knees. "Wynne, I . . ."

"Yes?"

He looked at her for a long time. His eyes were troubled, his brows drawn together. Several times she thought he would speak, but he stopped himself. Was he still angry with her for leaving Waverley? He didn't look it; he looked, as he said, repentant.

He held out his hand.

Wynne came forward slowly, watching his face. "Did you have something to say?"

"I love you."

She turned away. That wasn't what she had expected to hear.

Drew rose and followed her to the window, where she stood staring out at the black void and the reflections from inside the room. She could see him approach, watch his hands move to hold her shoulders, caress her arms. She watched him circle her waist and hold her securely, tenderly. And she knew he was watching her.

"I shouldn't love you, you know. There's no future in it," she whispered.

"I want to tell you about how I felt when I watched you leave that morning. A part of me left with you. I saw you turn back to the window, knowing that you couldn't see inside. Why would you do that if you didn't care?"

"Oh, Drew. I do care. I do love you. But can't you see that it's not fair to you. You deserve someone with whom there's a future."

He simply shook his head and continued. "When you left no message for me, I was confused. I was worried, yet Smythe wouldn't tell me where you were or what you were doing. Do you know how frantic I felt when you didn't return?"

"I'm sorry. I should have told you I was leaving," Wynne confessed. "But, Drew, please understand that I'm not accustomed to confiding in anyone. I've not had to answer to anyone for six years."

Drew rested his chin against her hair and pulled her closer. "I know, love. I know. But it's difficult for me to accept. I've never known a woman like you—so independent and capable."

"Your other women are shy, retiring creatures who cannot decide which bonnet to wear without your expert guidance?" Wynne asked with a hint of sarcasm born from jealousy.

"Definitely. All of them," Drew teased.

Wynne turned to look at him. "There really was no one in England?"

"No," he replied truthfully. "Oh, I'll admit that I've known my share of women. But I wasn't ready to settle down yet."

"Not even with James's mother? I still don't understand why you didn't marry her."

"You will someday, love."

She felt his lips move against her hair. "Until I met you, I'd never found a woman I could spend the rest of my life with—raising my children, waking beside me each morning, growing old together."

"That sounds like a fairy tale. I don't believe most people are like that."

"Maybe not most, but some are. My parents, for example. They're entirely devoted to one another, enjoy each other, yet raised four children together."

"Parents?"

"Yes. Most of us have them, you know."

Wynne frowned at his choice of words. Was he making a comment on his own status, or was this another remark about their relationship? "I just thought your father . . . didn't live with your mother."

She saw Drew's confused look in the mirror-like glass. "I think you're confusing my life stories, love. I didn't live with James's mother, but my parents have been married for forty years."

"Umm. You have three . . . what? Brothers? Sisters?"

"Two brothers and a sister," Drew admitted. "I'm the youngest."

"Ah, that explains it. I was wondering how you got to be so terribly spoiled and conceited."

Drew gave her a look of exaggerated hurt. "Spoiled and conceited? How can you say that?"

Wynne laughed, leaning back against his solid strength and enjoying this sharing. "You know that I can never stay upset with you, don't you? Even when you leave without authorization, become dreadfully drunk in public, and practically admit our relationship to the servants. You know that you will be forgiven."

"I know no such thing! Besides, I did have authorization. Smythe wrote a letter for me," Drew smugly replied.

Wynne laughed again. "You're still spoiled."

"Aye, that I am. Spoiled for love of you. You've ruined me for any other," he sighed.

"For now," Wynne returned.

"Forever," Drew stated firmly, and he turned her around to prove his point. His lips took hers fiercely, demanding a response she was more than willing to give.

17

Wynne's bay mare stamped impatiently at the soft, marshy earth, shaded by a dense stand of trees and honeysuckle.

She'd been waiting for Barton MacClintock all afternoon. Riding out first thing this morning, she saw no sign of the blackmailer, so she returned home for lunch. Drew was supervising the sawing, splitting, and planking of the timber and wouldn't be home before supper. If he knew what she planned, he would certainly try to stop her.

Wynne swatted at the honey bees and pulled the small watch from the pocket of her riding habit jacket and opened the cover. Fifteen minutes past three o'clock. Both the clearing around the lodge and the stream were empty and silent. She rubbed a persistent ache in her knee from the sidesaddle and shifted her weight.

Tightening the reins, she touched her heel to the mare's side and turned her around. Soon they were cantering away from the copse of trees and back toward Waverley.

Let the man contact me, she thought. I'll not wait for

him another minute. As soon as she saw him, she would tell him in no uncertain terms that the deal was off. Let him try to coerce her again; she'd outwitted better men in the past and would probably do so in the future.

The *Virginia Gazette* said that the fighting on the frontier had moved to the north and would probably stay there. Oh, there were occasional Indian attacks along the western frontier, but they were to be expected. It was the threat of a well organized, French-backed uprising that terrified the settlers. And Barton MacClintock was directly responsible for that very real threat.

He wasn't the only one, but he was the one who was using Waverley to transport his illegal cargo. No more, Wynne thought. No more women like Sarah Williams would suffer because Elizabeth Wynne Carr did not have the backbone to say no.

Wynne slowed the mare to a trot, then a walk, as she entered the stableyard. Her face set in a grim look of determination, she barely noticed that the servants avoided her with silent wariness as she dismounted and marched into the house.

The summer days slipped into a comfortable routine at Waverley. There was maintenance to be done on the buildings, fences to be repaired, foals to be weaned, and the all-consuming task of weeding and caring for the tobacco. Drew could be seen daily, riding the fields, working beside the men and supervising the projects. Wynne ventured out often, and together they made such a striking couple that the field hands would occasionally stop their work and watch them ride by. She remained blissfully ignorant of the rumors, while Drew suppressed them whenever possible and treated Wynne with every respect due the mistress of a large plantation.

Wynne went to visit her husband on a regular basis, of

which the household staff was aware. She made a point to tell Drew when she left, so a repeat of the Williamsburg journey was not made. And each time she entreated him not to follow her or interfere.

Drew gritted his teeth and watched her ride away each time. Smythe would tell him nothing further and whenever asked, would give him a quelling glance and walk away.

One day, after Wynne had left on her regular visit to Samuel Carr, an unexpected rider came to Waverley. He was a flushed young man, dusty and obviously unaccustomed to the long ride from Williamsburg.

Smythe came forward to answer the door.

"Pardon me, but I am looking for Andrew Leyton. I have reason to believe he is a bonded servant at Waverley."

"Yes, Mr. Leyton is here. What business to you have with him?"

"I'm sorry, but I must speak only to Lo . . . Mr. Leyton."

"As a bonded servant, Mr. Leyton has no authority to conduct any business without his owner's knowledge and consent."

"I am not here to conduct any business with . . . Mr. Leyton."

"Then why are you here, Mr. . . . ?"

"Fielder. Henry Fielder, of the firm of Craddock and Barnaby." He shifted on his feet, clutching a leather satchel in his left hand.

"I'm not familiar with the firm, Mr. Fielder. Are you from Williamsburg?"

"London. Craddock and Barnaby are solicitors for the Earl of Morley," Fielder replied cautiously.

Smythe was silent for several long moments.

"I really do need to speak with Andrew Leyton."

Just then Drew rode in from the fields, noticing the strange horse tied in front of the house. He reined in and dismounted as Smythe and the unknown man turned to watch him.

His hair was tousled from the wind, his skin deeply tanned and his physique lean, vigorous, and muscular. He was the picture of health, and Henry Fielder released a long-held breath of relief. "Thank God," he murmured.

Drew scowled at the man standing beside Smythe. He stopped before them.

"Mr. Leyton, this man is Henry Fielder of the firm Craddock and Barnaby. From London. He is here to see you," Smythe recounted.

"Really? How interesting." Drew brushed past the two men. "Smythe, Mr. Fielder and I will be in the study. Please see that we are not disturbed."

With that, Drew held the door open and watched as the startled but silent Henry Fielder preceded him into the house.

Drew led the way through the main hall as Henry gazed in awe at the splendor of Waverley. For an isolated plantation, it was as elegant as any London house. Its appeal lay more in the tasteful decor than the richness of furnishings, but it obviously had been carefully decorated with an owner's love.

Drew closed the study door after Henry Fielder entered, motioned for the man to be seated, then walked to the windows to ensure no eavesdroppers lurked outside. He turned and addressed the solicitor's representative.

"My father hired your firm?"

"Yes, my lord, he—"

"Please, do not address me as 'my lord' while I'm here. I've not disclosed my background."

"But my . . . Mr. Leyton, surely your rank would have ensured better treatment! Your family has been distraught to think of you being sold into bondage. Your father has been searching for the truth since your disappearance. He had investigators on your disappearance almost immediately. You knew that he had already invested significant efforts in discovering the location of the highwayman?" At Drew's nod, he continued, "He was apprehended shortly after you were taken from the Tower. With the proper persuasion, he revealed that he had robbed the carriage the night you were taken into custody. The remaining jewels from his earlier robberies were discovered in his hiding place, and all charges against you were dismissed."

"Really? Then I am a free man?"

"Yes, my . . . Mr. Leyton. Your father sent me to locate you as soon as the dismissal was final." Henry stopped his dialogue and pulled a packet of papers from the satchel. "I have it right here."

He handed the thick envelope to Drew, who accepted it almost with reluctance. He held it for a moment, savoring the feel of the fine-grained cowhide, the weight, the freedom it represented.

Drew walked to the desk and sat in Wynne's chair before opening the packet. Folded inside was a letter from his father, penned in his customary brusque style with authoritative language that left no doubt as to his feelings. Drew hoped the House of Lords never discovered that the Earl of Morely considered the judicial system to be populated by "stupid jackasses."

There were hundreds of pound notes, letters from his mother, brothers, and sister, his estate manager and the solicitors. He saved those for later. Slowly, almost reverently, he removed the official document that proclaimed him innocent of all previous charges and a free man.

As he read the briefly worded sentences, he realized what this truly meant. He was free. He could turn around and walk away from Virginia, from Waverley, from Wynne, and no man could stop him. He was free.

He closed his eyes, momentarily forgetting Henry Fielder. Free? Hell, he wasn't free. He would never be free of those luminous green eyes, that rarely bestowed but beautiful smile, the memories of the passionate nights in her arms. He opened his eyes and looked at Henry Fielder.

"Is there any other message from my father?"

"Only that he has a ship available for your transportation back to England. It's docked at Norfolk, at your disposal," Fielder related. "When would you like to leave, my lord?"

"Leyton . . . not 'my lord,'" Drew reminded him.

"Sorry, sir. Would you like to leave today?" Henry asked, apparently impatient to be gone from the colonies and safely back in London.

Drew folded the documents, letters, and currency and placed them back in the leather envelope. "No, not today."

"Mr. Fielder, remain here for a moment." Drew walked out of the study in search of Smythe. A few minutes later he was back. "I've made arrangements for you to spend the night with us. I'm sure you're tired from your journey."

"But, Mr. Leyton, surely you wish to be gone from here?"

"Smythe will show you to a room. We have dinner at eight. At that time you will meet Mrs. Carr, the mistress of Waverley." Drew paused and fixed Fielder with what he knew was an intense look. "I'm not going into extreme detail, Mr. Fielder, but let me inform you that my position here at Waverley is more than a common bondsman. Mrs. Carr is unaware of my status in England, although she does know that I was accused of being a highwayman. She doesn't know who my father is, and I intend for her to remain ignorant of that fact." He paused again for effect. "Is that clear?"

"Yes, yes, but . . ."

"Do *not* tell anyone why you are here. Tell them instead that you're passing through to purchase land north of the Pamunkey. You're simply spending the night at Waverley. Do you understand?"

"Yes, but . . ."

"Good," Drew said, sighing in relief. "Remember, not one word to anyone."

He turned away then, toward the study door, and waited for Henry Fielder to precede him into the hall. "Smythe!" he called. The butler appeared. "Mr. Fielder is ready to go to his room, Smythe. Would you please show him up?"

Smythe gave Drew a very controlled look of disapproval, but complied.

Drew watched the two men go up the stairs. Henry Fielder paused once and turned back to gaze at Drew, questions burning in his eyes. The youngest son of the Earl of Morley had no answers for now.

Wynne arrived from her visit to her paralyzed husband late that afternoon. Samuel's faithful servant continued to administer the daily dosage of mercury that had been prescribed many years before as the only treatment for his disease. She was emotionally and physically tired; Samuel's condition was no better or worse and the stress of concealing her relationship with Drew from everyone on the plantation was beginning to show.

Wynne made her way slowly to her room, her footsteps heavy on the stairs. She was tired so often lately, and she knew the reason. Without a doubt, she carried Drew's child. She liked to think it had been conceived that night at Chriswell's Ordinary, where Drew had so sweetly apologized and they'd so thoroughly loved each other until dawn.

Drew never asked about the pregnancy. She wasn't sure that he was even aware of it. By mutual agreement they didn't discuss the topic. And yet he continued to come to her bed almost every night and she continued to welcome him.

If there was no discussion of the fact that she was with child, there would be no reason to stop those pleasurable visits. She still couldn't admit to herself that Drew was the focal point in her life. Having him was as important as having his child. She was beginning to wonder if she could ever give him up.

At the top of the stairs she found Millie coming from one of the guest rooms. "What are you doing in there?"

"We have a guest, Mistress Carr. A Mr. Henry Fielder. Smythe said to make up a guest room for him," the maid explained.

"Henry Fielder? I don't remember the name," Wynne mused. "Is he from this area?"

"No ma'am. He's on his way across the Pamunkey to purchase some land. He's just spending the night."

"Very well, Millie. I'll meet Mr. Fielder later. I think I'll retire to my room for a while," Wynne said tiredly. She walked toward her suite. "Has the cook been informed?" she asked without turning back to the maid.

"Yes, ma'am. Everything's been taken care of."

Drew stood over the bed and gazed lovingly at the woman sleeping there. She had faint circles under her eyes and she'd lost some weight as the summer advanced. It was the baby, he knew. She was carrying his child.

The thought both terrified him and caused him great

joy. To create a child, a new life, with Wynne was the greatest miracle he could imagine. Never to be able to claim her as his own was the most tragic thing he could comprehend. How could he leave her now that she was to bear his child?

He knew he couldn't. When he'd discovered the reason for Henry Fielder's visit, a thousand thoughts had raced through his head. But the strongest, most vital one was that he couldn't leave Wynne. Not for a hundred pardons or a king's ransom.

He understood her reasons for not discussing the pregnancy. She'd never admitted that they had a future together. Never, in all the nights they had made love or all the afternoons spent under a canopy of green leaves, had she referred to "their" child or said one thing to make him believe she would change her mind. She'd never again asked him to stay with her, never to leave, as she did at the inn that evening when he went to Williamsburg searching for her.

If she admitted she was with child, there would be no reason for making love. No reason—except the truth. She wasn't ready for that yet.

And so they remained silent on the subject. He'd promised not to bring up the issue. He wondered how long she could disguise her waistline or pretend her tiredness was caused by the heat or her activities.

Wynne stirred, coming awake slowly and focusing on his face as he sat beside her on the bed. She raised her arms.

Drew complied with her silent plea, holding her tenderly. "Did you sleep well, love?"

"Umm, yes. I don't know why I'm so tired."

"Yes, I know. It must be the heat," Drew replied. They both smiled.

"We have a guest," she stated.

"Yes. Henry Fielder. I met him earlier," Drew said truthfully. "He's staying the night. I hope you don't mind."

"No, of course not."

"Do you feel like having supper together?"

"Yes, I'm fine. Really. I feel much better after having a nap." She sat up and plumped a pillow behind her, leaning against the headboard.

"Then I'll leave you to dress." He winked and grinned. "Unless, of course, you'd care for some company right now."

Wynne laughed. "No, not now, Mr. Leyton. Would you ask Millie to come up?"

Drew reached down and kissed her lightly. "I'll tell her, love." He rose from the bed and moved to the door. "I'll see you at eight."

Wynne waved goodbye from the bed, smiling and looking very pleased with the world. She tempted him so much that Drew almost joined her in the big bed. Almost.

Dinner was a quiet and refined exercise in polite conversation and exchanged compliments. Henry Fielder, like Drew, lavishly praised Annie's cooking. The house was commented upon and Wynne told Mr. Fielder of the task of bringing the furnishings from England, the Orient, and India together in what was the wilderness some twenty years ago.

After dessert, Wynne asked the men if they would care for brandy and cigars. They declined the tobacco, but asked Wynne to join them for refreshments. They moved to the formal parlor, where Smythe served them fine French brandy, no doubt smuggled into Virginia at great expense.

Drew deliberately prolonged the conversation until Wynne was discreetly hiding yawns behind her tea cup. He smiled at her attempts and she smiled back.

"If you gentlemen will excuse me, I believe I shall retire," she announced.

Henry Fielder was on his feet in an instant. "Thank you for a most enjoyable evening, Mrs. Carr."

"You are very welcome, Mr. Fielder. We don't have guests often, and your company is most appreciated." Drew rose and watched Wynne speak cordially to the solicitor. He knew she was waiting for him to announce that it was time for them to retire also, but he was going to disappoint her this once. He knew from her raised eyebrow that she waited for him to speak.

"I believe I shall finish my brandy, Mistress Carr. It's a most enjoyable vintage."

"Indeed? I have heard it said that careful aging is the secret." Her tone was light, but to him, her voice sounded sultry, inviting.

"Yes, I'm sure you are right on that point," he agreed with a smile for her alone.

Drew glanced at Henry Fielder and saw a look of shocked surprise on the man's face. So he hadn't missed the flirtatious tone of Wynne's remark. Damn, but the woman picked the most inopportune times to try her feminine wiles.

"Well, gentlemen, again, good night."

"Good night, Mistress Carr," Drew drawled. He would teach her a lesson later about flirting with him. It would be a very thorough and enjoyable task.

"Good night, Mrs. Carr. A pleasure."

Wynne walked up the stairs. Was he no longer interested in her bed? Never before had he lingered when she so obviously desired his presence. Perhaps it was the baby. Perhaps there was something different—something he found unappealing about her body.

In her room Wynne stood before the cheval mirror, trying to assess her appearance. Her cheekbones were more pronounced, her breasts slightly fuller and more sensitive, but other than that, she could see no difference. Her stomach was only slightly rounded and her waist was the same size—if she laced it into a corset.

How would Drew feel about her in a month? In two months? Would he still desire her as much then? If tonight was any indication, the answer was no.

With a sob Wynne whirled away from the mirror and crossed to her dressing table. Slowly, methodically, she removed the pins from her carefully arranged hair and placed them on the small silver tray. She removed the dress, washed her face, and pulled off the chemise and petticoats.

Wynne jerked the nightgown over her head and turned down the wick in the lamp, sniffing back a sob. Only the candle on the nightstand still burned, as it did every night after Millie came in and prepared the chamber for bedtime.

After settling into bed and covering her legs with the light sheet, she shifted until becoming comfortable. It was a hot August, with at least one more month of heat before fall began. She rubbed her hands protectively over her stomach, searching for some evidence of the child she so desperately wanted.

A child would give her life meaning and diversity, would disrupt the routine and bring laughter to Waverley. And then, next year, perhaps she could have another baby. Her agreement with Drew would be complete; he would leave. He wouldn't stay after realizing she was serious about not marrying him, even if she could. She'd protected her heritage with cunning plans and skills, and she'd continue to do so, for herself and her children and the memories of those she'd loved and lost. She turned to her side and cried herself to sleep.

* * *

Downstairs, Drew finished his brandy and poured another for himself and Henry Fielder. He was sure the solicitor wasn't going to be pleased to hear his announcement, but there was no helping that.

"Mr. Fielder, I've given my revised status much consideration. I realize you were expecting me to accompany you back to London immediately, but there are . . . circumstances that prevent me from leaving Virginia now."

"My lord . . . er, Mr. Leyton, I believe I understand."

Drew stared at the blushing man for a moment before continuing. "I don't expect word of my position here at Waverley to leave these walls. Do I have your word?"

"Yes, my lord. Of course."

"Good," Drew breathed. "It's my intention to stay here for as long as I need to. If circumstances do not meet my expectations within a reasonable amount of time, I assure you that I'll return to England immediately. In any case, I've prepared a letter for my father"—Drew paused and pulled an envelope from his inside coat pocket—"which I'll entrust to your care. Please see that he receives it as soon as possible."

Henry Fielder accepted the thick envelope. "Do you wish me to return on the ship your father sent for you?"

"Yes," Drew replied immediately. "If . . . when I return, I'll book my own passage." He finished the last of his brandy. "You'll also need to leave a letter of credit in Williamsburg. Do you have a firm that you deal with there?"

"Yes. In an office near the Governor's Palace."

"Good," Drew replied, setting his brandy snifter down on the engraved brass tray. "Then if I need anything, I'll know who to contact." He paused and looked at the solicitor.

"Is there anything else, my lord?"

"No, Mr. Fielder. I believe that covers everything." It was done. He was staying.

"Then I will take my leave for the evening. Good night, my lord."

"Good night, Mr. Fielder."

Drew waited until he heard the door to Henry Fielder's room close before blowing out the lamps and closing the doors to the parlor. There was no moon tonight and only the usual wall sconce was left burning. Smythe had already retired.

He made his way quietly to Wynne's bedchamber, turning the knob and opening the door slowly. It was incredibly dark inside the warm room and he waited a moment for his eyes to adjust before removing his clothes.

Wynne stirred when she felt the delicious sensation of Drew's hot kisses along her cheek and neck. He removed the sheet, raising the gown and stroking her pliant legs.

The blackness of night was an aphrodisiac; she could see nothing but his outline as he knelt beside her, but she would know his touch anywhere. Her skin burned, but not from the August heat. It was the magic of this man, the incredible way he made her respond. She wondered again if she could ever let him go.

18

Drew dismounted and placed a warning hand over the muzzle of his chestnut gelding. The horse's ears were pricked forward, intently watching a barge being poled up the creek. Drew watched also, his eyes narrowed as he viewed the three men on the boat. Two moved from back to front, handling the poles expertly and obviously concentrating on their slow advance. The third man looked familiar. His wiry frame leaned against one of the crates stacked in the center of the barge, partially covered with oiled canvas. Drew impatiently waited for the barge to move closer.

It was Barton MacClintock, the man who had visited Wynne several months ago, Drew realized. What in the bloody hell was a tobacco factor doing on a barge in a secluded creek away from plantations and towns? Drew wagered a hundred pound note that the man didn't have anything in those crates that was remotely related to tobacco.

MacClintock's eyes narrowed as he studied the creek-bank. Drew crouched further into the dense foliage. He prayed his horse stayed quiet and still until the barge was well away from his hiding place.

Suddenly, one of the boatmen slipped and cursed. Mac-Clintock's attention focused on the man and he motioned for him to be silent. He looked back to the forest. Drew was ready to swear that Barton MacClintock was looking right at him when he heard a rustling of the dry leaves and saw a squirrel dart across the ground and up a tree.

MacClintock saw it too. Apparently satisfied that the squirrel was the only thing catching his attention, he turned his back on Drew's hiding place and talked quietly to the men.

Later, after the barge had passed by and gone around a bend in the creek, Drew removed his hand from the soft muzzle of his gelding and backed him out of the hiding place. His booted feet barely disturbed the soft moss of the forest. His thoughts, however, were rushing through his head like dry leaves in a whirlwind.

Wynne knew about MacClintock, of that Drew was almost certain. He began to remember what she'd said about the Scotsman—about how he shouldn't be concerned about the man—that she would deal with him. How had she dealt with him? By allowing him access to Waverley land?

What was in those damn crates? If they'd been farther north or west, he would have suspected a weapons shipment to the French. But the French were fighting on the northern lakes and in the forests west of New York, if the months-old newspapers he'd read were accurate. There were no French in the settled areas of Virginia.

The only threats to Virginians were Indian raids in the west, near the mountains. Skirmishes like the one in which Sarah Williams's husband had been killed. Sarah . . . that was it!

Drew mounted quickly and urged the chestnut into a gallop. The gelding was sweating heavily, lathered across his wide chest and blowing hard when they reached the stable. Drew dismounted and led the horse inside the dark barn, calling for Riley. The older man hurried forward.

"Sir?"

"Please take care of him for me, Riley. I have an important errand at the house." Drew handed the reins to the stableman and turned to walk away. Before he reached the opening, he turned back. "And, Riley, you had best saddle another mount for me. I may have to leave again quickly."

"Sure thing, Mr. Drew," Riley replied, clearly puzzled by those instructions.

Wynne was coming in from the garden with a basket of cut flowers over her arm. Her dress of pale green was unencumbered by farthingales or stiff petticoats, and the slight breeze molded the skirt over the very slight but noticeable swell of her stomach.

Would she ever admit her pregnancy? Drew wondered. She was as silent on that fact as she'd been about Barton MacClintock. Slowing his pace, Drew watched her as she walked along the brick path.

God, how he loved her. He now understood the guilt over Sarah Williams and the secrecy about Wynne's dealings with MacClintock, but he still didn't know why she dealt with the man. Did she need money? Drew didn't think so, since he was familiar with the books for the plantation. Were there other expenses of which he was not aware? Did she owe money that was not recorded in the ledgers he viewed almost every day?

Wynne looked up and saw him, started to smile, then stopped.

"We need to talk," he said, taking her arm in a firm grip.

"Is something amiss?"

"We'll talk inside, if you please."

Wynne preceded him into the study, where he closed the door and checked the area outside the windows. She took a chair in front of the desk and placed her basket of flowers on the floor.

"Will you please tell me what's wrong?" she asked.

Drew unfolded his arms and sat in the chair opposite her. He paused for a moment before beginning. "Did you know that Barton MacClintock is using Waverley to transport something—probably illegally?"

She had a look of stunned confusion on her face. She paused to clear her throat. "What are you talking about?"

Drew tried to control his temper, but it was a tenuous task. "Right now, as we speak, there's a barge being poled upstream through Waverley property."

Wynne's eyes bulged with undisguised interest before she could control her expression. "So?"

Drew rose from the chair and paced in front of the fireplace. "Damn it, Wynne. This whole thing with Mac-Clintock is a mystery. I know there's something between you two. I've seen him here. I've heard your evasive answers about his business. Are you trying to tell me that you knew nothing of the nature of his trips on Waverley property?"

Wynne dropped her gaze to the colorful basket of flowers.

"Wynne! Answer me."

"Yes . . . he told me that he was using Waverley property! Does that answer your question?"

"Hardly," Drew scoffed. He stopped and glared at Wynne. "What is he smuggling?"

"I don't know . . . exactly."

Drew took a deep breath and tried to control his anger. "All right, let me tell you what I think. I believe there are weapons in those crates. I believe they're for the Indians on the frontier." He paused for a moment. "What do you think?"

"You're right. He's smuggling weapons," she murmured.

Drew ran a hand over his face, then combed it through his hair. "How long has this been going on?"

"Not long."

"How long?"

"Late spring."

"Before I came to Waverley?" Drew asked quietly.

"No . . . no, it was after," Wynne replied, staring at the fountain and garden.

"Wynne, love, look at me."

Her troubled green eyes turned to him. "Yes?"

"Does Barton MacClintock's smuggling have anything to do with me?" At her questioning look, he continued. "I mean, is there any connection between MacClintock's using your land and my indenture?"

"No, of course not," Wynne replied. "Why would you think that?"

Drew moved close and hunched down in front of Wynne. He took her cold hands in his larger, warmer ones. "I'm just trying to understand. I want to know what's going on here."

"It's very . . . complicated," she murmured.

"Tell me. Make me understand."

She took a long breath before beginning. "Barton Mac-Clintock visited here before you came. He wanted to talk about contracting for my crops and I told him it was too soon. He came back several weeks later." Wynne shifted in the chair, sitting up straighter. She gave a small laugh. "He told me he'd discovered my husband was . . . ill. He'd seen him. He would stay quiet about it if I went along with his scheme to transport his goods upstream."

"He blackmailed you?"

"Yes, I suppose that is what you call it." Wynne raised her tormented eyes to his. "I had no choice, or so I thought. I couldn't let anyone else find out about Samuel. I knew I would lose everything."

"And now? What do you think?"

"I don't know!" she cried. "Nothing has really changed, yet I know I can't let MacClintock use my land for something so evil."

Drew knelt before her chair and took her into his arms. She trembled with emotion, her hands grasping his arms as though she could anchor herself against the tumult.

"I went to Williamsburg to confront him. I was going to tell him that he had to stop."

"What happened?" Drew asked, stroking her back.

"He wasn't there. I left a message that he should meet me in one week. He never showed up."

"This has to stop, love," Drew stated firmly.

"I know. I tried," Wynne said, snuggling against his shoulder.

"Is that the only reason you went to Williamsburg—to confront MacClintock?"

"Well, yes," Wynne replied, confused by his question. She pushed back slightly in his embrace. "Why do you ask?"

"I want the whole story, Wynne. What else did you do in Williamsburg?"

"That's really none of your business," she indignantly stated, pushing back further.

"I'm making it my business," Drew stated, holding her firmly.

"All right then, I'll tell you." She drew in a deep breath. "I post letters from various places to Samuel's business associates and solicitors."

Ah, Drew thought. She was providing proof that Samuel Carr was alive and well. "And I suppose you visit people occasionally, mentioning that Samuel is doing this and that."

"Yes. I've tried to think of everything."

"You're very clever. I didn't realize how devious you could be," Drew remarked casually.

"You're furious, aren't you? Well, don't judge me, Drew, unless you've been in my situation. I did what I had to do." Wynne pushed away and stood up, walking to the window. "You don't understand how helpless I felt at first. I'd been engaged to another, a man I thought I could love . . . until I found him raping a slave. I hit him . . . scarred him for life. His father could have ruined us. That's the way of powerful men, isn't it?" She gave a bitter laugh. "Then my father died. I married Samuel to protect this plantation and my future. It was no love match. My God, he was as old as my father."

Wynne turned back to Drew and fixed him with a bold stare. "But don't be deceived by that. I cared for Samuel, and he cared for me. He was more like . . . an uncle. When he became paralyzed, I thought my life would be changed forever. I had visions of the magistrate taking away the plantation, my possessions, my freedom. I was frightened. Anyone—any stranger—could have been named my guardian. But more likely it would have been the magistrate or his son . . . the man I scarred for life.

"I did what I had to do," Wynne repeated. "I told Samuel that I wanted to have children, what I had planned, and although he couldn't reply, I feel that he agreed with my decision. He's had the best care I could give him. I don't think he suffers much. I do go to visit him," she admitted. "It's all I can do," Wynne whispered, hugging her arms.

Drew rose from his knees and came to stand in front of her. "I'm not judging you for what you did then. Hell, I'm not even judging you now. I realize you had your reasons. But, Wynne, this is illegal. It's treasonous." He moved closer and lightly clasped her arms. "You could be hanged for this," he said, looking intently into her eyes. "That I cannot allow."

"I'll tell him. It will stop," Wynne replied.

"There's no need. I'll take care of it. I just wanted you to make the decision."

"But . . ."

"One more thing, love." Drew paused and softened his gaze. "Are you in any other trouble . . . ?"

"What do you mean?"

"Are you having trouble with money? Was MacClintock giving you any money for using Waverley?"

"Of course not!" Wynne pushed away angrily. "How can you think I'd take money from that weasel?"

"I just asked," Drew replied. "If you needed money, I wouldn't blame you for . . ."

"How very magnanimous of you!" she scoffed. "You were judging me. Don't bother denying it."

"I was *not* judging you," Drew said. "I'm simply trying to explain that if you needed money, perhaps I could help."

Wynne whirled away. "Ha! You think I should take money from a convicted felon, a highwayman, and not from a Scottish tobacco factor. Besides, where would you get money? Would you return to robbing stages and carriages?"

Drew's earlier anger returned full force. "I am not a highwayman! I already explained that. And he is not *just* a tobacco factor. We both know that." Drew advanced until he had Wynne backed into a corner. "I made an honest offer."

"I don't need your money!" Wynne almost shouted.

Smythe appeared at the door, opening it wide enough to ask, "Mistress Carr? Is there anything amiss?"

Wynne paused only a moment before replying. "Yes, Smythe, there is. Mr. Leyton is being . . . difficult." She looked directly at Drew, moved to the mantel, opened a carved teak box, and pointed a firearm at Drew. "This pistol is primed, Mr. Leyton." She backed away from the fireplace toward the door.

Wynne handed the intricately engraved dueling pistol to the startled butler. "Smythe, I am entrusting Mr. Leyton to your care. Please make sure he does not follow me." She whirled through the door and was gone before either man could react.

Drew started to move and Smythe reacted. He leveled the pistol at Drew's chest.

"Please stay where you are, Mr. Leyton," he requested.

"Like hell. Get out of my way," Drew growled.

"Sorry. I cannot do that. The mistress requested that you do not follow her, and I will do whatever is necessary to see that you comply."

"Smythe, you don't understand. I believe she's gone to confront a man who is . . . who may do her harm. She hasn't fully considered this. She's acting on impulse, and right now her judgement isn't too good."

Smythe seemed to consider Drew's words, but the pistol did not waver. "Who is this man?"

"Barton MacClintock."

"He's a tobacco factor. How could he harm her?"

"Damn it, Smythe! I don't have time to explain everything to you. Will you let me leave?"

Smythe shook his head. "No."

Drew turned and walked to the side window, the one facing away from the garden. He heard hoofbeats before he saw Wynne ride away on the horse Riley had saddled for him. Drew's fist hit the window facing.

"Smythe, I must go after her. She's in danger."

"Just explain this danger to me."

"I don't have time! I must leave."

"Why would MacClintock harm Mistress Carr?" Smythe asked, seemingly unperturbed by Drew's ravings.

Drew stood directly in front of Smythe, in front of the pistol. "He's smuggling. She knows about it. She, in her impetuousness, is going to tell him to stop. Does that satisfy your curiosity?"

"Not entirely, but I admit you may have cause for concern."

"I'm leaving." Drew tried to push past the butler, but Smythe backed up and motioned with the pistol. "Not yet."

Drew stopped. He didn't think Smythe would shoot him but he wasn't certain. Perhaps now was the time to tell the butler.

"Look, Smythe. Wy . . . Mistress Carr just ran out of here and jumped on a horse. Right?" At the butler's nod, he continued, "She is in no condition to do that."

"I realize she was upset, but—"

"You don't understand. I mean physically she's in no condition."

"She looked perfectly healthy to me."

Drew stared at the ceiling. Lord, give me strength, he prayed. "She's pregnant."

Smythe's normally well composed features dissolved. His mouth fell open. "I didn't know," he whispered. "There had been rumors, but . . ."

"Well, now you do," Drew replied. "Do you see that I must protect her? No telling what harm MacClintock could do to her . . . or the child."

"She wanted a child very much," Smythe murmured.

"Yes, she did." Drew walked forward and took the pistol from Smythe's hand, tucking it into his waistband. "I'm going after her. If we don't return shortly, send the men after us. She rode toward the creek—upstream from the pasture that hasn't been cleared."

"Yes . . . yes, of course," Smythe replied, clearly shaken.

Drew rushed out of the study. Minutes later, he leaped on a horse and thundered out of the barn.

Wynne galloped over the fields, giving little thought to impending motherhood. All she could recall were Drew's words that Barton MacClintock was now on her property—within her grasp. She urged the horse onward.

The creek was just ahead; she could see the water glistening through the yellow and green leaves as the midday sun beat down. She pulled the lathered horse to a stop and listened. Nothing but birds and insects could be heard.

She followed the stream, keeping to the cleared areas where possible, or animal paths when necessary. Just as long as she could travel quickly. The trees along the streambed would keep MacClintock from seeing her until she wanted to be discovered. Then she would confront him.

The slower pace gave her time to think. She had acted impulsively, it was true. While Drew ranted and questioned, all she could think about was escaping his presence and going to MacClintock. Smythe's intervention had been most timely. Wynne smiled as she remembered that the ancient dueling pistol was not primed and loaded as she had boasted. She frowned as she imagined Drew's reaction to that fact.

Wynne looked around and was surprised to see that she

had followed the meandering stream in a half-circle, closer to the house and the hunting lodge. The water split less than a mile ahead, one branch forming a small pond that was sheltered from sight. This was probably where Mac-Clintock stopped.

She heard the movement of the barge through the water before she saw it. The shadows of many trees made the features of the men indistinguishable, but she could recognize MacClintock by his size. The other men were giants compared to the Scotsman, who was standing forward and looking ahead. The poling continued and MacClintock turned to walk back to the cargo.

The barge was moving very slowly, so Wynne rode as close as possible and dismounted. She draped the reins over a bush and walked to the tree line. The hunting lodge was now visible and the barge seemed to be preparing to stop. Wynne walked quickly away from the trees and hurried forward to intercept MacClintock. She knew the other men could be a problem, so she hoped the Scotsman could be caught alone. Would he become violent? The thought hadn't crossed her mind until now.

She had no weapon. Perhaps she should stop by the hunting lodge and get one from Sethti. Surely there was a sword, a dagger, or something from Samuel's military career. But then, if MacClintock knew she was anticipating trouble, he could become unreasonable. No, it was better to approach this as two civilized people.

Wynne stopped near the pool, crouched behind a flowering quince bush, and waited for the barge to arrive. Mac-Clintock whispered an order and the men spoke in hushed tones as they poled toward shore. The front of the barge bumped the bank and MacClintock jumped to the ground. Wynne's heart raced as she waited for him to move away from the boatmen.

She didn't have to wait long. MacClintock spoke softly to the men. "I'm going to look around. Stay near the barge until I return." She heard his footsteps on the dry grass and loose pebbles as he moved up the slight slope. He was coming toward her hiding place.

Wynne crouched lower, holding her breath. She was too close to reveal her presence. She would have to follow him until he was away from the two men.

MacClintock walked directly toward the hunting lodge. Wynne peeped around the bush, saw his retreating figure, then rose from her hiding place and followed at a safe distance.

MacClintock walked around the quiet lodge, keeping out of sight, she supposed, in case anyone was looking out of one of the six windows. Wynne waited for MacClintock in back of the lean-to. It didn't take long for him to make the circle.

Surprise showed briefly in his eyes as she stood calmly before him. Her head held high, Wynne defiantly glared at the Scot. An insincere smile appeared on his face.

"Well, well. What is the reason for this visit, Mrs. Carr?"

"It's very simple, MacClintock. I want you to stop using my property."

MacClintock moved closer, circling around Wynne. "And why would I want to do that?"

"Because I'll report you to the magistrate if you don't. And they will believe me, Mr. MacClintock, because I have proof that Samuel Carr is alive and well."

"Proof? Don't be stupid. He's right inside that building— and he's definitely not well."

Wynne moved away from the rock wall of the lodge. "Nonetheless, I can prove that Samuel has recently been in Virginia and is on his way to the Caribbean. You can't disprove that, so I *will* be believed."

"You can't be so certain," MacClintock stated, his eyes narrowing.

"Leave. Don't come back here or I *will* have you arrested."

MacClintock edged closer. "I don't think so," he replied, and lunged for Wynne.

19

MacClintock grabbed Wynne's arm and pulled her off balance. She stumbled toward him, suddenly aware of the vulnerability of her situation. The baby! She must not allow her baby to be harmed.

"Let me go, MacClintock," Wynne ordered. "Just take your hands off me and get off my property."

The Scotsman was a few inches shorter than Wynne, but his wiry frame was amazingly strong as he held her upper arms in a powerful grip. Wynne stood firm, trying to control her increasing fear.

"No . . . no, I don't think I'll let you go," he said. "You see, I believe that you will carry out your threat. You'd tell the magistrate, and even if he couldn't prove anything against me, there would still be suspicion. I can't afford that." He acted quickly, moving behind Wynne and twisting her arms backwards.

"Come along with me, Mrs. Carr. I have some friends I want you to meet."

Wynne began to panic as MacClintock pushed her forward.

Once they got to the barge, it would be three against one. She resisted all she could without falling, but he was stronger, and her efforts didn't stop him. Her feet slipped on the slick grass and rustling leaves, and it was all she could do to keep from screaming.

"Quit fighting me, damn it!" MacClintock warned. "I'll go easier on you if you don't give me any trouble."

Go easier? Good lord, what did he have in mind? Wynne couldn't stop a cry as he twisted her arm upward. They were moving toward the barge; it was just down the slope. Just a few more steps and the boatmen would notice them.

She heard the hoofbeats before she saw the horse in an all-out run, bearing down upon them. Drew flung himself from the back of the snorting animal as MacClintock increased the pressure. Drew had come for her!

"Garr! Roberts! Get up here!" the Scotsman yelled. "Stay back," he warned Drew.

The two burly boatmen ran up the bank and stood together, unarmed but looking extremely dangerous nonetheless.

"MacClintock! Let her go."

"Garr, go to the right. Roberts, around to the left. Wait for my order."

Wynne cried out at the odds. "Drew, no!"

"Let her go," Drew repeated.

MacClintock answered by shoving Wynne down the slope toward the barge. She fell to her knees, but caught herself as MacClintock let go of her arms to follow her descent. She stayed there, on her hands and knees, trying to plan her next move.

"Stop right there. Move over," Drew said to the boatmen.

Wynne looked up to see Drew had drawn a pistol and was

pointing it at the two men who stood together, their heavy arms dangling, their eyes confused. Oh God, not the pistol from the study . . . surely he would have checked it first!

"Don't just stand there!" MacClintock ordered the men. "Get that gun away from him!"

"Don't try it," Drew warned. "I can only get one of you, but which one?"

MacClintock leaned down and jerked Wynne to her feet. "Don't do anything foolish." He reached around her neck in a viselike grip that almost stopped her breathing. "I can snap her neck before you can get me, even if you do shoot one of them."

Drew advanced on the men, his eyes unwavering. "Get back to the barge," he ordered. "I'm not bluffing. I'd just as soon kill one of you."

Garr and Roberts exchanged glances, then retreated toward the barge.

"Stop it, you fools!" MacClintock yelled, but the men had already stepped aboard.

"Now," Drew continued, "get out of here."

The men looked only briefly at their angry employer before picking up their poles.

Drew looked at Wynne, his face a picture of anger. She knew he could see fear and pain in her own eyes. MacClintock's arm was choking her while his other hand held her arm twisted behind her back. She knew her rounded stomach would be clearly visible as the gown pulled and bunched around her.

"If you harm her, I'll kill you, MacClintock," Drew warned. "Now let her go and you can leave with your men."

MacClintock backed up, pulling Wynne with him. They were almost to the water. The barge was perhaps thirty feet away now.

He turned until Wynne was fully between him and Drew. She struggled weakly, but could offer little resistance. A small whimper escaped her lips.

"Get back on your horse and throw the pistol down. I'll let her go," he shouted to Drew.

"No." Drew advanced slowly.

Wynne detected a sudden tightening of MacClintock's muscles as Drew walked forward. Good Lord, but the Scotsman was mad—with fear. And Drew kept advancing. If anything happened to him . . .

"Let her go," Drew repeated yet again. "I'm getting impatient with you, MacClintock. If one hair on her head is harmed, I'll tear you apart with my bare hands."

Suddenly MacClintock pushed her away so quickly and violently that she landed in the shallow water face down. She immediately pushed upward, struggling with the wet fabric of her clothing. MacClintock had already pulled a knife from his boot.

"Drop the knife," Drew ordered, but MacClintock ignored him. He poised the blade, aiming at Drew's heart.

Drew fired. There was a hollow click.

Wynne yelled, "Drew, no!" She lunged forward, tackling MacClintock around the knees just as he was about to release the knife. It fell harmlessly in the mud of the creek-bank.

Drew ran forward and grabbed the Scotsman, who had been released by Wynne but hadn't gained his balance. Wynne sat up and looked frantically for the knife in the sticky black mud.

Drew shook MacClintock like a dog with a rat. He flung the Scotsman away from the creek, up the bank and into the thick cushion of honeysuckle. He leaped on the man, his powerful hands closing around the Scotsman's throat. MacClintock clawed at Drew's hands and arms, but was no match for the bondsman's longer reach and greater strength. The Scot's left hand reached downward, toward his boot.

Wynne screamed, "Drew, watch out! A knife!" just as MacClintock pulled a second blade from the left boot. An evil grin appeared on his face as he prepared to plunge it into Drew.

Wynne's hand touched something. The hilt of the first knife! It was covered in grime, but to her, it was the most welcome sight she had seen in a long while.

Drew and MacClintock continued to grapple for the knife until the Scot got a knee and a foot between their bodies and pushed with all his strength. Drew was flung off and rolled down the bank, at least ten feet from Wynne.

MacClintock advanced, the blade of the knife gleaming in the shafts of sunlight as he stalked his prey. Drew rose and kept his eyes on MacClintock as he moved away from the water, uphill, trying to get a better position. Wynne saw that a section of the creekbank had broken away. Drew angled toward it.

"Watch out!" she cried.

Drew stumbled and MacClintock lunged forward. Drew's body hit hard, his back across a fallen log. He raised his arms to protect himself.

Suddenly, Wynne rushed forward, reacting instinctively, protecting someone she loved. At that moment she hated MacClintock for causing her more torment. She raised the knife high, the hilt firmly clasped. She brought it down hard into the Scot's back, slicing through the flesh with amazing ease.

Drew saw the look of surprise on MacClintock's face, but he didn't associate it with Wynne until the Scot rolled away. She stood there, her arm still poised, her eyes glazed in shock. Drew looked down the slope and saw MacClintock's body slip into the creek.

Drew rose awkwardly and opened his arms to Wynne. She fell forward, almost knocking him over again in her haste. Sobbing into his chest, she gripped him tightly. The swell of her stomach pressed against him.

"It's all right now," Drew whispered.

Drew pushed her away slightly so he could see her face. "Are you injured, love? Are you hurt?"

Wynne shook her head. "No, I don't think so." She ran her hands over the muddied overskirt, the soaked petticoats. "No, nothing serious."

Drew clasped her tightly, burying his face in her hair. "And the baby?"

Wynne stiffened for a moment, then relaxed. "Fine."

"Thank God," Drew responded, his voice hardly above a whisper.

They stood there for a few minutes, gaining strength and composure from each other. Drew almost forgot his anger.

He pulled away first. "You had Smythe hold me with an unloaded pistol?"

"Of course," Wynne sniffed. "You don't think I would have a primed weapon pointed at you, do you?"

"The thought did cross my mind."

"Well, I wouldn't." Wynne paused. "I didn't realize you would follow so soon, or that you would try to use the pistol." She looked deeply into his eyes. "I'm glad you came."

Drew crushed her to his chest again. "So am I, sweetheart. So am I." He paused and stroked her back. "You shouldn't have run off. I would have taken care of MacClintock."

"It was my problem," Wynne murmured, "my responsibility."

Drew sighed. There was no talking to the woman sometimes. She was too damned independent.

"Is he . . . ?"

Drew looked at the creek. There was no sign of Mac-
Clintock's body. "I'll look."

Drew waded into the shallow water, downstream from
the area where the Scotsman had fallen. Nothing. Even the
barge was gone.

"There's no trace. I suppose his body drifted off."

"I thought we should at least bury him," Wynne said in
a small voice.

Drew tried to reassure her. "Think of it as a burial at
sea." He paused and looked into her eyes. "There's nothing
else to do."

"I know."

"Are you ready to go home?"

"Yes, I'm ready."

Drew took a long look at the small house when he
retrieved his horse. He would wager this was Samuel Carr's
residence. Now wasn't the time to confront her. He led the
horse back to her.

"We'll ride double back to your horse. Where did you
leave him?"

Wynne pointed downstream. "Not far."

Wynne turned to look once more at the stream. A shudder passed through her body. Drew tried to reassure her.
"We'll be home soon."

Wynne looked away from the site of the violent struggle.
"How long have you known about the baby?"

Drew's face relaxed as he smiled down at Wynne. "For
about as long as you have."

"Oh."

He placed Wynne carefully on the saddle, then mounted behind her. He held her close, his own nerves suddenly

raw in the aftermath of the violence. God, she could have been killed. Wynne and his baby.

"Are you happy about the baby, love? I know you wanted this child so badly."

Wynne nodded.

"When I saw MacClintock holding you, hurting you, it made me a little crazy. If he had harmed either you or the child, I would have killed him." He looked at her tired features. "Do you believe me?"

"Yes . . . yes, I do."

Wynne was quiet for so long that Drew thought she had fallen asleep. Drew pulled his horse to a stop when he found her mount, still loosely tied to the bush. "Drew?"

"Yes, love?"

"Are *you* happy about the baby?"

Drew hugged her tightly. Wynne tilted her face up and his lips took hers in a fierce kiss. He kissed her until she was breathless and weak.

"Yes, I'm happy about the baby," he finally whispered. "I love both of you very much."

"I love you too," she whispered.

His arms relaxed around her, holding her, protecting her.

20

Wynne had sent Faye and Smythe to Williamsburg again, this time with new tapes of her measurements for the seamstress. None of her gowns fit anymore, especially since she had no more corsets. Drew had taken all of them away when he discovered that she was attempting to cinch her waist into some of the more tight-fitting garments.

She leaned her head against the chair back and sighed, closing her eyes. She'd been sewing for several hours. Her fingers were cramped and a headache caused by eyestrain was beginning. The tiny nightgown lay unfinished on her lap.

"Mistress Carr! Mistress Carr!" Millie called as she ran up the stairs. She burst through the door, not stopping to knock. "Something terrible must have happened."

Wynne rubbed her tired eyes. "Millie? What's the matter with you?"

"It's that Indian man, Sethti. He's downstairs, all upset and mumbling in that language of his. I can't make out a thing."

The maid rambled on, but Wynne wasn't giving her attention. Everyone knew Sethti lived in the hunting lodge, since he'd been with Samuel in India. Wynne explained that Sethti couldn't travel with Samuel due to acute seasickness, so he stayed at Waverley. Wynne suspected that Cook knew about Samuel, since she prepared the food that was sent to the lodge several times a week. And of course John might know since he delivered supplies to Sethti. But no one ever said anything to her or, to her knowledge, to anyone else.

Sethti stood in the hall, his hands clasped in front and his eyes darting around the house. "Sethti? What is it?" Wynne asked as she neared the bottom of the steps.

"Missy! Please, I must speak with you."

"Of course. Come into the study." She led the Hindu into the room where she'd so often sat with Drew.

They took chairs in front of the fireplace. Wynne tried to appear calm, but inside she'd come to an appalling conclusion.

"He is dead, missy," Sethti announced, his eyes pooling with unshed tears.

Wynne covered her face with her hands and hung her head. Dead. Dear God, but it was finally over. The emotions that thought caused—horror, curiosity, relief— whirled through her head.

"How did it happen, Sethti?"

He looked frightened for a moment, then replied, "I do not know. He was fine last night. This morning," he shrugged, "he did not awaken."

Died in his sleep. Wynne let out a breath.

"Did he appear to be in any pain?" she reluctantly asked.

"Oh, no, missy. He just looked . . . asleep."

"Good. I mean, I'm glad he didn't suffer." Good Lord. Samuel was dead. She was a widow. A pregnant widow.

"Missy? Last night, there was something I should tell you."

Wynne's head jerked up. "What is it?"

"There was a man looking around the lodge. I was inside, but I saw him. He looked in the window of the bedroom." Sethti paused. "I know he saw Carr sahib."

"This man," Wynne began, "what did he look like?"

"I know this man, missy. He is the bonded man, Mr. Leyton. John told me of this man when he repaired the roof."

"Are you sure?"

"Yes, missy. He is a tall man," Sethti indicated, "and walks like the Maharaja of Rajasthan."

"Yes, that's Mr. Leyton," Wynne whispered, her mind racing. What could this mean?

Sethti interrupted her thoughts. "I will go and prepare the body of Carr sahib for burial."

Wynne looked at the Indian man who had been with her husband for so many years. He'd crossed the oceans to remain with Samuel and had tended him faithfully both before and after his illness. Now he would tend him one final time. "Yes, Sethti," she answered softly.

After the Indian man left, Wynne remained in the study and began a list of things that must be done. Since everyone knew that Samuel had gone to the Caribbean, she must develop a story about him coming home and dying unexpectedly. Or perhaps she could say that he'd died aboard ship and been returned home for burial. But she must get his death certified; otherwise, she wouldn't have the status of a widow, and could still find herself placed under a guardian. With the will Samuel had written six years ago, her status would be fairly well assured. However, neither she nor Samuel had thought about children when they drafted the will. As the "father," Samuel would have to name a guardian. And that, of course, hadn't happened. Lord, why hadn't she taken care of that before now?

Wynne rose and opened a cabinet, locating the brandy. She poured herself two fingers' worth in a crystal snifter and downed it in one gulp. It burned, but it served the purpose she intended. Her head cleared and her tense muscles relaxed.

Drew visited Samuel last night, she mused. And now Samuel was dead.

Drew wanted to marry her, of that she was certain. And always she could use the excuse of already being married. No more. She was a widow. Had Drew become so desperate that he would kill Samuel? The thought was abhorrent, yet not entirely unrealistic. He'd been angry enough to kill Barton MacClintock.

Drew returned to the kitchen for lunch. The tobacco was all cut and hanging in the curing barns, where it would remain for three to six weeks before it could be shipped. He was dead tired.

"Hello, Annie. What's for lunch?" Drew looked in the bubbling pot the cook swung away from the hearth.

"Beef stew," Annie replied, stirring the thick mixture. "How's the tobacco comin' along?"

"Fine. Just fine," Drew stated, rubbing his neck and shoulders.

"Mistress Carr wants to see ye," Annie informed him, turning to look at Drew over her shoulder. "Said to tell ye as soon as ye came in." Annie covered the pot and swung it close to the fire. "This heat could be the death of a body," she said, wiping her perspiring brow with the large apron.

Annie straightened and looked at the bondsman. "Do ye want a bowl of stew before ye see the mistress?"

"I'm hungry enough to eat the whole pot, Annie," he replied jokingly.

"Sit yerself down, then. I'll have it for ye in just a minute."

"What else is happening?"

Annie removed some pewter bowls from the cabinet. "We had some excitement this mornin'." She placed the bowls on the table, along with spoons and a mug of cider for Drew. "That Indian servant of Mr. Carr's came here this morning, ranting and raving in that gibberish he speaks. Said he had to see the mistress right away."

"What about?"

"Don't know yet," Annie said, wiping her hands. She used the corner of the apron to remove the iron pot and place it on the table.

Drew stared unseeing at the bowl as Annie dished out the stew. The servant had probably seen him last night when he visited the hunting lodge. Wynne no doubt wanted to reprimand him for looking for Samuel Carr. Well, he had seen Wynne's husband. Just as Wynne had said, Samuel was very ill. Wynne had not lied about that

"Drew?"

He looked up to see Annie gazing questioningly at him. "I said, do ye want anything else?"

"No, Annie, thank you," he replied automatically.

Drew ate quickly and silently, then went immediately to the study. He found Wynne sitting at the desk, staring out the window.

"Annie said you wanted to see me."

Wynne jumped at his voice and turned quickly to the door, where he stood just inside the study. She didn't say anything. Instead, she motioned for him to be seated.

Drew could see that she had been crying. Her beautiful face was so sad. There were faint circles under her eyes and she was still too thin.

"You went to see Samuel last night." It was a statement,

not a question. Her face showed little emotion, just lingering sadness.

"Yes." What else could he say?

"He's dead."

Samuel Carr dead? He'd appeared awake last evening. The Indian servant obviously took excellent care of him.

"Well," Wynne began, "do you have anything to say?"

"What would you like me to say, Wynne? That I'm sorry? I never knew the man, but he was your husband and you felt some affection for him. For your sake, I'm sorry."

"Is that all?"

"No, I must admit that it might be for the best. He was an old man, and a very ill one. Maybe he's better off now," Drew responded quietly.

Wynne took a deep breath and looked at the garden. He followed her gaze, almost able to see heat rise from the dried grass, flowers and trees, shimmering yellow and red in the midday sun. She looked back at him. "Did you kill him?"

It had never crossed his mind—to kill her husband.

"Well, did you?"

"No, love. I did not kill Samuel Carr."

Wynne looked away again, staring out the window.

Drew filled in the silence. "You don't trust me."

"I . . . I'm just not sure."

He bolted out of the chair, angry and frustrated. How could she even think that he could commit such a cold-hearted crime? "Damn it, Wynne. I didn't kill your husband!"

"You had a reason to kill him. You were there last night. He died last night," she recited, just as she would list off the daily assignments to the staff. "You may have thought that I would marry you if Samuel was dead."

"I didn't kill Samuel. I went to the creek last evening to

see if there was any sign of MacClintock's body. There wasn't. While I was there, I thought I'd see if that was where Samuel lived. I saw him and then I left. That's all."

"Tell me you don't still want to marry me. Tell me that you wouldn't get control of Waverley if we married. Tell me that you wouldn't want to be the father of this child I carry!"

"I can't! You know it's all true. I do want to marry you. I don't give a damn about Waverley. I do want this child, but mostly I want you."

Wynne's composure broke. "Samuel's death seems too convenient, too timely to be an accident."

"And so you accuse me?" Drew responded. "I'm to be accused again, convicted without even a trial by a jury of my peers?"

"And who would your peers be?" Wynne cried heatedly. "Thieves and liars. Murderers and highwaymen? Tell me, who can judge you better than I?"

"Your judgement is sadly lacking if you think I could kill a helpless man to gain this," Drew replied, stretching his arms wide to indicate Waverley.

"Maybe it is. I just know that you would have everything to gain and little to lose by Samuel's death."

Trying to control his anger, Drew paced the study. He felt betrayed, more so than when the tavern wench falsely accused him and he was arrested. Because this betrayal was by the woman he loved, and whom he thought really loved him. There was only one way to show Wynne he didn't covet this plantation.

"I can prove that I'm not a convicted highwayman. I can prove that I have no interest in Waverley."

Wynne looked at him skeptically. "What kind of proof could you possibly have?"

"It's obvious that I'll have to show you," he scoffed.

"You know, love, at one time you said you trusted me. You *swore* that you believed me. Was that a lie?"

Wynne shook her head in denial. "No, not then."

Drew's fist hit the desk. "Then why now? What have I done to deserve this?"

"I don't know," Wynne whispered. "I just don't know anymore."

Drew turned around, walking quickly out the door.

"Where are you going?"

"To my room. There's something you must see to believe, I think."

He strode quickly down the hall, through the family parlor, and took the stairs two at a time. He stormed into his room and pulled the bottom drawer of the chest open.

Oblivious to his surroundings, he searched through the papers from the leather envelope. He threw hundreds of pound notes on the bed along with letters. He settled on an official parchment and turned around, startled to see that Wynne had followed him.

"Here. Let me read this to you," he stated coldly. He cleared his throat before beginning. "Let it therefore be known that the charges of robbery against Andrew Philip Leyton, Baron Rother, Lord-Lieutenant of East Sussex, having no basis in fact, are hereby dismissed, and that Lord Leyton is to be considered free and without implication regarding this matter."

Wynne staggered back against the doorframe. "When did you get that?" she asked in a small voice.

"Do you remember Henry Fielder?"

"Yes," she whispered.

"He is a solicitor hired by my father. He was to find me and return me to England."

"But that was . . . over a month ago."

Drew laughed cruelly. "Yes, over a month. I've been free

to leave at any time." He turned to the bed and indicated the currency scattered over the quilt. "My father even sent a ship to fetch me back to London."

"Your father?" Wynne asked softly.

"Yes, my father, the Earl of Morley," Drew answered. "You do remember my saying I was the youngest son? Well, he takes care of all his children."

He saw her sag against the doorframe but he was so angry that it barely registered.

"Your father . . . an earl?"

"Yes," Drew returned coldly, "my legitimate father."

"Oh, God," Wynne whispered.

"It's a little late for prayer," Drew scoffed. "And let me set you straight on some other issues also." He turned away to fold the parchment and letters, then calmly stacked the pound notes back in the envelope. "I don't need Waverley to make me a wealthy man. My estate in England makes more than this plantation each year. I could best your profits with one good cargo on my ships. So you see, *love,* I don't need your property. I have plenty of my own."

Over the blood pounding fiercely in his head, Drew heard a thud and turned quickly. Wynne's limp body draped across the floor, her head resting at an odd angle against the doorframe. "God, *nooo!*" he yelled.

21

Drew sat in a chair beside Wynne's bed, his hand holding hers so that he could feel the beat of her pulse. She lay so still; only her shallow breathing indicated that life still flowed in her veins. Her pale face appeared almost as white as the sheets, and her hair, which usually shone like gold, cascaded over the pillow in dull, unbound strands.

She had been like this since their confrontation in the early afternoon. He rubbed the blue-green veins in the back of her hand and willed his strength to flow through his fingertips into her unconscious body.

He had sent a man on a fast horse to Charles City for a doctor right after she collapsed. John told him it would take about six hours, so they should be returning any time. In fact, he thought, glancing at the clock on the mantel, they should already have been here.

While the doctor was here, Drew intended for him to look at Samuel Carr and certify his death. He wanted proof that the man died of natural causes—that he'd been ill for years. Wynne would no doubt be furious, but it was the truth. He wanted no more lies between them.

He only wanted her to get well, to smile at him again and speak his name with love. Because despite her accusations, he couldn't believe that she really meant them. No, she loved him, and their love wasn't so fragile that one argument, even a serious one, would destroy it.

Drew moved his chair closer, never releasing her hand. His eyes moved over her body, clad in a soft white nightgown and covered by a light sheet against the night air. His other hand followed, resting on the swell of her stomach. "Dear Lord, please don't let her lose this child," he prayed. He bowed his head onto the mattress, mentally and physically exhausted.

Sometime later he was awakened by the door opening. He blinked, disoriented at first. Then he saw John standing just inside the bedroom with a man Drew assumed was the doctor. He was short, fatherly in appearance, with eyeglasses perched on his nose. Drew rose stiffly from the chair, reluctantly letting go of Wynne's hand and removing his hand from her rounded stomach.

"Mr. Drew, this is Dr. Adams."

"Doctor," Drew said softly, afraid of wakening Wynne. "I was expecting you some hours ago."

"I was tending one of my patients. Couldn't be avoided. Now, what seems to be the problem here?"

So Drew told him about Wynne, about all the things she had been through: the stress of managing the plantation, the conflict with MacClintock, the pregnancy. He left out some of the more scandalous details and he didn't mention Samuel's illness or death.

At the end of Drew's monologue, the doctor stood near the bed, looking down at Wynne, and placed his hand over her stomach, pressing gently. He glanced at Drew, his grey eyes shrewd. "Where's the lady's husband?"

"Dead. He died last night or early this morning. I want you to examine his body—to tell us why he died."

"Do you suspect something unusual about his death?"

"No, I don't." Drew looked down at Wynne's white face. "But she does."

"I think you should tell me the rest of this story."

Drew did, as tactfully as possible. He told the doctor about being transported to Virginia. He admitted that Samuel had been ill for years, but asked the doctor to examine Samuel's body for himself.

"I will, but first I want to examine the lady a little closer."

Sometime later, the doctor made his way slowly down the stairs. Drew rushed forward to meet him in the hall. He no longer cared who knew about his feelings for Wynne. He was tired of pretending to be nothing more than her bondsman or overseer. It was time for everyone to know who he was and that he would soon be her husband.

He and the doctor talked for some time in the study. He insisted that Dr. Adams spend the night since the hour was so late, and after the man had retired to one of the guest rooms, Drew returned to Wynne's bedroom, where he resumed his vigil—one hand holding hers, the other resting lightly on his child.

Wynne came awake slowly, disoriented and feeling battered. She opened her eyes and saw the canopy of her bed, illuminated by a candle that created a golden glow in the night. She felt a weight on her abdomen and sensed Drew's presence before she turned to look beside the bed.

His dark head rested on the white sheet, one hand grasping hers and the other resting on her stomach. His breathing was deep and regular. She dared not move.

How long had he been there? For that matter, how long had she been unconscious? She tried to focus on the clock; it was past midnight.

Drew moaned in his sleep, his head turning on the bed and his hands tightening their grasp. Wynne involuntarily shuddered.

He awoke immediately, sitting upright and staring at her. There was no smile or greeting from him, only the intense stare that looked as though he could see into her soul. Wynne looked away and tried to fight back the tears.

Slowly, as though he knew she was frightened, he reached over, stroked her cheek, and turned her head to him with the lightest touch. He whispered, "Wynne, how do you feel?"

She tried to turn away, but his fingers exerted a gentle pressure. God, could he see how she regretted what she'd said? How scared she was? It was too much—Samuel's death, Drew's hateful revelations. She blinked once, then twice. A tear ran down her face and dropped to the pillow.

"Don't cry, sweetheart," Drew said softly. "I'm so sorry I made you ill."

"No . . ." Wynne whispered, her voice breaking. "May I have some water, please?"

Drew released her hand and she watched him pivot away from the bed. A porcelain pitcher and goblet waited on the nightstand, along with a damp cloth folded on a lacquered tray and a brightly burning candle. Drew poured some water and moved back beside her.

Placing a strong arm behind her, he lifted her shoulders slightly and brought the glass to her lips. She couldn't meet his eyes; she couldn't stand to see the accusation she knew would be there.

When she finished drinking, Drew lowered her carefully. "Can you talk now?"

Wynne nodded. "I don't know what to say," she murmured.

"Say you forgive me, love. Say that you'll feel better soon."

Wynne turned her head and slowly raised her eyes to meet his caring look. She shook her head, tears threatening again. "There's nothing to forgive. It's I who must ask for forgiveness."

"You were upset. You didn't know what you were doing."

Wynne shook her head again. "No, you're wrong. I knew what I was doing."

Drew rose and walked to the window. "What are you saying?"

Wynne was silent for a long time. Drew turned around and looked at her, his eyes glowing in the candlelight. Finally, she spoke in a low voice that was tinged with sorrow.

"I *believed* you might have killed Samuel. I honestly did. I've always believed the worst, and now . . ." She ended in a sob, unable to continue.

Drew moved back to the bed. She couldn't repress the urge to cringe, to shrink away from his penetrating stare.

"What are you really saying? Do you still believe that I murdered a helpless man?"

Wynne would not meet his eyes. "I don't know," she whispered. "I don't think so in my heart, but when I think about it rationally . . ."

"Which will you accept—your heart or your head?"

"I don't know! I've been terrible to you, and now this," Wynne sobbed.

"Please don't cry," Drew said, sitting down. "Please, you'll only make yourself ill."

"I can't help it," Wynne moaned. "I've always told myself you were only after Waverley. That you wanted to better yourself by marrying me. Don't you see? It made it easier to understand, whether it was true or not."

"And now?" Drew asked. "What do you think now?"

"That you really wanted to marry me. That you didn't want Waverley at all. And that I've made a terrible mistake by bringing you into all this." She gestured with her hand, then let it fall limply to the mattress.

"It's all my fault," she continued. "It seemed so simple—so foolproof. Buy a bondsman. Get pregnant. Have a child. Free him, send him away." Wynne scornfully laughed. "Simple? I had no idea what I was doing. And now I've hurt you, Samuel is dead, and I will bring a child into this world who will never know his father." Wynne's voice broke and she buried her face in the pillow.

"It doesn't have to be like that," Drew calmly stated.

Wynne sobbed harder.

Drew tried to turn her, to face her. She resisted. "Wynne, listen to me. You *will* marry me. Our child will have my name."

Wynne denied his offer, shaking her head. "No," she cried, "I can't marry you now. Don't you see? Your offer is made out of compassion and you could never really trust me."

"Our love isn't so fragile that it would cease to exist."

"No."

"Think of the baby, Wynne. The child will need a father."

"No, please, I can't!" Wynne's voice rose in near hysteria.

"Love, please calm down," Drew said softly. "We won't speak of it any more tonight. You need to rest and regain your strength." He straightened the sheets and pulled her hair free, arranging it on the pillow.

"I'll leave you now. Millie can stay with you if you would like."

"No, that's not necessary," Wynne murmured. "I'll sleep now."

"Do you want anything else?"

Yes, she felt like crying. I want to start over. I want to pretend none of this ever happened. But it was real. And she had caused it by her selfish, childish wants.

How many people had been hurt because of her actions? How many more would be hurt? It was almost more than she could bear. Please, please leave before I start crying again, her mind screamed.

"I'll let you sleep," Drew said. He turned down the lamp on the table and moved to the door. Wynne could barely see him in the dim light of the single candle. "I'll be in my room if you need me."

"Thank you . . . for everything," Wynne whispered.

Drew turned, walked out, and closed the door softly.

Dr. Adams spent the night, checked on Wynne again the next morning, and then talked to Drew.

"I think she's simply exhausted and in shock." He shook his balding head. "Rest will be her best medicine—that and good food. Perhaps a bit of red wine would help."

"What about the baby?" Drew asked.

"The baby is well settled and doesn't seem to have suffered."

"When do you think she'll feel better again?"

"It's hard to say. If she doesn't get a fever . . ."

"What do you mean, a fever?"

"Well, sometimes when the mind is disturbed, a brain fever develops. I don't believe her condition is that serious."

That gave Drew another possibility to worry over. Nonetheless, he told the doctor that Samuel Carr must be examined and a certificate of death provided.

Samuel's body had been moved to the cold cellar below the kitchens, so the doctor went down there with Drew and John in attendance. After examining the dead man, the doctor sent for Sethti, explaining that he wanted to question him about the dosage of medication Samuel was receiving for his condition.

The Indian servant arrived within the hour, obviously nervous. After asking only a few questions, Dr. Adams patted the man on the shoulder and sent him back to the hunting lodge, explaining that the burial could take place as soon as arrangements could be made.

"So, Dr. Adams, what caused Samuel Carr's death?" Drew asked as they walked back to the study.

"Mercury poisoning. It built up in his system over the years. The servant said he'd been treating him with it ever since they left India, some twenty years ago. His gums were slightly blue and his teeth loose. It's a sure sign of poisoning. Of course, if that hadn't killed him, the syphilis would have. Poor man must have lived through hell." The doctor shook his head.

Drew released a long-held breath. At least no one was responsible for Samuel's death.

"I've got to wonder about the health of the lady, though. I didn't examine her for it, but if her husband was infected, then——"

"She's not," Drew stated firmly.

"Sometimes it's not so apparent. The baby——"

"She's not," Drew stated again. He stopped on the walkway, making sure he was out of hearing of anyone. "She and her husband had never been intimate. There is absolutely no chance she has the disease."

"So that's the way of it."

"My intention is to marry her as soon as possible."

"Then she is agreeable?"

Drew shifted uncomfortably. "Not at the moment."

The doctor placed a fatherly hand on Drew's shoulder. "Let me give you some advice. If you want to keep this quiet, marry her before the baby is born and declare the child as yours. If you wait until after the birth, the child will be considered Samuel Carr's unless declared a bastard. I don't think you want that."

"No, not that."

"The colonial laws are less strict than those of England. There, a fine might be assessed along with public humiliation. Here, a simple statement is usually accepted if the parents marry."

"I'm well familiar with the English laws. However, I haven't had the opportunity to talk to anyone about the colonial edicts. I believe I'll send someone to Williamsburg, to the law firm that represents my father's interests."

"Might be a good idea."

"She'll see reason soon enough. She has an extremely logical mind." Which had gotten her into this situation in the first place, Drew thought.

The doctor nodded. "Make the lady see that it's the right thing to do. She's apparently been trying to do too much. She must have felt under so much pressure, and quite frankly, I can't think too highly of you for contributing to her anxiety by having an affair with her when—"

"Don't assume things you know nothing of, Doctor."

"I know you claim the child."

"That child is all she wanted," Drew admitted. His eyes scanned the house, the gardens, the fields visible behind the fencerows. "And this plantation. She didn't want a man in her life. She's had control over her life too long to trust anyone else."

"Well, convince her any way you can. You know, it's

been said that more flies are taken with a drop of honey than a gallon of vinegar."

"I'll remember that, Doctor," Drew said.

Smythe and Faye arrived late that afternoon. Drew saw the wagon turn the corner of the house and stop near the kitchen. When he walked out of the study to intercept Smythe, several servants were unloading the purchases. Faye, with a show of authority, supervised the disposition of each bundle, bag, and box. Smythe looked on with barely concealed interest. Drew would have found it amusing if he were not so distressed.

"Smythe," Drew greeted the butler tersely, "I need to speak with you immediately."

Drew turned away and marched into the study, confident that the other man would follow. When Smythe hurried into the study a few minutes later, Drew was sitting behind the desk, feeling perfectly at home there. In front of him were two packets of documents. Smythe faced the desk and raised an eyebrow.

"Samuel Carr is dead," Drew stated without emotion. "It happened three days ago. Mercury poisoning, Dr. Adams diagnosed."

"And Mistress Carr? How is she taking it?"

Drew looked away from the butler's steady gaze. "She . . . she is not well. Mr. Carr's death did not affect her as much as . . ."

"Yes, Mr. Leyton? What else has happened?"

Drew took a deep breath. "She thought I killed the man, Smythe."

There was silence in the room after Smythe's sudden indrawn breath. His eyes flared briefly, then settled with his usual decorum on Drew. "And are you guilty, Mr. Leyton?"

"It seems we've had this conversation before." He paused and rubbed his furrowed brow. "No, I did not kill him. The Indian servant saw me looking in the window the night he died. He told Mrs. Carr. She assumed the rest." Drew shrugged. "We argued . . ."

"You and the Indian servant?"

"No. Mrs. Carr and I had an argument over her assumption that I would be capable of killing her husband. There's something else I must show you."

Drew opened the leather envelope that contained his freedom. He handed Smythe the parchment proclaiming his innocence, then watched as the butler read the document from the House of Lords.

Smythe's eyes raised to meet Drew's. "There is more?"

Drew nodded. "When I told her who I was—that I was free—the shock was too much for her. She fainted. I had Dr. Adams from Charles City come out and he confirmed that she was suffering from exhaustion and shock."

Smythe nodded.

"She blames herself for too much, Smythe. She feels guilt, of all things, over the way I have been treated. She is quite unreasonable on that point. And there are other circumstances . . ."

"Which I suppose you would not care to disclose?" Smythe finished for Drew.

"That's right. Suffice it to say that she has rejected my proposal of marriage."

Smythe's eyebrows raised another notch. "Then what is to be done?"

"She cannot run this plantation, not in her present condition. She hasn't been out of bed all day, since she fainted yesterday."

Drew walked over to the brandy decanter and poured himself a healthy portion. He took a sip, then another, before continuing. "I will stay. I still intend to marry her, despite her objections." She needs me, Drew wanted to shout, but he sipped his drink in silence.

"I will go up to see the mistress now," Smythe said.

"I'll go up with you," Drew replied and drained his brandy.

The two men left the study, curiously united in their concern for the woman lying upstairs.

The next days were two of the longest Drew had ever experienced. Wynne hadn't left her bed except to tend to her body's needs, and then only with help from her maid. It was as if the vibrant spark of life was gone from her eyes, the laughter was gone from her lips, and love had fled her heart.

Drew had sent for Lady Grayson, thinking that she was the one person who might be able to make Wynne see the importance of accepting his proposal—if not for herself, then for the child and Waverley. Lady Grayson arrived just before the burial of Samuel Carr, so Drew didn't have time to talk to her about Wynne's condition right away.

Wynne hadn't felt well enough to attend the small funeral that Smythe had arranged for her husband. The servants and Drew were in attendance, along with Lady Grayson. It was a quiet, solemn affair at the family graveyard located on the land that had belonged to Wynne's father, Colonel Palmer. Samuel was laid to rest beside Nanny Richards and Smythe ordered a large stone marker from Charles City to mark his grave.

Drew met with Lady Grayson that evening in the parlor, explaining Wynne's condition, the details of Samuel's death, and his changed status. She seemed to take it all with inherent grace, her concern for Wynne evident in her desire to help.

"You can say what you like, but I believe that the truth is that you are both two healthy young people who found yourselves together. Now, don't start denying it again. I don't doubt that you love her and that she loves you. My advice is to woo her with loving kindness and passionate declarations."

"She already rejected my offer of marriage," Drew scoffed.

"And how did you make this offer? On bended knee with flowers and kisses? Or did you make it sound like a business arrangement that was the best thing all around?"

"Well, I . . ."

"Just as I thought," Lady Grayson said, smiling. She rose from her chair. "I will go up and see her now. You stay here and think about how to win her love permanently." She walked toward the door, but stopped before entering the hall. "Good arguments never won a heart. If you truly love her, then make her see that. A woman doesn't want to be considered a burden, nor does she wish to marry simply for the sake of a child. Convince her, Drew. Don't be so honorable and logical that you lose sight of why you are in this situation in the first place."

Drew watched her leave, thinking of what she had said and what Dr. Adams had said. Wynne loved him, but in all these months, she hadn't let her love override her desire for independence. What would sway her now?

Wynne lay abed after Lady Grayson left, trying to focus on what her new neighbor and friend had said about why the marriage should occur. Lady Grayson admitted that she knew Drew's family in England, but she hadn't said anything before because she had promised Drew.

But, a small voice of reason asked, what if you had

known? Would you feel any different about him, love him any more? No, but that wasn't the point. She'd always been able to rationalize that he was unsuitable, that he only wanted Waverley. That was no longer true.

She'd used him, tried to place him from her mind and heart, accused him repeatedly of everything from avarice to murder, yet still he remained. Wynne turned, burying her head beneath a pillow.

Yet the images would not be blocked. Without the soft light of afternoon to distract her, she was free to remember . . . and to feel. She recalled the way Drew's blue eyes burned in passion, the way his lids lowered as he bent to kiss her, the way his nostrils flared in anger, and the way his lips softened in amusement. He was a complex man: a man who was versatile and adaptable. And he had been hers ever so briefly.

Unacknowledged, a spark of life began to burn. She'd truly lived and experienced a range of emotion she wasn't aware of previously. And she'd loved, and still loved, a man who did what he thought was best. The father of her child was a man of whom she could be proud.

If she married Drew, people would talk. They would say that Drew was the father of her child even if she denied it. By marrying him, she would only be confirming their suspicions, and she had no intention of letting her child grow up with the scorn of society. She knew firsthand how much that hurt. She could not subject her child to that.

And if she kept putting Drew off, kept refusing to marry him, eventually he would go away. He would go back to England, to his family and title and land. They might never forget each other, but there would be the memories, and they could each start their lives again.

She must get well, for herself and for the child. She'd grieved long enough for Samuel; she'd felt guilty over her treatment of Drew. It was time to rejoin the world.

Wynne rolled over, blinking in the light. She'd get up, order a bath, dress, and have dinner downstairs. She would show Drew and Lady Grayson that she was going to be fine.

She swung her legs over the side of the bed and sat up slowly, awkwardly. Bracing one hand on the nightstand and pushing up from the mattress with the other, she tried to rise. The room swam alarmingly; tiny lights exploded in her head.

She moaned as she eased back on the mattress, then collapsed against the pillows. She couldn't even get out of bed, much less convince anyone that she could manage the plantation. Helpless, as weak as a newborn kitten, they would all say that she was foolish to ignore Drew's offer. Marry him, they would say, and let him bear the burden. She wanted to scream. How could Drew love her after all she had done, all she had said? And how could she marry him, never knowing why he gave her his name?

22

Wynne sat in the front parlor, watching the approach to Waverley for Drew's return. It had been five days. She'd expected him back from Williamsburg in four. She'd hoped he would return in three.

She returned her attention to the baby's gown, which she embroidered in blue and yellow. She was reluctant to hope, but she really wished for a son. Someone who would inherit Waverley and be able to hold it for the future.

Wynne smoothed her hair back, then stretched. The child seemed to grow daily. She felt awkward and uncomfortable much of the time. She could no longer ride. She looked in the mirror and saw only her expanding middle.

The sound of a coach approaching stopped her musings. She folded the baby's gown quickly and placed it on her chair, then hurried to the window to look at the drive. A strange carriage was slowing down. It was a fine vehicle; its glossy blue lacquer was highlighted with gold trim. The matched greys pulling the vehicle were almost as fine as the carriage itself.

Wynne smoothed her hair and shook the wrinkles from her high-waisted gown as she stood at the window. Outside, the breeze swirled fallen leaves of gold, orange, red, and brown. The autumn sun was bright and Wynne squinted as it reflected off the glare of the carriage. She waited impatiently for her visitor to alight.

The carriage stopped. Several moments passed before the door was opened a crack. Then it was flung back and a gentleman's leg appeared. Wynne concentrated on the well muscled calf and slowly raised her eyes. It was Drew, looking for all the world like the aristocrat he was.

Her breath stopped and she again felt the folly of her schemes. He was in his element now, standing proud beside a fine coach, dressed in splendor with confidence etched in his fine features. He didn't belong in a backwoods plantation, giving in to the whims of a woman who had caused him such grief.

His gaze came to rest on the house and Wynne knew the moment he noticed her standing at the window. His expression was carefully controlled as his eyes rested on her. Her figure almost in profile, she held the drapes back with one hand and had the other resting over her middle. She could almost imagine being his wife, eagerly awaiting his return as she nurtured their child. It was a dream: nothing more than a foolish dream, she knew, just as her earlier plan had been.

Wynne noticed his frown and assumed that he wasn't happy to see her. She turned away from the window, tears brimming in her eyes. Without further thought to the small gown she had been embroidering or his return, which she had so eagerly awaited, she fled up the stairs before Smythe came forward to open the doors.

Drew burst inside, bringing with him the suppressed anger and frustration of an eight-hour carriage ride.

"How is she?"

"Improved," Smythe replied in a tentative voice. "Although I believe she is still . . ."

"Still what, man? Has she been ill?"

"No, not ill. She just doesn't seem to be herself."

Drew walked into the front parlor. The baby's gown was on the chair where she'd left it. He retrieved it, fingering the tiny stitches and smiling at the softness of the fabric.

"Mistress Carr went upstairs," Smythe informed him.

Drew turned back to the carriage, still holding the gown. Minutes later he returned with a large package that was swathed in protective muslin. He paused for a moment, as if undecided where to place it. Finally, he turned back to the front parlor and set the package down on a marble-topped table by the fireplace.

"Please see that this is not disturbed, Smythe. Have those other packages taken to the family parlor. And ask Mistress Carr if she will join me for dinner."

"Yes, sir."

Drew left, his strides sure and steady as he headed for the study. "I do not wish to be interrupted," he announced over his shoulder.

"Yes, sir," Smythe replied again as Drew closed the door to the study.

Late that evening, after Wynne joined Drew for a rather strained and silent dinner, Drew asked the household staff and Riley to join him in the family parlor. Wynne apprehensively agreed to come, not knowing what Drew had in mind.

However, when she saw the packages, she guessed at least part of his intent. He stood by the staircase while the servants filed into the room and perched on the chairs and settees. They looked uncomfortable and uncertain, while

Drew smiled at them like a benevolent lord.

Wynne was the last to be seated. When she had settled her skirts of gold and brown and raised her eyes to Drew in question, he began to speak.

"I wanted to bring you together tonight to thank you for making my stay at Waverley pleasant, in spite of the circumstances of my arrival here in the colonies. This doesn't mean that I'm leaving Waverley. I wanted to explain my status and express my gratitude.

"I was originally transported here as a bondsman based on accusations of robbery in England. I was innocent of those charges. It has now been proved that I was indeed not guilty and all charges were dismissed. I'm a free man.

"Now that Mr. Carr has passed away, I realize that some of you may be apprehensive about the future of Waverley. I've contacted the solicitors of my father, the Earl of Morley, here in Virginia. They have assured me that Waverley will be safe from any interference. You may rest assured that your positions here are as secure as they were before Mr. Carr's death. That is, of course, based on Mrs. Carr's approval of your performance," he added with a meaningful glance at Wynne. "She is, and shall continue to be, your mistress.

"I do not intend to encroach upon her authority. However, Mrs. Carr has been under much stress and it is my only intention to help with the administration of the estate in whatever way I can. So"—Drew stepped away from the stairs and went to the table where the packages were stacked—"I have a token of my thanks for each of you."

Drew passed out the presents to the startled servants. First he handed a box to Annie. Wynne perched on the edge of her seat so she could watch Annie open the package. Inside was a beautiful and frivolous bonnet, as cheerful in appearance as Annie was in disposition. A matching shawl completed her gift. She grinned and tearfully hugged Drew, who looked gracious but uncomfortable.

Next he presented smaller boxes to both Faye and Millie. Inside were small vials of cologne and scented soap. Both maids thanked him and compared fragrances.

For Riley he had purchased a bottle of the finest French brandy, no doubt illegally imported into the colony. Wynne said nothing about that, however, and smiled at the childlike expression of glee on Riley's weathered face.

Smythe seemed surprised to receive a gift and even more unsure of how to respond. He very carefully lifted the lid of the inlaid wooden box and removed a pipe, meticulously carved to resemble a lion's head. It was a beautiful work of art as well as a functional masterpiece.

"How did you know?" Smythe inquired.

Drew shrugged. "The smoke from your room late at night. I recognized it as pipe tobacco."

"Thank you," Smythe solemnly said.

"You're welcome."

Wynne looked around the room at the smiling faces of her staff. Sitting there together, she could almost believe they were a family. Drew had a way about him that appealed to almost everyone.

She stood after a moment. "Thank you for coming tonight. Please feel free to stay as long as you would like. I will say good night." Drew caught up to her before she had started up the staircase. "Did you think I had nothing for you?"

"Me?" Wynne replied, stunned. "No . . . that is, I didn't expect anything."

"Well, I brought you something anyway. I thought perhaps we could retire to the front parlor." Drew took her arm and guided her away from the stairs, through the main hall, and into the more formal room.

He steered her toward the pale green brocade settee and then retrieved the large package from the marble-topped table. A jumble of emotions raced through her. It had been so long since someone had given her a gift. Mostly, however, she was curious.

He stood there in front of her, obviously unsure of where to put the box. He finally placed it on the settee beside her, told her to wait a moment, and moved the table directly in front of her. He put the box back on the table and sat down beside her.

"I have something to ask you, love," Drew said softly, taking her hand.

She shivered slightly, but didn't know whether it was from the chill in the room or his touch. "Yes?" she replied, slightly breathless.

"Will you marry me?"

Wynne shook her head in denial. "I already told you—I can't."

"Listen, Wynne. Samuel Carr is gone. I know that the usual period of mourning is not observed here in the colonies. I would be able to get a special license in any case."

"I can't." Wynne turned to him. "You don't really want to marry me. I know that. You just want to do the right thing."

"It's more than that and you know it."

Wynne shook her head again. "I've done some terrible things. I've lied, schemed, broken my marriage vows, killed a man . . ."

"No, you didn't."

"I've done all those things; you know I have."

"You didn't kill a man."

"Drew, why are you doing this to me?" she sobbed.

"You saw me stab . . . him. Is that the kind of woman you want to marry?"

Drew pulled her into his arms. "What? A loyal, courageous woman who would kill to save the man she loves? Yes, that's exactly the kind of woman I want for my wife."

"No . . . it's no good. I can't marry you! You can't love me."

Drew stroked her back. "Please don't get upset. I can't understand your reasons. I know we can have a future together."

Wynne whispered into his chest, "I'm sorry. I'm so sorry."

Drew stroked his fingers along her cheek and tilted her face up. He looked long and deep into her eyes, placing one finger over her lips. "Don't say any more, love." He paused, outlined her lips, then replaced his finger with his firm mouth and kissed her gently.

They clung together for only a moment before Wynne pulled away. Her reaction to him was as startling now as it had been over six months ago.

Drew looked at her silently for another moment, then reached for the package. "I have something for you." He pulled off the muslin cover.

Wynne's hands covered her cheeks and she let out a gasp. "It's beautiful!"

"Look inside," he coaxed.

Wynne sat forward on the settee and tentatively opened the etched glass doors of the jewel case. A melody drifted through the room, and Wynne turned to him, her heart singing along with the notes. "Do you know the music?"

"No," Drew shook his head. "I'm sorry to say that I don't." He smiled at her. "Open the top drawer."

She did so, slowly, afraid of what she would find. When

the emerald ring was revealed, Wynne jumped back, startled by the magnificent gems.

Drew chuckled. "I've never known a woman to react so violently to jewels. Here," he said, reaching for the ring. "I was hoping this could be a betrothal ring, but it can just as well be . . ."

"No!" Wynne exclaimed. "I mean, I can't accept this."

"Of course you can." He slipped it on her finger.

"No, really, I can't," Wynne insisted, gazing with longing at the brilliant stones on the third finger of her left hand. "You shouldn't have."

"Well, I did," Drew responded. "Open the other drawers."

"No . . . you didn't," Wynne said.

Drew grinned.

So Wynne opened each drawer of the jewel case, not believing that these jewels were intended for her. It was more than she could ever expect in a lifetime, much less at one sitting. And the pieces! Drew had obviously chosen each one with care and love. There was a three-strand choker of pearls and a beautifully carved cameo brooch.

When the last drawer was opened and Wynne saw the magnificent sapphire and diamond necklace, she gasped aloud. Tears came to her eyes when she gazed at the stones. Blue, just like his eyes. She clutched the necklace to her breast.

"Don't cry, love. They're only pieces of jewelry."

"Only pieces of . . . ? They're wonderful! But, Drew, I cannot accept them. There's a fortune in jewels there," Wynne protested, gesturing at the case. "I can't accept them."

"You can and you will," Drew insisted. "If you don't want them, they're yours to sell, give away, whatever."

"But I could never!" Wynne's mind rebelled at the thought of parting with anything Drew gave her.

"Then keep them," he murmured, placing another light kiss on her lips. "I want you to have them."

"You have given me so much," Wynne whispered.

"And you've given me much also," Drew insisted gently. "Your tenderness and care," he murmured against her slightly parted lips. "Your innocence," he touched his lips to hers. "A child," his hand moved to her waist, bringing her close. "And more, if you would admit it." Drew kissed her fiercely, passionately, desperately.

A whimper escaped her even as she clung to him.

"Don't cry. I can't stand it when you cry."

"I'm sorry," Wynne sobbed. "I seem to cry at the slightest thing." Like confessions of undying love and a fortune in jewels, her mind added.

"It's all right," Drew soothed, rubbing her back. "Everything will be fine."

"I want to believe you, truly I do," she confessed.

"Then just get well and don't worry so much. You want to have a healthy baby, don't you?"

"Oh, yes," Wynne sighed. "More than anything else."

Drew picked up the sapphire necklace, placing it around her neck and clasping it efficiently. The gold was cold against her skin at first, but as she tenatively touched it, it began to warm, almost as if it was a part of her.

"It doesn't exactly match this gown," Drew remarked.

"It's lovely." Wynne traced the flower patterns of the jewels. "You shouldn't have . . . but I must admit that I love everything you gave me."

"Even the child?"

Wynne looked deeply into his sapphire-blue eyes. "Especially the child." She kissed him briefly and would have broken away, but his hands grasped her arms and held her close.

"Wynne, there's something I have to tell you."

His face was suddenly serious, no longer animated with expectation as it had been when she opened the jewel box drawers. "What is it?"

"I was serious when I said you hadn't killed a man." He paused, his eyes intense, making her suddenly very uncomfortable. "Barton MacClintock is alive."

She felt the blood drain from her face. The room blurred for a moment and all she felt were Drew's hands holding her securely. "How?" she whispered.

"I don't know, love. I only know that I saw him in Williamsburg. I think he saw me too. I tried to follow him, but he got away."

"Then you can't be sure. Maybe it was a man who looked something like—"

"It was him," Drew stated firmly. "He was across the street from me, then he crossed and started off toward Capitol Landing Road. It was MacClintock."

"No . . . I stabbed him. He slipped into the river."

Drew shook his head, then lightly stroked her arms. She was suddenly cold, shivering in the evening air. "I think the boatmen must have put him on the raft. That's why I never found his body, even when I went back to look."

"But he hasn't been here . . . to Waverley." Barton MacClintock alive! The nightmare wasn't over after all.

"My guess is that he's been recuperating from his wound. That would have taken a while."

Wynne shuddered, unable to forget the feel of the knife sinking into his flesh.

"I'm sorry, love. I shouldn't have reminded you of that," Drew murmured, pulling her close, holding her against his chest.

"I don't know what to say," she mumbled into his waist-coat. "You're sure?"

Drew kissed the top of her head. She felt his lips move. "I'm sure."

"He could come back, couldn't he?"

"I think it's very likely."

Wynne wanted to hide, to slink away from all that was happening and pretend this latest threat didn't really exist. But of course she couldn't. Somehow, she had to protect herself . . . and her baby. As if the child knew she was thinking of him, he began to move vigorously.

"The baby—"

"My God, you're not ill! Wynne, I—"

"No, he's just active. Oh, Drew, I'm so scared. Not for myself, but for the child. MacClintock will come here, I know he will. He's a mean man and he'll want revenge." Her voice broke with a sob.

"Wynne, there's only one thing to do. I didn't want to pressure you into this, but marrying me is the best option. You know I can't stay here forever, on Waverley, without people talking about your reputation. I can't pretend to be a bondservant any longer."

"No, that wouldn't be fair," Wynne murmured. Marry him? She had so many good reasons not to do that. But MacClintock! How could she protect herself and the plantation against the man if he were intent on revenge? "But I'd just be forcing you into another situation . . . another problem. I swore I wouldn't do that."

"You're not forcing me, love. I *want* you. I always have; you know that."

"I once called you spoiled. I accused you of thinking you could always get what you want."

"I remember," Drew chuckled.

"Maybe I was right. Maybe you do always get what you want."

"This isn't the way I wanted it to be. I wanted you to

have a choice. But MacClintock could threaten you; he could harm our child. I can't allow that, even if it does take away your freedom of choice."

"I understand," Wynne murmured.

"Does that mean you'll marry me?"

Wynne pulled back so she could look into his eyes. He was so sincere that she didn't doubt his intentions. He'd always been honest with her, except about his true status. Even that she understood. Lady Grayson said Drew was an honorable man, just like his father. He'd always tried to do the noble thing, even if it meant concealing his title and living the life of a bondsman.

"Yes," she finally whispered. "I'll marry you."

He looked at her fiercely for another minute. Were those tears in his eyes, the eyes that matched the necklace that rested heavily around her neck? Then he was crushing her to him, almost pulling her off the seat of the sofa with the force of his embrace.

"You won't be sorry, love. We'll make this marriage work. I'll protect you against MacClintock, against anything or anyone that threatens you or my child."

"I just wanted a simple life, Drew," she murmured against his chest. "I wanted to run this plantation and live in peace with my neighbors. I wanted a child to love and who would love me in return. Was that so much to ask?"

"No, but you deserve so much more. You deserve to have everything, and I'll do my best to see that you do." He pulled back and Wynne wearily met his eyes.

"Waverley will be yours when we marry. That's the way it works." A man's law, she thought bitterly, regardless of the fact that she had successfully run the plantation for six years.

"No. Waverley will continue to be yours."

Wynne shook her head, confused by his words. "What

do you mean, Waverley will be mine? I know you won't physically try to take it away or do anything for spite. I think more of you than that."

"That's not what I mean. When I was in Williamsburg, I drafted a document guaranteeing your control of Waverley. You'll have the power to make all decisions concerning the staff, the crops—everything you now do. If you want me to help, I will, but Waverley will be yours."

"But . . . why?"

Drew smiled tenderly. "Because, love, you are Waverley. You're part of the forests and fields, the sunshine and shadows that make up the land. I can no more envision you separate from this land, this house, than I can now imagine myself living anywhere else."

Did he mean it? He intended them to live here, on her property? "Drew—" she began, then her voice broke.

"Everything will be fine. Together we'll take care of Mac-Clintock. Our child will grow up here, along with all the others we'll no doubt have. I love you, Wynne. I want to spend my life with you, and I want you to feel the same way."

With a quick movement, he stood, then reached down, placed one of her arms around his neck, and lifted her from the couch as if she weighed no more than that jewel case.

"Drew, I'm too heavy," she feebly protested. It felt so good to be held against him, to rest her cheek on his chest and hear his heartbeat pound reassuringly beneath her ear.

"More nonsense." He kissed her forehead. "I'm taking you to bed."

"But—"

"No 'buts.'" He strode out of the formal parlor and into the hallway, passing an open-mouthed Smythe at the foot of the stairs.

"Mistress Carr is retiring, Smythe. Please see that the

jewel case is locked up." Drew climbed a few stairs, then stopped. "And send Millie up in a few minutes."

Wynne relaxed against him. By the time he opened her door and laid her carefully on the bed, she was almost asleep.

"Drew?"

"Yes?"

"I love you."

"I know. I've always known." He kissed her tenderly, gently. "I love you too." Smoothing her hair back where it had pulled loose on the sides, he gazed at her so sweetly that Wynne felt the tears threaten. "Things will work out, Wynne. Everything will be fine."

"I want to believe you. Truly I do."

"Then trust me. Believe in our love. When I had nothing else to believe in, it gave me hope. You are my anchor, Wynne, my port in the storms of life. Always remember that."

"Oh, Drew, that's beautiful. I don't deserve—"

"Sleep, love. We'll talk tomorrow. The solicitor will be here with the agreement, but you need to rest."

"I will," she promised, thinking again of his vow to let her control Waverley. If she had been forced to make a choice, would she have been so willing to give up Waverley for him? He deserved that kind of love, that kind of selfless devotion. Suddenly, she wanted to give him that kind of love, to show him how much she cared. She reached up and grasped his hand.

"Drew, I do love you," she said almost desperately.

"I know love, I know." He held her hand briefly, then placed it back on the mattress.

Wynne heard the sound of the door open just then. Millie stepped into the room. "Mistress Carr?"

Drew stepped back from the bed. "I was just leaving."

"Drew?"

"What?"

How could she express what she felt? It seemed as though what she could say was not enough, that she couldn't express her feelings. Lord, but she was tired . . . and confused. "Nothing. Just . . . good night."

He stood there for another minute, then, as if he chose to ignore Millie's presence, he stepped forward, leaned over, and kissed her forehead. "Everything will be fine, love."

Wynne closed her eyes. She hoped so. She would pray that it were so.

23

The solicitor, Mr. Walter Herschel, arrived the following day. He brought the document guaranteeing Wynne's control of Waverley during her lifetime and to her children in perpetuity. Wynne signed it at her desk in the study, her hand trembling slightly as she gripped the quill. Events had moved so quickly that she was still having difficulty adapting to everything.

At times it seemed unreal that she and Drew could be married at all, much less in six weeks. The banns had to be read for three Sundays prior to the ceremony, a detail that Drew insisted upon to show the highest degree of propriety. And Wynne wanted to wait until after the tobacco shipment left Norfolk so Drew wouldn't be rushed. The ceremony itself would take place in the family parlor. Wynne planned to have a small reception upstairs in the ballroom for the staff. Lady Grayson had agreed to stand beside her at the wedding.

Drew smiled at her as she finished signing the document. "Do you have any questions?"

"No . . . I don't think so." Wynne glanced at the two

men, who looked as though they now expected her to leave. Well, she didn't have any further business with them anyway. "If you'll excuse me, I believe I shall go upstairs."

"Of course, Mrs. Carr. My condolences on the loss of your late husband," Mr. Herschel said, then gave a quick glance at Drew. "And my congratulations upon your impending marriage."

What a strange conversation, Wynne mused. Most widows had at least an adequate period of mourning. She hadn't even ordered any black gowns or dyed any of her new ones. It seemed inappropriate to wear black during her brief betrothal to Drew. But then, she'd never actually felt *married* to Samuel.

"Why don't you rest, love?" Drew said in a concerned voice as he took her elbow and walked her toward the stairs. "If you need me, I'll be in the study for a while, meeting with Mr. Herschel."

"Of course." What other business did he have with the solicitor? If it concerned Waverley, perhaps she should stay. But then, Drew would have told her if it concerned her plantation. And she was still tired. She felt his eyes on her back as she climbed the stairs to her room.

During the next weeks, as the tobacco cured and Wynne recovered from her illness, visitors began to drift toward Waverley. First there were a few matrons from neighboring plantations who came to express their sympathy over Samuel Carr's passing. Others had heard the banns at church. Their eyes widened as they saw Wynne's obvious pregnancy and then fairly bulged as they saw Drew saunter through the house. They quickly excused themselves after remembering other errands, then exchanged shocked glances as they boarded their carriages.

Wynne turned back to the house with a feeling of dread. It seemed the gossip was bound to start. She tried to ignore what she knew would have implications for her child later.

Some of Samuel Carr's business associates came from Williamsburg, never realizing that his widow was in truth the "associate" they had corresponded and invested with over the last several years. Their comments, while outwardly comforting, held a trace of innuendo that Wynne failed to fully recognize. She only knew she felt increasing apprehensive about her situation.

Mr. Herschel came back to meet with Drew one day, and they remained sequestered in the study for most of the afternoon. Drew politely asked the man to spend the night.

The next morning at breakfast, Drew and the solicitor were speaking in hushed tones as Wynne descended the stairs and walked toward the dining room. Her steps slowed as she recognized a few words.

". . . and the rumors are getting more vicious," the solicitor informed him.

There was crash, like a fist hitting the table. Wynne stopped completely, her attention absolute.

"God damn it!" she heard Drew curse. "Those narrow-minded hypocrites!"

There was silence for a moment. Wynne stood perfectly still, half expecting the next words.

"You must admit, my lord, that the situation is rather . . . unusual."

Drew scoffed. "What would they have me do, pray tell? Should I just abandon the lady as her time grows near? Move away just weeks before our wedding? Should I ignore that the tobacco must be transported in less than a month?"

"No, my lord, but perhaps some other arrangements could be made to prevent this gossip. Perhaps a proper chaperone . . . "

"I'm acting as her estate manager," Drew said. "There's nothing improper about that."

"No," the solicitor tenatively responded, "but it is quite unusual for an English lord to act as an estate manager for his former owner while he awaits their marriage."

There was silence. Wynne felt as if she had been kicked in the stomach. Her breath was constricted and there was almost a physical pain around her heart.

She heard the clink of china and silverware as the two men continued their breakfast. Slowly she resumed her walk toward the dining room, composing her features in a mask of cool politeness.

Both men stood when she entered. The solicitor's face was flushed and his look was that of a small child who'd been caught with his hand in a cookie jar. Drew had composed his features, but Wynne could detect anger in the set of his jaw.

"Good morning," she said.

Drew moved around to pull out her chair at the foot of the table. "I believe I will serve myself first," Wynne said, turning away to the sideboard.

Drew waited while she carefully mounded small portions of the hearty food on her plate. He seated her and walked around to his chair.

"You remember Mr. Walter Herschel from Williamsburg?"

"Of course. How are you, Mr. Herschel?" Wynne automatically asked.

"It is a pleasure to see you again, Mrs. Carr."

"Please, don't let me interrupt your conversation."

"Oh, we were just discussing some trivial items."

"Indeed?" Wynne responded with a raised eyebrow as she looked at Drew.

"I was just telling Mr. Herschel about how well you had managed this plantation before my arrival."

"Really?"

"Indeed," Drew replied.

The two men glanced at each other as Wynne began to eat her breakfast.

"How long are you staying, Mr. Herschel?" Wynne asked as she sipped her coffee.

"I'll be leaving as soon as Lord Leyton signs some contracts."

Wynne turned to Drew. "Are they concerned with the tobacco shipments?"

"Yes, they are. I've secured a ship in a caravan that will be leaving Norfolk in three weeks. That gives enough time to finish the curing and packing."

"Is the transport protected?"

"There are five armed ships from His Majesty's fleet accompanying the six merchantmen. It should be very safe."

"Would you go to Norfolk to see the shipment on its way? Since you've made all the other arrangements, you might as well see the shipment off."

Drew looked at her lovingly, but with a question in his eyes. Did he realize he was taking over her plantation just as he had vowed he wouldn't do? She'd always made arrangements for tobacco shipments, at least for the last six years. Let *him* go to Norfolk. She wasn't sure she wanted to be around him anyway. Besides, it would be nice to have the house quiet, to herself.

"I don't think that would be such a good idea."

"Why?"

"Have you forgotten our Scottish friend?"

She blanched at the reminder of Barton MacClintock.

"Yes, I had."

"If you like, I can hire armed guards. It might be a good idea anyway."

"I won't have my home turned into an armed camp!"

"Well, what do you propose?"

"I didn't realize my opinion was important at this late stage," she bitterly replied, noticing the flare of anger in his eyes.

"Wynne . . ." he warned.

"Never mind," she said, setting her cup down. "If you gentlemen will excuse me, I'm feeling rather fatigued." With that she rose and walked from the dining room, back straight and head held high.

Drew waited impatiently for Wynne to join him for dinner that evening. When she didn't arrive, he asked Smythe to make sure she was well.

The butler returned in less than five minutes. "Mistress Carr is sorry she does not feel well enough to join you for dinner. She is having a tray sent to her room."

Drew frowned and returned to the dining room, where he attacked a large serving of beef roast, potatoes, and other vegetables. He declined the delicate custard and retired upstairs, cursing the stubborn woman who refused to confront their problems.

Still, he had to admit as he climbed the stairs, she was unwell. That was why he'd not consulted her on many of the decisions concerning Waverley. He didn't want to add to her problems. Wynne had always been an active and tireless woman who handled large responsibilities with ease. Now she was listless much of the time. She was tired and occasionally irritable. Drew supposed that most pregnant women suffered similar afflictions, but he wasn't certain since he'd never spent a great deal of time around one. His sisters-in-law went into seclusion during their confinement and his brothers never discussed the subject. His sister, although married, had not yet conceived. And with Sally, he hadn't really paid any attention to her until after his son was born, except to ensure she had adequate care.

And so he remained a bachelor who was, typically, ignorant of the subject.

The door to his room was open and a candle was burning on the nightstand. Faye, he supposed, who came each evening to turn down his bed and deliver his laundered or mended clothes, had already been here. There was a movement to his left. Wynne stood in the near-darkness of the candlelit evening, still wearing the soft blue robe with a white knitted shawl draped over her shoulders.

"We need to talk," she said in a hoarse whisper.

Drew paused for a moment, then closed the door and moved forward. "Why didn't you come down for dinner?"

"I . . . wasn't hungry."

"You aren't ill?"

She shook her head. "No, I'm fine."

Drew advanced until he rounded the foot of the bed. Wynne took a step backward. "What are you doing?" she murmured.

Drew didn't answer with words. Instead, he pulled Wynne forward and wrapped his arms securely around her. Her eyes were wide as his lips descended.

"What . . ."

"Be quiet and kiss me," he ordered.

It was a forceful, hungry kiss. The frustration of the past two months surfaced fully as Drew molded his lips over Wynne's, urging her compliance as his tongue traced the

line where her lips were pressed together. They parted with
a moan of surrender from Wynne.

"God, I've missed you," he whispered between kisses.
He turned her slightly, moving toward the bed. Her legs
had just touched the edge of the mattress when she
gasped, "Drew . . . no."

He pushed her gently onto the mattress so she was sitting on the high bed. "Yes," he murmured, nipping at her
neck and twining his fingers through her hair.

He continued the assault on her senses, using insistent
but mild pressure which made her recline on the bed.

"Do you remember this?" he asked as he cupped her
breast and teased the nipple to hardness. "Are you hungry
for this?" he asked as he kissed her deliberately into compliance.

Wynne moaned again, more from her response than in
answer to his demands. Her gown had almost magically
opened past her waist as Drew's roaming hands moved
over her rounded stomach. His lips followed there also,
pressing compelling kisses over each inch of exposed
flesh.

Her hands alternately pressing against his shoulders and
grasping his hair, Wynne was caught in a whirlwind that
lifted away from realities and swirled her thoughts into dis-
jointed sensations.

"The baby," she gasped. "We must not . . . the baby."

Drew's hand moved down, behind her thigh, and he
lifted her leg over his. "I'll be gentle," he promised. "I want
you so much."

"No!" she cried, twisting away. "Stop it!"

Drew rolled to his back and raked a hand through his
hair. His breath was uneven, his obviously aroused body
full of tension and frustrated desire. "Why?"

Wynne struggled to sit up, pulling her gown together as

she scooted off the bed. She walked on shaky legs to the other side of the room. "I came here to talk, not to . . ."

"Make love? I thought we loved each other," Drew scoffed. "You said you'd try," he whispered.

Wynne shivered at his tone. "I'm not sure this is such a good time to talk." Not now. Not when he was in this kind of mood.

Drew sat up and scowled. "What does that mean?"

Wynne took a long, deep breath. "It means that perhaps we should have this conversation at a later date."

"Like when? Before or after the wedding?"

"I'm going back to my room," Wynne responded, walking toward the door.

Drew was up in a flash, grasping her arm. "Don't run away, Wynne. You never were a woman to run away from a problem."

Wynne stopped, closed her eyes for a moment, then opened them and turned to look him fully in the eyes. "Yes, you're right. I've been bold. I've made some rather daring and harmful suggestions, haven't I? I schemed and meddled myself, and you, right into this present situation." She took another breath before continuing. "And look at what happened," she said quietly. "Just look at what has happened," she whispered tearfully.

"Wynne, don't," Drew pleaded. "We've been over this before. Reliving the past won't change anything."

Wynne shook her head. "How can I help but relive the past when I think about MacClintock being alive, possibly wanting to kill me? It rather makes the past an important issue."

"I told you I'd protect you from MacClintock."

"But that's not the only thing, Drew. Just two weeks ago I signed a document that your solicitor wrote, giving me control of Waverley. How many decisions have I made regarding Waverley in the last two weeks? Have I had the opportunity to participate in any discussions of my tobacco crop or its transport to England? No. You've taken care of everything, haven't you?"

"You resent me for trying to make your life easier?" Drew asked incredulously. "I was trying to spare you the burden—"

"It's *my* burden. It's been mine for more than six years.

"I want to share it with you. I thought we were going to share our lives and the life of our child."

"You're not sharing . . . you're taking over!"

Drew walked toward the windows, raking a hand through his hair. "You were so ill. I thought it would be best to just take care of the details."

"Well, next time, ask."

"Does that include sharing your bed? Will I have to ask for that also?"

"I can't talk any more now," Wynne stated. "There are many things we need to discuss, but not now."

"We have to talk sooner or later."

"I know," she whispered, "but not now." Wynne pulled her arm away, opened the door, and walked quickly back to her bedroom, half afraid that Drew would follow her.

24

Michael Grayson arrived the next day before lunch, shivering in the cold weather that had arrived with much bluster the night before. Drizzling rain had continued throughout the morning, turning the dirt to mud. Michael removed his boots near the front door and slipped into some shoes Smythe provided.

Wynne heard him talking to the butler and came down the stairs as fast as possible, relieved to see a friendly face.

"Mr. Grayson," she greeted him, holding out her hand. "It's so good to see you."

"The pleasure is mine." She saw his eyes go almost immediately to her large middle, covered by the thickly quilted petticoats of her high-waisted dress. "Did your mother tell you?"

"She mentioned it," he said, frowning. "Is your child due soon?"

Wynne shook her head. "The end of February. Although I can hardly imagine waiting that long."

"It must be very difficult for you."

"You mean since Samuel's death?"

"Yes, of course."

"Or did you mean something else?" She watched his eyes flash with . . . what? Anger, pity, scorn?

"Is Lord Leyton still here?"

"He's in the study, I believe. He's been helping me since—"

"I heard the banns read."

"Oh."

Michael took a step toward her. "If he's forcing you . . ."

"He's not," a harsh, deep voice said from farther back in the hall.

Wynne whirled around, half afraid, half angry at his tone.

"Mr. Grayson and I were just having a conversation."

"It concerns me," Drew said with finality.

Wynne raised her nose in what she hoped was a dismissing look. "Just because we were talking *about* you doesn't mean that it *concerns* you."

He walked right up to her and placed an arm around her rigid shoulders. "Whatever concerns my betrothed concerns me."

She wanted to hit him, truly she did. Or throw something at him, or yell at him. Was she to have no privacy? He'd taken away the administration of Waverley. Was he now proposing to take away her freedom as well? She'd just see about this!

Wynne pivoted in his grasp and placed a hand on his chest. "Mr. Grayson and I are going to have tea in the parlor, in front of the fire, where my guest can warm himself after his long, cold ride. If you would care to join us, I'm sure we would welcome your company." She turned away then, ordering a fire to be laid in the parlor. Smythe hurried away to do her bidding, no doubt relieved to be away.

Walking toward the parlor, she turned back and asked, "Are you coming, Mr. Grayson?" She looked at Drew and found him watching her, a glow to his eyes and a smile on his lips.

Then, to her dismay, he advanced on her, lifted her hand, and kissed her knuckles. With a gleam in his eye that she knew occurred only when he was teasing or aroused, he whispered, "I'm glad you're feeling better, love."

He released her hand and faced Michael. "Mr. Grayson, I hope you have a pleasant visit. Perhaps I can join you in a while, as soon as I finish my business."

Wynne stood there, amazed at his sudden change in mood, until Drew walked back down the hall and closed the study door. Only after Michael grasped her elbow and asked if she would like to go into the parlor did she allow a smile to break free. Maybe there was hope after all.

After they were seated, the tea served and the fire roaring, Michael told her of the reason for his visit.

"Mother was against disturbing you, but she's taken ill with the same malady that many of the staff suffer from. It doesn't appear to be serious, but involves some congestion of the lungs and a slight fever. With so many of our people unable to work and Mother ill, I thought it best to see if you could spare some servants for a few days."

"Of course I can! I'm glad to be of help. I only wish I could come myself, but . . ."

"I understand."

His remark sounded curt. Again Wynne had the feeling that she was being judged. "I don't understand. If you find my . . . condition so repellent, why ask for my help?"

"Repellent? How can you even think that!"

Wynne shrugged, looking down at the stitching on her

overskirt. "It's obvious you feel uncomfortable around me."

Michael grasped her hand. She looked up into his eyes: caring, sensitive eyes.

"Not you, Mistress Carr," he said softly. "I have great respect for you. No, it's him that I find lacking. He should have known this was a disastrous course. If he tried to ruin your name, he couldn't have found a more effective means."

"The gossip is that bad?"

"You know how people love to talk." Michael shrugged. "Until the next bit of slander comes along, I'm afraid you and Lord Leyton are the current topics."

Wynne looked into the fire, at the dancing, cheerful flames. "This was entirely my idea. You mustn't fault D— Lord Leyton."

"I'm afraid I must."

"I would despair if this became a barrier between my family and yours."

"It won't," he vowed. "As I said, until the next bit of news comes along."

"Then," Wynne added with a sad smile, "perhaps I'll pray for some great, timely scandal."

A spark flared in Michael Grayson's eyes only briefly, but it made Wynne wonder what it meant. "You may just get your wish, my lady."

My lady! She hadn't thought of that. In a few weeks she would be Lady Leyton. It was a staggering idea. She smiled at Michael, but she wasn't sure if it was a reassuring one at all.

Wynne dispatched Faye, some kitchen help and laundresses to the Graysons' plantation that same day, having her wagon follow him back to his home. She left instructions for Faye to be in charge, consult with Lady Grayson, and return when they were no longer needed. She then promptly put Andrew Leyton and Michael Grayson out of her mind.

Or she tried. It was strange, but she didn't feel at all lethargic now. Helping her neighbors, knowing they supported her, had given her reassurance and direction.

Drew's odd behavior in the hallway this morning caused her several moments of trepidation. She knew that now was the time to have the talk they'd been postponing for so long. Drew had gone to the curing barn after having lunch with her and Michael. Since it was now late afternoon and no longer raining, Wynne decided to take a walk. She missed being active. She decided to visit the stables and see the horses. They always lifted her spirits with their soft brown eyes and velvet muzzles.

Drew pulled the chestnut to a halt outside the stable and heard the sound of a woman's laugh from the side of the barn. Tying the reins to a fencepost, he walked around the paddock and saw her.

Wynne's booted feet rested on the lowest rail. She was wrapped in a thick, dark blue wool cloak that swirled in the wind. The hood was pushed back and her unbound hair drifted about her head like sheaves of wheat in the summer breeze. Her delicate nose and ears were pink from the cold air, but her spirits seemed decidedly high as she watched Roger's Folly frolic in the enclosure.

The seven-month-old colt snorted, bucked, and galloped around the small paddock, excited by the crisp air, full of energy and life. A smile formed on Drew's face as he watched Wynne watch the colt.

As if she felt his gaze, Wynne turned and looked at him. "Hello!" she greeted cheerfully.

Drew walked forward until they were standing so close

he could smell the jasmine fragrance that was so much a part of her.

He thought briefly of kissing her, but remembered the last time he'd impulsively tried to make love to her. Perhaps it would be best to go slowly. Lord, but that was a task. It had been so long and she looked so beautiful.

Her eyes sparkling with life, she murmured, "You've been gone a long time."

"Yes, it has been a long time," he replied suggestively.

Wynne blushed and looked away. "I meant to the curing barn. I thought you might be back earlier."

He shrugged. "I wanted to check on the fires. It's going to be a cold night."

"Is the tobacco curing well?"

"As far as I can tell. John swears it is."

Wynne nodded. "He should know."

"Will you have dinner with me tonight?"

"Yes," she answered, watching the colt.

"Will you talk to me tonight?"

"Yes," she again answered, turning to look into his eyes. "Tonight . . ." she said, unconsciously imitating his capitulation so many months ago.

Drew smiled, putting his own meaning to her words. "I'll see you at dinner then." Unable to resist touching her, even if for a brief moment, he lifted her hand and placed a kiss on her palm. "Until later," he said meaningfully and strolled away.

After dessert and coffee, Wynne turned to Drew. "Can we talk upstairs later?"

Drew reached over and took her hand. "How much later? I don't think I can wait much longer, love. The look in your eyes, the smile on your lips— you're driving me crazy."

"Give me thirty minutes," she said, rising from the chair. "Will you come to my room?"

"You know I will," he whispered as he bent to kiss her shoulder. "Thirty minutes seems forever."

Wynne tenderly laid her hand upon his cheek. "Forever is a long, long time." Again, she spoke words that had been said months before.

"Not nearly long enough," Drew looked into her eyes. "I'll be upstairs soon, love."

Wynne walked slowly up the stairs, trying to be as graceful as possible despite her bulk. Did he remember each of their conversations as she did, repeating the words he'd said before to assure her he still felt the same? It was impossible to know for sure, but she had thought it would be just like Drew to show her that way that he still loved her, had always loved her.

Inside her bedroom, she opened the bottom drawer of the chest and removed the pale green gown. Fortunately, the gown was loose and flowing, which would allow her to wear it despite her expanding figure. At first, right after they'd made love, she had thought she'd never wear the gown again. Now she realized that she wanted to erase the memory of how their first time ended and replace it with the promise of their future together.

Drew knocked lightly on the door before turning the knob and entering. Several candles burned, giving a cozy light that was enhanced by the fireplace. Wynne reclined on the bed, propped up by several pillows.

"You look like a bride."

Laughing lightly, she replied, "A fat bride!"

"A beautiful, pregnant bride then." He grinned. His face became more serious as he sat beside her on the bed. "You're even more beautiful than I remembered. I thought of you so much today. About what we've been to each other, the things we've shared. When you were ill for so long, I worried that you might never fully recover, that I might never see you smile again." He took her lips in a loving kiss. "I love you so much."

She responded without hesitation, much to Drew's delight. It was as though the last few months of strain had been swept away.

"Love me, please," she whispered against his lips. She held him tightly, but not with desperation. No, this felt more like passion and love; he gloried in her response.

"It's been too long, love," he whispered in near pain.

"I want you," she simply stated, "and I don't know now why it took me so long to say those words again. I've always loved you. You were right about us all along." She paused for a moment, lying back against the pillows and pulling him to her. "I'm so glad you were right."

Drew moaned and held her tightly, kissing her fiercely. "I love you," he whispered over and over as his hands roamed her body. He restrained his ardor, gently removing her gown, looking into her eyes for any sign of hesitance or discomfort. There was none. Only passion and love were reflected there.

"Oh, Drew, please love me," she pleaded, burying her head beside his on the pillow.

"We have all night, love," he promised.

Wynne's languid body was pliant in his hands as he lifted them higher toward their goal. She watched him from half-closed lids as his steady rhythm caused the most exquisite sensations to build. She saw the muscles of his chest and shoulders tense with the strain of holding back, his arms bulge as he held her hips, his eyes glow from love, and then she gave herself over to release she knew would never be repeated.

* * *

Wynne awoke to the comfort of Drew's embrace. She was firmly nestled against his relaxed body and his deep, steady breath stirred the strands of hair along her nape.

Wynne turned to see the clock on the mantel. Two o'clock. She watched Drew in sleep for several moments, until he stirred and smiled into her serious expression.

"Hello," he murmured sleepily. "You look like an angel."

Wynne smiled in return, thinking he had never looked so handsome as he did now, relaxed and full of love. She wanted this closeness to last forever, and it would, if only they never had to get out of bed again. Her smile faded as she thought of Michael Grayson's comments about gossip and then remembered Henry Fielder's remarks at the breakfast table.

"What's wrong? Are you feeling all right?"

"For Heaven's sake, Drew, must you constantly ask me how I feel?" Wynne teased, trying for the lightest tone possible.

"What is it then?"

She rolled over onto her back, pulling the sheet with her. "Michael Grayson mentioned the gossip that is circulating about us . . . about the banns, my pregnancy—"

"Damn."

"Is that all you can say?"

"Talk like that never lasts. It will be as stale as last year's ale before our child is walking."

"Do you honestly believe that?" Wynne scoffed. "This society has little to gossip about. A scandal like this will *never* die down. Do you hear me? Never," she almost screamed. "My child would never be able to have friends or take his rightful place on Waverley with that stigma attached. And ignoring it will not make it go away!"

"No one would ever question the paternity of *my* child," Drew said angrily.

"See! You admit it's your baby. You'll be admitting it to all the world when we marry. Why can't you see how that will affect our child?"

"I fully intend to acknowledge our child. You must know that I could never have people go on half-believing Samuel Carr is the father. And our child will carry *my* name, just as you will." He shook his head. "I now understand what one of the Greek writers meant when he said, 'I can't live either without you or with you.' It seems we have a dilemma that doesn't want to resolve itself."

Wynne felt the color drain from her face. Her old fears rushed back—the scorn of others, the loneliness of being ostracized, made her heart cry out in compassion for their unborn babe.

"Wynne," Drew said gently, pushing himself up to hold her loosely, "don't worry about the paternity of our child. It's a settled issue. If you trust me, you'll accept this."

"I . . . I do trust you. I'm just afraid, not for myself, but for our child. I know how it feels—"

"No one—do you hear me—no one will openly question our child or scorn him. You forget, my family will be behind us. And you have friends here. Lady Grayson and her son will stand beside us. You must trust that things will work out."

"I'll try," she whispered.

"You should sleep, love."

"Yes, I suppose you're right. Although I do want you to know that I feel fine."

His hand crept under the sheet, splaying across her abdomen. The baby kicked and moved inside. A grin split Drew's face as he felt the activity.

"It seems our child is anxious to meet his father."

Wynne smiled, stroking his hair back behind his ears. "I think you've already been introduced," she murmured, feeling a blush creep across her cheeks.

25

There was a tradition of having a send-off party after the shipment of tobacco left the docks at Norfolk. This year Lady Grayson had a formal ball at her plantation, Fairfield, to celebrate the event. Wynne heard about it from acquaintances who were passing through. They mentioned that it was a shame Wynne couldn't attend, but in her condition . . . Their words had trailed off, leaving her no doubt of their true sentiments. She was glad she had been unable to attend the ball, which had occurred several days before. She didn't want to hear any more unkind remarks.

Wynne sat at her desk in the study, studying the flames in the fireplace. Drew insisted that the rooms be kept comfortably warm so she wouldn't catch a chill. He was as concerned as an old woman.

He had also heard about the event. She had encouraged him to attend alone, but he would hear nothing of it. Wynne believed he still guarded her against MacClintock, although they never spoke of the man who had apparently come back from the dead. She noticed that wherever she went around the garden or stable, anytime she was away from the house, someone was close by. She suspected they carried firearms, but said nothing to Drew.

She wanted nothing to spoil the intimacy they had found in the last two weeks. Ever since the night when he'd come to her room, their relationship had changed yet again to one of sharing, companionship, and love. She still worried about gossip and rumors, but tried to keep her anxiety from Drew, since he simply wouldn't believe that it would be a problem in the future. She obviously could not convince him that Virginia was vastly different from London, so she let that one subject remain undiscussed.

In less than a week they would be married. Her gown was ready and Annie would start on the food in a few days. With the tobacco already shipped, there was little to concern her except impending marriage and motherhood. Drew encouraged her to review the books, make plans for next season, and help as much as she could with winter preparations.

It was such a relief to know he had only assumed those responsibilities when he thought her unable. As she looked back on her behavior during the last two months, she realized that she *hadn't* been able to run the plantation during her illness. Drew had known that and tried to spare her the burden. At last her suspicion had been lifted and she could see him as he was, love him as he deserved.

Drew told her he had arranged for a permanent estate manager for his properties in England. He had resigned as Lord-Lieutenant of East Sussex, but he was still Baron Rother, a title that would pass to their son someday, even if they never lived in England. The title had been a dormant one that went with the estate Drew purchased in Sussex. He had petitioned the House of Lords to reinstate the title to him, since the last Baron died without heirs. Wynne laughed as she remembered how the topic had come up. They'd been lying in bed, a plate of scones perched atop of her stomach, when she asked if his family was so full of titles that even the youngest son got one.

"Are you accusing me of being spoiled again?" he'd asked.

"No," she replied. "I'm *certain* you're spoiled. I just wonder about the title you never use."

"I suppose I'm not accustomed to it yet. You see, my father encouraged me to have it reinstated so I could more fully participate in politics. It's a family tradition," he explained, licking a few crumbs off her collarbone.

"I'm afraid we've already started a new family tradition."

"And what would that be, love?"

"Spending an inordinate amount of time abed," she'd replied, sighing deeply as his tongue traced lower.

"Now that's the kind of tradition I'd like to continue," he whispered, pushing the scones aside.

She'd finally gotten her nap, but not until much later and not until she was so sated that sleep was a natural outcome. Lord, but she loved that man.

Mail came from Williamsburg the next day; Drew received a letter from his parents and Wynne got the latest copy of the *Virginia Gazette*. In it was an article on the Graysons' ball. Wynne almost didn't read it, but curiosity overcame bitterness and she leaned back against the sofa in the family parlor and pored over each word.

It wasn't about the ball so much as it was a revelation! Lady Grayson announced that she was in truth the Dowager Countess of Wellston! Of all the things Wynne expected, this was the most startling. Her neighbor, the mild and kind Lady Grayson, had been married to a powerful earl for almost twenty years. The paper went on to explain that the current earl, the earl's son by a previous marriage, lived in London and on the family estate, Wellsley.

What news! Then it hit her. The light in Michael Grayson's eyes the last time he visited had been because he *knew* this would cause a ripple in Tidewater society. It would make Wynne's behavior seem like yesterday's news. He must have encouraged his mother to admit her title, or told her of Wynne's dilemma, and Lady Grayson volunteered to create the scandal. No doubt the biddies who thrived on gossip would flock to Lady Grayson's plantation to associate themselves with a member of the nobility who had such ties to the mother country. Surely no one had heard of a countess who kept her standing in society a secret. Her reasons alone would keep them guessing for months.

She had to tell Drew. She pushed herself up from the sofa and walked into the study, where Drew was bent over some correspondence

"Drew! You must hear this."

He looked up, amusement in his blue eyes. "What is it, love?

"Lady Grayson is in truth the Dowager Countess of Wellston! She must have created the scandal herself to take public speculation off me. Isn't that the most wonderful thing a friend could do?" She waved the paper in the air before letting it settle on the desk.

Drew smiled, picked up the *Gazette*, and began to read. He looked up in a minute, grinning like a small boy. "Didn't I tell you everything would be fine?"

"You knew about this?" Wynne sputtered.

"No, but I'm not surprised. Lady Grayson was a friend of my mother's when they were both debutantes. It only makes sense that she made a suitable match also."

Wynne rolled up the paper and hit him on the head with it. "You are the most irritating man! I think this is grand news and you take it all in stride. Can't you at least pretend some excitement?"

Drew bounded out of the chair and was around the desk in a heartbeat. "I'll tell you what gets me excited," he growled. "That spark of mischief and life in your eyes." He grabbed her, pulling her against his body, as close as she could get in her condition. "Would you like me to show you how excited?"

"Drew!" She feigned outrage, pushing against his chest. "Behave yourself. We're not even married yet!"

He laughed loud and long. She finally joined in, reveling in the exuberance she felt. Things were going to be all right, just as Drew said.

"Do you know, love, I think Lady Grayson was giving us a wedding present."

Wynne looped her arms around his neck. "I think it's a marvelous gift."

The wedding took place three days later, in the evening. They exchanged vows in front of an Anglican minister. It was a short event, which was considered in good taste due to the bride's condition and her supposed state of mourning. Out of respect for Samuel's memory, Wynne wore a mauve gown, simple in design and free of excessive frills. Drew looked dashing and dignified in a new frock coat he'd ordered while in Williamsburg.

As Lady Grayson stood beside her, Wynne couldn't stop tears from pooling in her eyes. She looked over at her friend and neighbor during the clergyman's recitation and mouthed a silent "thank you."

She still couldn't believe it. The emerald and diamond

ring was placed on her finger as Drew vowed to love, honor, and protect her. It was more than she had ever hoped, all the dreams she'd ever imagined and more.

Christmas came and went, celebrated quietly with small gifts for each other and several for the baby, who continued to grow at what seemed to Wynne to be an alarming rate. She and Drew made love on Christmas Eve, but since then she'd been so uncomfortable that they no longer shared that intimacy. Drew held her at night, whispering how much he loved her and how he longed to see their son or daughter.

Wynne thought about that in January when, during a quiet afternoon as she walked down the stairs to the study, she felt a gush of water that soaked her petticoats and a severe cramp that made her gasp before sinking to the step.

It was several hours later but it felt like days, when Annie looked up from wiping Wynne's face.

"What is it?" she asked in a weak voice.

"Mr. Leyton . . . his lordship! He's running toward the house."

Wynne closed her eyes and clenched her fists against the gripping pain. Her legs drew up and the spasm intensified. Would this baby ever come? It had been hours; it seemed like days.

She'd hoped Drew would return from the field every minute. She wanted his strong arms to hold her and his tender caresses to soothe her. Where in the world could he have been?

"Annie," she whispered, "are you sure?"

Before the cook could answer, the bedroom door burst open and Drew's figure filled the portal. His face was white from the cold, his breath coming in short gasps as though he'd been running.

She gasped his name.

"Wynne," he mouthed in reply, but no sound came forth.

Annie rushed forward, filling the gap. "Mr. Drew! Ye shouldn't be here. Now, sir, I didn't mean here at the house. I meant up here, in the bedroom. Why don't ye go back . . ."

Her voice trailed off as Drew walked slowly, steadily toward the bed. Wynne's eyes never left him; his eyes never left her. "Wynne," he whispered again. He reached out his hand.

Another spasm of pain racked Wynne. She gasped and gripped the sheet until her knuckles turned white. Wynne looked exhausted; after the pain subsided she lay as still as death on the white sheets, her eyes closed and her breathing regular. Drew quietly asked Annie to leave them for a while, and the cook reluctantly agreed. "Call me if her pains get regular—or if they get any worse."

Drew pulled a chair up to the bed as Wynne opened her eyes. "I thought you'd never get home."

Why had she gone into labor so soon? That was what really terrified Drew—that something was wrong with her or the baby. He'd heard that babies born early had problems, didn't survive . . . Lord, but he was scared.

"Wynne? Do you remember when Colonel Nanny was having trouble foaling?" He waited until Wynne gave a small nod. "I want to feel your stomach to see how the baby is turned. Will you let me do that?"

"Of course," she whispered. "Everything will be fine now," she repeated Annie's words. Just then, another pain gripped her and she grasped his hand with amazing force.

Drew held her hand with his right and placed his left over her distended stomach. "Try to relax, love," he coaxed. "Breathe deeply . . . slowly. That's it."

In a moment, the spasm passed and Wynne sank back to the bed. Drew sat on the mattress and lifted the sheet. "I'm going to feel the baby now," he said, and firmly moved his hands over her abdomen.

He wasn't sure, but it seemed that there were too many feet and elbows and bulges. He carefully felt the child, trying to ensure the head was in the right place. It was hard to tell. He scowled.

"What is it?" Wynne demanded, concern evident as she tried to raise herself. "What is wrong with my baby?"

"I'm not sure, love, but there may be . . ."

"What? Tell me—what is it?"

"There may be more than one baby."

Wynne was silent for so long, Drew thought she may have misunderstood. He began, "I said, there may be—"

Wynne's sudden laughter was unexpected and, to Drew, unwarranted. "Wynne? What's the matter?"

"Two . . . babies!" she managed to say before succumbing to more laughter. There was a desperate tone to the sound, though, and Drew heard it.

Annie came back into the room, but Drew refused to leave. Wynne wanted him here, and he was determined to see that she and the baby, or babies, were all right. Over two hours later, the first child was born—a girl. About one minute later, a boy made his appearance.

Later, with Wynne cleaned up, the sheets changed and the babies resting in the cradle, Drew took a moment to look at the babies—his children. A rush of pride filled him.

"They are beautiful, aren't they, Annie?"

"Aye, they're beauties. Fine children, the kind to make

anyone proud." Annie walked over to the cradle. "Ye made her happy, Drew, and that's a fine thing to do.

Drew took one more look at the now sleeping mother and babies. "I don't ever remember being this hungry." Except aboard the transport ship, he amended to himself.

"Let's go see what we can come up with, lad," Annie offered. "I had started some venison stew before . . ." Her voice trailed off as the two made their way out of the bedroom, closing the door quietly.

An announcement of the babies' births was sent to the *Virginia Gazette* by Smythe as soon as the roads were negotiable. As a consequence, by the time Andrea Elizabeth and Philip Winston were one month old, and despite the fact winter weather prohibited much travel, a surprising number of Virginia residents paid their respects.

Wynne was certain that the neighbors would have started to talk about the paternity of the children, since they'd been reminded of the former gossip. That was usually enough to start it up again. However, the next paper they received from Williamsburg had an article about Michael Grayson. It seemed that Lady Carolyn wasn't the only one hiding a title. It was revealed that he was a viscount, the owner of a Welsh estate and ancient title inherited from his mother's family.

"Viscount Penmae," Drew said, rolling the title around like a cherry pit in his mouth. "No wonder I didn't recognize his name."

"What do you mean?"

"We were at Cambridge together, although I graduated several years ahead of him. He recognized me, but I couldn't place him. Now I know why."

"I'm still amazed—at Lady Carolyn and now this."

"They are wonderful friends."

"Perhaps you are right. Gossip may not be a problem."

"I'm glad to see that you are finally beginning to trust me," Drew replied with a gleam in his eye.

"Oh, I trust you. I just don't assume that you know *everything*, my lord," Wynne teased.

"Mouthy wench," he muttered. "I can hardly wait to take you to task over that remark."

"My lord, I can hardly wait either."

26

It seemed strange to have the minister back to the house just three months after the wedding to christen the babies, but that was exactly what happened. Not only was it the christening, but Drew and Lady Carolyn had turned it into a social event for the entire county and more.

Wynne struggled to get into the pale pink gown she had chosen for the occasion. Even though Millie had tightened her new corset until it was almost painful, the gown barely fastened. No wonder, Wynne mused. All she did any more was play with the babies and eat the rich food Annie insisted on preparing.

Looking into the cheval mirror, Wynne was startled to see her breasts rising precariously above the neckline. She nursed the babies and her milk seemed to agree with them so much that they were rapidly gaining weight, their early birth no longer noticeable.

Drew was so proud of them. Wynne smiled. He spent all his available time in the nursery or her room, talking to them. He promised them ponies next summer, and visits to England, and all kinds of presents. She was glad they were too young to understand all the things he said. When he made the outrageous promises, she would only smile and shake her head.

"It's time, milady," Millie stated as she came back into the bedroom. "Everything looks real nice. His lordship said if you don't make an appearance right now, he'll come and get you himself." Millie giggled.

"Good gracious! Well, his threats don't bother me." She walked over to the jewelry case and found the sapphire and diamond necklace. "Help me fasten this, Millie."

She only hoped that society was as accepting as Drew and the Graysons said they would be. The ballroom had been festooned with ribbons and laden with food and drink. It was costing a fortune, but Drew swore it was the way to impress the neighbors. "Act as if it's the most natural thing in the world," he had advised. "Imagine that you invite them over every week." To Wynne, who had not entertained the neighbors in almost seven years, it seemed more than odd.

She twirled around, the farthingales of her dress holding the material away from her body. "How do I look, Millie?"

"Just beautiful, ma'am . . . I mean, your ladyship."

Mary was sitting in the nursery with the babies. Wynne opened the door a crack and looked in on them. Both were sleeping soundly. Mary sat in the rocker, sewing by the light of the window. Wynne pulled the door closed, ready to face the society that had caused her so much grief.

* * *

Wynne walked into the ballroom slowly, looking like an angel. A very earthly angel. Drew's breath caught in his throat, since each soft step of her slippered feet seemed to jar her breasts infinitesimally closer to spilling out of her bodice. He suppressed a frown; it wasn't her fault she was swollen from nursing the babies. He just wished they weren't in such a public setting where any man could openly ogle the display.

"My love," he murmured as she stepped in front of him, smiling. "Do you have no gowns that cover more of your charms?"

Wynne raised an eyebrow and looked down at her cleavage. "No, my lord. It seems they are all like this one."

"Then we will make a trip to the seamstress as soon as possible. I'm afraid I might mistake you for one of the other delicacies and devour you in front of our guests."

She blushed then, a high pink color that went exceptionally well with the gown.

"Our guests are arriving," she said. In a lower voice, she added, "behave yourself!"

Drew laughed, taking her elbow and turning to greet their guests. If he managed to make it through the entire evening without ravishing his wife, he would call it a success.

The feast started after a toast and continued for several hours. Spirits were high as the wine and ale flowed. Wynne mingled among their guests, assuming with ease the role she had so recently acquired.

"This is a lovely party, your ladyship," one of the "biddies," as Wynne called them, said.

It was all Wynne could do to bite her tongue and give a civil reply. "I'm so glad you could come," she murmured in reply, searching the crowd for Lady Carolyn. The other woman was so short that it was difficult to see her among the other guests.

She finally located her and waved. Lady Carolyn moved through the crowd, grasping Wynne's hand when she got within reach.

"It's a marvelous party, my dear. Everyone is quite taken with your husband."

Wynne saw him standing near the mirrored wall, talking to a group of planters. Yes, he fit in here, just as she hoped. Love and pride flowed through her.

"Your heart's on your sleeve," Lady Carolyn admonished.

"I can't seem to help myself. I love him more than I ever thought possible."

"I'm so happy for you, my dear." Lady Carolyn gave her hand a little squeeze.

"I want to thank you again for everything you've done, revealing your identity, coming to my aid . . ."

"I was glad to. When Michael came home that day and told me how sad you seemed, it just broke my heart. What's the secret of one old lady compared to giving you a chance at happiness?"

"Oh, I'm so happy, Lady Carolyn. So very happy." Her eyes went to Drew again. He was laughing at some jest. "Our life is just about perfect."

A few minutes later Wynne left the party to feed the babies. She called for Millie to help her, but her maid was busy replenishing the punch bowl. Faye offered to help instead. Wynne waved to Drew, then, when no one was looking, blew him a kiss across the room. His eyes seemed to burn right through the gown.

Andrea had just awakened from a nap, but Philip was still sleeping as Wynne and Faye walked into the nursery.

"Why don't you go downstairs and get something to eat,

Mary? Faye and I will visit with the children a while," Wynne offered.

"Thanks, ma'am. I think I'll see what Annie has left in the kitchen."

"I may bring the babies into the ballroom after I feed them," Wynne said. "Why don't you wait a while before you come back up? Just go ahead and enjoy yourself."

Wynne picked up Andrea after Mary left, walked over to the rocker, and then remembered why she'd asked Faye to help her; the bodice of this dress unbuttoned down the back.

"Faye, would you mind unfastening the gown?"

A moment later, Wynne nursed her hungry daughter. Faye waited by the window, apparently embarrassed by Wynne's nursing of the baby.

"So that's what the bondsman did to you," MacClintock's voice said coldly.

Faye spun around and gasped at the intrusion. Wynne felt the blood leave her face. She pulled her baby closer to her, terrified that she would faint. MacClintock! He lived, just as Drew said!

Andrea gave a small whimper.

"Keep your brat quiet if you want it to live," the Scotsman threatened. "Move away from that chair. Over there, by that fine little piece"—he motioned toward Faye with the knife he held.

Wynne, terrorized by the gleam of the large blade, stood still.

"Move now or you'll feel this blade sooner than I had planned."

Wynne moved sideways, keeping her eye on MacClintock as she made her way to the crib. Philip was still quiet, so she assumed he slept. Andrea wriggled in her arms. Debating with herself, Wynne finally decided to put the baby back in the crib. If she had to fight MacClintock, she could not afford to be encumbered by her daughter. She tugged her bodice in place.

"Hurry up," MacClintock said.

She placed the baby on the mattress and gave her the soft cloth toy. "Move away from those brats," MacClintock ordered. "Over there." He motioned toward an inner wall, away from the windows. "You too," he said to Faye, who was practically shaking in fear.

"Do you know I almost died? I would have, too, if those good-for-nothing bargemen hadn't fished me from the creek. I hid for a long time, not knowing what kind of lies you told the magistrate."

"Nothing we could have said about you would be a lie, unless it was a compliment."

"Vicious, aren't you? Well, you won't be so feisty in a few minutes."

"You don't scare me, MacClintock. Drew will be here in a moment and he'll kill you for sure this time."

The Scotsman backed toward the hall door, closed it securely, and turned the lock. "Take her dress off her," he ordered Faye.

The maid cast a trembling glance at Wynne, who stood proud and strong facing the threat. "Take it off her or I'll start with you!"

"Drew will kill you for this," she repeated.

"He will be a dead man," he threatened. "While I'm here, I think I'll finish off those brats too. They are his, aren't they?"

Wynne said nothing, her throat suddenly constricted.

"Well," he yelled, "aren't they?"

"No."

"You lie, bitch!" MacClintock screamed, before remembering to be quiet. "I know they're his," he hissed. And he started walking toward the crib.

*   *   *

Drew fidgeted as he talked with his new neighbors. He knew Wynne had gone to feed the babies, and that took quite a while, but he was anxious for her to return. During the past six weeks since the twins' births, he would sit for long minutes as she nursed the babies. Usually she sat in the rocker with one baby at a time to her breast. It was a beautiful scene, especially in the morning with the winter sunlight filtered through the pale curtains of the nursery windows.

He wondered if she was nursing the babies right now. If he left the party and went into their bedroom, would he be able to open the connecting door to the nursery and see the same scene? He shifted again in his chair, his body responding to the image of Wynne with the bodice of the pale pink dress pushed down.

He acted on impulse, telling the men, "I'll be back in a moment. I'm going to check on my wife."

It was torture, he knew, to watch her like this. They hadn't made love since the babies' birth. Despite Wynne's vows that she felt fine, he noticed that she occasionally winced.

Drew reached the double doors of the master suite and treaded quietly through their bedroom to the nursery. He turned the knob slowly, not wanting to startle Wynne or the children, in case they slept.

A man's scream pierced the quiet.

Barton MacClintock had taken three steps toward the crib before Wynne lunged at him. Only Faye's restraining hand kept her from being slashed by the knife he arced quickly toward her movement.

"Please, ma'am. Don't do anything foolish," Faye pleaded.

Wynne turned to look at the maid, her eyes frantic but her voice calm. "You're right." A small movement at the corner of her eye caused her to pause. The door to her bedroom had moved! It was a tiny crack, but it had not been open earlier. There must be someone there!

She turned to MacClintock. "I'll do whatever you want if you will just not harm my babies. I'll go with you. In fact, we should probably leave. Let's leave the house right now, before anyone finds out you're here." Wynne backed toward the partially open door.

"I like it here just fine. We have a problem, though. You." He motioned to Faye. "Get over here."

"No . . . please," Faye pleaded.

MacClintock moved forward, grabbing Faye's wrist and dragging her toward the middle of the room. Constantly keeping an eye on Wynne, he pulled both of Faye's hands behind her back and used one of the babies' cloth diapers to secure them. He pushed Faye to the floor and efficiently bound her feet.

"Just to make sure you stay quiet," he said as he used another cloth to gag the maid. "I don't want any interruptions while I have a little fun."

"Why don't we go into the other room?" Wynne offered.

"Why don't you just take that pretty little thing off?" he answered. "I like the idea of having you right here, on the floor, while the little ones watch. If you're real good, I might even let the brats live," he jeered.

"You don't really want to do this, MacClintock," Wynne argued.

"Don't try to talk your way out of this. You should have been nicer to me when you had the chance." He continued to advance, away from the crib and closer to the door.

He lurched forward, catching the shoulder of her dress with one hand as he brought the knife to Wynne's neck with the other. His thin fingers bit into her shoulders as he pulled her down, ripping the fabric. "On your knees," he ordered as he pressed the blade to her throat.

Wynne's legs almost gave out, she was so frightened. Slowly, her eyes never leaving MacClintock's face, she bent her knees and winced when the knife cut into her flesh.

"Faster," he demanded, his breath coming fast. "Get down on the floor." He grabbed the front of her dress and pulled. It split down the front and Wynne could not suppress a cry.

"I want you to know what it feels like to think you are dying. You do know that I will kill you, don't you?" he muttered.

Wynne looked away, slowly turning her head so she could see the doorway, which was at a right angle to MacClintock. He might be able to see movement. She had to get his attention away from whoever was on the other side. She prayed it was Drew.

"I'll go along with you," Wynne offered in a shaking voice. She was kneeling on the floor, so she slowly lowered her body, twisting so MacClintock would have to turn to face her. She moved back slightly, keeping her eyes on the Scotsman.

"That's more like it. Now," he threatened, one hand going to the drawstring holding up his breeches, "I'll see what that meddlesome lord found so pleasing."

"I don't think so," a deep voice stated from behind MacClintock.

Instead of whirling, as Drew expected him to do, MacClintock fell forward, grabbing for Wynne. Drew leveled the pistol, which he kept with him at all times, at the Scot. He couldn't fire; he might hit Wynne.

The knife slashed out as Wynne tried to protect herself. It cut into the fleshy part of her hand below the little finger. She cried out, blood running down her forearm as she tried to get away from MacClintock.

"Drop the knife, MacClintock," Drew ordered, moving into the room.

Wynne struggled against the Scot. He held one of her arms, but he couldn't watch both Drew and her at the same time. She twisted with all her strength, trying to get away from him long enough for Drew to take a shot.

"Be still, bitch," he ordered. He brought the knife around, trying to get it against her neck. As he turned, Wynne brought her knee up into his groin with all her might.

His cry of pain mingled with Wynne's as the knife came down again, this time slashing her thigh. She brought her knee up again and pushed him away, rolling aside. She heard the deafening sound of Drew's pistol.

The babies' cries split the sudden quiet of the nursery. Drew ran forward to ensure MacClintock was really dead this time as Wynne rose shakily to her feet. Her dress was split down the front past her waist and hung from one shoulder. Blood dripped from her hand and ran down her thigh, soaking the silk petticoats underneath.

"Hush, my loves," she murmured to the infants. "It's all right now. Mother is here," she whispered, trying to reassure the babies without picking them up. Her legs were curiously weak and she felt lightheaded as she leaned over the crib.

Drew rushed over to Faye and removed the gag and

restraints on her hands and legs. The sounds of people run-ning up the stairs caused him to act quickly. "Let Mary and Lady Carolyn in here. Just those two. Hurry!"

Drew walked to the crib and stood beside Wynne, plac-ing an arm around her. "Are they well? Did he harm them?"

"No," Wynne replied, her voice faint.

"You were very brave, my love." He tried to turn her, but she wanted to stay by the crib.

"No! I want my babies. I want . . ." She reached toward them. Blood dripped onto Philip's gown. She froze, a scream building inside.

Drew whirled her around and stared into her white face. He saw her eyes roll back and felt her body start to go limp. He swung her into his arms as she slumped against him.

Moments later, Mary and Lady Carolyn, followed by Faye, ran into the nursery. Mary rushed toward the chil-dren and gasped when she saw the blood on Philip's gown. "Mr. Drew!" she yelled. Drew had just placed Wynne on the bed in her room.

Seeing where Mary was staring, he reassured the woman. "It's Wynne's blood, Mary. The babies are not harmed. Just scared. Please take care of them for us. I must see to Wynne."

He hurried back to the bedroom, but Faye was already there, sponging the blood from Wynne's body as Lady Grayson pressed a cloth to the cut on her hand.

"She has another cut on her thigh," he told Faye.

The gash on Wynne's leg was deeper, but it was a clean, straight cut. "It will probably need stitches," Drew com-mented. "Faye, go get Annie. Tell her to bring whatever she needs to set some stitches. And if she has anything medici-nal in her kitchen, have her bring that also."

Annie bustled into the room minutes later, her arms full

of wicker baskets and bundles. "Move aside," she ordered Drew. "I know what needs to be done!"

She did, Drew admitted an hour later as he studied her handwork. The stitches were neat, the bleeding had stopped, and Wynne was clean and dressed in a soft white nightgown. All he could do now was wait for her to awaken. Annie had fixed a sleeping and pain potion, but Wynne needed to awaken to swallow the mixture.

"Lord Leyton?" Smythe spoke from the doorway to the nursery. "What would you like me to do with the body?"

Drew turned to look at the butler. He wished he could kill MacClintock all over again, only this time it would be much, much more painful. No quick shot through the heart. The man deserved to suffer.

"Wrap it up and put it in the cold house. Have someone take it to Williamsburg tomorrow in the wagon. I had already informed the governor that MacClintock was alive and threatening Wynne. There should be no problems about his death."

Smythe turned to leave, then paused. "Will the mistress recover?"

"She'll be fine," Drew answered, turning back to look at the figure in the bed. Her eyes were open.

"My love, oh, love. You scared ten years from my life today," Drew whispered.

"The babies . . ."

"They're both fine. You must drink this, love. Annie fixed it for your pain. It will help you sleep."

Wynne's eyes focused on the glass he brought to her lips. She took a small sip, then raised her good hand to restrain him. "Is he dead?"

Drew smiled into her pale features. "Yes, this time he's dead." He reached down to push an errant strand of hair away from her temple.

"Good." She closed her eyes.

He held the glass up to Wynne's lips. "It will help you," he promised as she drained the mixture.

He sat beside the bed while the potion worked, watching as Wynne drifted to sleep.

27

"*If I don't get out of this bed soon,* I will become mad!"

"And if you try to walk on that leg, you will become crippled!"

Wynne crossed her arms over her abundant breasts and glared with flashing green eyes that dared Drew to argue with her. The little witch! She wanted to argue!

"I'm tired of lying in this bed, having the babies brought to me, having meals brought to me, having sponge baths given to me. I want *out,* and I want out *now.*"

"Elizabeth Wynne, don't you even consider getting out of that bed by yourself," Drew warned. Although they should be in the middle of a serious confrontation, he felt his mouth begin to twitch with the trace of a smile. He tried to look completely serious and intimidating. He tried to look threatening. He was not, even in his opinion, doing a very good job.

"I will get out of this bed when I am . . . am . . . *damn* good and ready!"

Trying to appear shocked by her language, and trying equally hard not to laugh, Drew placed his hands on his hips and did his best imitation of a fatherly figure. "I should wash your mouth out with soap for that. Better yet, perhaps you need a good thrashing!" He advanced on the bed.

"Don't you dare!" Wynne warned as she tried to move away. "I'll scream this house down. I'll carve you into little pieces. I'll—"

"What you need is some company," Drew explained, crawling onto the mattress. "Maybe I'll thrash you first, then give you what you really need."

"You wouldn't!"

"I might."

He crawled closer, until he was leaning over her. Pouncing like a cat, he grabbed both wrists and held her lightly against the headboard of the bed. He rested on his side, one knee slowly insinuating itself between her legs.

"You're not really angry with me," he stated confidently.

"I am! I'm terribly, terribly angry. And disappointed. And I don't like you at all," Wynne asserted.

"Liar. Shall I kiss you and prove my case?" Drew threatened, leaning closer.

"No!"

He moved his leg, rubbing the sensitive area between her thighs. "Well," he whispered, "shall I prove I am right?"

"Yes," she replied, turning her head away from his hovering lips. "You are right."

"That's better," he smiled, moving back slightly.

"I'm only terribly angry—not terribly, terribly," Wynne teased.

"Why, you . . ."

"Don't you dare harm me. I'm injured. You could do irreparable damage to my person."

Drew bent close again, whispering into her ear. "I'd like to do a lot of things to your person, but damage? Never! Shall I tell you what I would like to do?"

"No . . . ," she murmured in a small voice.

"You're lying again."

Wynne smiled into his teasing face. "You're right."

They laughed. Drew was certain she was feeling completely well now. She might have been bored, but the shadows were gone from her eyes. For that he was eternally grateful.

"If you're a good girl this evening, I'll carry you downstairs for breakfast tomorrow. Would you like that?"

"What do I have to do to be a good girl?"

"Eat all your supper, don't give Millie any trouble, and let me watch you nurse the twins later."

"Is that all?" Wynne asked nonchalantly.

"No," he said thoughtfully, his body already painfully aroused. "That's not quite all."

"Good," she whispered, pulling his head down for a kiss.

Later that evening, Drew held Andrea as Wynne nursed Philip. She was leaning against the pillows, wearing a pink frilly garment that made her look delicate and desirable. For the first time since the babies' birth, he wished that they would hurry and finish their dinners. He had plans for their mother.

Within a few minutes, with both babies asleep in a guest bedroom that had been converted to a nursery after MacClintock's death, Drew pulled up the sheet and slipped naked into bed.

"I feel strange," Wynne whispered, snuggling deeper under the covers.

"What do you mean?"

"Well . . . it's been so long."

"It certainly has," he growled.

"And I've had two babies."

"Yes," he said, reaching for her, pulling her closer to his warm body.

"And we're married now."

"So? Is that supposed to make it different? Besides, we've made love since we've married."

"Well, yes, but I was pregnant then."

Drew rested his head on her shoulder and moaned. "Wynne, love, what's wrong?"

She thought about it for a moment, finding it difficult to put her uneasiness into words. "Drew, if you had never come to Virginia, if we had never met, what would you be doing now?"

"What kind of question is that?"

"I want to know." She rolled toward him, resting a hand on his smooth, muscled chest. "I suppose I want to know that you haven't just made the best of the situation you found yourself in. That this is where you truly want to be."

"My love, you are all I ever wanted."

"But would you have chosen me if you'd had a chance? After all, I *did* choose you—I bought you."

He stroked her hip, his fingers warm magic through the silk of her gown. "You forget, love, that I could have left at any time. If I'd told you who I was, offered you a large reward for returning me to my family, wouldn't you have accepted?"

"I . . . don't know."

"But surely a simple bondservant wouldn't have meant that much to you then."

"Drew, you were never a simple bondservant."

"But you didn't love me then . . . or did you?"

"Well," she whispered, twining an arm around his neck, "perhaps I did."

"And perhaps I didn't leave because I loved you. All I know is that from the very first moment I saw you standing in the study, your soft green eyes and shining blond hair, looking all vulnerable and appealing, I was a changed man."

"You thought I was soft and vulnerable! I was trying to look stern and authoritative. How can you—"

His kiss silenced her, thoroughly and effectively. When he finally broke away, they were both breathing hard.

"Tell the world what a hard, strict mistress you are, love. I'll never give away your secret. But for me, only for me, be the woman I fell in love with, the woman who cried at night, who loves newborn foals and wriggling babies, who had a legacy to carry on. Be mine, love, for now and always."

"Oh, Drew, I will . . . for now and always." She held him close as he worked that magic, the tears of joy that pooled in her eyes making the candlelight seem like a thousand stars in the dim bedroom. She made a wish on every one, knowing that beside the man she loved, each wish would be granted, each dream fulfilled.

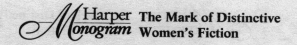

COMING NEXT MONTH

A FOREVER KIND OF LOVE by Patricia Hagan

A sweeping novel of romance, suspense, mystery, and revenge, set in the turbulent reconstruction period following the Civil War. This bestselling author tells a story of two lovers drawn together in the blaze of passion amidst a world aflame with prejudice and deceit.

THE SEASON OF LOVING by Helen Archery

A delightful Christmas romance set in Regency England. On her way to visit a family friend, Merrie Lawrence's gig runs into the Earl of Warwick's curricle. Discovering Merrie is his mother's houseguest, the earl takes an immediate dislike to her, only to discover later his overwhelming interest.

THE BASKET BRIDE by Phyllis Coe

An enthralling historical romance spun from the historic event of the "Basket Brides" who came from France in the 18th century to help settle Louisiana.

ONE MAN'S TREASURE by Catriona Flynt

Adventure, intrigue, and humor are hallmarks of this delightful historical romance. Ruth McKenna travels to Flagstaff, Arizona, to make peace with her brother, but she's too late—someone has killed him. The only person to help her is big, redheaded Gladius Blade. A nosy, hard-headed woman only adds to Blade's problems. But when he falls in love with her, he knows he is in for real trouble.

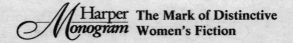 **Harper Monogram** The Mark of Distinctive Women's Fiction

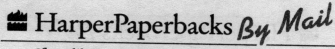

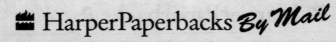

YESTERDAY'S SHADOWS
by Marianne Willman

Bettany Howard was a young orphan traveling west searching for the father who left her years ago. Wolf Star was a Cheyenne brave who longed to know who abandoned him—a white child with a jeweled talisman. Fate decreed they'd meet and try to seize the passion promised. 0-06-104044-4

MIDNIGHT ROSE by Patricia Hagan

From the rolling plantations of Richmond to the underground slave movement of Philadelphia, Erin Sterling and Ryan Youngblood would pursue their wild, breathless passion and finally surrender to the promise of a bold and unexpected love. 0-06-104023-1

WINTER TAPESTRY
by Kathy Lynn Emerson

Cordell vows to revenge the murder of her father. Roger Allington is honor bound to protect his friend's daughter but has no liking for her reckless ways. Yet his heart tells him he must pursue this beauty through a maze of plots to win her love and ignite their smoldering passion. 0-06-100220-8

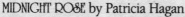